PRIZE STORIES

1·9·9·4

·THE·

O. HENRY

AWARDS

Edited and wit[ ] W9-AZR-827

an Introduction by

William Abrahams

DOUBLEDAY

NEW YORK LONDON TORONTO SYDNEY AUCKLAND

PUBLISHED BY DOUBLEDAY
a division of Bantam Doubleday Dell Publishing Group, Inc.
1540 Broadway, New York, New York 10036

DOUBLEDAY and the portrayal of an anchor with a dolphin
are trademarks of Doubleday,
a division of Bantam Doubleday Dell Publishing Group, Inc.

Library of Congress Cataloging-in-Publication Data
Prize stories. 1947–
New York, N.Y., Doubleday.
v. 22 cm.
Annual.
The O. Henry awards.
None published 1952–53.
Continues: O. Henry memorial award prize stories.
1. Short stories, American—Collected works.
PZ1.011   813'.01'08—dc19   21-9372
                                               MARC-S

ISBN: 0-385-47117-3
ISBN: 0-385-47118-1 (pbk.)

April 1994

1 3 5 7 9 10 8 6 4 2

First Edition

CONTENTS

Publisher's Note   ix

Introduction by William Abrahams   xi

FIRST PRIZE: Alison Baker, "Better Be Ready 'Bout Half Past
Eight"
The Atlantic, January 1993   1

SECOND PRIZE: John Rolfe Gardiner, "The Voyage Out"
The New Yorker, January 18, 1993   26

THIRD PRIZE: Lorrie Moore, "Terrific Mother"
The Paris Review, No. 124 (1992)   53

Stuart Dybek, "We Didn't"
Antaeus, Spring 1993   94

Marlin Barton, "Jeremiah's Road"
Shenandoah, Spring 1993   108

Kelly Cherry, "Not the Phil Donahue Show"
The Virginia Quarterly Review, Summer 1993   129

Elizabeth Cox, "The Third of July"
   Story, Summer 1993   146

Terry Bain, "Games" —
   The Gettysburg Review, Summer 1993   159

Amy Bloom, "Semper Fidelis"
   Antaeus, Spring 1993   168

Michael Fox, "Rise and Shine"
   Raritan, Summer 1992   180

David McLean, "Marine Corps Issue"
   The Atlantic Monthly, May 1993   196

Elizabeth Graver, "The Boy Who Fell Forty Feet"
   The Stanford Humanities Review, Vol. 2, No. 1 (1993)   216

Susan Starr Richards, "The Hanging in the Foaling Barn"
   The Thoroughbred Times, March 19, 1993   229

Janice Eidus, "Pandora's Box"
   Witness, Vol. VII, No. 7 (1993)   243

Judith Ortiz Cofer, "Nada"
   The Georgia Review, Winter 1992   260

Mary Tannen, "Elaine's House"
   Epoch, Vol. 42, No. 2 (1993)   272

Dennis Trudell, "Gook"
   The Chariton Review, Spring 1993   286

Helen Fremont, "Where She Was"
   Ploughshares, Winter 1992–93   304

Elizabeth Oness, "The Oracle"
American Short Fiction, Summer 1993   313

Katherine L. Hester, "Labor"
Indiana Review, Fall 1992   337

Thomas E. Kennedy, "Landing Zone X-Ray"
New Letters, Vol. 58, No. 4 (1992)   346

Biographies and Some Comments by the Authors   360

Magazines Consulted   374

PUBLISHER'S NOTE

This volume is the seventy-fourth in the O. Henry Memorial Award series, and the twenty-eighth to be edited by William Abrahams.

* * *

In 1918, the Society of Arts and Sciences met to vote upon a monument to the master of the short story: O. Henry. They decided that this memorial should be in the form of two prizes for the best short stories published by American authors in American magazines during the year 1919. From this beginning, the memorial developed into an annual anthology of outstanding short stories by American authors, published, with the exception of the years 1952 and 1953, by Doubleday.

Blanche Colton Williams, one of the founders of the awards, was editor from 1919 to 1932; Harry Hansen from 1933 to 1940; Herschel Brickell from 1941 to 1951. The annual collection did not appear in 1952 and 1953, when the continuity of the series was interrupted by the death of Herschel Brickell. Paul Engle was editor from 1954 to 1959, with Hanson Martin coeditor in the years 1954 to 1960; Mary Stegner in 1960; Richard Poirier from 1961 to 1966, with assistance from and coeditorship with William Abrahams from 1964 to 1966. William Abrahams became editor of the series in 1967.

In 1970, Doubleday published under Mr. Abrahams's editorship *Fifty Years of the American Short Story*, and in 1981, *Prize Stories of the Seventies*. Both are collections of stories selected from this series.

The stories chosen for this volume were published in the period from the summer of 1992 to the summer of 1993. A list of the magazines consulted appears at the back of the book. The choice of stories and selection of prizewinners are exclusively the responsibility of the editor. Biographical material is based on information provided by the contributors and obtained from standard works of reference.

INTRODUCTION

The twenty-one stories gathered here represent, individually and all together, a level of achievement that would be notable at any time, but especially so when eighteen of the authors are newcomers to the O. Henry Awards. The presence here of Alison Baker, John Rolfe Gardiner, Marlin Barton, Kelly Cherry, Elizabeth Cox, Terry Bain, Amy Bloom, Michael Fox, David McLean, Elizabeth Graver, Susan Starr Richards, Judith Ortiz Cofer, Mary Tannen, Dennis Trudell, Helen Fremont, Elizabeth Oness, Katherine L. Hester, and Thomas E. Kennedy testifies better than any assertions of mine to the continuing strength, variety, and necessity of the American short story.

We are six years from the end of the century: it seems reasonable to predict that the centennial will bring a spate of critical and historical studies tracing the evolution of the art of the story over the past hundred years. Most welcome they will be, but my intention in these introductory remarks is nowhere so ambitious: I want simply to say something about where the story is in our time.

For a start I notice how well everyone writes, and with what an admirable and serene disregard for what's fashionable— Is there a style of the year? I don't think so. A good number of these (though certainly not all) are *contemporary* stories—their themes and characters belong recognizably to the here and now. When a story is set in the Second World War, say, as in John Rolfe Gardiner's "The Voyage Out," or in the 1950s, as in Stuart Dybek's "We Didn't," one has the sense of the writer drawing upon—inventing or restoring or re-imagining—past experience, not necessarily specifically so, but with a view and an understanding of the experience now that might not have been apparent then.

Gardiner's and Dybek's stories are essentially serious, yet in each an unexpected note of comedy is sounded, sardonic and satiric in "The Voyage Out," rueful and farcical in "We Didn't." So too in Lorrie Moore's "Terrific Mother," where the comic and tragic are powerfully juxtaposed. And it is worth remarking on the number of other writers here—Terry Bain, Elizabeth Oness, and Mary Tannen, to name only a few —who have found their subject in the comic aspect of life in the 1990s.

"Humankind," as T. S. Eliot reminded us, "cannot bear too much reality." In an age when the tragic and the terrible are a continuing part of everyday existence, it is not surprising, then, that the comic spirit should emerge so conspicuously in the contemporary short story as an attempt to tell the truth: we laugh to be wise.

I hope this is not too portentous a way to introduce Alison Baker's "Better Be Ready 'Bout Half Past Eight," to which I have awarded First Prize this year. I have found it utterly original in its content, and as such peculiarly a story of the 1990s—it is hard to imagine it in its airy, affable, hilarious, and truthful substance coming into being until now. Questions of gender and concerns about sexual identity are not usually dealt with in these comic or seriocomic terms, and I can envision readers (chiefly those to whom the 1990s have not yet happened) made uncomfortable by Baker's story and the levels of truth it explores, who will shrug it aside as fantasy or worse. After all, there are still readers at large who would banish *Huck Finn* from our public libraries. Ms. Baker is a not unworthy descendant of Mark Twain. She has the gift of laughter, and I venture to predict that her story will be read into the next century.

Special thanks to Arabella Meyer at Anchor Books for her invaluable assistance.

—William Abrahams

PRIZE STORIES
1994
THE O. HENRY
AWARDS

Alison Baker

BETTER BE READY 'BOUT
HALF PAST EIGHT

"I'm changing sex," Zach said.

Byron looked up from his lab notebook. "For the better, I hope."

"This is something I've never discussed with you," Zach said, stepping back and leaning against the office door. "I need to. Do you want to go get a beer or something?"

"I have to transcribe this data," Byron said. "What do you need to discuss?"

"My sexuality," Zach said. "The way I feel trapped in the wrong body."

"Well, I suppose you were right," Byron said.

"Right?" Zach said.

"Not to discuss it with me," Byron said. "It's none of my business, is it?"

"We've been friends a long time," Zach said.

"Have you always felt this way?" Byron said.

Zach nodded. "I didn't know it was this I was feeling," he said. "But I've been in therapy for over a year now, and I'm sure."

"You've been seeing Terry about *this*?"

Byron had given Zach the name of Terry Wu, whom he himself had once consulted professionally.

Zach nodded again.

"He's terrific. He knew the first time he met me what I was."

"What were you?" Byron said.

"A woman," Zach said.

Had he missed any signs? Byron sat frowning at the computer screen. Then he stood, shoved his hands into his pockets, and stared out the window. He could see the sky and the top of the snow-covered hills. On this floor all the windows started at chin level, so you couldn't see the parking lot or the ground outside; you could see only distances, clouds, and sections of sunrise.

He walked up and down the hall for a while. The surrounding labs buzzed with action, students leaning intently over whirring equipment, technicians laughing over coffee. Secretaries clopped through the hall and said, "Hi, Dr. Glass," when they passed him. He could ignore them, because he had a reputation for being absentminded; he was absorbed in his research, or perhaps in a new poem. He was well known, particularly in scientific circles, for his poetry. He edited the poetry column of a major scientific research journal. He judged many poetry-writing competitions, and he had edited anthologies.

What had he missed?

Worrying about it was useless. Zach's sexuality wasn't his concern. "Just as long as it doesn't interfere with work," he would say. "I can't have people's personal lives taking over the lab."

But in fact he didn't believe in the separation of work and home. "If your love life's screwed up, you're probably going to screw up the science," he'd said more than once when he sent a sobbing technician home, or gave a distraught graduate student the name of a counselor. As a result, his workers did sacrifice, to some extent, their personal lives; they came in on weekends or at night to see to an experiment. The dictum, even if artificial, seemed to work.

"Go on home," he imagined himself saying to Zach, patting him on the shoulder. "Come back when it's all over."

But that wouldn't work. For one thing, the fretting wouldn't end. For another thing, Zach wouldn't be Zach when he came back. He would be a woman Byron had never met.

"He's putting you on," Emily said. She was sitting at the table, ostensibly editing a paper on the synthesis of mRNA at the transcriptional level in the Drosophila Per protein, but whenever the spoon Byron held approached Toby's mouth, her own mouth opened in anticipation.

"Nope," Byron said, spooning more applesauce from the jar. "He wanted to tell me before he started wearing makeup."

"If Zach thinks that's the definition of women, he's headed for trouble," Emily said. "I suppose he's shaving his legs and getting silicone implants too."

"Not to mention waxing his bikini line," Byron said.

"Oh, God," Emily said, laughing. "I don't want to hear any more." She handed Byron a washcloth, and Byron carefully wiped applesauce off Toby's chin. "How would you know you were the wrong sex?"

"Woman's intuition?" Byron said.

"Very attractive," he said the next morning, when Zach walked into the lab wearing eye shadow.

"Don't make fun of me, okay?" Zach said.

Byron felt embarrassed. "I didn't mean anything," he said. "I mean, it's subtle and everything."

Zach looked pleased. "I've been practicing," he said. "You

know what? My younger brother wears more makeup than I do. Is this a crazy world or what?"

"Yeah," Byron said. He'd met Zach's brother, whose makeup was usually black. "Are you doing this gradually? Or are you sort of going cold turkey? I mean, will you come in in nylons and spike heels some morning?"

"Babe," Zach said, "I've been getting hormones for six months. Don't you notice anything different?"

He put his hands on his hips and turned slowly around, and Byron saw discernible breasts pushing up the cloth of Zach's rugby shirt. Byron felt a little faint, but he managed to say, "You're wearing a bra."

Zach went over to look in the mirror behind the door. He stood on tiptoe, staring intently at his breasts for a moment, and then, as he took his lab coat off the hook, he said, "God, I'm starting to feel good."

"You are?" was all Byron could manage. He was wondering how to say, without hurting Zach's new feelings, Don't call me babe.

All day he tried not to look at Zach's breasts, but there they were, right in front of him, as Zach bent over the bench, or peered into the microscope, or leaned back with his hands behind his neck, staring at the ceiling, thinking.

"I'm heading out," Byron said to Sarah in midafternoon.

"Are you okay?" she said, looking up from the bench. "You look a little peaked."

"I'm fine," Byron said. "I'll be back in the morning."

But once out in the parking lot, sitting in his car, he could think of no place he wanted to go. He hung on to the steering wheel and stared at the Mercedes in front of him, which had a Utah license plate that read IMAQT. A woman, of course.

Well, it's not *my* life, he thought. Nothing has changed for me.

. . .

"I haven't had this much trouble with breasts since I was sixteen," he said to Emily as they sat at the kitchen table watching the sunset.

"How big are they?" Emily said.

"Jesus, I don't know," Byron said.

"Bigger than mine?" she said.

Byron looked at Emily's breasts, which were bigger since she'd had Toby. "No," he said. "But I think they've just started."

"You mean he'll keep taking hormones till they're the size he wants?" Emily said. "I should do that."

"You know," Byron said, "what I don't understand is why it bothers me so much. You'd think he's doing it to spite me."

"Going to meetings will be more expensive," she said.

"What do you mean?" Byron said.

"Honey," Emily said, "if Zach's a woman, you won't be sharing a room. Will you?"

"Oh," Byron said. "Do you think it will make that much difference?"

"You're already obsessed with his breasts," Emily said. "Wait till he's fully equipped."

Byron leaned his head on his hand. He hadn't even *thought* about the surgical procedure.

"I think you're letting this come between us," Zach said the next day.

"What?" Byron said.

"We've been friends a long time. I don't want to lose that."

"Zach," Byron said, "I don't see how things can stay the same."

"But I'm still the same person," Zach said.

Byron was not at all sure of that. "Well, how's it going?" he finally said.

Zach seemed pleased to be asked. He sat down on the desk and folded his arms. "Really well," he said. "The surgeon says the physiological changes are right on schedule. I'm scheduled for surgery starting next month."

"Starting?" Byron said.

"I'm going to have a series of operations," Zach said. "Over several months. Cosmetic surgery for the most part."

"Zach," Byron said, "maybe it's none of my business, but don't you feel—" He cast about for the right way to say it. "Won't the operations make you feel, uh, mutilated?"

Zach shook his head. "That's what it's all about," he said. "They won't. To tell you the truth, in the past year or two I've come to feel as if my penis is an alien growth on my body. It's my *enemy*, Byron. This surgery's going to liberate me."

Byron crossed his legs. "I don't think I can relate to that," he said.

"I know," Zach said. "My support group says nobody really understands."

"Your support group?" Byron said.

"Women who've had the operation," Zach said, "or are in the process. We meet every week."

"How many are there?"

"More than you'd think," Zach said.

"So," Byron said. "Are you—I mean, should I call you 'she' now?"

Zach grinned. "I've been calling myself 'she' for a while. But so far nobody outside my group has."

"Well," Byron said. He tried to look at Zach and smile, but he couldn't do both at once. He smiled first, and then looked. "I'll work on it," he said. "But it's not exactly easy for me either, you know."

"I know," Zach said. "I really appreciate your trying to understand." He stood up. "Back to work," he said. "Oh." He turned around with his hand on the doorknob. "I'm changing my name, too. As of next month I'll be Zoe."

"Zoe," Byron said.

"It means 'life,' " Zach said. "Mine is finally beginning."

. . .

"It means 'life,' " Byron said mincingly to Toby as he pulled the soggy diaper out from under him. " 'Life,' for Christ's sake."

Toby smiled.

"What's he been for thirty-eight years—dead?" Byron said. He dried Toby and sprinkled him with powder, smoothing it into the soft creases. As he lifted Toby's feet to slide a clean diaper underneath him, a stream of pee arced gracefully into the air and hit Byron in the chest, leaving a trail of droplets across Toby's powdered thighs.

"Oh, geez," Byron said. "Couldn't you wait ten seconds?" He reached for the washcloth and wiped the baby off. Then he wiggled the little penis between his thumb and forefinger. "You know what you are, don't you?" he said, leaning over and peering into Toby's face. "A little man. No question about that."

Toby laughed.

After he'd put Toby into the crib, Byron went into the bathroom, pulling his T-shirt off. He caught sight of himself in the mirror and stood still. With the neckband of the shirt stuck on his head, framing his face, the shirt hung from his head like a wig of green hair.

He took his glasses off to blur the details and moved close to the mirror, looking at the line of his jaw. Was his jaw strong? Some women who had what were called "strong features" were quite attractive. Byron's mother used to say that Emily was built like a football player, but Byron had always thought she was sexy.

He put his glasses on and stepped back, bending his knees so that only his shoulders showed in the glass. With long hair around his face, and a few hormones to change his shape a little, he'd make a terrific woman.

He opened the medicine cabinet and took out one of Emily's lipsticks. He leaned forward and spread it on his mouth,

and as he pressed his lips together, a woman's face material-
ized in the mirror. Byron's heart came to a standstill.

It was his mother.

"It was the weirdest thing," he said. "I never looked like her
before. Never."

"You never cross-dressed before," Zach said, continuing to
stare at the computer screen. "What's going on with this
data?"

"Of course I never cross-dressed," Byron said. "I still don't
cross-dress. I just happened to look in the mirror when my
shirt was on my head."

Zach looked up at him and grinned. "And there she was,"
he said. "You would be amazed what we find out about ourselves when we come to terms with our sexuality."

"Oh, for God's sake," Byron said. "I was taking my shirt
off. I wasn't coming to terms with anything."

"That's fairly obvious," Zach said, tapping at the keyboard.

"Jesus!" Byron said. "Do those hormones come complete
with bitchiness? Or is your period starting?"

Zach stared at him. "I can't believe you said that," he said.

Byron couldn't believe he'd said it either, but he went on.
"Everything's sexuality with you these days," he said crossly.
"I'm trying to tell you about my mother and you tell me it's
my goddamn sexuality."

Zach stood up and stepped away from the desk. "Look,"
he said, folding his arms, "it's called the Tiresias syndrome.
You're jealous because I understand both sexes. By cross-
dressing—whether you go around in Emily's underwear or
just pretend you've got a wig on—you're trying to identify
with me."

For a long moment Byron was unable to move. "What?" he
finally said.

"You can't handle talking about the things that really matter, can you?'' Zach said. ''As soon as we get close to personal feelings, you back off.''

''Feelings,'' Byron said.

''You're a typical man when it comes to emotions,'' Zach said.

''And you're a typical woman,'' Byron said.

Zach shook his head. ''You are in trouble, boy.''

''*I'm* in trouble?'' Byron said. ''Looks to me like you're the one with the problem.''

''That's the difference between us,'' Zach said. ''I'm taking steps to correct my problem. You won't even admit yours.''

''My problem is you,'' Byron said. ''You are a fucking prick.''

''Not for long,'' Zach said.

''Once a prick, always a prick,'' Byron shouted.

After Zach walked out the door, Byron sat down at his desk and stared at the data Zach had pulled up on the screen, but its sense eluded him. Finally he spun his chair around and put his feet up on the bookcase behind him, and reached for a legal pad.

He always wrote his poetry on long yellow legal pads. He had once tried to jot down some poetic thoughts on the computer, but they had slipped out of his poem and insinuated themselves into a new idea for a research project, which in fact developed into a grant proposal that was later funded. The experience had scared him.

He stared up at the slice of sky that was visible from where he sat, and held the legal pad on his lap for more than an hour, during which time he wrote down thirteen words. When Sarah stuck her head into the office and said, ''See you tomorrow,'' he put the pad down and left work for the day.

Driving home, he thought about his dead mother, Melba Glass. She had never liked Emily, but once Byron was married, his mother stopped saying snide things about her. She asked them instead. "Honey," she'd say, "isn't Emily a little *strident?*"

"What do you mean, 'strident'?" Byron would snarl, and she would say she'd meant nothing at all, really, young women were just *different* these days. Byron would narrow his eyes at her, but later, when he'd driven his mother to the train station and waved her off, the idea would come back to him. Emily *was* vociferous in her opinions. And not particularly tolerant of her mother-in-law's old-fashioned tendencies.

"Why doesn't your mother *drive?*" she'd say.

"Why should she?" he'd say. "She never needed to."

"She needs to now, doesn't she?" Emily would say.

"Why should she?" Byron would repeat, and for a couple of days he would react to everything Emily said as if she were being highly unreasonable, and *strident.*

What would Emily say if he told her that his dead mother had appeared to him? Worse, that he had appeared to himself as his dead mother?

Emily would lean over Toby's crib in the dark. "I'll be Don Ameche in a taxi, honey," she'd sing. "Better be ready 'bout half past eight."

"How are you? Three of you now. Ha!" Terry Wu said.

"Three of me?" Byron said.

"You have a little baby?" Terry said.

"Oh! Toby! Terrific! And Emily. I see. Sure, we're fine. Really. Everything's terrific."

A concerned look seized Terry Wu's face. "Do you protest too much?" he said, and he leaned forward, pressing his fingertips together.

"Protest?" Byron said. "That's not why I'm here."

"Maybe no, maybe yes," Terry said, but he leaned back again.

"No, it's my, uh, colleague. You know, Zach."

"Ah," Terry said.

"I seem obsessed," Byron said weakly.

"You are obsessed with your colleague?"

"With his sex," Byron said.

"His sex?" Terry said.

Byron felt himself blushing. "I can't get used to the idea that he's a woman."

Terry nodded again. "Each one is a mystery."

"No, it's just—why didn't I know?"

"Did you know your wife was pregnant when she conceived?"

"What does that have to do with it?" Byron said.

"Well," Terry said, "you were there when it happened, in fact you did the deed, and yet you didn't know about it."

"Terry, I think that's something else."

Terry shrugged. "Are you in love with your colleague?"

"Of course not." He was becoming angry. "What are you getting at?"

"I am trying to elicit a coherent statement from you," Terry said. "So far all you have managed to tell me is that you are obsessed with your colleague and are not in love with her. I am having trouble following your flight of ideas."

"Look." Byron stared down at his feet. "Someone whom I have known for more than twenty years has overnight turned into a woman. It's shaken my understanding of reality. I can no longer trust what I see before my eyes."

"Yet you call yourself a scientist," Terry said thoughtfully. "It is simply a matter of surgery and hormonal therapy, isn't it? Changing one form into another by a well-documented protocol?"

Byron stared at him. "That's not what I mean," he said.

Terry clasped his hands together happily. "Yet a magical process is involved as well! An invisible and powerful force! Something that is beyond our understanding! But"—he put his hands on his desk and stared into Byron's eyes—"even your poetic license will not allow you to accept it?"

"My poetic license?" Byron said.

"Are man and woman so different, so unrelated, that no transformation is possible? It's this Western culture," Terry said in disgust. "In my country, people exchange sexes every day."

Byron wondered if he had understood Terry correctly.

"Suppose your little baby comes to you in twenty years and says, 'Daddy, I am now Chinese.' Will you disown the child, after twenty years of paternity? No! He will still be the son you love."

"Chinese?" Byron said.

"I fear our time is up," Terry said. He stood up and held his hand out. Byron stood too, and shook it. "Good to see you again. Would you like to resume these discussions on a regular basis? I can see you at this time every week."

"I don't think so," Byron said. "I just wanted this one consultation."

"Glad to be of service," Terry said. "No charge, no charge. Professional courtesy. Someday I may need an experiment!" He chuckled. "Or a poem."

"A shower?" Byron said.

"Isn't it a kick?" Emily said. "Gifts like garter belts and strawberry douches."

"That's sick," he said.

"Oh, come on, honey. His men friends are invited too." She put down the screwdriver she'd been using to put together Toby's Baby Bouncer and leaned over to kiss Byron's knee. "It'll be fun."

"Why don't we just play red rover?" Byron said. "All the girls can stand on one side and yell, 'Let Zach come on over.' "

"You act as if you've lost your best friend," Emily said.

"I *am* losing him. I've known him for twenty years and

suddenly I find out he's the opposite of what I thought he was."

"Ah," Emily said, and she sat back against the sofa. "Here we go. Men and women are the exact opposite."

"Don't you start," he said. "I don't need an attack on the home front."

"I'm supposed to comfort you, I suppose." Emily said. "Sympathize with you because your good buddy's going over to the enemy."

"Well?" Byron said. "Aren't you secretly glad? Having a celebration? Letting him in on all your girlish secrets?"

Emily shook her head. "We're talking about a human being who has suffered for forty years, and you're jealous because we're giving him some lacy underpants? You're welcome to some of mine, if that's what you want." She smiled at him.

"Suffered?" Byron said. "The dire fate of living in a male body? A fate worse than death, clearly."

"Why are you attacking *me?*" Emily said.

"I'm not attacking you," he said. "I'm just upset." He scooted closer to her and put his arms around her, laying his head against her breasts. "What if I lost you, too?"

"Sweetheart," Emily said, "you're stuck with me for the duration."

"I hope so," Byron said. He turned his head and pressed his face against her. "I certainly hope so." His voice, caught in her cleavage, sounded very far away.

"Nearly twenty years ago," Byron said softly, holding Toby in his arms as he rocked in the dark, "when Daddy and Uncle Zach were very young—"

Toby, who was gazing at his eyes as he spoke, flung out a fist.

"He was still Uncle Zach at the time," Byron said. He tucked the fist into his armpit. "Anyway, we used to ride out to the quarries outside Bloomington to go swimming. You've never been swimming, but it's a lot like bobbing around in Mummy's uterus."

Toby's eyes closed.

"We used to ride our bikes out there after we'd finished our lab work," Byron said. "Riding a bike in the summertime in southern Indiana is a lot like swimming too. The air is so full of humidity you can hardly push the sweat out your pores.

"So we would ride out there in the late afternoon, and hide our bikes in the trees, and go out to our favorite jumping-off place," Byron said. "And Daddy and Uncle Zach would take off all their clothes, and get a running start, and jump right off the edge of the cliff into space!"

Toby made a sound.

"Yes, the final frontier," Byron said. "And we would hit the water at the same instant, and sink nearly to the bottom of the bottomless pit, and bob up without any breath. It was so cold."

He frowned. What kind of story was this to tell his son? Toby was asleep now, but in a few years he'd complain. He'd want plot, and character development.

"That was poetry, son," Byron whispered. He stood up and laid the sleeping baby on his stomach in the crib. Tomorrow morning Emily would put Toby in his new Baby Bouncer, and Toby Glass would begin to move through the world on his own.

"What are you giving her?" Sarah said.

"Who?" Byron said, looking up from his calculations.

"Zoe," Sarah said. "We're giving her silk underwear from Frederick's of Hollywood. Do you know her bra size?"

"Sarah," Byron said, pushing his chair back and crossing his arms, "why on earth would I know Zach's bra size?"

"Oooh," Sarah said. "Touchy, aren't we? You *are* friends." She stood there watching him as if, Byron thought, she was daring him to deny it.

"There are some things you just don't discuss in the locker room," he said.

"Oh," Sarah said. "Well, what are you getting her?"

"I haven't thought about it," Byron said.

"Don't you think you *ought* to think about it?"

It was his mother's voice, and for a moment Byron thought his mother had spoken, there in his office. It was just what she would have said. She would look at him over her glasses, a long, questioning look. "Why not something personal? Intimate? You two have known each other a long time."

"Mom, you don't get something intimate for another guy," he would say.

"Oh, Byron, Byron. You should be more flexible, dear. You sound like your father." Every time she had said it she meant it as a reproach, but Byron was always rather pleased.

He wished sadly that he *could* talk to his mother. She never even knew that he had a son of his own. He looked at the picture of Toby on the desk and thought, she would be disappointed to see how much he looks like Emily's father.

He pictured her sitting in the chair beside his desk, her legs crossed. She had had very nice legs. She always insisted on buying expensive stockings at Dellekamps'. "When I worked at Du Pont," she told him more than once, holding out her foot and gazing at her delicately pointed toes, "they gave us all the stockings we wanted, but they were nylon."

"Mom," Byron said aloud, "I don't want to give him anything."

And as if he had disappointed her again, he saw her sadly pick up her purse from the floor and stand up.

"Just let me tell you this, Byron," she said. "If you don't support Zoe at this time in her life, you'll regret it forever."

She stepped toward him, shaking her finger at him.

"Forever, Byron."

He sighed, and looked at the legal pad lying in wait on the

desk. His mother had once told him she used to write poetry, but he had never read any of it.

"I wonder what happened to all my mother's poems," Byron said.

Emily looked up from the paper she was reading and stared at him thoughtfully, chewing on the end of her red pencil. "It wasn't very *good* poetry," she said.

"How do you know?" he said.

She frowned. "Byron, sometimes I think you live in a cocoon."

"You read it?" Byron said in amazement.

"Sure," she said. "You know, little poems about love, flowers, the moon." She shook her head, looking at the paper in her lap. "This guy should try poetry," she said.

"Why didn't she let me read it?" Byron said. He glanced at the television screen, where a woman was talking about teenage reproductive strategies in abusive households. "Em. What happened to it?"

"She threw it away," Emily said. "She thought it was too embarrassing to keep."

"Why did she talk to *you* about it?" Byron said.

"We had to talk about something," Emily said.

"Maybe your mother is right," Byron said. "Maybe I have no idea what's going on in the world." He peered into the rear-view mirror at Toby, who was snoring softly in his car seat and paying no attention.

Byron had thought in the beginning that being a scientist would increase his understanding of the world, and the world's understanding of itself. But instead as his work grew more specialized over the years and his expertise became narrower, his brain seemed to be purging its data banks of extraneous information and shutting down, one after another, his receptors for external stimuli. He had been so caught up in chronicling the minuscule changes taking place in the gels and tubes of his laboratory that the universe had changed its very nature without his even noticing. The world had a new arrangement that everyone else seemed to understand very well: even his poetry had simply served to keep him self-absorbed, oblivious of what must be reality.

Actually, he rather liked the idea of living in a cocoon while the world became a wilder and more exotic place. Sirens wailed, cars throbbing with bass notes roared past him with mere children at the wheel, dead women appeared in mirrors, and men changed into women; but Byron and Toby Glass putted across town safe and snug inside a cocoon.

"What do *I* know?" Byron thought. "What *do* I know?"

"Can I help you?" said a heavily scented woman with beige hair. Her lips were a carnivorous shade of red, and her eyelids were a remarkable magenta.

"I'm looking for a gift," Byron said.

"For Baby's mother?" the woman said.

"Who?" Byron said.

"Baby's mother," she said, and with a long scarlet fingernail she poked at the Snugli where Toby Glass was sleeping peacefully against Byron's stomach.

"Oh," Byron said. "No. This is for a shower."

"Oh, I love showers!" the woman said. "What kind?"

"Sort of a coming-out shower."

"We don't see many of those," she said. She turned to survey her wares. "Are you close to the young lady?"

"I used to be," Byron said. "But she's changed."

"*Plus ça change,*" the woman said. "Something to remember you by. Something in leather?"

"Well, I don't know," Byron said, nervously stroking the warm curve of Toby's back. "I thought maybe stockings?"

The woman frowned. "You mean like pantyhose?"

"I guess not," he said.

"I know." The woman tapped Byron's lower lip with the red fingernail. "Follow me." She led him to the back of the store and leaned down to pull open a drawer. "For our discerning customers. A Merry Widow." She held up a lacy black item covered with ribbons and zippers.

"Wow," Byron said. "I didn't know they still made those."

"They are *hot*," the saleswoman said. She held it up against her body. "Imagine your friend in this!"

"I can't," Byron said.

"Do you know her bra size?" the woman asked.

"I'm not sure it's final yet," Byron said.

"Oh," the woman said. "Well. Maybe some perfume." Byron followed her back to the front of the store, where she waved her hand grandly at a locked glass cabinet. "These are very fine perfumes, from the perfume capitals of the world. Paris, Hong Kong, Aspen. This one is very popular—La Différence."

"That's good," Byron said. "I'll take some of that."

"Oh, excellent choice!" The woman patted his cheek before she reached into her cleavage and drew out a golden key to unlock the perfume cabinet.

"While Ginny rings that up, would you like to try on some of our makeup?" said another salesperson.

"No, thanks," Byron said.

The woman pouted at him. "You *should*," she said. "Lots of men wear it. Girls go crazy for it." She patted a stool in front of the counter. "Sit down."

Byron sat, and she removed his glasses. "You'll look *terrific*," she said. She leaned toward him, her lips parted, and gently massaged his eyelid with a colorful finger. " 'Scuse me while I kiss the sky," she sang softly, stroking the other one. Then she drew on his eyelid with a long black instrument. "This is Cream-So-Soft," she told him. "It is *so* easy to put on." She drew it across the other eyelid, and finally she brushed his eyelashes with a little brush and stood back. "There," she said. "You are a *killer.*"

Toby began to gasp into Byron's shirt. The makeup woman swooped down. "Oooh," she said. "Little booper's making hungry noises." She lifted her eyes to Byron. "Bet I can stall him."

"You can?" Byron said.

"Babies *love* this," she said. She maneuvered Toby out of the Snugli and sat him down facing her on Byron's lap. She began to sketch on his face with the Creem-So-Soft while Toby stared silently at her nose. "There!" She picked Toby up and held him for Byron to examine.

Toby beamed and waved his limbs. He was adorned with a black moustache and a pointy black goatee.

"Oh, how darling," Ginny said, coming back from the cash register. "Will this be cash or charge?"

Byron looked at the bill she handed him. "Charge," he said. "I thought this store went out of business a long time ago."

"Lots of people say that," Ginny said.

"What have you done to the baby?" Emily said when Byron walked in the door.

"Babies like this," Byron said. "It's a preview of what he'll look like in twenty years."

"He's going to be a beatnik?" Emily said. She took Toby from Byron's arms. "Don't you think you're rushing things a little?"

Byron sighed. "They grow up so fast," he said. He kissed the top of Toby's head, and then kissed Emily. "How do you like the new me?"

Emily looked at him. "Did you get your hair cut?" she said.

"Em, I'm wearing makeup," Byron said.

"Oh," she said. "So you are." She held Toby up and sniffed at his bottom. "Daddy didn't change your dipes," she said, and she carried him off to his room.

Byron went into the bathroom to look at himself. His eyelids were a very bright purple. He picked up Emily's Barn
Red lipstick and carefully covered his lips with it. Then he
took off his glasses.

"You know who you look like?" Emily said, appearing beside him in the mirror. "Your mother. Honest to God. If you
had one of those curly little perms, you could pass for your
own mother." She peered into the mirror, stretching her upper lip with her forefinger. "Do you think I should shave my
moustache?"

"No," Byron said. "It's sexy." He slid his hands under her
arms and over her breasts. "Let's go to bed."

"No, thanks," Emily said. She picked up her Creem-So-Soft
and started to outline her eyes. "I have no desire to sleep with
your mother."

"You never did like my mother," Byron said.

"Not a lot," Emily said.

"I think I'll go over to the lab," Byron said. He kissed her
cheek, leaving a large red lip print.

"Hold still," Emily said. She wet a washcloth, and as she
scrubbed his lips he had a sudden vision of his mother scrub-
bing at grape juice the same way thirty-five years ago.
"There. Now you look like my husband again."

He looked in the mirror. His stinging lips were still pinker
than normal. "Is wearing makeup always so painful?"

"Always," she said. "We do it for love."

Byron liked weekends at the lab, he liked weekdays, too,
when students and technicians wandered in and out of one
another's labs borrowing chemicals, and all the world seemed
engaged in analyzing the structures and chemical interactions
of various tissues. But weekends, when the offices were
empty and the halls were quiet, and only the odd student
padded back and forth from the bathroom, had a cozy, private feeling. Byron could think better in the silence, and he

felt close to other scientists, who had given up time in the outside world to bend lovingly over their benches and peer into microscopes, hoping to add to the world's slim store of truth. Both the lab work he did and the poetry he wrote on weekends seemed to spring from a deeper level: a place of intuition and hope that was inaccessible when he was distracted by bustle. On weekends he caught glimpses of the world he hoped to find, where poetry and science were one, and could explain the meaning of life.

"The meaning of life," he said aloud, and wrote it down on his legal pad. Then he turned and typed it on the keyboard, and it appeared in amber letters on the screen in front of him. He smiled and pushed back in his chair, and put his feet on the desk. Poem or experiment? Either one!

He felt that he was on the threshold of an important discovery.

"Why are you doing this?"

Byron opened his eyes. It was Zoe, leaning against the doorjamb. It was definitely and absolutely Zoe; she could no longer be mistaken for a man. He stared at her; what *was* it? The hair, the clothes, the jaw, the way the arms were folded: all were utterly familiar. What had happened?

"The makeup," Zoe said. She shook her head. "You're trying to be something you're not."

He had forgotten about the purple eye shadow and the mascara, but he said, "How do you know what I'm not?"

"It's just that you're so conservative," Zoe said.

"No," he said. "I'm really quite wild. I'm just handicapped by my many fears."

"You?" Zoe said.

He nodded. "But you're wild through and through."

Zoe shook her head. "I'm conservative at the core. That's always been my major problem." She gazed out the window at the white hills. "You know the only thing I regret? I'll never have any children now."

"You could adopt."

She shook her head. "They won't have my genes."

"You never really know your children anyway," Byron said.

Zoe sighed. "Tell me honestly. Did Emily teach you how to put that eyeliner on?"

Byron smiled. "No," he said. "In fact she learned from me."

Zoe narrowed her eyes and stared at him for a moment, and then sat down on a stool. "I'm thinking of going to law school."

"Are you serious?" he said. "You'd leave the lab?"

"Sure. Patents is the way to go."

"You'd leave me?"

Zoe reached over and seized the tablet. "Poetry, poetry, poetry," she said. "Always with you it's the poetry. Anyone would think you're too distracted to work."

"You think any of this is easy?" Byron said.

"None of it," she said, and they sat together for a while without talking. "Are you coming to my shower?"

"Aren't showers supposed to be a surprise?" Byron said.

Zoe shrugged. "I hate surprises. I told Sarah she could give me a shower only if she invited men, too."

"I got you a gift." Byron was surprised to feel suddenly shy. "But is there anything you'd really like?"

"Will you come see me in the hospital?"

Byron nodded.

Zoe smiled. "Actually, you look good in makeup," she said. "It redefines your features. You look stronger."

"It's the same old me, though," Byron said. "I'm not any stronger than before."

"I really am thinking of law school," Zoe said. "I need to change my life."

"Changing your sex isn't enough?"

"No. That's who I've been all along."

"Oh," Byron said, and all at once he felt very sad, and exhausted. He put his feet up on the desk, and they sat there in silence, gazing at the part of the world they could see through the window.

After a while he told Zoe about Toby's trip to Dellekamps'. "And then," he said, "I'm sitting on a bench in the mall giving him his bottle, and I look up and these two old ladies are staring at him. 'That is dis*gust*ing,' one of them says. And the other one gasps and grabs her arm and points at me. And they both back away looking horrified."

Zoe began to laugh.

"And then a man and a little girl walk by, and the little girl says, 'Daddy, is that a homeless person?' And the father says, 'No, dear, that's a man with problems.' "

"Oh," Zoe gasped, holding her ribs.

Byron wiped the tears from his own cheeks, and when he looked at his hand, he saw that it was smeared with mascara. "I had no idea," he said, "no idea why these people were saying these things. I'd forgotten about my makeup. And Toby just looked normal to me."

"Stop," Zoe said, bending over and clutching her stomach.

"And finally a man comes up to me with his hands on his hips and says, 'You ought to be ashamed.' "

"I'm dying," Zoe croaked. "I can't breathe. Oh." She jumped from the stool and ran through the door. "I have to pee."

"You," Byron called after her, "should be ashamed." He listened to the squeegeeing of her sneakers as she ran down the empty hall, and to the familiar creak of the hinges as she pushed open the door to the men's room.

"Glad you could make it, glad you could make it," Terry Wu said, shaking Byron's hand vigorously.

"Did you doubt that I would?" Byron said.

"You're a busy man," Terry said. "So often the cells can't wait." He leaned forward and whispered, "I am giving her a vibrator." Aloud, he said, "The muscles of the calves ache when one first wears high heels."

"That is so true," Emily said. She smiled at Terry Wu and pulled Byron away. "That guy gives me the creeps," she said.

"Honey, you're being xenophobic," Byron said. "Things are different in his country."

They pushed their way through the crowd, Byron cupping one hand protectively around Toby's head to keep him from being squashed in his Snugli.

"There you are!" Sarah appeared in front of them. "Isn't the turnout great?" She waved her arm at the crowd.

Emily hugged her. "Did you get it?" she said.

Sarah nodded. "I never spent that much on a bra in my life."

"How did you know what size to get?" Byron asked.

"I asked her," Sarah said. She led them over to where Zoe stood beside a gift-covered table. "Here are the Glasses!"

"I'm so glad you could come," Zoe said. She kissed Emily on the cheek and prodded Toby's bottom with a glistening red-tipped forefinger. "How's my little beatnik godbaby?"

"Zoe, you look gorgeous," Emily said. "Really. You look so —you."

"Next I'm going to have electrolysis on my facial hair," Zoe said.

"You look pretty good as you are," Byron said. He wondered when the time would come that Zoe would kiss *his* cheek. "I bought you some perfume, but I ended up giving it to Emily."

"Thank goodness," Zoe said. "I'm allergic to everything but La Différence, anyway."

"One of these days," Byron said, "I'll write you a poem."

"He's never done that for me." Emily waved her hand at the table in front of them. "Look at all this loot."

They stared at the pile of presents. "I can't wait to open them," Zoe said. "I've always wanted a shower."

"Isn't it wonderful to get what you always wanted?" Byron put his arm through hers and squeezed it, and he could feel her breast against his triceps as she squeezed back, her muscles hardening briefly against his own.

He felt a rush of pleasure. On his left Emily reached for a bacon-wrapped chicken liver; on his right his oldest friend in the world gently disengaged her arm from his to touch the hands of the dozens of people who had come to wish her well; and from his shoulders, like a newly discovered organ of delight, hung the little bag full of Toby Glass.

Toby Glass, who could grow up to be anything!

The musicians in the string quartet hired for the occasion began to tune their instruments, leaning toward each other, listening, nodding gravely. The cellist moved her stool a little closer to the violinist; the violinist held her instrument away from her neck as she shook back her long red hair, and then replaced it firmly under her chin. Suddenly, as if spontaneously, each player lifted her bow and held it poised in the air for a long moment, until at some prearranged and invisible signal they plunged their bows toward the strings of their various instruments and began to play.

John Rolfe Gardiner

THE VOYAGE OUT

Tony Hoskins, at twelve, was an intellectual child, wary of sensation. Not a prodigy exactly, but at the head of his form at Cacketts School. He could declaim on several tales from Chaucer, and on the paths of the planets, even on the curious journeys of human sperm and ovum, although he hadn't a clue about finding a girlfriend or about what might be asked of him in pleasing one.

On this day he was saying all the wrong things. First to his father: "Daddy, at least I'll be sailing on a British ship, under a British flag."

"Actually not," he was told. "It's an American vessel. You'll be all right."

This was before the German began to aim his torpedoes at Yanks, before his subs began to hunt in wolfpacks.

"Not to worry," his father went on. "You'll be in convoy."

Why a convoy if no need to worry? His father, in Royal Army lieutenant's uniform, bare of medals, could not answer.

Hoping to put his religion in order before embarkation, Tony looked to his mother. "Tell me again, what's the Trinity?" he said unexpectedly just before the ship pulled out.

"Tiresome boy," she said. "Three in one and one in three. If you don't understand that, you shan't have a chocolate."

Again he was confused; his mother's simplistic formulation seemed at odds with her piety. Hardly off the gangplank, his legs rubbery with fear, he didn't want candy, only assurance that this huge and blunt-prowed merchant ship with a woman's name, the Ellen Reilly, riding high in the water, would come to safe port across the Atlantic and that his new school would be tolerable.

He saw other parents retreating, crying into handkerchiefs, stumbling off the boat and along the dock, giving their boys up to the sea and a new world. The drawn lips of his father and mother began to quaver as they turned away. And enemies appeared beside him, his second-form mates Booth and Jeffries, full of questions:

"Do the lifeboats have engines?"

"Is it daytime in Canada?"

"Will we take a secret course to avoid submarines?"

The same boys who despised him in the classroom, who had called him "twit" and "wonkie" for his privileged conversations with the masters, were hovering around him. Why should he nurse their fears?

And here came Rasson-Pier, who was older, a fifth former who had once caned Tony for impudence. Rasson-Pier told them all to shut up. He said the lot of them should be ashamed for leaving their country in wartime. And if it were up to him he'd be in uniform, not in retreat.

"Hoskins, you're in my cabin," he announced. "See that the beds are made taut."

Rasson-Pier, tall, well muscled, and lording it over the others from Cacketts, with gray eyes under blond bangs, and sufficient beard to be permitted a razor in his kit.

Riding down the channel from Folkstone, Tony tried to use his father's advice: "Think of the ship as the floating island of a country still at peace." Over on their left was France, which he knew to be alive with Germans; on the right, his own island, which, after dark, would be under attack again from the air.

Only three weeks earlier, Tony's headmaster, strolling across his playing fields at night, had been killed by a bomb far off its city target. A miraculous and devastating event, a direct hit on school morale. In the ensuing rearrangements of the school year, Tony and six other boys, and Mr. Pardue, history master of the stunned academy, had been booked on this empty supply ship—refugees for resettlement in a Canadian boarding school.

The Ellen Reilly came clear of the coast and swung to the west. There was no convoy, only open sea. Tony took the blank journal his father had given him that morning (with the advice of writing five hundred words a day at bedtime) and threw it over the side.

"You mustn't be angry," Pardue admonished. "It will only be fourteen days." But Tony gestured at the zigzag wake of the ship, the pattern of fear they were leaving on the sea behind them.

"Never mind," Pardue told him, "you'll be at their organ in two weeks. Maybe some of your Chopin, eh?"

"Maybe some of his Chopin, eh?" The other boys played with the line, but anxiety cracked their voices.

In the boys' new school, an oddity of brick and stone nestled in farm fields to the west of Toronto, they came to be known as "The Boys from Cacketts," or "The Boys from Cacketts Minus One," after the tragedy at sea, while their teacher shepherd became "Pastor Pardue" among his new colleagues, who found him to be a total loss as an instructor, and a fount of useless homily: "There are no ifs in history."

They were set apart as a curious subculture among the relatively coarse population of Canadian boys—a little band with a higher order of fealty to the King, and led in intellect by the youngest, the pale scholar Tony. He was allowed into the school chapel each afternoon to practice at the organ, while the others were led off to a field to fight over a leather ball or flail away with cricket bats. Tony had come with two copies of his medical excuse, proof of his asthma—one to be filed in the school infirmary, and the other for his pocket. Thus reprieved from athletic torment, he was free to demonstrate his case that the body's only sensible purpose is to carry around the brain.

On October 28, 1941, Lieutenant Gerald Hoskins dashed off a note, from his office in the London Cage, to his son, Tony, at the Charter Bridge School:

Dearest Tony,

Horrible, horrible. We had the awful news before your letter arrived. There are not enough tears in the world to answer for the loss of a child. And such a well-favored boy by all reports. You must be numb. Our only response to such an untimely death can be surpassing love for those who survive. Try to think of our love for you.

You say the Trinity was revealed to you on the crossing. Very well, but remember you are stuck to the planet by gravity, and from an Oriental perspective you may be upside-down, worshipping the devil. But no more—the Colonel is calling.

P.S. No, we don't keep animals here. Nor are there Nazis in dank cells. "London Cage" is simply the informal name given to this interrogation center. From time to time I will write you from my office here, where I won't have your mother looking over my shoulder. The address here must remain unknown to you. Your letters should be posted home.

A second letter from the Lieutenant to his son, dated November 15, 1941:

Dearest Tony,

Nothing from you this month. Our assumption must be that you have settled in and found a schedule suited to your special needs. We have a report from Dean Hastie, who tells us your academic proficiency is "not balanced by contribution to community."

While offering the excuse of your harrowing journey, he cites you for sarcastic remarks about the Canadian students, for shirking work in the school garden, and resisting dress regulations.

Though your mother and I agree that shorts are not suited to the climate, the answer is to bundle heavily on top. Wear the sweater, scarf, and cap as prescribed in the school manual. You know that long trousers come in the third form, just as they do at Cacketts.

You may have heard on the wireless that we are managing quite well in the air. When I am not translating or writing interrogation reports, they have me reading prisoners' mail. There, I've told you a little secret, and you must keep it to yourself.

A sympathy committee has been got up here. We take turns visiting the Rasson-Piers. When you have a moment you will write them whatever you can muster of David's last days. Perhaps something you found heroic in him, or you could express your wonder at his potential. As the last to see him you are a target of their curiosity. They have questions beyond the police type, which they are too discreet or grief-bound to ask. It will be your job, now or later, to anticipate and console.

It's too awful to think he might have been showing off acrobatically so close to the side. Showing off for whom? one asks, since no one saw him go overboard. So dreadful for all of you, wondering if he were hiding somewhere or actually lost at sea.

We hope the investigation has ended and we pray for your

happiness. Or, I should say, your mother prays and I beg of fate. Have you been faithful to your journal? It will be a revelation to you in time to come.

After the blank journal had gone over the side, Mr. Pardue had gone to his cabin to fetch a substitute, another bound notebook with marbled cover.

"Your father told me how much this means to him," he said to Tony. "I've put some starter lines in for you." He pointed to the first page:

> For every trouble under the sun,
> There be a remedy or there be none.
> If there be one, try and find it,
> If there be none, never mind it.

"You take it from there," he said, smiling.

Before they left the channel someone had puked. And now the boys' stomachs felt the rise, fall, and side shift of the Atlantic's heavy quartering waters. The first officer promised only more discomfort. "That's right—we're empty," he announced on the boat deck. "And the higher she rides, the further she rolls."

He had come from the bridge to lay down ship's rules for the Cacketts boys. At mealtime they would go to the mess deck, officers' side. The rest of the day they would remain in their cabins doing schoolwork. For exercise, they could walk the main deck, but only with Mr. Pardue's supervision. The bridge and hold of the ship were off-limits. The boys must stay out of the crew's cabins and out of the galley, or risk losing a hand to the steward's cleaver.

The officer had no sooner turned back when Rasson-Pier performed the first of his handstands on the ship's railing. Upside-down, he had winked at Tony as the ship rocked in a rising swell.

"See that, Hoskins?" The older boy's hand was on Tony's shoulder as they went to their cabin. "You can count on me, you see. I'll be watching out for you. You have nothing to fear from the chaps in Canada."

Dean Hastie at the Charter Bridge School to the parents of Tony Hoskins in Brasted, Kent, November 30, 1942:

We normally write to parents of the boys from Cacketts at the end of each term. However, the head and I felt it would be wrong to delay in reporting that Tony is in a fair way to surpassing school records for third-form boys in Mathematics, Latin, and History of the Empire. He might achieve similar distinction in Composition if he could be kept to assigned topics.

We should recommend your son for immediate advancement to fourth form if his social and emotional maturity were up to the same marks. As you know, at Charter Bridge we strive to develop the fully rounded boy. We had expected that in his second year here Tony would have put new-boy diffidence behind him and joined with a will in some extracurricular pursuit.

Perhaps Tony has mentioned the motto cut in stone over our chapel door. "Remember Now Thy Creator in the Days of Thy Youth." We take the charge seriously, so you must not misunderstand when I say the religious conversion your son experienced on his journey here is troubling in its intensity. Our chaplain cannot shake him from his testimony that the Trinity was revealed to him on the ocean as three glowing balls. We see no joy in his faith.

I must tell you that the transfer has not been a complete success. The boys from Cacketts tend to remain a clique, though they sometimes quarrel among themselves. Your son does not seem to be a member, even of this separate band. We sense a residual grieving here for the loss of their young idol, and a weight of unfinished business. One boy has suggested that Tony's original account of the events at sea may not be reliable. And now, more than a year after the fact, our Mr. Pardue comes forward to say that your son may have kept a journal which might clear him of all suspicion. We wouldn't think of invading his privacy without warrant. Perhaps you would advise him to open relevant pages to our scrutiny.

A brighter note. Our musical instructor is leaving Charter Bridge this month, and we are asking Tony to fill in as chapel organist for Sunday service and Wednesday vespers. It's our little scheme to get him more involved.

On the journal's first page Pardue's verse has been scribbled over and splashed with ink:

Sept. 23, 1941. Aboard the Ellen Reilly: The ship is black, red, and rusty. Sailed 1420 Greenwich. R.-P.'s stunt behind Pardue's back takes everyone's breath. Supper: mashed potatoes, bright-yellow gravy of uncommon viscosity, and salty fish, white and cooked to a mush like the potatoes. One serving of greens a day; we missed them by coming aboard too late for lunch.

Tonight Jeffries came into our cabin crying. He wanted to know why I was put with R.-P. R.-P. said wouldn't the Germans love to see him like that. Jeffries left sniveling. R.-P. asked me down from my upper to play cards on his bunk. Twenty-one. No money, playing for favors, he said. I lost terribly, what do I owe him? R.-P. has torch with extra dry cells. He will allow me to use it to keep my notes. Says he's at sea in Latin. Quite so! And I, a second former, might help.

Booth came in shaking with fear. The idiot thinks he heard a torpedo propeller passing under us. No one can sleep.

A year after the crossing, the notebook was more useful to Tony as a chronology of odd particulars than as a thoroughgoing journal—a skeleton on which his memory hung the dangerous flesh, the things he would never have written down. For example, the way Rasson-Pier's tone had changed after lights-out from cold command to simpering—as if he were taking the part of a woman in a play.

With the notion of water rushing in to drown him in his sleep, Tony had sneaked out of his cabin in the middle of the first night and wandered through dim-lit passages, down metal stairways, into empty cargo compartments. Somewhere close to the throbbing center of the ship he heard a horse whinny and a lion roar. Alarmed by what he took to be his own inventions, he became confused in retreat, and spent an unconscionable time finding his cabin again.

From Lieutenant Gerald Hoskins at the London Cage to Tony Hoskins at the Charter Bridge School, April 13, 1943:

Yes, we support your refusal to show any part of the journal. Violation of your private thoughts is tantamount to rape of the spirit.

There is mischief here, too. I'm sorry to say we are no longer speaking with the Rasson-Piers since they find more comfort in the gossip of the Jeffrieses, passed along by their son Arthur. A poisonous little chap, I'd guess, but you would know better than I.

Yes, traits in an individual can be correlated with national origin, the pieties of Mr. Pardue to the contrary notwithstanding. It's quite possible that the impulsive and vainglorious side of David Rasson-Pier was passed along by the father's French parents. As to the question of cultural distinction, consider the opening lines of two letters which crossed my desk this week, the first from a German: "Dear Mother, The most awful thing has happened. We have been captured by the English and are being held in Oran, waiting transfer to a prison camp in America."

The second from an Italian: "Dear Mama, The most wonderful thing has happened. We have been captured by the English and will soon be on our way to the United States."

Don't mistake me, I'm not advocating one attitude over the other. But if your Pardue doubts the relevance of my example, I suggest he visit the prison camp in Bowmanville. I'm told the Germans there are goose-stepped by their officers to the mess hall, where Italians happily prepare the food and banter about the women waiting for them in the town.

No, we do not hold it against the Dean for denying you further use of the chapel organ. Really! A two-octave glissando at the end of "God Save the King" while the school waited for amen! Did you expect to get away with that?

Guard your journal.

September 25, 1941, aboard the Ellen Reilly:

This whole ship trembles with the thump of its engines. Diesels, I'm told. Above this constant drumming is the day-long rattle of electric paint chippers as the crew works at their endless chore of scraping and painting. They'll go from bow to stern, then start all over again.

No one actually studied today. In spite of the din, fell asleep over my books. R.-P. woke me before Pardue came in. Anyone caught napping during study time gets twenty-four-hour cabin confinement. I've been made tutor of second and third formers. Pardue says those not prone to seasickness must minister to those who are. He is. So is Jeffries. I am not.

Booth apologized for rudeness. As R.-P. has taken my part, others are shifting colors, too, seeking my favor. At present, most of them are unable to function. While they moan in their bunks, I explore.

Dolphins weaving under the prow. Watched them for most of an hour before slipping below again. One of the crew stopped me. Only wanted to talk. This was Sam, an able-

bodied seaman, who is missing two fingers, and limps. Asked
did I know there were unfortunates below. Heard animals
again in lower cargo compartments. Couldn't find them.

Night walk. The deck was dark but for moonlight. No outside lights permitted. Passageways only faintly lit. Memorized numbers on doors and did not get lost. No one believes
I saw a black-haired girl in bathing costume. She was rattling
a cup of coins and chanting something sad, as if practicing to
be a beggar. Someone called from another compartment,
"Raklo! Raklo!" and she stood still as a stone. If R.-P. doesn't
believe any of this, why does he keep asking how old the girl
was and what she looked like? Very young. Her skin a mot-
tled ochre.

Someone filched my breakfast orange. R.-P. boxed Booth's
ear. Doesn't matter who did it, he says, just doesn't want it
happening again.

Tony had put aside pen and notebook when Rasson-Pier offered his soft invitation.

"Do you want to come down to my bunk?" All the courage
and bluster vanishing again.

"No."

"For a little visit?"

"No."

"You're to be kind to those who aren't feeling well."

He didn't believe the older boy was sick, only dodging the
books for another day, with the sympathy of Pardue.

"No."

From Dean Hastie at the Charter Bridge School to the parents
of Tony Hoskins in Brasted, Kent, May 21, 1943:

Looking toward vacation, we are suggesting that Tony not
remain in dormitory with Mr. Pardue and the other boys
from Cacketts. We would not want a repeat of last summer's

incident. With your permission, Tony will spend the interim at the Croyston farm, which provides the school with milk and eggs.

A picture of the family is enclosed. In truth, I think the Croystons would welcome an appropriately innocent companion for their shy daughter, Margaret, and your son seems well suited for the job. Though the family won't provide intellectual stimulation, they keep a wholesome life, devout yet not without humor.

Tony will be expected to help with farm chores, perhaps just the thing for the continuing melancholy. A break from the high academic standard to which he holds himself, and from his difficult religion. May I quote him? "The faith at Charter Bridge is to true faith as water is to wine." Perhaps the justification for his little musical joke on the school.

We have not discounted homesickness—the long, unnatural separation from the two of you. Too, the Rasson-Pier case will not go away. As I explained months ago, the initial investigation produced little but tears and mystery. Should we discourage the family from persisting? So many loose ends. From their distance can they be sure the appropriate questions were asked? Our Cacketts boys have kept the stew at a boil.

You ask again for the facts free of the children's fantasy. The ship's log reported the child missing on October 1, 1941. Captain Andrew Shad made inquiries and established that David had been given to reckless displays of daring. He concluded one of these must have been the boy's final act.

The Ellen Reilly made its first port, Halifax, on October 7. Our boys disembarked and were detained there two days for questioning, first by the R.C.M.P., later by a visiting magistrate from London. Before the investigation was completed and the Captain's finding upheld, the ship had already taken on grain and tinned food, and sailed the night of October 8 for Baltimore. There the loading of war supplies was com-

pleted. With the same officers and crew the boat turned back
for England on October 14.

We now believe there was another element on board the
Ellen Reilly between England and North America, a group
kept apart from legitimate ship's company but sighted several times if we are to believe the Jeffries boy and your own
child. A band of Polish performers? Gypsies? Lithuanian
Jews? How they came to be on the ship and where they disembarked are as open to speculation as their nationality.

We had, too, the crass report of a seaman named Sam, put
off the boat in Halifax for the theft of a pair of shoes. He was a
rough sort who befriended several of our boys and enter-
tained them with bawdy talk in his quarters, which they
knew were off-limits.

This Sam testified to having seen passengers in the hold.
He fouled his account with details of a dark young lady, little
more than a child by his word, offering her favors to several
of the crew. If people didn't believe him, he said, they could
ask our boys what she'd do.

As to the mysterious travellers, whether Captain Shad gave
them passage as a humanitarian gesture or for his own profit
is unclear. Their arrival was not recorded by Canadian immi-
gration. Shad, who survives as a master in the merchant
marine (the Ellen Reilly went down in January, off the
Azores), does not deny that such a group could have been
stowaways during his command.

We are told that the docks in Halifax are too closely pa-
trolled for any such band to have disembarked without papers. They may never have come ashore in North America
unless they were spirited off the ship in Baltimore. The
United States was not yet at war, and security was doubtless
lax. This seems a remote possibility but so does their very
existence on board. Given the curious tatterdemalion migra-
tions and urgencies of wartime, their passage is not beyond

belief. Perhaps sympathy, reinforced by coin, eased the path into America.

Again we ask you to urge your child to come forward with his journal, if it exists, and any relevant information that might soothe the family. We have again advised the Rasson-Piers against a crossing.

Though we find Tony a difficult boy, the faculty is interested by him, and, if I may say so, fond of him. We would see nothing unnatural in an infatuation he may have had for David Rasson-Pier. These things are common as hiccups among schoolboys, and are left behind as naturally as they arrive.

Our comptroller reminds me that we have not received your share of reparations for the water damage in Tony's room last August. We appreciate your faith in Tony's innocent part. However, a clear culprit was not found, and all the boys from Cacketts must share the cost of repair.

September 26, 1941, aboard the Ellen Reilly:

Ocean calm but Sam says we're headed into "weather to pump the boys' stomachs again." Complimented me for my sea legs. Told him R.-P. is faking it to avoid the books. If he were sick, how could he use the ship's rail for a gymnast's horse? He spins his legs right around over the side. Jeffries, Phillips, and Booth have all seen him do it. Gives me the willies. Booth said he wouldn't care if R.-P. lost his balance.

Found another route to the forward cargo bay. Hid in a crate and watched the show. Bales of hay set out in a circle. There appears to be a family circus travelling with us. Preparing its act for America? A small black bear was brought in, muzzled and growling softly. Is this the noise I took for a lion's roar? Can bears survive on ship's rations? There is also a miniature pony that whinnies like a full-grown horse.

I suppose the man must throw knives every day or get out

of practice. Tonight the girl was pitiable, with her chin fallen to her chest, and her arms stretched wide, like Christ on the cross, and surrounded by the steel blades delivered in rapid order. By her father? Her brother?

A woman unleashed the bear and placed it on the seat of a small bicycle. Maybe upset by the motion of the ship, it could not keep the pedals going and tumbled over.

R.-P. says I must pay my gambling debt. I'm sure he cheated me.

Tony had recorded nothing of what happened the next day, or the following night when, after lights-out, Rasson-Pier had climbed into the upper bunk with him, whispering urgently, "The others needn't know."

He wrote nothing of his haunted sleep, of this famous athlete poking around behind him with his stupidly swollen thing.

From Captain Gerald Hoskins at the London Cage to Tony Hoskins at the Charter Bridge School, September 20, 1943:

Dearest Tony,

Your mother and I would transfer you to another school in an instant if it were reasonably within our power. Our distance, our ignorance of alternatives, and the dean's reluctance to recommend "some inferior academy" all work against us. It is an outrage that your notebook was stolen. We have demanded an apology from Hastie. He seems to us a great blandifier. Believe me, you have nothing to fear from him but his dangerous good will.

It is out of the question for you to return to England now. The Americans have only just begun to appreciate the logic of convoys. In the meantime their coastal waters have become a continent-long fireworks display, with U-boats sinking tankers and supply ships at will. Hardly a time to play "Red Rover, Red Rover, Let Tony Come Over."

There is nothing to be ashamed of in your account of the crossing save the occasional grammatical lapse, though eyebrows are raised at the mention of gambling. The hounds have what they've bayed for, a dry bone. Now let them bury it.

The Dean says you worked admirably for the Croystons and amazed their church youth fellowship with the force of your testimony. I know your mother's letters are full of admiration for your spiritual awakening. She warns me not to disrupt your faith with petty sophistry. Still, I can't approve a dogma which condemns to perdition all those beyond its pale. This is *entre nous*.

It's no special boast to tell you I've been promoted to Captain. All officers here at the Cage have taken one step up. So, nothing heroic, though I am credited with devising a new purgative for the tight-lipped Germans. I stamp their papers N.R. (*Nach Russland*, to Russia) and their mouths run a torrent.

From Dean Hastie at the Charter Bridge School to the parents of Tony Hoskins in Brasted, Kent, January 24, 1944:

Again the school offers its full apology to you and your son. That Tony's journal should have been taken from his room is altogether unacceptable. That pages were copied and distributed is despicable.

We don't know who stole the notebook. It appeared in the office of our school paper, the *Charter Sentinel*, where the editor, one of our senior boys, cut a stencil of certain pages and ran them off on the mimeograph machine. This misguided chap, who comes to us from Detroit with a warped notion of press freedom, has been relieved of all journalistic duty.

I now believe it was a mistake to badger Tony for his record of the voyage. The notes have only raised the anxiety of the Rasson-Piers, who insist they could not be the work of a twelve-year-old. In their new anguish they suspect the cruel mischief of an adult—a post-dated fabrication supporting the police report of a foolhardy, self-inflicted death.

The family's theory was reinforced by your son's admission that the notebook was not the original, lost at sea, but a substitute provided by Mr. Pardue. Thus, he too is a subject of suspicion. The evidence of a missing page, the ragged edge in the journal, where a sheet was torn from it, adds to our confusion. The more so, since this was apparently part of the entry for October 2, 1941, the day after David's disappearance was first recorded.

We have assured the family that the original notes are in Tony's skilled hand, and that your son is capable of the vocabulary and sentiment, even the occasional poetic flourish. We couldn't swear to the dating of the entries, but have no reason to doubt their honesty. The headmaster and I were disturbed by references to gambling, punishable at Charter Bridge by immediate expulsion. However, we accept Tony's word that nothing of value was to be exchanged, only favors.

That the mysterious travellers below-decks are transformed into a Gypsy circus seems a wild leap of imagination. Our school physician advises me that the mind under stress (all the Cacketts boys have acknowledged their numbing terror of submarines) may take refuge in illusion.

A copy of the mimeographed notes is now in the hands of the police, who have asked to speak with Tony once more. Be assured that the school's attorney will again be on hand to prevent investigative bullying. If Tony chooses to tell them he remembers nothing, that will suffice. We pray for a return to academic tranquillity.

September 28, 1941, aboard the Ellen Reilly:

The rattle of the paint chippers stopped for a merciful hour this morning. Pardue took advantage of the relative quiet, calling a meeting in his cabin to rally spirits. He never rose from his bunk. The air was horrid.

Our workbooks will be collected tomorrow, though there is not a word or cipher in most of them. Took Pardue some tea this morning and was caught out by Phillips watching from the door of his room. Phillips says it will all come out when we reach Canada, all the broken rules. And there will be whippings. Told him there is no corporal punishment at Charter Bridge. He seemed much relieved. He asked what R.-P. talks about and does he do stunts in the cabin.

Pardue whined pitifully for me to take his tray away. The smell of toast and margarine was making him ill again. Jeffries tried to trip me at his doorway. Called me "suck-bottom."

I can tolerate the pitch and roll of the ship. Also, the further one descends through the lower decks, the less one notices the roll. Sam says the people below are stealing food. The galley is missing a dozen tins of beef. Bear provender? Captain Shad is furious and says we've been roving through his ship against orders. I'm the one. I suppose the others would rather die in their cabins.

I have seen a periscope like a black needle in the waves behind us.

October 1, 1941, aboard the Ellen Reilly:

R.-P. did not return to the cabin last night. A search for him began this morning. Certain we won't find him.

There followed a line obliterated, washed over with ink. How many times had he been asked, "If you wrote 'certain,' were you not certain?" And "Why did you cross this out?" Why should he tell them, "I did not cry with the rest"?

. . .

On the evening of September 29, Rasson-Pier followed Tony
down through the maze of passages to the performance
chamber, complaining repeatedly of the grease stains the
metal stairways were leaving on his trousers.

"Periscope? Girl in a bathing costume? What next, Hoskins?"

"Why didn't Pardue put Phillips with you?" Tony asked
him. "Someone more your age."

"I asked for you," he said. "Thought it might give you a
boost."

The hero of the Cacketts playing fields had asked for *him?*
Anxious about displeasing Rasson-Pier again, he prayed the
girl would be there.

She was sitting on a bale, with her back to them. A long
black dress appliquéd with red and orange rings gave the
effect of contouring her ample young figure in tight-fitting
bracelets.

"Run along," Rasson-Pier ordered. "I'll speak to her alone."

"She doesn't speak English," Tony said. "I could try a little
French for you."

Why had he wanted to be helpful? He was only pushed
aside.

The girl turned and stared at them without modesty. Before
Rasson-Pier could sit beside her, she had risen, taken his arm,
and was leading him away through the hatch at the far end of
the compartment. Perhaps a fortune-teller, Tony thought,
leading him to a private place to read his palm.

From Dean Hastie at the Charter Bridge School to the parents
of Tony Hoskins, Brasted, Kent, January 26, 1944:

I dare to presume a friendship has developed between us in
our pursuit of your son's welfare. This letter following close
on the heels of the last is prompted by a surprising turn in the
Rasson-Pier case. There is now a theory the boy may be alive.

We are told by the police that there was a family row before the voyage, a shouting match in which David called his parents such names as "pale cowards" and "funny little people." He threatened never to come back if they packed him off to Canada. This was followed by one of his acrobatic demonstrations, a walk on his hands down a stone stairway in front of their home in Kent. Certainly a thoughtless display in front of his troubled parents.

The imaginations of the Rasson-Piers must be racing along with the flow of news and rumor from the families of our Cacketts contingent. I'm told that "Gypsy circus" is oxymoronic, that, while Gypsy children are often sent out to beg, the families never perform or work for money, unless it be in telling the future.

The Rasson-Piers now cling to the frail chance that a rebellious David might have been drawn to, or charmed away by, this band that must have intended to land in America. That they may have seen profit in his gymnastic virtuosity. But who is to say they were Gypsies? Haven't they also been called Lithuanian Jews and Polish performers?

I turn again to Tony's situation. Why do the other children continue to torment him? If the authorities don't trust his written account, how will they credit his oral testimony?

Your child has taken refuge in his faith. All worthy counsel, he avers, comes from the three-person God, though we know he looks daily to his letter box for guidance from you. Your son has lost weight. We try to see that he eats well.

From Captain Gerald Hoskins at the London Cage to Tony Hoskins at the Charter Bridge School, February 15, 1944:

Dearest Tony,

We're proud of you. Stick to your guns, and ask yourself this: Why would they have you impeach yourself? What good could come of it? Can the lost boy be brought back? If you find yourself in a compromising box, don't jump out in public. If there is something to say that can cause only humiliation, take it to this higher being of yours, all three of him if necessary. I am dead serious. Take proper nourishment, and hold on. You will cross this way in victory the moment the Atlantic is secure.

Early on September 30th. Rasson-Pier had come back to the cabin quite exhausted.

"They don't wash, you know," he said. He sighed and fell asleep. Tony covered for him through the morning, calling "Studying, please" when the others knocked for their morning chats.

At noon, Rasson-Pier was awake and irritable.

"Who doesn't wash?" Tony asked him.

But the older boy was looking into the future. "If you say anything of what's happened in this cabin, I'll report your funny business when I caned you at Cacketts."

"What business?"

"The way you enjoyed it. Even more without trousers."

"I never. Whatever do you mean?"

"Yes, well, who will they believe?" He fell back on his bunk. "Perhaps I'll tell them anyway," he said.

He slept again for several hours, woke, and asked, "What if she's given me the disease?"

"What disease?"

"You sap. The one that takes your brain."

"I believe there's a cure for that."

The older boy nodded slowly.

"Don't look for me tonight" was the last Tony heard him say.

If the girl's odor displeased him, if he thought her infected, why had he gone to see her again? Goatish, Tony had heard his mother say, but would not a goat demand exclusively a mate of opposite gender?

. . .

The October 1st journal entry had concluded: The ship went a drunken path through the glowing sea when the sky was torn into three ragged black sheets by lightning.

Tony had stayed out on the open deck that evening in order to avoid his roommate. Standing at the stern, he watched the serpentine course of the ship recorded in the roiled wake. With the first bolt of lightning, he swung around and saw a figure far up the deck balanced upside down and turning with his hands on the rail, his legs, at that instant, over the side. And someone was standing there, close to him, perhaps the girl. All went black and a moment later they were all brilliantly lit by a second bolt. The spinning body was disconnected from the rail, floating out into the night.

So obvious of Rasson-Pier. Showing off for the girl. Performance was the only language they had in common. Tony made his way forward in the dark, but the two of them had vanished. No time to applaud the trick; the next act of his floating circus had already begun. A spectral ball was gliding down the stay that ran from antenna mast to the bow. It split into two glowing spheres, and then there were three of them, evenly spaced, moving back and forth along the taut metal line. He watched for several minutes until they merged into one again and disappeared.

October 2, 1941, aboard the Ellen Reilly:

Is he pestering the dolphins? Sawn into rude portions by sharks? Have I seen the spirit of God in triplicate?

The next page had been torn from the notebook.

From Tony Hoskins at the Croyston farm to his parents in Brasted, Kent, August 23, 1944:

The summer has flown. I am two inches taller. Six feet! The second haying is finished. I was allowed to work the rake, an old-fashioned thing once pulled by a horse, this season by an ancient tractor, petrol being available. For two weeks, I've been sitting on the metal seat of the rake and lifting its tines at each windrow with a hand lever. As a result my right arm is appreciably muscled, and I must do something to bring the left into balance.

Yesterday a man came to replace some rotten boards in the north end of the haymow. I was asked my estimate of the barn's height at the point of the gable. I could tell them quite precisely, I said, by measuring the shadow of the barn and that of a pole of known length, then applying simple geometry. By the time I gave my answer, Mr. Croyston had made a calculation of his own and the carpenter was on his way to the lumberyard. My figure was off by half a foot, Mr. Croyston's correct to the inch. So my fancy education is a thing of some amusement here, though Margaret is keen to share my books and ideas.

Last Thursday I was asked to escort her to a "young people's" in the village. It's not the social gathering it sounds. There is some flirtation, but only so much as is possible when you are seated in church pews under the eyes of a preacher.

Between hymns, each boy and girl is expected to rise, in turn, and share a faith-affirming experience. I think I blushed awfully when the minister's eyes fell on me, but I was able to stand and tell again of the three balls of fire over the deck of the Ellen Reilly. By the end of my story the pastor's eyes were brimful, and I was embarrassed for him. Margaret, seated to my right, took my hand when I sat down again.

From Captain Hoskins at the London Cage to Tony Hoskins at the Charter Bridge School, September 10, 1944:

A note to tell you that civilians are crossing again! Given proper escort, it appears to be safe. I've made inquiries, and will find a berth for you the moment space is available on a secure ship. You've been so long there under brutish circumstances. It would be cruel of us to leave you longer than is prudent for your safety. We know that there is still talk of your journal's missing page. I fear the gossips will never give it up.

From Tony Hoskins at the Charter Bridge School to his parents in Brasted, Kent, October 5, 1944:

Please do not book passage for me. I'm content and intend to finish here.

Fair questions have been raised, and there is something I want to clear up about the voyage out. When I saw David Rasson-Pier spinning above the ship's rail, I thought he'd learned a new trick. It never occurred to me he was out of control. Not until it was far too late to give an alarm.

The following day I returned to the same place on the deck. Looking down, I saw a row of three lifeboats suspended over the side. One could speculate about David's having possibly fallen onto the canopy covering one of these and climbing back onto the deck below. But the chance is so minuscule. Believe me, he perished at sea. It's too late to raise another slim hope that can only give anguish.

If you must know, the page torn from the journal held my thoughts on the family below decks. Particularly the girl, and Rasson-Pier's use of her. I did not invent the girl. Think of her under a rain of knives, and try to imagine throwing knives at me for a living.

The Dean is quite mistaken about Gypsies. They frequently take itinerant work, and are known for their rapport with animals, notably as trainers of circus acts. And when I went down in the ship, I heard *"Raklo Raklo!"* called out like a crow's warning. It's the Gypsy word for a non-Gypsy boy. I doubt I will see her again, or know what befell her, but we were all Gypsies on that voyage, I now believe, and I would cry *"Raklo!"* now to those who did not make the crossing. Our chaplain says the war has blown seed, good and bad, to all points of the compass, and it remains to be seen what will germinate. High hopes for me. But what of the rootless Gypsies? I like to think of the girl and her family moving across America, performing, escaping from one camp to the next.

I'm confident her troupe survives. Almost as certain as I am that David Rasson-Pier is dead. The passage of time has not weakened my resolve not to write to his family. You will have to guess at my reasons.

About my "hard faith," as Hastie calls it. You shouldn't think I ever believed the fireballs over the ship's deck were the actual embodiment of the Trinity. I took them, rather, as a phenomenal sign of Mother's faith. No more periscopes after that. They helped me complete the crossing without going mad. And why should that sign be erased now, by some scientific explanation? Really, for men who profess faith, some of my instructors are quite hopelessly literal.

For all that, I like the teachers here quite as well as the masters at Cacketts. The Atlantic may, as you say, be secured for Allied shipping. Nevertheless, I don't wish to return to England before graduation from Charter Bridge.

From Dean Hastie at the Charter Bridge School to the parents of Tony Hoskins in Brasted, Kent, November 20, 1944:

We shall never hope to understand this war's random terror, why we are spared here in our snug academy while refugees from all walks are driven pillar to post. I do believe we can now take hope in these few boys from Cacketts who were washed up on our shores. I am their Dean, yet I sense that they are children no more. The heat of war has fired them, and they shine with a new hardness and brilliance. Especially your son.

You would not recognize Tony. His second summer on the Croyston farm did wonders. He is quite filled out in athletic proportion, and happy as we have never seen him. It will please you to hear, too, that your son has found common ground with students and masters alike, and can be seen on occasion roughhousing and joking with his mates from Cacketts.

Something has cleared the air. There is less ostentation in his religious assertion. I don't think the other boys ever believed he was guilty of any complicity in the Rasson-Pier tragedy. Rather, they resented his claim to a private audience with God on the voyage out. Without boasting, we give our faculty credit here, in particular our Department of Physical Science. Mr. Theonel believes his lecture on electricity was responsible. As he says, "Knowledge must rush in where dispelled superstition leaves a vacuum." Tony now concedes that the three balls of light he saw on the ship's antenna must have been static electricity, the phenomenon called "St Elmo's fire."

We think it gave him comfort to learn from our History instructor that early mariners also believed they witnessed holy bodies in the rigging of their ships—the *corpus sancti*, or corposants, as they called them. Tony will be returning to you with a new maturity. Once more, he has our permission to practice his music on the chapel organ. Eventually, I'm sure, he'll be trusted to play for our services again.

The third anniversary of David Rasson-Pier's disappearance will not have escaped your notice. It was observed here by a special prayer at evening vespers, and a reading of this note from the family: "We believe our son perished at sea by his own dangerous devices. To those children who survive, we offer our blessing. Your useful lives must be our monument to David's memory." The school is much relieved by their sad but sensible resignation.

The Charter Bridge students filing in to the final chapel service of the year were surprised to see Tony Hoskins seated at the organ. Excited, they squirmed and whispered in their pews, as if assured of a sacrilege to spice the imminent summer rebellion.

They were disappointed to hear scarcely a hint of the expected irreverence. Buttercup's theme floated over "Faith of Our Fathers," so cleverly hidden in tempo and contrapuntal disguise that no one but the new music instructor was wise to it. From the choir he winked approval at his richly gifted student.

Lorrie Moore

TERRIFIC MOTHER

Although she had been around them her whole life, it was when she reached thirty-five that holding babies seemed to make her nervous—just at the beginning, a twinge of stage fright swinging up from the gut. "Adrienne, would you like to hold the baby? Would you mind?" Always these words from a woman her age looking kind and beseeching—a former friend, she was losing her friends to babble and beseech —and Adrienne would force herself to breathe deep. Holding a baby was no longer natural—she was no longer natural— but a test of womanliness and earthly skills. She was being observed. People looked to see how she would do it. She had entered a puritanical decade, a demographic moment—whatever it was—when the best compliment you could get was: You would make a terrific mother. The wolf whistle of the nineties.

So when she was at the Spearsons' Labor Day picnic, and when Sally Spearson had handed her the baby, Adrienne had burbled at it as she would a pet, had jostled the child gently, made clicking noises with her tongue, affectionately cooing, "Hello punkinhead, hello my little punkinhead," had reached to shoo a fly away and, amidst the smells of old grass and the fatty crackle of the barbecue, lost her balance when the picnic bench, dowels rotting in the joints, wobbled and began to topple her—the bench! The wobbly picnic bench was toppling her! And when she fell backward, spraining her spine— in the slowed quickness of this flipping world she saw the clayey clouds, some frozen faces, one lone star like the nose of a jet—and when the baby's head hit the stone retaining wall of the Spearsons' newly terraced yard and bled fatally into the brain, Adrienne went home shortly thereafter, after the hospital and the police reports, and did not leave her attic apartment for seven months, and there were fears, deep fears for her, on the part of Martin Porter, the man she had been dating, and on the part of almost everyone, including Sally Spearson who phoned tearfully to say that she forgave her, that Adrienne might never come out.

Those months were dark and cavernous with mourning. Martin Porter usually visited her bringing a pepper cheese or a Cabash couscous cup; he had become her only friend. He was divorced and worked as a research economist, though he looked more like a Scottish lumberjack—graying hair, redflecked beard, a favorite flannel shirt in green and gold. He was getting ready to take a trip abroad. "We could get married," he suggested. That way, he said, Adrienne could accompany him to northern Italy, to a villa in the Alps set up for scholars and academic conferences. She could be a spouse. They gave spouses studios to work in. Some studios had pianos. Some had desks or potter's wheels. "You can do whatever you want." He was finishing the second draft of a study of first world imperialism's impact on third world monetary systems. "You could paint. Or not. You could not paint."

She looked at him closely, hungrily, then turned away. She still felt clumsy and big, a big beefy killer in a cage, in need of the thinning prison food. "You love me, don't you," she said. She had spent the better part of seven months napping in a leotard, an electric fan blowing at her, her left ear catching the wind, capturing it there in her head, like the sad sea in a shell. She felt clammy and doomed. "Or do you just feel sorry for me?" She swatted at a small swarm of gnats that had appeared suddenly out of an abandoned can of Coke.

"I don't feel sorry for you."

"You don't?"

"I *feel* for you. I've grown to love you. We're grown-ups here. One grows to do things." He was a practical man. He often referred to the annual departmental cocktail party as "standing around getting paid."

"I don't think, Martin, that we can get married."

"Of course we can get married." He unbuttoned his cuffs as if to roll up his sleeves.

"You don't understand. Normal life is no longer possible for me. I've stepped off all the normal paths and am living in the bushes. I'm a bushwoman now. I don't feel that I can have the normal things. Marriage is a normal thing. You need the normal courtship, the normal proposal." She couldn't think what else. Water burned her eyes. She waved a hand dismissively, and it passed through her field of vision like something murderous and huge.

"Normal courtship, normal proposal," Martin said. He took off his shirt and pants and shoes. He lay on the bed in just his socks and underwear and pressed the length of his body against her. "I'm going to marry you, whether you like it or not." He took her face into his hands and looked longingly at her mouth. "I'm going to marry you til you puke."

They were met at Malpensa by a driver who spoke little English but who held up a sign that said VILLA HIRSCHBORN, and when Adrienne and Martin approached him, he nodded and said, "Hello, *buon giorno*. Signor Porter?" The drive to the villa took two hours, uphill and down, through the countryside and several small villages, but it wasn't until the driver pulled up to the precipitous hill he called *La Madre Vertigi-noso*, and the villa's iron gates somehow opened automatically then closed behind them, it wasn't until then, winding up the drive past the spectacular gardens and the sunny vineyard and the terraces of the stucco outbuildings, that it occurred to Adrienne that Martin's being invited here was a great honor. He had won this *thing*, and he got to live here for a month.

"Does this feel like a honeymoon?" she asked him.

"A what? Oh, a honeymoon. Yes." He turned and patted her thigh indifferently.

He was jet-lagged. That was it. She smoothed her skirt, which was wrinkled and damp. "Yes, I can see us growing old together," she said, squeezing his hand. "In the next few weeks, in fact." If she ever got married again, she would do it properly. The awkward ceremony, the embarrassing relatives, the cumbersome, ecologically unsound gifts. She and Martin had simply gone to City Hall, and then asked their family and friends not to send presents but to donate money to Greenpeace. Now, however, as they slowed before the squashed-nosed stone lions at the entrance of the villa, its perfect border of forget-me-nots and yews, its sparkling glass door, Adrienne gasped. *Whales*, she thought quickly. *Whales* got my crystal.

The upstairs "Principessa" room, which they were ushered into by a graceful, bilingual butler named Carlo, was elegant and huge—a piano, a large bed, dressers stenciled with festoons of fruit. There was maid service twice a day, said Carlo. There were sugar wafers, towels, mineral water and mints. There was dinner at eight, breakfast until nine. When Carlo bowed and departed, Martin kicked off his shoes and sank into the ancient, tapestried chaise. "I've heard these 'fake' quattrocento paintings on the wall are fake for tax purposes only," he whispered. "If you know what I mean."

"Really," said Adrienne. She felt like one of the workers

taking over the Winter Palace. Her own voice sounded booming. "You know, Mussolini was captured around here. Think about it."

Martin looked puzzled. "What do you mean?"

"That he was around here. That they captured him. I don't know. I was reading the little book on it. Leave me alone." She flopped down on the bed. Martin was changing already. He'd been better when they were just dating, with the pepper cheese. She let her face fall deep into the pillow, her mouth hanging open like a dog's, and then she slept until six, dreaming that a baby was in her arms but that it turned into a stack of plates, which she had to juggle, tossing them into the air.

A loud sound awoke her. A falling suitcase. Everyone had to dress for dinner, and Martin was yanking things out, groaning his way into a jacket and tie. Adrienne got up, bathed and put on pantyhose which, because it had been months since she had done so, twisted around her leg like the stripe on a barber pole.

"You're walking as if you'd torn a ligament," said Martin, locking the door to their room, as they were leaving.

Adrienne pulled at the knees of the hose, but couldn't make them work. "Tell me you like my skirt, Martin, or I'm going to have to go back in and never come out again."

"I like your skirt. It's great. You're great. I'm great," he said, like a conjugation. He took her arm and they limped their way down the curved staircase (Was it sweeping? Yes! It was sweeping!) to the dining room, where Carlo ushered them in to find their places at the table. The seating arrangement at the tables would change nightly, Carlo said in a clipped Italian accent, "to assist the cross-pollination of ideas."

"Excuse me?" said Adrienne.

There were about thirty-five people, all of them middle aged, with the academic's strange, mixed expression of merriment and weariness. "A cross between flirtation and a fender bender," Martin had described it once. Adrienne's place was at the opposite side of the room from him, between a historian writing a book on a monk named Jaocim de Flore and a musicologist who had devoted his life to a quest for "the earnest andante." Everyone sat in elaborate wooden chairs, the backs of which were carved with gargoylish heads that poked up from behind either shoulder of the sitter, like a warning.

"De Flore," said Adrienne, at a loss, turning from her carpaccio to the monk man. "Doesn't that mean 'of the flower'?" She had recently learned that *disaster* meant "bad star" and she was looking for an opportunity to brandish and bronze this tidbit in conversation.

The monk man looked at her. "Are you one of the spouses?"

"Yes," she said. She looked down then back up. "But then so is my husband."

"You're not a screenwriter, are you?"

"No," she said. "I'm a painter. Actually more of a printmaker. Actually, more of a—right now I'm in transition."

He nodded and dug back into his food. "I'm always afraid they're going to start letting *screenwriters* in here."

There was an arugula salad, and osso bucco for the main course. She turned now to the musicologist. "So you usually find them insincere? The andantes?" She looked quickly out over the other heads to give Martin a fake and girlish wave.

"It's the use of the minor seventh," sniffed the musicologist. "So fraudulent and replete."

"If the food wasn't so good, I'd leave now," she said to Martin. They were lying in bed, in their carpeted skating rink of a room. It could be weeks, she knew, before they'd have sex here. "*So fraudulent and replete*," she said in a high nasal voice the likes of which Martin had heard only once before, in a departmental meeting chaired by an embittered, interim chair who did imitations of colleagues not in the room. "Can you even use the word *replete* like that?"

"As soon as you get settled in your studio, you'll feel better," said Martin, beginning to fade. He groped under the covers to find her hand and clasp it.

"I want a divorce," whispered Adrienne.

"I'm not giving you one," he said, bringing her hand up to his chest and placing it there, like a medallion, like a necklace of sleep, and then he began softly to snore, the quietest of radiators.

They were given bagged lunches and told to work well. Martin's studio was a modern glass cube in the middle of one of the gardens. Adrienne's was a musty stone hut twenty minutes farther up the hill and out onto the wooded headland, along a dirt path where small darting lizards sunned. She unlocked the door with the key she had been given, went in, and immediately sat down and ate the entire bagged lunch —quickly, compulsively, though it was only nine-thirty in the morning. Two apples, some cheese, and a jam sandwich. "A jelly bread," she said aloud, holding up the sandwich, scrutinizing it under the light.

She set her sketch pad on the work table and began a morning full of killing spiders and drawing their squashed and tragic bodies. The spiders were star shaped, hairy, and scuttling like crabs. They were fallen stars. Bad stars. They were earth's animal-try at heaven. Often she had to step on them twice—they were large and ran fast. Stepping on them once usually just made them run faster.

It was the careless universe's work she was performing, death itchy, and about like a cop. Her personal fund of mercy for the living was going to get used up in dinner conversation at the villa. She had no compassion to spare, only a pencil and a shoe.

"Art *trouvé?*" said Martin, toweling himself dry from his shower, as they dressed for the evening cocktail hour.

"Spider *trouvé*," she said. "A delicate, aboriginal dish." Martin let out a howling laugh that alarmed her. She looked at him, then looked down at her shoes. He needed her. Tomorrow she would have to go down into town and find a pair of sexy Italian sandals that showed the cleavage of her toes. She would have to take him dancing. They would have to hold each other and lead each other back to love or they'd go nuts here. They'd grow mocking and arch and violent. One of them would stick a foot out, and the other would trip. That sort of thing.

At dinner she sat next to a medievalist who had just finished his sixth book on *The Canterbury Tales.*

"Sixth," repeated Adrienne.

"There's a lot there," he said defensively.

"I'm sure," she said.

"I read deep," he added. "I read hard."

"How nice for you."

He looked at her narrowly. "Of course, *you* probably think I should write a book about Cat Stevens." She nodded neutrally. "I see," he said.

For dessert Carlo was bringing in a white chocolate torte, and she decided to spend most of the coffee and dessert time talking about it. Desserts like these are born, not made, she would say. She was already practicing, rehearsing for courses. "I mean," she said to the Swedish physicist on her left, "until today, my feeling about white chocolate, was: Why? What was the point? You might as well have been eating goddamn *wax*." She had her elbow on the table, her hand up near her face, and she looked anxiously past the physicist to smile at Martin at the other end of the long table. She waved her fingers in the air like bug legs.

"Yes, of course," said the physicist, frowning. "You must be —well, are you one of the *spouses?*"

· · ·

She began in the mornings to gather with some of the other spouses—they were going to have little tank tops printed up —in the music room for exercise. This way she could avoid hearing words like *Heideggerian* and *ideological* at breakfast; it always felt too early in the morning for those words. The women pushed back the damask sofas, and cleared a space on the rug where all of them could do little hip and thigh exercises, led by the wife of the Swedish physicist. Up, down, up down.

"I guess this relaxes you," said the white-haired woman next to her.

"Bourbon relaxes you," said Adrienne. "This carves you."

"Bourbon carves you," said a redhead from Brazil.

"You have to go visit this person down in the village," whispered the white-haired woman. She wore a Spalding sporting goods T-shirt.

"What person?"

"Yes, what person?" asked the blonde.

The white-haired woman stopped and handed both of them a card from the pocket of her shorts. "She's an American masseuse. A couple of us have started going. She takes lire or dollars, doesn't matter. You have to phone a couple days ahead."

Adrienne stuck the card in her waistband. "Thanks," she said, and resumed moving her leg up and down like a toll gate.

For dinner there was *tachino a la scala*. "I wonder how you make this?" Adrienne said aloud.

"My dear," said the French historian on her left. "You must never ask. Only wonder." He then went on to disparage sub-altered intellectualism and dormant tropes.

"Yes," said Adrienne, "dishes like these do have about them a kind of *omnihistorical reality*. At least it seems like that to me." She turned quickly.

To her right sat a cultural anthropologist who had just come back from China where she had studied the infanticide.

"Yes," said Adrienne. "The infanticide."

"They are on the edge of something horrific there. It is the whole future, our future as well, and something terrible is going to happen to them. One feels it."

"How awful," said Adrienne. She could not do the mechanical work of eating, of knife and fork, up and down. She let her knife and fork rest against each other on the plate.

"A woman has to apply for a license to have a baby. Everything is bribes and rations. We went for hikes up into the mountains, and we didn't see a single bird, a single animal. Everything, over the years, has been eaten."

Adrienne felt a light weight on the inside of her arm vanish and return, vanish and return, like the history of something, like the story of all things. "Where are you from ordinarily?" asked Adrienne. She couldn't place the accent.

"Munich," said the woman. "Land of *Oktoberfest*." She dug into her food in an exasperated way then turned back toward Adrienne to smile a little formally. "I grew up watching all these grown people in green felt throwing up in the street."

Adrienne smiled back. This was how she would learn about the world, in sentences at meals; other people's distillations amidst her own vague pain, dumb with itself. This, for her, would be knowledge—a shifting to hear, an emptying of her arms, other people's experiences walking through the bare rooms of her brain, looking for a place to sit.

"Me?" she too often said, "I'm just a dropout from Sue Bennet College." And people would nod politely and only sometimes ask, "Where's that?"

The next morning in her room she sat by the phone and stared. Martin had gone to his studio; his book was going fantastically well, he said, which gave Adrienne a sick, abandoned feeling—of being unhappy and unsupportive—which made her think she was not even one of the spouses. Who was she? The opposite of a mother. The opposite of a spouse.

She was Spider Woman.

She picked up the phone, got an outside line, dialed the number of the masseuse on the card.

"*Pronto,*" said the voice on the other end.

"Yes, hello, *per favore, parle anglese?*"

"Oh, yes," said the voice. "I'm from Minnesota."

"No, kidding," said Adrienne. She lay back and searched the ceiling for talk. "I once subscribed to a haunted-house newsletter published in Minnesota," she said.

"Yes," said the voice a little impatiently. "Minnesota is full of haunted-house newsletters."

"I once lived in a haunted house," said Adrienne. "In college. Me and five roommates."

The masseuse cleared her throat confidentially. "Yes. I was once called on to cast the demons from a haunted house. But how can I help you today?"

Adrienne said, "You were?"

"Were? Oh, the house, yes. When I got there, all the place needed was to be cleaned. So I cleaned it. Washed the dishes and dusted."

"Yup," said Adrienne. "Our house was haunted that way, too."

There was a strange silence in which Adrienne, feeling something tense and moist in the room, began to fiddle with the bagged lunch on the bed, nervously pulling open the sandwiches, sensing that, if she turned just then, the phone cradled in her neck, the baby would be there, behind her, a little older now, a toddler, walked toward her in a ghostly way by her own dead parents, a nativity scene corrupted by error and dream.

"How can I help you today?" the masseuse asked again, firmly.

Help? Adrienne wondered abstractly, and remembered

how in certain countries, instead of a tooth fairy, there were such things as tooth spiders. How the tooth spider could steal your children, mix them up, bring you a changeling child, a child that was changed.

"I'd like to make an appointment for Thursday," she said. "If possible. Please."

For dinner there was *vongole in umido,* the rubbery, wine-steamed meat prompting commentary about mollusk versus crustacean anatomy. Adrienne sighed and chewed. Over cocktails there had been a long discussion of peptides and rabbit tests.

"Now lobsters, you know, have what is called a hemi-penis," said the man next to her. He was a marine biologist, an epidemiologist, or an anthropologist. She'd forgotten which.

"Hemi-penis." Adrienne scanned the room a little frantically.

"Yes." He grinned. "Not a term one particularly wants to hear in an intimate moment, of course."

"No," said Adrienne, smiling back. She paused. "Are you one of the spouses?"

Someone on his right grabbed his arm, and he now turned in that direction to say why yes he did know Professor so-and-so . . . and wasn't she in Brussels last year giving a paper at the hermeneutics conference?

There came *castagne al porto* and coffee. The woman to Adrienne's left finally turned to her, placing the cup down on the saucer with a sharp clink.

"You know, the chef has AIDS," said the woman.

Adrienne froze a little in her chair. "No, I didn't know." Who was this woman?

"How does that make you feel?"

"Pardon me?"

"How does that make you feel?" She enunciated slowly, like a reading teacher.

"I'm not sure," said Adrienne, scowling at her chestnuts. "Certainly worried for us if we should lose him."

The woman smiled. "Very interesting." She reached underneath the table for her purse and said, "Actually, the chef doesn't have AIDS—at least not that I'm aware of. I'm just taking a kind of survey to test people's reactions to AIDS, homosexuality and general notions of contagion. I'm a sociologist. It's part of my research. I just arrived this afternoon. My name is Marie-Claire."

Adrienne turned back to the hemi-penis man. "Do you think the people here are mean?" she asked.

He smiled at her in a fatherly way. "Of course," he said. There was a long silence with some chewing in it. "But the place *is* pretty as a postcard."

"Yeah, well," said Adrienne, "I never send those kinds of postcards. No matter where I am I always send the kind with the little cat jokes on them."

He placed his hand briefly on her shoulder. "We'll find you some cat jokes." He scanned the room in a bemused way and then looked at his watch.

She had bonded in a state of emergency, like an infant bird. But perhaps it would be soothing, this marriage. Perhaps it would be like a nice warm bath. A nice warm bath in a tub flying off a roof.

At night she and Martin seemed almost like husband and wife, spooned against each other in a forgetful sort of love—a cold, still heaven through which a word or touch might explode like a moon, then disappear, unremembered. She moved her arms to place them around him, and he felt so big there, huge, filling her arms.

The white-haired woman who had given her the masseuse card was named Kate Spalding, the wife of the monk man, and in the morning she asked Adrienne to go jogging. They

met by the lions, Kate once more sporting a Spalding T-shirt,
and then they headed out over the gravel, toward the gardens. "It's pretty as a postcard here, isn't it?" said Kate. Out
across the lake the mountains seemed to preside over the mi-
nutiae of the terra cotta villages nestled below. It was May
and the Alps were losing their snowy caps, nurses letting
their hair down. The air was warming. Anything could happen.

Adrienne sighed. "But do you think people have *sex* here?"

Kate smiled. "You mean casual sex? Among the guests?"

Adrienne felt annoyed. "*Casual* sex? No, I don't mean *casual* sex. I'm talking about difficult, randomly profound, Sears
and Roebuck sex. I'm talking marital."

Kate laughed in a sharp, barking sort of way, which for
some reason hurt Adrienne's feelings.

Adrienne tugged on her socks. "I don't believe in casual
sex." She paused. "I believe in casual marriage."

"Don't look at me," said Kate. "I married my husband because I was deeply in love with him."

"Yeah, well," said Adrienne. "I married my husband because I thought it would be a great way to meet guys."

Kate smiled now in a real way. Her white hair was grand-
motherly, but her face was youthful and tan, and her teeth
shone generous and wet, the creamy incisors curved as ca-
shews.

"I'd tried the whole single thing but it just wasn't working," Adrienne added, running in place.

Kate stepped close and massaged Adrienne's neck. Her
skin was lined and papery. "You haven't been to see Ilke from
Minnesota yet, have you?"

Adrienne feigned perturbance. "Do I seem that tense, that
lost, that . . ." and here she let her arms splay spastically.
"I'm going tomorrow."

. . .

"He was a beautiful child, didn't you think?" In bed Martin held her until he rolled away, clasped her hand and fell asleep. At least there was that: a husband sleeping next to a wife, a nice husband sleeping close. It meant something to her. She could see how through the years it would gather power, its socially sanctioned animal comfort, its night life a dreamy dance about love. She lay awake and remembered when her father had at last grown so senile and ill that her mother could no longer sleep in the same bed with him—the mess, the smell—and had had to move him, diapered and rank, to the guest room next door. Her mother had cried, to say this farewell to a husband. To at last lose him like this, banished and set aside like a dead man, never to sleep with him again: she had wept like a baby. His actual death she took less hard. At the funeral she was grim and dry and invited everyone over for a quiet, elegant tea. By the time two years had passed, and she herself was diagnosed with cancer, her sense of humor had returned a little. "The silent killer," she would say, with a wink. "The *silent killer.*" She got a kick out of repeating it, though no one knew what to say in response, and at the very end she kept clutching the nurses' hems to ask, "Why is no one visiting me?" No one lived that close, explained Adrienne. No one lived that close to anyone.

Adrienne set her spoon down. "Isn't this soup *interesting?*" she said to no one in particular. "*Zup-pa mari-ta-ta!*" Marriage soup. She decided it was perhaps a little like marriage itself: a good idea that, like all ideas, lived awkwardly on earth.

"You're not a poetess, I hope," said the English geologist next to her. "We had a poetess here last month, and things got a bit dodgy here for the rest of us."

"Really." After the soup there was risotto with squid ink.

"Yes. She kept referring to insects as 'God's typos' and then she kept us all after dinner one evening so she could read from her poems, which seemed to consist primarily of the repeating line, 'The hairy kiwi of his balls.' "

"Hairy kiwi," repeated Adrienne, searching the phrase for a sincere andante. She had written a poem once herself. It had been called "Garbage Night in the Fog" and was about a long sad walk she'd taken once on garbage night.

The geologist smirked a little at the risotto, waiting for Adrienne to say something more, but she was now watching Martin at the other table. He was sitting next to the sociologist she'd sat next to the previous night, and as Adrienne watched she saw Martin glance, in a sickened way, from the sociologist, back to his plate, then back to the sociologist. "The *cook?*" he said loudly, then dropped his fork and pushed his chair from the table.

The sociologist was frowning. "You flunk," she said.

"I'm going to see this masseuse tomorrow." Martin was on his back on the bed, and Adrienne was straddling his hips, usually one of their favorite ways to converse. One of the Mandy Patinkin tapes she'd brought was playing on the cassette player.

"The masseuse. Yes, I've heard," said Martin.

"You have?"

"Sure, they were talking about it at dinner last night."

"Who was?" She was already feeling possessive, alone.

"Oh, one of them," said Martin, smiling and waving his hand dismissively.

"Them," said Adrienne coldly. "You mean one of the spouses, don't you. Why are all the spouses here women? Why don't the women scholars have spouses?"

"Some of them do, I think. They're just not here."

"Where are they?"

"Could you move," he said irritably, "you're sitting on my groin."

"Fine," she said and climbed off.

. . .

The next morning she made her way down past the conical evergreens of the terraced hill—so like the grounds of a palace, the palace of a moody princess named Sophia or Giovanna—ten minutes down the winding path to the locked gate to the village. It had rained in the night, and snails, golden and mauve, decorated the stone steps, sometimes dead center, causing Adrienne an occasional quick turn of the ankle. A dance step, she thought. Modern and bent-kneed. Very Martha Graham. *Don't kill us. We'll kill you.* At the top of the final stairs to the gate she pressed the buzzer that opened it electronically, and then dashed down to get out in time. YOU HAVE THIRTY SECONDS, said the sign. TRENTA MINUTI SECONDI USCIRE. PRESTO! One needed a key to get back in from the village, and she clutched it like a charm.

She had to follow the Via San Carlo to Corso Magenta, past a hazelnut gelato shop and a bakery with wreaths of braided bread and muffins cut like birds. She pressed herself up against the buildings to let the cars pass. She looked at her card. The masseuse was above a *farmacia*, she'd been told, and she saw it now, a little sign that said, MASSAGGIO DELLA VITA. She pushed on the outer door and went up.

Upstairs through an open doorway, she entered a room lined with books: books on vegetarianism, books on healing, books on juice. A cockatiel, white with a red dot like a Hindu wife's, was perched atop a picture frame. The picture was of Lake Como or Garda, though when you blinked it could also be a skull, a fissure through the center like a reef.

"Adrienne," said a smiling woman in a purple peasant dress. She had big, frosted hair and a wide, happy face that contained many shades of pink. She stepped forward and shook Adrienne's hand. "I'm Ilke."

"Yes," said Adrienne.

The cockatiel suddenly flew from its perch to land on Ilke's shoulder. It pecked at her big hair, then stared at Adrienne, accusingly.

Ilke's eyes moved quickly between Adrienne's own, a quick read, a radar scan. She then looked at her watch. "You can go into the back room now, and I'll be with you shortly. You can take off all your clothes, also any jewelry—watches, or rings. But if you want you can leave your underwear on. Whatever you prefer."

"What do most people do?" Adrienne swallowed in a difficult, conspicuous way.

Ilke smiled. "Some do it one way; some the other."

"All right," Adrienne said and clutched her pocketbook. She stared at the cockatiel. "I just wouldn't want to rock the boat."

She stepped carefully toward the back room Ilke had indicated, and pushed past the heavy curtain. Inside was a large alcove, windowless and dark, with one small bluish light coming from the corner. In the center was a table with a newly creased flannel sheet. Speakers were built into the bottom of the table, and out of them came the sound of eery choral music, wordless *oohs* and *aahs* in minor tones, with a percussive sibilant chant beneath it that sounded to Adrienne like, "Jesus is best, Jesus is best," though perhaps it was "Cheese, I suspect." Overhead hung a mobile of white stars, crescent moons and doves. On the blue walls were more clouds and snowflakes. It was a child's room, a baby's room, everything trying hard to be harmless and sweet.

Adrienne removed all her clothes, her earrings, her watch, her rings. She had already grown used to the ring Martin had given her, and so it saddened and exhilarated her to take it off, a quick glimpse into the landscape of adultery. Her other ring was a smokey quartz, which a palm reader in Milwaukee —a man dressed like a gym teacher and set up at a card table in a German restaurant—had told her to buy and wear on her right index finger for power.

"What kind of power?" she had asked.

"The kind that's real," he said. "What you've got here," he said, waving around her left hand, pointing at the thin silver and turquoise she was wearing, "is squat."

"I like a palm reader who dresses you," she said later to Martin in the car on their way home. This was before the incident at the Spearson picnic, and things seemed not impossible then; she had wanted Martin to fall in love with her. "A guy who looks like Mike Ditka, but who picks out jewelry for you."

"A guy who tells you you're sensitive, and that you will soon receive cash from someone wearing glasses. Where does he come up with this stuff?"

"You don't think I'm sensitive."

"I mean the money and glasses thing," he said. "And that gloomy bit about how they'll think you're a goner, but you're going to come through and live to see the world go through a radical physical change."

"That was gloomy," she agreed. There was a lot of silence and looking at the night-lit highway lines, the fireflies hitting the windshield and smearing, all phosphorescent gold, as if the car were flying through stars. "It must be hard," she said, "for someone like you to go out on a date with someone like me."

"Why do you say that?" he'd asked.

She climbed up on the table, stripped of ornament and the power of ornament, and slipped between the flannel sheets. For a second she felt numb and scared, naked in a strange room, more naked even than in a doctor's office, where you kept your jewelry on, like an odalisque. But it felt new to do this, to lead the body to this, the body with its dog's obedience, its dog's desire to please. She lay there waiting, watching the mobile moons turn slowly, half-revolutions, while from the speakers beneath the table came a new sound, an electronic, synthesized version of Brahms's lullaby. An infant.

She was to become an infant again. Perhaps she would become the Spearsons' boy. He had been a beautiful baby.

Ilke came in quietly and appeared so suddenly behind Adrienne's head, it gave her a start.

"Move back toward me," whispered Ilke, "move back toward me," and Adrienne shifted until she could feel the crown of her head grazing Ilke's belly. The cockatiel whooshed in and perched on a nearby chair.

"Are you a little tense?" she said. She pressed both her thumbs at the center of Adrienne's forehead. Ilke's hands were strong, small, bony. Leathered claws. The harder she pressed the better it felt to Adrienne, all of her difficult thoughts unknotting and traveling out, up into Ilke's thumbs.

"Breathe deeply," said Ilke. "You cannot breathe deeply without it relaxing you."

Adrienne pushed her stomach in and out.

"You are from the Villa Hirschborn, aren't you?" Ilke's voice was a knowing smile.

"Ehuh."

"I thought so," said Ilke. "People are very tense up there. Rigid as boards." Ilke's hands moved down off Adrienne's forehead, along her eyebrows to her cheeks, which she squeezed repeatedly, in little circles, as if to break the weaker capillaries. She took hold of Adrienne's head and pulled. There was a dull, cracking sound. Then she pressed her knuckles along Adrienne's neck. "Do you know why?"

Adrienne grunted.

"It is because they are over educated and can no longer converse with their own mothers. It makes them a little crazy. They have literally lost their mother tongue. So they come to me. I am their mother, and they don't have to speak at all."

"Of course they *pay* you."

"Of course."

Adrienne suddenly fell into a long falling—of pleasure, of surrender, of glazed-eyed dying, a piece of heat set free in a room. Ilke rubbed Adrienne's earlobes, knuckled her scalp like a hairdresser, pulled at her neck and fingers and arms, as if they were jammed things. Adrienne would become a baby, join all the babies, in heaven where they lived.

Ilke began to massage sandalwood oil into Adrienne's arms, pressing down, polishing, ironing, looking, at a quick glimpse, like one of Degas's laundresses. Adrienne shut her eyes again and listened to the music, which had switched from synthetic lullabyes to the contrapuntal sounds of a flute and a thunderstorm. With these hands upon her, she felt a little forgiven and began to think generally of forgiveness, how much of it was required in life: to forgive everyone, yourself, the people you loved, and then wait to be forgiven by them. Where was all this forgiveness supposed to come from? Where was this great inexhaustible supply?

"Where are you?" whispered Ilke. "You are somewhere very far."

Adrienne wasn't sure. Where was she? In her own head, like a dream; in the bellows of her lungs. What was she? Perhaps a child. Perhaps a corpse. Perhaps a fern in the forest in the storm; a singing bird. The sheets were folded back. The hands were all over her now. Perhaps she was under the table with the music, or in a musty corner of her own hip. She felt Ilke rub oil into her chest, between her breasts, out along the ribs, and circularly on the abdomen. "There is something stuck here," Ilke said. "Something not working." Then she pulled the covers back up. "Are you cold?" she asked, and though Adrienne didn't answer, Ilke brought another blanket, mysteriously heated, and laid it across Adrienne. "There," said Ilke. She lifted the blanket so that only her feet were exposed. She rubbed oil into her soles, the toes, something squeezed out of Adrienne, like an olive. She felt as if she would cry. She felt like the baby Jesus. The grown Jesus. *The poor will always be with us.* The dead Jesus. Cheese is the best. Cheese is the best.

· · ·

At her desk in the outer room, Ilke wanted money. Thirty-five thousand lire. "I can give it to you for thirty thousand, if you decide to come on a regular basis. Would you like to come on a regular basis?" asked Ilke.

Adrienne was fumbling with her wallet. She sat down in the wicker rocker near the desk. "Yes," she said. "Of course."

Ilke had put on reading glasses and now opened up her appointment book to survey the upcoming weeks. She flipped a page, then flipped it back. She looked out over her glasses at Adrienne. "How often would you like to come?"

"Every day," said Adrienne.

"*Every day?*"

Ilke's hoot worried Adrienne. "Every *other* day?" Adrienne peered hopefully. Perhaps the massage had bewitched her, ruined her. Perhaps she had fallen in love.

Ilke looked back at her book and shrugged. "Every other day," she repeated slowly as a way of holding the conversation still while she checked her schedule. "How about at two o'clock?"

"Monday, Wednesday and Friday?"

"Perhaps we can occasionally arrange a Saturday."

"Okay. Fine." Adrienne placed the money on the desk and stood up. Ilke walked her to the door and thrust her hand out formally. Her face had changed from its earlier pinks to a strange and shiny orange.

"Thank you," said Adrienne. She shook Ilke's hand, but then leaned forward and kissed her cheek; she would kiss the business out of this. "Good-bye," she said. She stepped gingerly down the stairs; she had not entirely returned to her body yet. She had to go slow. She felt a little like she had just seen God, but also a little like she had just seen a hooker. Outside she walked carefully back toward the villa, but first stopped at the gelato shop for a small dish of hazlenut ice cream. It was smooth, toasty, buttery, like a beautiful liqueur, and she thought how different it was from America, where so much of the ice cream now looked like babies had attacked it with their cookies.

"Well, Martin, it's been nice knowing you," Adrienne said smiling. She reached out to shake his hand with one of hers and pat him on the back with the other. "You've been a good sport. I hope there will be no hard feelings."

"You've just come back from your massage," he said a little numbly. "How was it?"

"As you would say, 'Relaxing.' As I would say—well, I wouldn't say."

Martin led her to the bed. "Kiss and tell," he said.

"I'll just kiss," she said, kissing.

"I'll settle," he said. But then she stopped and went into the bathroom to shower for dinner.

At dinner there was *zuppa alla paesana* and then *salsicce alla griglia con spinaci*. For the first time since they'd arrived, she was seated near Martin, who was catercorner to her left. He was seated next to another economist and was speaking heatedly with him about a book on labor division and economic policy. "But Wilkander ripped that theory off from Boyer!" Martin let his spoon splash violently into his *zuppa* before a waiter came and removed the bowl.

"Let us just say," said the other man calmly, "that it was a sort of homage."

"If that's 'homage,'" said Martin, fidgeting with his fork, "I'd like to do a little 'homage' on the Chase Manhattan Bank."

"I think it was felt that there was sufficient looseness there to warrant further explication."

"Right. And one's twin sibling is simply an explication of the text."

"Why not," smiled the other economist, who was calm, probably a supply-sider.

Poor Martin, thought Adrienne. Poor Keynesian Martin, poor Marxist Martin, perspiring and red. "Left of Lenin?!" she had heard him exclaiming the other day to an agriculturalist. "Left of *Lenin?!* Left of the Lennon Sisters, you mean!" Poor godless, raised-an-atheist-in-Ohio Martin. "On Christmas," he'd said to her once, "we used to go down to The Science Store and worship the Bunsen burners."

She would have to find just the right blouse, just the right perfume, greet him on the chaise lounge with a bare shoulder and a purring, "Hello, Mister Man." Take him down by the lake near the Sfondrata chapel and get him laid. Hire somebody. She turned to the scholar next to her, who had just arrived this morning.

"Did you have a good flight?" she asked. Her own small talk at dinner no longer shamed her.

"Flight is the word," he said. "I needed to flee my department, my bills, my ailing car. Come to a place that would take care of me."

"This is it, I guess. Though they won't fix your car. Won't even discuss it, I've found."

"I'm on a Guggenheim," he said.

"How nice!" She thought of the museum in New York, and a pair of earrings she had bought in the gift shop there but had never worn because they always looked broken, even though that was the way they were supposed to look.

". . . but I neglected to ask the foundation for enough money. I didn't realize what you could ask for. I didn't ask for the same amount everyone else did, and so I received substantially less."

Adrienne was sympathetic. "So instead of a regular Guggenheim, you got a little Guggenheim."

"Yes," he said.

"A Guggenheimy," she said.

He smiled in a troubled sort of way. "Right."

"So now you have to live in Guggenheimy town."

He stopped pushing at a sausage with his fork. "Yes. I heard there would be wit here."

She tried to make her lips curl, like his.

"Sorry," he said. "I was just kidding."

"Jet lag," she said.

"Yes."

"Jetty laggy." She smiled at him. "Baby talk. We love it." She paused. "Last week of course we weren't like this. You've arrived a little late."

He was a beautiful baby. In the dark there was thumping, like tom-toms, and a piccolo high above it. She couldn't look, because when she looked, it shocked her, another woman's hands all over her. She just kept her eyes closed, and concentrated on surrender, on the restful invalidity of it. Sometimes she concentrated on being where Ilke's hands were—at her feet, at the small of her back.

"Your parents are no longer living, are they?" Ilke said in the dark.

"No."

"Did they die young?"

"Medium. They died medium. I was a menopausal, afterthought child."

"Do you want to know what I feel in you?"

"All right."

"I feel a great and deep gentleness. But I also feel that you have been dishonored."

"Dishonored?" So Japanese. Adrienne liked the sound of it.

"Yes. You have a deeply held fear. Right here." Ilke's hand went just under Adrienne's ribcage.

Adrienne breathed deeply, in and out. "I killed a baby," she whispered.

"Yes, we have all killed a baby—there is a baby in all of us. That is why people come to me, to be reunited with it."

"No, I've killed a real one."

Ilke was very quiet and then she said, "You can do the side-lying now. You can put this pillow under your head; this other one between your knees." Adrienne rolled awkwardly onto her side. Finally Ilke said, "This country, its pope, its church, makes murderers of women. You must not let it do that to you. Move back toward me. That's it."

That's not *it*, thought Adrienne, in this temporary dissolve, seeing death and birth, seeing the beginning and then the end, how they were the same quiet black, same nothing ever after: everyone's life appeared in the world like a movie in a room. First dark, then light, then dark again. But it was all staggered so that somewhere there was always light.

That's not it. That's not it, she thought. But thank you.

When Adrienne left that afternoon, seeking sugar in one of the shops, she moved slowly, blinded by the angle of the afternoon light but also believing she saw Martin coming toward her in the narrow street, approaching like the lumbering logger he sometimes seemed to be. Her squinted gaze, however, failed to catch his, and he veered suddenly left into a *calle*. By the time she reached the corner, he had disappeared entirely. How strange, she thought. She had felt close to something, to him, and then suddenly not. She climbed the path back up toward the villa and went and knocked on the door of his studio, but he wasn't there.

"You smell good," she greeted Martin. It was some time later and she had just returned to the room to find him there. "Did you just take a bath?"

"A little while ago," he said.

She curled up to him, teasingly. "Not a shower? A bath? Did you put some scented bath salts in it?"

"I took a very masculine bath," said Martin.

She sniffed him again. "What scent did you use?"

"A manly scent," he said. "Rock. I took a rock-scented bath."

"Did you take a bubble bath?" She cocked her head to one side.

He smiled. "Yes, but I, uh, made my own bubbles."

"You did?" She squeezed his biceps.

"Yeah. I hammered the water with my fist."

She walked over to the cassette player and put a cassette in. She looked over at Martin, who looked suddenly unhappy. "This music annoys you, doesn't it?"

Martin squirmed. "It's just—why can't he sing any one song all the way through?"

She thought about this. "Because he's Mr. Medley-head?"

"You didn't bring anything else?"

"No."

She went back and sat next to Martin, in silence, smelling the scent of him, as if it were odd.

For dinner there was *vitello alla salvia*, baby peas and a pasta made with caviar. "Nipping it in the bud," sighed Adrienne. "An early frost." A fat, elderly man arriving late pulled his chair out onto her foot, then sat down on it. She shrieked.

"Oh, dear, I'm sorry," said the man, lifting himself up as best he could.

"It's okay," said Adrienne. "I'm sure it's okay."

But the next morning, at exercises, Adrienne studied it closely during the leg lifts. The big toe was swollen and blue, and the nail had been loosened and set back at an odd and unhinged angle. "You're going to lose your toenail," said Kate.

"Great," said Adrienne.

"That happened to me once, during my first marriage. My husband dropped a dictionary on my foot. One of those subconscious things."

"You were married before?"

"Oh, yes," she sighed. "I had one of those rehearsal marriages, you know, where you're a feminist and train a guy, and then some *other* feminist comes along and *gets* the guy."

"I don't know." Adrienne scowled. "I think there's something wrong with the words *feminist* and *gets the guy* being in the same sentence."

"Yes, well—"

"Were you upset?"

"Of course. But then, I'd been doing everything. I'd insisted on separate finances, on being totally self-supporting. I was working. I was doing the child care. I paid for the house, I cooked it, I cleaned it. I found myself shouting, "This is feminism? Thank you, Betty!""

"But now you're with someone else."

"Pre-taught. Self-cleaning. Batteries included."

"Someone else trained him, and you stole him."

Kate smiled. "Of course. What, am I crazy?"

"What happened to the toe?"

"The nail came off. And the one that grew back was wavy and dark and used to scare the children."

"Oh," said Adrienne.

"Why would someone publish six books on Chaucer?" Adrienne was watching Martin dress. She was also smoking a cigarette. One of the strange things about the villa was that the smokers had all quit smoking, and the nonsmokers had taken it up. People were getting in touch with their alternative centers. Bequeathed cigarettes abounded. Cartons were appearing outside people's doors.

"You have to understand academic publishing," said Martin. "No one reads these books. Everyone just agrees to publish everyone else's. It's one big circle jerk. It's a giant economic agreement. When you think about it, it probably violates the Sherman Act."

"A circle jerk?" she said uncertainly. The cigarette was making her dizzy.

"Yeah," said Martin, re-knotting his tie.

"But six books on Chaucer? Why not, say, a Cat Stevens book?"

"Don't look at me," he said. "I'm in the circle."

She sighed. "Then I shall sing to you. Mood music." She made up a romantic, Asian-sounding tune and danced around the room with her cigarette, in a floating, wing-limbed way. "This is my Hopi dance," she said. "So full of hope."

Then it was time to go to dinner.

The cockatiel now seemed used to Adrienne and would whistle twice, then fly into the back room, perch quickly on the picture frame and wait with her for Ilke. Adrienne closed her eyes and breathed deeply, the flannel sheet pulled up under her arms, tightly, like a sarong.

Ilke's face appeared overhead in the dark, as if she were a mother just checking, peering into a crib. "How are you today?"

Adrienne opened her eyes to see that Ilke was wearing a pin that said: Say a Prayer. Pet a Rock.

Say a Prayer. "Good," said Adrienne. "I'm good." Pet a Rock.

Ilke ran her fingers through Adrienne's hair, humming faintly.

"What is this music today?" Adrienne asked. Like Martin, she too had grown weary of the Mandy Patinkin tapes, all that unshackled exuberance.

"Crickets and elk," Ilke whispered.

"Crickets and elk."

"Crickets and a elk and a little harp."

Ilke began to move around the table, pulling on Adrienne's limbs and pressing deep into her tendons. "I'm doing choreographed massage today," Ilke said. "That's why I'm wearing this dress."

Adrienne hadn't noticed the dress. Instead, with the lights now low, except for the illuminated clouds on the side wall, she felt herself sinking into the pools of death deep in her bones, the dark wells of loneliness, failure, blame. "You may turn over now," she heard Ilke say. And she struggled a little in the flannel sheets to do so, twisting in them, until Ilke helped her, as if she were a nurse and Adrienne someone old and sick—a stroke victim, that's what it was. She had become a stroke victim. Then lowering her face into the toweled cheek plates the brace on the table offered up to her (the cradle, Ilke called it), Adrienne began quietly to cry, the deep touching of her body, melting her down to some equation of animal sadness, shoe leather and brine. She began to understand why people would want to live in these dusky nether zones, the meltdown brought on by sleep or drink or this. It seemed truer, more familiar to the soul than was the busy complicated flash that was normal life. Ilke's arms leaned into her, her breasts brushing softly against Adrienne's head, which now felt connected to the rest of her only by filaments and strands. The body suddenly seemed a tumor on the brain, a mere means of conveyance, a wagon; the mind's go-cart taken apart, laid in pieces on this table. "You have a knot here in your trapezius," Ilke said, kneading Adrienne's shoulder. "I can feel the belly of the knot right here," she said, pressing hard, bruising her shoulder a little, and then easing up. "Let go," she said. "Let go all the way, of everything."

"I might die," said Adrienne. Something surged in the music and she missed what Ilke said in reply, though it sounded a little like, "Changes are good." Though perhaps it was "Chances aren't good." Ilke pulled Adrienne's toes, milking even the injured one, with its loose nail and leaky underskin, and then she left Adrienne there in the dark, in the music, though Adrienne felt it was she who was leaving, like a person dying, like a train pulling away. She felt the rage loosened from her back, floating aimlessly around in her, the rage that did not know at what or whom to rage though it continued to rage.

She awoke to Ilke's rocking her gently. "Adrienne, get up. I have another client soon."

"I must have fallen asleep," said Adrienne. "I'm sorry."

She got up slowly, got dressed, and went out into the outer room; the cockatiel whooshed out with her, grazing her head.

"I feel like I've just been strafed," she said, clutching her hair.

Ilke frowned.

"Your bird. I mean, by your bird. In there—" she pointed back toward the massage room—"*that* was great." She reached into her purse to pay. Ilke had moved the wicker chair to the other side of the room so that there was no longer any place to sit down or linger. "You want lire or dollars?" she asked and was a little taken aback when Ilke said rather firmly, "I'd prefer lire."

Ilke was bored with her. That was it. Adrienne was having a religious experience, but Ilke—Ilke was just being social. Adrienne held out the money and Ilke plucked it from her hand, then opened the outside door and leaned to give Adrienne the rushed bum's kiss—left, right—and then closed the door behind her.

Adrienne was in a fog, her legs noodly, her eyes unaccustomed to the light. Outside, in front of the *farmacia*, if she wasn't careful, she was going to get hit by a car. How could Ilke just send people out into the busy street like that, ducks for the kill, fatted calves, a farewell to arms? Her body felt doughy, muddy. This was good, she supposed. Decomposition. She stepped slowly, carefully, her Martha Graham step, along the narrow walk between the street and the stores. And when she turned the corner to head back up toward the path

to the Villa Hirschborn, there stood Martin, her husband,
rounding a corner and heading her way.

"Hi!" she said, so pleased suddenly to meet him like this,
away from what she now referred to as "the compound."
"Are you going to the *farmacia?*" she asked.

"Uh, yes," said Martin. He leaned to kiss her cheek.

"Want some company?"

He looked a little blank, as if he needed to be alone. Perhaps he was going to buy condoms.

"Oh, never mind," she said gaily. "I'll see you later, up at
the compound, before dinner."

"Great," he said, and took her hand, took two steps away,
and then let her hand go, gently, midair.

She walked away, toward a small park—il Giardino Leo-
nardo—out past the station for the vaporetti. Near a particularly exuberant rhododendron sat a short, dark woman with a
bright turquoise bandanna knotted around her neck. She had
set up a table with a sign: CHIROMANTE: TAROT E FACCIA. Adrienne
sat down opposite her in the empty chair. "Americano," she
said.

"I do faces, palms or cards," the woman with the blue scarf
said.

Adrienne looked at her own hands. She didn't want to
have her face read. She lived like that already. It happened all
the time at the villa, people trying to read your face—freezing
your brain with stoney looks and remarks made malicious
with obscurity, so that you couldn't read *their* faces, while
they were busy reading yours. It all made her feel creepy, like
a lonely head on a poster somewhere.

"The cards are the best," said the woman. "Ten thousand
lire."

"Okay," said Adrienne. She was still looking at the netting
of her open hands, the dried riverbed of life just sitting there.
"The cards."

The woman swept up the cards, and dealt half of them out,

every which way in a kind of swastika. Then without glancing at them, she leaned forward boldly and said to Adrienne, "You are sexually unsatisfied. Am I right?"

"Is that what the cards say?"

"In a general way. You have to take the whole deck and interpret."

"What does this card say?" asked Adrienne, pointing to one with some naked corpses leaping from coffins.

"Any one card doesn't say anything. It's the whole feeling of them." She quickly dealt out the remainder of the deck on top of the other cards. "You are looking for a guide, some kind of guide, because the man you are with does not make you happy. Am I right?"

"Maybe," said Adrienne, who was already reaching for her purse to pay the ten thousand lire so that she could leave.

"I am right," said the woman, taking the money and handing Adrienne a small, smudged business card. "Stop by tomorrow. Come to my shop. I have a powder."

Adrienne wandered back out of the park, past a group of tourists climbing out of a bus, back toward the Villa Hirschborn—through the gate, which she opened with her key, and up the long stone staircase to the top of the promontory. Instead of going back to the villa, she headed out through the woods toward her studio, toward the dead tufts of spiders she had memorialized in her grief. She decided to take a different path, not the one toward the studio, but one that led farther up the hill, a steeper grade, toward an open meadow at the top, with a small Roman ruin at its edge—a corner of the hill's original fortress still stood there. But in the middle of the meadow, something came over her—a balmy wind, or the heat from the uphill hike, and she took off all her clothes, lay down in the grass and stared around at the dusky sky. To either side of her the spokes of tree branches crisscrossed upward in a kind of cat's cradle. More directly overhead she studied the silver speck of a jet, the metallic head of its white stream like the tip of a thermometer. There were a hundred people inside this head of a pin, thought Adrienne. Or was it, perhaps, just the head of a pin? When was something truly small, and when was it a matter of distance? The branches of the trees seemed to encroach inward and rotate a little to the left, a little to the right, like something mechanical, and as she began to drift off, she saw the beautiful Spearson baby, cooing in a clown hat, she saw Martin furiously swimming in a pool, she saw the strewn beads of her own fertility, all the eggs within her, leap away like a box of tapioca off a cliff. It seemed to her that everything she had ever needed to know in her life she had known at one time or another, but she just hadn't known all those things at once, at the same time, at a single moment. They were scattered through, and she had had to leave and forget one in order to get to another. A shadow feel across her, inside her, and she could feel herself retreat to that place in her bones where death was and you greeted it like an acquaintance in a room; you said hello and were then ready for whatever was next—which might be a guide, the guide that might be sent to you, the guide to lead you back out into your life again.

Someone was shaking her gently. She flickered slightly awake to see the pale, ethereal face of a strange older woman leaning over, peering down at her as if Adrienne were something odd in the bottom of a tea cup. The woman was dressed all in white—white shorts, white cardigan, white scarf around her head. The guide.

"Are you—the guide?" whispered Adrienne.

"Yes, my dear," the woman said in a faintly English voice that sounded like the good witch of the north.

"You are?" Adrienne asked.

"Yes," said the woman. "And I've brought the group up here to view the old fort, but I was a little worried that you might not like all of us traipsing past here while you were, well—are you all right?"

Adrienne was more awake now and sat up to see at the end of the meadow the group of tourists she'd previously seen below in the town, getting off the bus.

"Yes, thank you," mumbled Adrienne. She lay back down to think about this, hiding herself in the walls of grass, like a child hoping to trick the facts. "Oh, my god," she finally said, and groped about to her left to find her clothes and clutch them, panicked, to her belly. She breathed deeply, then put them on, lying as flat to the ground as she could, hard to glimpse, a snake getting back inside its skin, a change, perhaps, of reptilian heart. Then she stood, zipped her pants, secured her belt buckle and, squaring her shoulders, walked bravely past the bus and the tourists who, though they tried not to stare at her, did stare.

By this time everyone in the villa was privately doing imitations of everyone else. "Martin, you should announce who you're doing before you do it," said Adrienne, dressing for dinner. "I can't really tell."

"Cube-steak yuppies!" Martin ranted at the ceiling. "Legends in their own mind! Rumors in their own room!"

"Yourself. You're doing yourself." She straightened his collar and tried to be wifely.

For dinner there was *cioppino* and *insalata mista* and *pesce con pignoli*, a thin piece of fish like a leaf. From everywhere around the dining room scraps of dialogue—rhetorical barbed wire, indignant and arcane—floated over toward her: "As an aesthetician, you can't not be interested in the sublime!" or "Why, that's the most facile thing I've ever heard!" or "Good grief, tell him about the Peasants' Revolt, would you?" But no one spoke to her directly. She had no subject, not really, not one she liked, except perhaps movies and movie stars. Martin was at a far table, his back toward her, listening to the monk man. At times like these, she thought, it was probably a good idea to carry a small hand puppet.

She made her fingers flap in her lap.

Finally, one of the people next to her turned and introduced himself. His face was poppy-seeded with whiskers, and he seemed to be looking down, watching his own mouth move. When she asked him how he liked it here so far, she received a fairly brief history of the Ottoman Empire. She nodded and smiled, and at the end he rubbed his dark beard, looked at her compassionately, and said, "We are not good advertisements for this life. Are we?"

"There *are* a lot of dingdongs here," she admitted. He looked a little hurt, so she added, "But I like that about a place. I do."

When after dinner she went for an evening walk with Martin, she tried to strike up a conversation about celebrities and movie stars. "I keep thinking about Princess Caroline's husband being killed," she said.

Martin was silent.

"That poor family," said Adrienne. "There's been so much tragedy."

Martin glared at her. "Yes," he said facetiously. "That poor, cursed family. I keep thinking, what can I do to help? What can I do? And I think, and I think, and I think so much I'm helpless. I throw up my hands and end up doing nothing. I'm helpless!" He began to walk faster, ahead of her down, into the village. Adrienne began to run to keep up. Marriage, she thought, it's an institution, all right.

Near the main piazza, under a streetlamp, the CHIROMANTE: TAROT E FACCIA had set up her table again. When she saw Adrienne, she called out, "Give me your birthday, signora, and your husband's birthday, and I will do your charts to tell you whether the two of you are compatible! Or—" She paused to study Martin skeptically as he rushed past. "Or, I can just tell you right now."

"Have you been to this woman before? he asked, slowing

down. Adrienne grabbed Martin's arm and started to lead
him away.

"I needed a change of scenery."

Now he stopped. "Well," he said sympathetically, calmer
after some exercise, "who could blame you." Adrienne took
his hand, feeling a grateful, marital love—alone, in Italy, at
night, in May. Was there any love that wasn't at bottom a
grateful one? The moonlight glittered off the lake like electric
fish, like a school of ice.

"What are you doing?" Adrienne asked Ilke the next afternoon. The lamps were particularly low, though there was a
spotlight directed onto a picture of Ilke's mother, which she
had placed on an end table, for the month, in honor of
Mother's Day. The mother looked ghostly, like a sacrifice.
What if Ilke were truly a witch? What if fluids and hairs and
nails were being collected as offerings in memory of her
mother?

"I'm fluffing your aura," she said. "It is very dark today,
burned down to a shadowy rim." She was manipulating
Adrienne's toes and Adrienne suddenly had a horror-movie
vision of Ilke with jars of collected toe juice in a closet for
Satan, who, it would be revealed, *was* Ilke's mother. Perhaps
Ilke would lean over suddenly and bite Adrienne's shoulder,
drink her blood. How could Adrienne control these thoughts?
She felt her aura fluff like the fur of a screeching cat. She
imagined herself, for the first time, never coming here again.
Good-bye. Farewell. It would be a brief affair, a little nothing;
a chat on the porch at a party.

Fortunately, there were other things to keep Adrienne
busy.

She had begun spray-painting the spiders and the results
were interesting. She could see herself explaining to a dealer
back home that the work represented the spider web of solitude—a vibration at the periphery reverberates inward (expe-

riential, deafening) and the spider rushes out from the center to devour the gong, the gonger and the gong. Gone. She could see the dealer taking her phone number and writing it down on an extremely loose scrap of paper.

And there was the occasional after-dinner sing-song, scholars and spouses gathered around the piano in various states of inebriation and forgetfulness. "Okay, that may be how you learned it, Harold, but that's *not* how it goes."

There was also the Asparagus Festival, which, at Carlo's suggestion, she and Kate Spalding in one of her T-shirts—*all right already with the T-shirts, Kate*—decided to attend. They took a hydrofoil across the lake and climbed a steep road up toward a church square. The road was long and tiring and Adrienne began to refer to it as the Asparagus Death Walk.

"Maybe there isn't really a festival," she suggested, gasping for breath, but Kate kept walking, ahead of her.

Adrienne sighed. Off in the trees were the ratchety cheeping of birds and the competing, hourly chimes of two churches, followed later by the single off-tone of the half hour. When she and Kate finally reached the asparagus festival, it turned out to be only a little ceremony where a few people bid very high prices for clutches of asparagus described as "bello, bello," the proceeds from which went to the local church.

"I used to grow asparagus," said Kate on their walk back down. They were taking a different route this time, and the lake and its ochre villages spread out before them, peaceful and far away. Along the road wildflowers grew in a pallet of pastels, like soaps.

"I could never grow asparagus," said Adrienne. As a child her favorite food had been "asparagus with holiday sauce." "I did grow a carrot once, though. But it was so small I just put it in a scrapbook."

"Are you still seeing Ilke?"

"This week, at any rate. How about you?"

"She's booked solid. I couldn't get another appointment. All the scholars, you know, are paying her regular visits."

"Really?"

"Oh, yes," said Kate very knowingly. "They're tense as dimes." Already Adrienne could smell the fumes of the Fiats and the ferries and delivery vans, the asparagus festival far away.

"Tense as dimes?"

Back at the villa, Adrienne waited for Martin, and when he came in, smelling of sandalwood, all the little deaths in her bones told her this: he was seeing the masseuse.

She sniffed the sweet parabola of his neck and stepped back. "I want to know how long you've been getting massages. Don't lie to me," she said slowly, her voice hard as a spike. Anxiety shrank his face: his mouth caved in, his eyes grew beady and scared.

"What makes you think I've been getting—" he started to say. "Well, just once or twice."

She leaped away from him and began pacing furiously about the room, touching the furniture, not looking at him. "How could you?" she asked. "You know what my going there has meant to me! How could you not tell me?" She picked up a book on the dressing table—*Industrial Relations Systems*—and slammed it back down. "How could you horn in on this experience? How could you be so furtive and un-truthful?"

"I am terribly sorry," he said.

"Yeah, well, so am I," said Adrienne. "And when we get home, I want a divorce." She could see it now, the empty apartment, the bad eggplant parmigiana, all the Halloweens she would answer the doorbell, a boozy divorcee frightening the little children with too much enthusiasm for their costumes. "I feel so fucking *dishonored!*" Nothing around her seemed able to hold steady; nothing held.

Martin was silent and she was silent and then he began to speak, in a beseeching way, there it was the beseech again, rumbling at the edge of her life like a truck. "We are both so lonely here," he said. "But I have only been waiting for you. That is all I have done for the last eight months. To try not to let things intrude, to let you take your time, to make sure you ate something, to buy the goddamn Spearsons a new picnic bench, to bring you to a place where anything at all might happen, where you might even leave me, but at least come back into life at last—"

"You did?"

"Did what?"

"You bought the Spearsons a new *picnic bench?*"

"Yes, I did."

She thought about this. "Didn't they think you were being hostile?"

"Oh . . . I think, yes, they probably thought it was hostile."

And the more Adrienne thought about it, about the poor bereaved Spearsons, and about Martin and all the ways he tried to show her he was on her side, whatever that meant, how it was both the hope and shame of him that he was always doing his best, the more she felt foolish, deprived of reasons. Her rage flapped awkwardly away like a duck. She felt as she had when her cold, fierce parents had at last grown sick and old, stick boned and saggy, protected by infirmity the way cuteness protected a baby, or should, it should protect a baby, and she had been left with her rage—vestigial girlhood rage—inappropriate and intact. She would hug her parents good-bye, the gentle, emptied sacks of them, and think, where did you go?

Time, Adrienne thought. What a racket.

Martin had suddenly begun to cry. He sat at the bed's edge and curled inward, his soft, furry face in his great hard hands, his head falling downward into the bright plaid of his shirt.

She felt dizzy and turned away, toward the window. A fog had drifted in, and in the evening light the sky and the lake seemed a singular blue, like a Monet. "I've never seen you cry," she said.

"Well, I cry," he said. "I can even cry at the sports page if the games are too close. Look at me, Adrienne. You never really look at me."

But she could only continue to stare out the window, touching her fingers to the shutters and frame. She felt far away, as if she were back home, walking through the neighborhood at dinnertime: when the cats sounded like babies and the babies sounded like birds, and the fathers were home from work, their children in their arms gumming the language, air shaping their flowery throats into a park of singing. Through the windows wafted the smell of cooking food.

"We are with each other now," Martin was saying. "And in the different ways it means, we must try to make a life."

Out over the Sfondrata chapel tower, where the fog had broken, she thought she saw a single star, like the distant nose of a jet; there were people in the clayey clouds. She turned, and for a moment it seemed they were all there in Martin's eyes, all the absolving dead in residence in his face, the angel of the dead baby shining like a blazing creature, and she went to him, to protect and encircle him, seeking the heart's best trick, *oh, terrific heart.* "Please, forgive me," she said.

And he whispered, "Of course. It is the only thing. Of course."

Stuart Dybek

WE DIDN'T

We did it in front of the mirror
And in the light. We did it in darkness,
In water, and in the high grass.
—"WE DID IT," YEHUDA AMICHAI

We didn't in the light; we didn't in darkness. We didn't in the fresh cut summer grass or in the mounds of autumn leaves or on the snow where moonlight threw down our shadows. We didn't in your room on the canopy bed you slept in, the bed you'd slept in as a child, or in the backseat of my father's rusted Rambler which smelled of the smoked chubs and kielbasa that he delivered on weekends from my Uncle Vincent's meat market. We didn't in your mother's Buick Eight where a rosary twined the rearview mirror like a beaded, black snake with silver, cruciform fangs.

At the dead end of our lovers' lane—a side street of abandoned factories—where I perfected the pinch that springs open a bra; behind the lilac bushes in Marquette Park where you first touched me through my jeans and your nipples, swollen against transparent cotton, seemed the shade of lilacs; in the balcony of the now-defunct Clark Theater where I wiped popcorn salt from my palms and slid them up your thighs and you whispered, "I feel like Doris Day is watching us," we didn't.

How adept we were at fumbling, how perfectly mistimed our timing, how utterly we confused energy with ecstasy.

Remember that night becalmed by heat, and the two of us, fused by sweat, trembling as if a wind from outer space that only we could feel was gusting across Oak Street Beach? Wound in your faded Navajo blanket, we lay soul-kissing until you wept with wanting.

We'd been kissing all day—all summer—kisses tasting of different shades of lip gloss and too many Cokes. The lake had turned hot pink, rose rapture, pearl amethyst with dusk, then washed in night black with a ruff of silver foam. Beyond a momentary horizon, silent bolts of heat lightning throbbed, perhaps setting barns on fire somewhere in Indiana. The beach that had been so crowded was deserted as if there was a curfew. Only the bodies of lovers remained behind, visible in lightning flashes, scattered like the fallen on a battlefield, a few of them moaning, waiting for the gulls to pick them clean.

On my fingers your slick scent mixed with the coconut musk of the suntan lotion we'd repeatedly smeared over one another's bodies. When your bikini top fell away, my hands caught your breasts, memorizing their delicate weight, my palms cupped as if bringing water to parched lips.

Along the Gold Coast, high rises began to glow, window added to window, against the dark. In every lighted bedroom, couples home from work were stripping off their business suits, falling to the bed, and doing it. They did it before mirrors and pressed against the glass in streaming shower stalls, they did it against walls and on the furniture in ways that required previously unimagined gymnastics which they invented on the spot. They did it in honor of man and woman, in honor of beast, in honor of God. They did it because they'd been released, because they were home free, alive, and private, because they couldn't wait any longer, couldn't wait for the appointed hour, for the right time or temperature, couldn't wait for the future, for Messiahs, for peace on earth and justice for all. They did it because of the

Bomb, because of pollution, because of the Four Horsemen of the Apocalypse, because extinction might be just a blink away. They did it because it was Friday night. It was Friday night and somewhere delirious music was playing—flutter-tongued flutes, muted trumpets meowing like tomcats in heat, feverish plucking and twanging, tom-toms, congas, and gongs all pounding the same pulsebeat.

I stripped your bikini bottom down the skinny rails of your legs and you tugged my swimsuit past my tan. Swimsuits at our ankles, we kicked like swimmers to free our legs, almost expecting a tide to wash over us the way the tide rushes in on Burt Lancaster and Deborah Kerr in their famous love scene on the beach in *From Here to Eternity*—a scene so famous that although neither of us had seen the movie our bodies assumed the exact position of movie stars on the sand and you whispered to me softly, "I'm afraid of getting pregnant," and I whispered back, "Don't worry, I have protection," then, still kissing you, felt for my discarded cutoffs and the wallet in which for the last several months I had carried a Trojan as if it was a talisman. Still kissing, I tore its flattened, dried-out wrapper and it sprang through my fingers like a spring from a clock and dropped to the sand between our legs. My hands were shaking. In a panic, I groped for it, found it, tried to dust it off, tried, as Burt Lancaster never had to, to slip it on without breaking the mood, felt the grains of sand inside it, a throb of lightning, and the Great Lake behind us became, for all practical purposes, the Pacific and your skin tasted of salt and to the insistent question that my hips were asking, your body answered yes, your thighs opened like wings from my waist as we surfaced panting from a kiss that left you pleading *oh Christ yes*, a yes gasped sharply as a cry of pain so that for a moment I thought that we *were* already doing it and that somehow I had missed the instant when I entered you, entered you in the bloodless way in which a young man discards his own virginity, entered you as if passing through a gateway into the rest of my life, into a life as I wanted it to be lived *yes* but O then I realized that we were still floundering unconnected in the slick between us and there was sand in the Trojan as we slammed together still feeling for that perfect fit, still in the *Here* groping for an *Eternity* that was only a fine adjustment away, just a millimeter to the left or a fraction of an inch further south through with all the adjusting the sandy Trojan was slipping off and then it was gone but yes you kept repeating although your head was shaking no-not-quite-almost and our hearts were going like mad and you said yes Yes wait . . . Stop!

"What?" I asked, still futilely thrusting as if I hadn't quite heard you.

"Oh, God!" you gasped, pushing yourself up. "What's coming?"

"Julie, what's the matter?" I asked, confused, and then the beam of a spotlight swept over us and I glanced into its blinding eye.

All around us lights were coming, speeding across the sand. Blinking blindness away, I rolled from your body to my knees, feeling utterly defenseless in the way that only nakedness can leave one feeling. Headlights bounded toward us, spotlights crisscrossing, blue dome lights revolving as squad cars converged. I could see other lovers, caught in the beams, fleeing bare-assed through the litter of garbage that daytime hordes had left behind and that night had deceptively concealed. You were crying, clutching the Navajo blanket to your breasts with one hand and clawing for your bikini with the other, and I was trying to calm your terror with reassuring phrases such as, "Holy shit! I don't fucking believe this!"

Swerving and fishtailing in the sand, police calls pouring from their radios, the squad cars were on us, and then they were by us while we sat struggling on our clothes.

They braked at the water's edge, and cops slammed out brandishing huge flashlights, their beams deflecting over the dark water. Beyond the darting of those beams, the far-off throbs of lightning seemed faint by comparison.

"Over there, goddamn it!" one of them hollered, and two cops sloshed out into the shallow water without even pausing to kick off their shoes, huffing aloud for breath, their leather cartridge belts creaking against their bellies.

"Grab the sonofabitch! It ain't gonna bite!" one of them yelled, then they came sloshing back to shore with a body slung between them.

It was a woman—young, naked, her body limp and bluish beneath the play of flashlight beams. They set her on the sand just past the ring of drying, washed-up alewives. Her face was almost totally concealed by her hair. Her hair was brown and tangled in a way that even wind or sleep can't tangle hair, tangled as if it had absorbed the ripples of water—thick strands, slimy-looking like dead seaweed.

"She's been in there a while, that's for sure," a cop with a beer belly said to a younger, crew-cut cop who had knelt beside the body and removed his hat as if he might be considering the kiss of life.

The crew-cut officer brushed the hair away from her face and the flashlight beams settled there. Her eyes were closed. A bruise or a birthmark stained the side of one eye. Her features appeared swollen—her lower lip protruding as if she was pouting.

An ambulance siren echoed across the sand, its revolving red light rapidly approaching.

"Might as well take their sweet-ass time," the beer-bellied cop said.

We had joined the circle of police surrounding the drowned woman almost without realizing that we had. You were back in your bikini, robed in the Navajo blanket, and I had slipped on my cutoffs, my underwear still dangling out of a back pocket.

Their flashlight beams explored her body causing its whiteness to gleam. Her breasts were floppy; her nipples looked shriveled. Her belly appeared inflated by gallons of water. For a moment, a beam focused on her mound of pubic hair which was overlapped by the swell of her belly, and then moved almost shyly away down her legs, and the cops all glanced at us—at you, especially—above their lights, and you hugged your blanket closer as if they might confiscate it as evidence or to use as a shroud.

When the ambulance pulled up, one of the black attendants immediately put a stethoscope to the drowned woman's swollen belly and announced, "Drowned the baby, too."

Without saying anything, we turned from the group, as unconsciously as we'd joined them, and walked off across the sand, stopping only long enough at the spot where we had lain together like lovers, in order to stuff the rest of our gear into a beach bag, to gather our shoes, and for me to find my wallet and kick sand over the forlorn, deflated-looking Trojan that you pretended not to notice. I was grateful for that.

Behind us, the police were snapping photos, flashbulbs throbbing like lightning flashes, and the lightning itself still distant but moving in closer, rumbling audibly now, driving a lake wind before it so that gusts of sand tingled against the metal sides of the ambulance.

Squinting, we walked towards the lighted windows of the Gold Coast, while the shadows of gapers attracted by the whirling emergency lights hurried past us toward the shore.

"What happened? What's going on?" they asked us as they passed without waiting for an answer, and we didn't offer one, just continued walking silently in the dark.

It was only later that we talked about it, and once we began talking about the drowned woman it seemed we couldn't stop.

"She was pregnant," you said, "I mean I don't want to sound morbid, but I can't help thinking how the whole time we were, we almost—you know—there was this poor, dead woman and her unborn child washing in and out behind us."

"It's not like we could have done anything for her even if we had known she was there."

"But what if we *had* found her? What if after we had—you know," you said, your eyes glancing away from mine and your voice tailing into a whisper, "what if after we did it, we went for a night swim and found her in the water?"

"But, Jules, we didn't," I tried to reason, though it was no more a matter of reason than anything else between us had ever been.

It began to seem as if each time we went somewhere to make out—on the back porch of your half-deaf, whiskery Italian grandmother who sat in the front of the apartment cackling before "I Love Lucy" reruns; or in your girlfriend Ginny's basement rec room when her parents were away on bowling league nights and Ginny was upstairs with her current crush, Brad; or way off in the burbs, at the Giant Twin Drive-In during the weekend they called Elvis Fest—the drowned woman was with us.

We would kiss, your mouth would open, and when your tongue flicked repeatedly after mine, I would unbutton the first button of your blouse revealing the beauty spot at the base of your throat which matched a smaller spot I loved above a corner of your lips, and then the second button that opened on a delicate gold cross—that I had always tried to regard as merely a fashion statement—dangling above the cleft of your breasts. The third button exposed the lacy swell of your bra, and I would slide my hand over the patterned mesh, feeling for the firmness of your nipple rising to my fingertip, but you would pull slightly away, and behind your rapid breath your kiss would grow distant, and I would kiss harder trying to lure you back from wherever you had gone, and finally, holding you as if only consoling a friend, I'd ask, "What are you thinking?" although, of course, I knew.

"I don't want to think about her but I can't help it. I mean it seems like some kind of weird omen or something, you know?"

"No, I don't know," I said. "It was just a coincidence."

"Maybe if she'd been further away down the beach, but she was so close to us. A good wave could have washed her up right beside us."

"Great, then we could have had a *menage à trois*."

"Gross! I don't believe you just said that! Just because you said it in French doesn't make it less disgusting."

"You're driving me to it. Come on, Jules, I'm sorry," I said, "I was just making a dumb joke to get a little different perspective on things."

"What's so goddamn funny about a woman who drowned herself and her baby?"

"We don't even know for sure she did."

"Yeah, right, it was just an accident. Like she just happened to be going for a walk pregnant and naked, and she fell in."

"She could have been on a sailboat or something. Accidents happen; so do murders."

"Oh, like murder makes it less horrible? Don't think that hasn't occurred to me. Maybe the bastard who knocked her up killed her, huh?"

"How should I know? You're the one who says you don't want to talk about it and then gets obsessed with all kinds of theories and scenarios. Why are we arguing about a woman we don't even know, who doesn't have the slightest thing to do with us?"

"I *do* know about her," you said. "I dream about her."

"You dream about her?" I repeated, surprised. "Dreams you remember?"

"Sometimes they wake me up. Like I dreamed I was at my *nonna's* cottage in Michigan. Off her beach they've got a raft for swimming and in my dream I'm swimming out to it, but it keeps drifting further away until it's way out on the water

and I'm so tired that if I don't get to it I'm going to drown.
Then, I notice there's a naked person sunning on it and I start
yelling, 'Help!' and she looks up, brushes her hair out of her
face, and offers me a hand, but I'm too afraid to take it even
though I'm drowning because it's her."

"God! Jules, that's creepy."

"I dreamed you and I were at the beach and you bring us a
couple hot dogs but forget the mustard, so you have to go all
the way back to the stand for it."

"Hot dogs, no mustard—a little too Freudian, isn't it?"

"Honest to God, I dreamed it. You go off for mustard and
I'm wondering why you're gone so long, then a woman
screams a kid has drowned and immediately the entire crowd
stampedes for the water and sweeps me along with it. It's like
one time when I was little and got lost at the beach, wander-
ing in a panic through this forest of hairy legs and pouchy
crotches, crying for my mother. Anyway, I'm carried into the
water by the mob and forced under, and I think, this is it, I'm
going to drown, but I'm able to hold my breath longer than
could ever be possible. It feels like a flying dream—flying
underwater—and then I see this baby down there flying, too,
and realize it's the kid everyone thinks has drowned, but he's
no more drowned than I am. He looks like Cupid or one of
those baby angels that cluster around the face of God."

"Pretty weird. What do you think it means? Something to
do with drowning maybe, or panic?"

"It means the baby who drowned inside her that night was
a love child—a boy—and his soul was released there to
wander through the water."

"You really believe that?"

We argued about the interpretation of dreams, about
whether dreams were symbolic or psychic, prophetic or just
plain nonsense until you said, "Look, you can believe what
you want about your dreams, but keep your nose out of mine,
okay?"

We argued about the drowned woman, about whether her death was a suicide or a murder, about whether her appearance that night was an omen or a coincidence, which, you argued, is what an omen is anyway: a coincidence that means something. By the end of summer, even if we were no longer arguing about the woman, we had acquired the habit of arguing about everything else. What was better: dogs or cats, rock or jazz, Cubs or Sox, tacos or egg rolls, right or left, night or day—we could argue about anything.

It no longer required arguing or necking to summon the drowned woman; everywhere we went she surfaced by her own volition: at Rocky's Italian Beef, at Lindo Mexico, at the House of Dong, our favorite Chinese restaurant, a place we still frequented because they had let us sit and talk until late over tiny cups of jasmine tea and broken fortune cookies earlier in the year when it was winter and we had first started going together. We would always kid about going there. "Are you in the mood for Dong, tonight?" I'd ask. It was a dopey joke, and you'd break up at its repeated dopiness. Back then, in winter, if one of us ordered the garlic shrimp, we would both be sure to eat them so that later our mouths tasted the same when we kissed.

Even when she wasn't mentioned, she was there with her drowned body—so dumpy next to yours—and her sad breasts with their wrinkled nipples and sour milk—so saggy beside yours which were still budding—with her swollen belly and her pubic bush colorless in the glare of electric light, with her tangled, slimy hair and her pouting, placid face—so lifeless beside yours—and her skin a pallid white, lightning-flash white, flashbulb white, a whiteness that couldn't be duplicated in daylight—how I'd come to hate that pallor, so cold beside the flush of your skin.

There wasn't a particular night when we finally broke up, just as there wasn't a particular night when we began going together, but I do remember a night in fall when I guessed that it was over. We were parked in the Rambler at the dead end of the street of factories that had been our lover's lane, listening to a drizzle of rain and dry leaves sprinkle the hood. As always, rain revitalized the smells of the smoked fish and kielbasa in the upholstery. The radio was on too low to hear, the windshield wipers swished at intervals as if we were driving, and the windows were steamed as if we'd been making out. But we'd been arguing as usual, this time about a woman poet who had committed suicide, whose work you were reading. We were sitting, no longer talking or touching, and I remember thinking that I didn't want to argue with you anymore. I didn't want to sit like this in silence; I wanted to talk excitedly all night as we once had, I wanted to find some way that wasn't corny-sounding to tell you how much fun I'd had in your company, how much knowing you had meant to me, and how I had suddenly realized that I'd been so intent on becoming lovers that I'd overlooked how close we'd been as friends. I wanted you to know that. I wanted you to like me again.

"It's sad," I started to say, meaning that I was sorry we had reached a point of sitting silently together, but before I could continue, you challenged the statement.

"What makes you so sure it's sad?"

"What do you mean, what makes me so sure?" I asked, confused by your question, and surprised there could be anything to argue over no matter what you thought I was talking about.

You looked at me as if what was sad was that I would never understand. "For all either one of us know," you said, "she could have been triumphant!"

Maybe when it really ended was that night when I felt we had just reached the beginning, that one time on the beach in the summer between high school and college, when our bodies rammed together so desperately that for a moment I thought we did it, and maybe in our hearts we had, although for me, then, doing it in one's heart didn't quite count. If it did, I supposed we'd all be Casanovas.

I remember riding home together on the El that night, feeling sick and defeated in a way I was embarrassed to mention. Our mute reflections emerged like negative exposures on the dark, greasy window of the train. Lightning branched over the city and when the train entered the subway tunnel, the lights inside flickered as if the power was disrupted although the train continued rocketing beneath the Loop.

When the train emerged again we were on the South Side and it was pouring, a deluge as if the sky had opened to drown the innocent and guilty alike. We hurried from the El station to your house, holding the Navajo blanket over our heads until, soaked, it collapsed. In the dripping doorway of your apartment building, we said goodnight. You were shivering. Your bra showed through the thin blouse plastered to your skin. I swept the wet hair away from your face and kissed you lightly on the lips, then you turned and went inside. I stepped into the rain and you came back out calling after me.

"What?" I asked, feeling a surge of gladness to be summoned back into the doorway with you.

"Want an umbrella?"

I didn't. The downpour was letting up. It felt better to walk back to the El feeling the rain rinse the sand out of my hair, off my legs, until the only places where I could still feel its grit was the crotch of my cutoffs and in each squish of my shoes. A block down the street, I passed a pair of jockey shorts lying in a puddle and realized they were mine, dropped from my back pocket as we ran to your house. I left them behind, wondering if you'd see them and recognize them the next day.

By the time I had climbed the stairs back to the El platform, the rain had stopped. Your scent still hadn't washed from my fingers. The station—the entire city, it seemed—dripped and steamed. The summer sound of crickets and nighthawks echoed from the drenched neighborhood. Alone, I could admit how sick I felt. For you, it was a night that would haunt your dreams. For me, it was another night when I waited, swollen and aching, for what I had secretly nicknamed the Blue Ball Express.

Literally lovesick, groaning inwardly with each lurch of the train and worried that I was damaged for good, I peered out at the passing yellow-lit stations where lonely men stood posted before giant advertisements, pictures of glamorous models defaced by graffiti—the same old scrawled insults and pleas: FUCK YOU, EAT ME. At this late hour the world seemed given over to men without women, men waiting in abject patience for something indeterminate, the way I waited for our next times. I avoided their eyes so that they wouldn't see the pity in mine, pity for them because I'd just been with you, your scent was still on my hands, and there seemed to be so much future ahead.

For me it was another night like that, and by the time I reached my stop I knew I would be feeling better, recovered enough to walk the dark street home making up poems of longing that I never wrote down. I was the D. H. Lawrence of not doing it, the voice of all the would-be lovers who ached and squirmed but still hadn't. From our contortions in doorways, on stairwells, and in the bucket seats of cars we could have composed a *Kama Sutra* of interrupted bliss. It must have been that night when I recalled all the other times of walking home after seeing you so that it seemed as if I was falling into step behind a parade of my former selves—myself walking home on the night we first kissed, myself on the night when I unbuttoned your blouse and kissed your breasts, myself on the night that I lifted your skirt above your thighs and dropped to my knees—each succeeding self another step closer to that irrevocable moment for which our lives seemed poised.

But we didn't, not in the moonlight, or by the phosphorescent lanterns of lightning bugs in your backyard, not beneath the constellations that we couldn't see, let alone decipher, nor in the dark glow that had replaced the real darkness of night, a darkness already stolen from us; not with the skyline rising behind us while the city gradually decayed, not in the heat of summer while a Cold War raged; despite the freedom of youth and the license of first love—because of fate, karma, luck, what does it matter?—we made not doing it a wonder, and yet we didn't, we didn't, we never did.

Marlin Barton

JEREMIAH'S ROAD

He is at it again. Jeremiah can't see him, but he hears him and knows that across the old roadbed that is nothing now but a ditch full of trees and brush—but used to carry people on mules and in wagons back in the long ago, carry them all the way over into Mississippi if they wanted to go that far—is that crazy boy walking around the trunk of a great dead white oak, first one direction and then the other, endless circle after endless circle in the dust of that sun-baked dirt yard. And he hollers all the while. Lord, how he hollers.

"*Gon' have to kill Luther! This nigger ain't talking! Ain't saying shit! Haa! Beat this nigger!*" The sound of the voice is violent. It is a rasp that suddenly breaks the quiet into pieces.

Jeremiah is sitting on his porch. He takes a long breath, shakes his head. As often as he has heard Luther, he is still not used to the sound. The hollering makes him nervous, unsettled, as if he is waiting on the bad news that must follow such a commotion. He wonders if maybe Marvin is out there by the tree, too, picking at Luther again. It is always worse when Marvin taunts Luther.

Jeremiah wishes the hollering would stop, and for a moment it does. There is a peaceful silence. He takes another deep breath, feels his stomach settle. He clasps his black hands together, stretches his arms and rubs his palms. The skin is rough there, dry. Age and work, he thinks. Too many years on God's earth and too many years of ploughing for Conrad Anderson. And not ploughing with no tractor neither. He stops rubbing his hands, holds them out, fingers spread, and looks at them, remembers how they felt on the worn plough handles, how thick the calluses were.

"Hit me again! Haa! Come on!"

In the winter he can see Luther. All the trees are bare and the bushes dead. Now all he can do is hear, but that is more than enough.

He used to go over across the old road and visit about every day, mostly with Verdel, but with the children, too, and then grandchildren. So many of them living there together. But Verdel has been dead for four years, and there are great-grandchildren now. And sometimes strangers. Faces he doesn't know and doesn't want to know. Mean faces from far away.

Luther is the youngest of Verdel's children. He has, besides Marvin, ten brothers and sisters and half-brothers and half-sisters, some still at home, some that Jeremiah hasn't seen in a long, long time. They are scattered. Up North. The same place where those strangers come from, where Marvin, and then Luther, came back from.

Jeremiah remembers when Luther was a wide-eyed little boy who could barely walk. And he remembers how Luther grew so fast and how he gave him pieces of penny candy, peppermint and gum, and little hard cookies until Luther got too old for that. "Tell Jeremiah 'Thank you, Luther,' " Verdel would say. The little boy would grin, and, like so many children, hid his face in his mama's skirt. Then, as Jeremiah would get up and start out across the old road, Luther would come up suddenly, grab his leg and say, "Thank you."

"Viet Cong gon' have to kill Luther! Luther ain't talking. Haa!"

Viet Cong, nothing, Jeremiah thinks. Detroit. Nothing but Detroit and that dope. Ain't been nowhere but Detroit. He has never been there, never been more than thirty miles from the house where he was born, but he knows about that place. Making cars and taking dope. Drive down here with that stuff, get a poor country nigger on it. Shuck! Didn't used to be.

He remembers when things started to change. Verdel was still alive, but sick so much she couldn't rule the roost like she once had. And Marvin, after so many years, had come back down from Detroit, away from his father. He was no longer that little boy that used to play down by the creek and show Jeremiah the mussels he dug up out of the sand. Marvin had a surly look about him. He was quiet, carried himself in a kind of slouch and barely moved, except when he was beating on Luther or one of the grandchildren. It wasn't playful fighting, like brothers do; it was mean. His sleepy eyes would open wide, and his arms would swing wild as he hit and slapped.

It is beginning to get dark now. The shadows are gone, melted into each other with the last of the sun's heat. The smell of evening comes. It is clean and a little cool, a trace of moisture in it, but not sticky as in the day. This is Jeremiah's favorite time. He lets the coolness settle on him like dew and thinks of the old days, remembers coming in from work about this time. He would have been chopping cotton, or if it was after Mr. Conrad quit planting he might have been getting a cow up or checking on a newborn calf. Even now, when he walks through the pasture to pay Mr. Conrad his rent, he likes to look over the young calves. They are so wide-eyed and spirited.

"Luther ain't talking! Kill this nigger. Put me in the ground!"

"Lord," Jeremiah whispers.

He looks up and sees Mary and Rosa coming home. They

are young with pretty brown skin and tight shapes. They live in the other side of his house. Sometimes one or the other will sit out and talk with him, most times not. Mary has an older brother that comes and takes him to Demarville to cash his check the third of every month. It is almost time again. Verdel used to make Marvin take him, but it wasn't long before she couldn't get him to do it anymore. He just got too sullen. Marvin used to tell him that he ought to put his money in the bank. "It my business what I do," he would tell Marvin.

The girls stop at the edge of the porch. Mary says that they have been up to the store and that it is a right nice evening, not too hot. They going to fix them some supper now, she says. They climb the steps and go inside. He watches them.

He sits a while longer. He doesn't hear Luther anymore. The spell has maybe worn off him for now, let him alone. He has probably gone inside, had enough of walking in circles for this day. Jeremiah sees again Luther's little-boy face, the wide eyes like a calf's, the shy smile. And he thinks about all the trips Luther has made up North the last several years. Gone for six months at a time. "Lord," he calls out. He hopes that maybe Luther will soon be asleep. He figures that it is only when Luther sleeps that his mind quits talking to him, at least where he can hear.

It is dark now. He sees the electric light shining out of Rosa and Mary's windows. It breaks through the rusted screens and strikes the gray, worn boards of the porch. When Mr. Conrad finally put electricity in the house Jeremiah told him that he didn't want it. "No sir! A coal-oil lamp all I need." He even had to argue, and was afraid Mr. Conrad would put electricity in anyway. But he didn't. Jeremiah likes the soft light that the flame from the wick puts out, the way the light is gently absorbed by the dark wood walls. There is a kind of glow, a luster, that is a constant in his mind. He can look at the lamp at night and remember the same light from his earliest memories. The light even has a smell to it that is gentle and so familiar. It eases him, and so often now he does not feel easy. He isn't sure why. He sometimes in the night feels as if he is lost out in deep woods, and the thing that bothers him most is that he knows they are the woods that he used to hunt in and know so well. He killed deer there, and squirrels, and hunted coons.

He gets up, walks inside and pulls the screen door to, latching it. His room is hot, and he leaves the heavy door open. There isn't much breeze but he wants to catch what little might come along. He has his windows open.

He undresses in the dark, washes his face over a wash-pan, and lies down on the bed. From there he can see the small fireplace and his chifforobe and a cane-bottom chair. The room has a dank smell to it that is also familiar. It pushes down on his senses. He can taste it, feel it on his skin.

After he has rested a minute he slides himself to the bed's edge, reaches underneath, feels for cool metal and pulls the .32 out to where it is right on the floor beside him. This has become one of his two nighttime rituals, the rituals he started when that low, uneasy feeling first began to come down on him. He doesn't know now when that was exactly. Four years ago? When Verdel died? Before that? He isn't sure. But something has come on him, a kind of uneasiness, fear even. A kind of night fear, like a child might have. Not a fear of any man or woman, something more than that, larger. But not death. Just something. As if he is lost out in those woods. Or as if maybe that old road has grown up so thick with trees and brush that he can't tell anymore where he lives. The old marks all gone. And he is just trying to get back to—somewhere.

He moves back onto the middle of his bed and begins his other ritual. He lets himself go limp, stares up at the ceiling, lets the darkness clear his mind, and waits for the old voices and the memories that go so far back. His father's voice is first tonight. And, for the first time in a long while, he hears it clearly. It sounds like it is supposed to, deep and full. "Don't you be going down there to Dawes Quarter. You stay away from them Dawes niggers. They sorry! I catch you down there, boy, I beat you. Better hear me good!"

And now his mother's voice, so gentle. "You leave him alone. He a good boy. He ain't going to get in no trouble. Now is you, Jeremiah?"

He remembers how dark his father's skin was, darker than his, dark as the blackened fireplace bricks. And he remembers the scars on his father's hands where the skin seemed to have boiled up and hardened. He remembers his mother's hands, too, such long brown fingers, the skin so much softer than it should have been for the work she did out in the fields. "How come your skin so soft, Mama?" he'd ask. "It my secret," she would say, and laugh.

He stretches. He is tired and can feel sleep coming on.

The only sounds are those of crickets and sometimes a night bird calling from a long way off.

"Jeremiah! Jeremiah!" His brother's voice now. He sees the little boy sitting on the floor. What does he want? To be carried? He picks him up, takes him outside under the long shade of the sycamore and lets him play there with a stick. They take turns scratching with it in the dirt. Jeremiah draws shapes, circles and squares, and his brother scratches through them.

How long has that been now? And when exactly was it that his brother died? Had the little boy gotten big enough where he could run, or was it before that? He used to know, but he disremembers now. And when was it that the first house burned? He can see the flames, hear the house falling in on itself. He can hear his mother's cries, her calling out to the Lord, like she did in church, like he does now sometimes. Was the fire before his father fell and missed work? Sometimes he disremembers when things happened back in that long ago.

And when he can't make the memories come back right, he feels sick inside, dizzy in his mind.

All dead, he thinks. And Pauline, his wife, took so long ago now. It is her voice that he always waits to hear. Some nights it comes, some nights it is too late in the coming.

He listens, lets his mind go back. He thinks that maybe there is still time tonight. And then: "We have more," he hears. "The Lord took this one, Jeremiah, but there be more. I promise you. Look at all the ones my Mama done had. I her daughter ain't I? I tell. . . ."

Now that *other* sound. He has waited for it. It pounds through the wall; it wails; its voices shout. Rosa and Mary sing with it, and it takes his mind over and steals the people and places he has known. "Shuck!" he says. There is nothing now but the room's darkness and that awful sound filling up his mind.

He starts to get up, but lies still. He thinks of the old road. He wishes sometimes that he could leave his house and his few things behind and walk down it, pick his way through the trees and brush until he can go no further.

"Kill this nigger! Put him in the ground," he hears, or thinks he hears, but how can he above the music?

"Open up this door again, bitch! Don't slam no door in my face."

In the first moment that Jeremiah is awake he thinks he hears his father. But the words aren't his father's, and he soon recognizes the voice. Marvin's. There is no music now, just shouting.

"Go on now! We ain't letting you back in. You didn't act right last time."

"Damn you! You know you owe Marvin. Brung you that stuff other night. I seen how it done you. Done you right. Now you can do me right!"

"You acting crazy. Leave us alone! We don't want you around tonight. You wild. Messed up."

Jeremiah has risen from the bed and is standing now behind the screen. Marvin can't see him and Jeremiah waits. He is ready. The room is dark, but at this moment he is sure of everything around him, as sure as the feel of the weight in his right closed hand.

"Fuck you, then! I don't need none of you." Marvin steps back from the door and leans against a post. He stands quiet, waiting, Jeremiah knows, to see if the door will open. Jeremiah waits, too. There is no sound. He remembers how Marvin used to beat Luther, how he moved when he hit, how his face narrowed in mean concentration. He knows that Marvin is concentrated on the door now in the same way.

In a few minutes, Marvin turns quietly and slips off the porch and through the brush. Jeremiah is surprised; he thinks Marvin would have had more patience. Jeremiah was ready to wait all night.

Morning. He awakens and his first thought is of cotton, long rows of it stretching not-yet-white around the side of a gentle sloping, but terraced, hill. And then he thinks of Marvin and last night and feels a tenseness in himself like he usually feels only when Luther has been hollering half the day. He wonders for a moment how his own child might have turned out. Better than Marvin he likes to think. Pauline said there would be more, but there weren't.

He hears morning sounds: birds and a cow lowing, then the tractor and bushhog out in the pasture. That new boy, he thinks. Mr. Conrad done hired him another one. Reckon how long he last? Didn't even show up Monday.

The tractor sputters, rattles. He looks out his window and sees gray smoke shoot up every now and then above the machine. Mr. Conrad tried to get him on that thing so many times after he bought it. Had even cussed him once. The same thing happened when Mr. Conrad bought a lawn mower with an engine. Jeremiah just sharpened the blades on the old one and went to work.

He dresses, puts on his hat and picks up his walking stick. The wood is worn smooth with handling. He walks to the county road and turns toward Riverfield. As usual, he doesn't use his stick to help him walk. He holds it crossways behind his back and catches the ends of it in the crook of each arm. It braces him, holds him. The young ones ride by sometimes, say, "Look at Jesus on his cross."

It is a long walk, but he finally gets to the little gathering of buildings. He stops at the post office first, picks up his check, puts it in his pocket, then walks on over to Mr. Conrad's store.

He walks inside and sits in a chair by the window. Miss May, Mr. Conrad's wife, is working today. She is sitting, resting for the moment. She runs a file across her nails. The store is quiet now, but a crowd will soon gather, the way it always does on check day. Mr. Conrad brings him a Coke. "How you feeling this morning, Jeremiah?"

"Fine," he says.

Mr. Conrad gets the things Jeremiah calls out: cheese, rag bologna, a can of peas. He charges these things. Tomorrow, after Jeremiah has cashed his check, he will come and pay his bill. He doesn't let Mr. Conrad cash his check. Mr. Conrad don't need to know everything. A man has a right to keep some things private.

"Have your bill ready for you in the morning, Jeremiah."

"Yes, sir," he says.

He picks up his bag, walks out of the store and hears the screen slam shut behind him. Several cars pull up to the store the moment he steps out. A crowd stands now in front of the post office. Check Day in Riverfield is beginning. He walks in front of the post office, headed in the direction of home. Suddenly, Marvin steps out of the crowd and in front of him, looking at him with cat's eyes that seem as if they have just opened from sleep. Marvin runs his hands down into his pockets, throws his head back, and rolls a toothpick from one corner of his mouth to the other. Part of Jeremiah wants to laugh at Marvin's strutting.

"You need to go to town today, don't you, old man? Yeah, I remember how Mama used to make me take you. 'Be nice,' she said. Shit."

Jeremiah doesn't speak. He stares past Marvin on down the road. He tightens his grip on the cane that he has shifted to his right hand. He waits.

"Tell you what Marvin gon' do for you. I gon' open my taxi service. That's right. You be my first customer today. For ten dollars and gas, I take you to Demarville. Let you cash your puny check. I know you don't be cashing it in there," he says, pointing to the store.

"Don't want nothing from you," Jeremiah says. He stands firm, feet planted solid. He waits.

Marvin laughs, then walks away, still laughing.

He is halfway home now. Two cars pass. He steps out of the way and into the tall weeds beside the road. Both cars blow by him in a fury of noise and hot wind. Later, another comes down the road, slower this time, and he hears the steady thump, thump, thump of loud music, and when it's close, the shouting voices and all that racket. Nate Johnson's boy, he thinks. Shuck!

He remembers other music, when he was a boy. A man sitting out on some porch with a guitar. Whose porch, though? he wonders. His own? The man makes the sound come out of that wooden box with the blade of a pocket knife. The music is painful-like, as if he uses that knife to cut the sound loose from those shining metal strings. The man plays so slow it seems as if the whole world is still. The wind doesn't even blow. When he puts his guitar down Jeremiah begs for more until his father tells him to *hush.*

Home isn't far now. He turns down the dirt road, sees a car parked beside his house. The old road used to run somewhere right along here, but he can't tell exactly where now. The trees are so thick. He can see it in his mind though. Black folks walking to and from town, someone riding a mule. A white lady in a buggy.

He gets home. Mary's brother, Henry, says, "Was wondering where you was."

"You a little early."

"I reckon so."

Jeremiah goes inside, puts his things away. Henry will take him to Demarville. Jeremiah wants to get his business taken care of.

He sleeps; it's late afternoon. He has been to town, come home and eaten his lunch of cheese and bologna and black-eyed peas. He usually sleeps about this time. The afternoons are quiet, sometimes quieter than the nights. But today he is awakened suddenly, startled from sleep by a machine gun sound. And then that violent pouring of words:

"Shoot me! Haa! I ain't talking. Kill this nigger. Kill Luther!"

The Fourth Day, he thinks. They done started already. It ain't even until tomorrow.

He gets up, walks out onto the porch. He hears laughing, boyish squeals from over across the way. More firecrackers explode. He walks down into the old road, slips up to the fence that runs along the other side of it and watches. He sees Luther, walking silent now around that oak, and the grandchildren and great-grandchildren. Marvin is among them, lighting the fuse and then running back with the rest of them, playing like a kid, as if maybe he never went off up North and came back all mean, messed up. Jeremiah remembers for a moment how he came on Marvin once down by the creek.

He saw him all of a sudden, as he did this morning. Only Marvin was just sitting there, peaceful-like, on a sandbar, his legs folded, looking at the water. "What you doing, Marvin?" he said. "Just thinking," Marvin answered. That was all, "Just thinking." He said it so peaceful-like. His eyes were closed. Jeremiah watched him a moment, then walked on off. Let him be. Maybe Marvin got troubles, he thought.

Now, across the fence, he sees those strange faces. Detroit faces. There are usually a few of them around, come to stay with Marvin and Luther. They worse than any Dawes Quarter nigger ever thought about being, he thinks. And Marvin right in there with them.

There are more strange faces than usual. It will be that way all over Riverfield, Jeremiah knows. All the ones that went off to Akron and Cleveland and Chicago come home for the Fourth Day with strange wives and husbands and children. And the ones that left act so different now. Ain't never should have left.

The door to Verdel's old house opens and Jeremiah stares in amazement at what he sees. It is as if he is looking at someone who has just left the ground of his own accord. A white boy steps from out of the house. He has long blond hair and wears a white shirt and white pants. A regular vision of white in the afternoon sun. What he is doing there Jeremiah can only wonder. Can't be good, he thinks.

All the rest of the afternoon he hears them. Fireworks keep going off; sometimes there is only a single explosion and then quiet, sometimes twenty or thirty go off in rapid bursts and drive Luther into fits. *"Kill me,"* he hollers. *"Luther don't tell nothing!"*

Later, Jeremiah hears the racing of a car engine. The sound starts off low and full; then when the engine is gunned it builds in fat spurts until there is nothing but the continual explosion that whines higher and higher, unbearably, through the trees and rises above the old road.

Jeremiah rubs his hands together, rocks his body quickly back and forth in his chair out on the porch. That uneasiness has crept into him and rises through his body. The night fear. He walks inside, even closing the heavy door, but he can still hear the sound and it is too hot to close the windows. He splashes water on his face, but the water is hot against his skin. It runs down his neck and makes his shirt stick.

He walks back outside, down the steps and over into the road. He peers through the brush and sees a car with its hood up. It's blue, an older make. The white boy and someone black with a fat stomach and no shirt on lean over the engine while Marvin sits behind the wheel and revs the motor, cussing when it idles low. Marvin stomps the gas pedal and turns and looks straight at Jeremiah. For a moment Jeremiah is afraid he's been seen. He waits, but Marvin's face shows no recognition.

Luther walks silent for now. It is Jeremiah who feels like yelling above the sound of the engine.

No music tonight. Mary and Rosa have gone out. The fireworks continually break the quiet, and Jeremiah can't sleep. He feels somehow as if he is waiting on something. Worst of all tonight, the old voices don't speak. Jeremiah strains, listens, sends his mind back, but hears nothing. Seems as if there is nothing there inside him.

The fireworks stop for a moment and without the voices there is only silence. He doesn't listen for them any longer. He feels the night fear in himself, and he waits for something else now as he lies on top of his quilt, something silent, something that he can't even imagine. He feels heavy, as if something's pushing down on top of him.

.   .   .

He awakens from a dream. Pauline was sitting before him, right there in the cane-bottom chair, pulling apart the seam of an old cloth sack that she wants to use. He hears the tearing sound again. Only, it's rougher this time. A creaking now, like the branches of pines in a strong wind. A shadow moves past. And another. Then not a shadow at all but a flash of white, and he raises up, knowing and gasping suddenly for the breath that is like a thick fluid now. This is no dream. A hard weight lands against him. He chokes and then feels a blow against his face, feels his cheek become hot and tastes the blood as it flows into his mouth in rivulets. "Don't kill him, don't kill the bastard!" he hears. Not a voice he knows. The hot dark body is on top of him, holding him. He remembers his pistol. It's lying there in the dark on the floor—loaded, ready, and so useless now. "Look in the chifforobe," another voice shouts. He doesn't know this one either. The white boy moves quick at the command. He is opening the chifforobe, rifling through it. He looks underneath, finds the metal box. Jeremiah knows how much he's about to lose. He tries to raise up again. Something metal strikes the back of his head. A hand grabs his face, palm in his mouth, and it pushes his head into the pillow. He can't breathe. He tastes the skin, it's full of grease, and bites into the slick flesh like an animal tearing meat. A scream. Two more blows against his head. "You old son of a bitch!" "Don't kill him! Come on," he hears, and the hulking weight is off him. The torn screen door slams and footsteps strike the porch; then he hears a slapping sound, nervous laughter and then nothing. He shakes, his head is filled with dizziness. He feels lost for a moment, as if he is gone too far out into those woods again and can find his way only if he stumbles onto a familiar landmark, an old dead tree, a creek maybe or an old road. He takes hard breaths. His lungs are still filled with liquid. The whole thing seems as if it lasted no longer than his dream. He looks to the cane-bottom chair, as if he will find Pauline there. He sees it lying overturned.

He opens the gate, almost stumbles, then walks on through. Mr. Conrad's lights aren't on. He chains the gate back and walks to the house, makes his way up onto the neatly kept porch. Two chairs and a bench sit among potted plants. He knocks several times, then leans against the door frame. He has made up his mind about what he will say. Sometimes you got to lie to tell the truth, he thinks.

He thought about going after them, following them through the trees and bushes in the old road. But he felt too dizzy and weak, felt as if he never would have made it up out of the old road without falling. So he rested, waited until his head cleared. But now, knocking on Mr. Conrad's door, he feels as if he should have stumbled after them. And if he couldn't make it, then so be it. He could die in that road. Ain't got long to live, anyway.

A light comes on and a door opens. Miss May is standing there in a robe; one hand holds it closed. A black hairnet covers her gray hair.

"What's happened, Jeremiah?"

From her expression he knows how bad he must look. He can still taste blood on his lip, and he catches the bitter taste of grease on his tongue every now and then.

"I been robbed, Miss May."

Her sleepy eyes seem to focus, and she looks frightened for a moment.

"Come inside," she says. "I'll get Mr. Conrad."

"No ma'am. I stay out here on the porch," he says. He feels suddenly dizzy.

She looks at him for an instant, as if to say, "You ought to come on in," then turns and walks back into the house. "It's Jeremiah," he hears her say.

In a moment Mr. Conrad is there, standing in a blue robe.

He opens the screen door. "Come in the house, Jeremiah. You been hurt."

"No, sir. I just set right here," he says. But Mr. Conrad holds the screen open still, and he can see Mr. Conrad begin to get aggravated the way he did when he found out that Jeremiah wouldn't drive the tractor. He cuts his eyes, frowns. "Come in where it's cool," he says. Jeremiah steps inside. "We'll get you a chair in the kitchen."

"No, sir," Jeremiah says. He could make it into the kitchen, but he sits down on the floor beside the door.

"All right, then," Mr. Conrad says. "Whatever you want." Miss May comes back, followed by their son and grandson. The son is already dressed, and the grandboy looks as if he's walking in his sleep. The four of them stand over Jeremiah, peer down at him. He hadn't wanted all this.

"How bad does your head hurt you, Jeremiah?" Miss May asks.

"It be all right."

"We'll call the doctor."

"I just want me some water."

"Don't you want the doctor to look at you?" she says.

"No'm," he says, and turns away.

"I'll get you some water, then." She walks into the kitchen.

Mr. Conrad and his son, who Jeremiah remembers as a little boy, ask at the same moment: "Who did this to you?" Their looks are grave, as if to say, "We will take care of this. Tell us who. Give us a name."

Jeremiah shuts his eyes. He thinks about what he has decided to say, remembers the blows against his head. He opens his eyes, looks at Mr. Conrad and then at his son. They are waiting. The grandboy stands behind them, waiting also, waiting to see what his father and grandfather will do about this. Jeremiah draws a breath slowly until it fills him.

"Marvin, Verdel's boy," he says, then looks blankly at his old, dry hands that hang limp between his knees.

. . .

The sheriff comes in a little while. Jeremiah hears the car pull up, and Mr. Conrad and his son tell him they will be right back, then walk outside. They leave the door open. He hears another car; a door slams. He listens for voices, but can't make them out. Finally, there are footsteps on the porch, and he hears the words "old man." He closes his hands, tightens them into fists, and remembers how they held the plough.

Mr. Conrad leads the sheriff inside. The sheriff is black. A white state trooper is with him.

"Tell the men what happened, Jeremiah," Mr. Conrad says.

He tells them how he woke up, how one of them held him down while the white boy got his money. Then tells them that he saw Marvin, heard his voice clearly.

"One of them was white?" the sheriff asks.

"Yes, sir. They was all over at Verdel's old house today. I seen them. Some strange black boys and that white boy. They was working on a car."

"What kind?" the trooper asks.

"Blue. Looked like one like Miss May used to have a while back. A Chevrolet, I believe. If I saw it again, I'd know it."

They go first to Verdel's old house. Jeremiah rides with the sheriff; the trooper is behind them, then Mr. Conrad and his son in a pickup. They pull up along side each other in the dirt yard. Jeremiah is sure that the ones that robbed him are long gone. The house is dark, but a dusk-to-dawn lamp shines from a pole.

"Any of these cars the one you saw them working on?"

"No, sir."

The sheriff gets out of the car, tells Jeremiah to stay put. The trooper and Mr. Conrad and his son follow the sheriff to the door. Jeremiah watches the four men. Suddenly he feels a tiredness come on him that is so complete he has to work to catch his breath. He feels as if he has been ploughing all day in the hot sun without a break, or as if he has been walking lost in the woods, walking one circle after another, trying to draw breath from the hot still air.

"Come on out here," he hears the sheriff say. One of Verdel's grandchildren steps out of the door, a girl of about fifteen. Jeremiah can't recall her name. She holds her arms wrapped around her middle, looks at her feet. She doesn't look once at Jeremiah sitting in the lighted car.

"Where's Marvin?" the sheriff says.

A window at the end of the house is opened a little wider. Jeremiah hears it being raised. A hand reaches out, hangs off the sill.

"Tell us where your brother is," the trooper says. "We need to talk with him."

"He my uncle, and I don't know where he at. I ain't see'd him."

"Jeremiah says he saw him over here today," the sheriff says.

She still does not look toward the car. "I ain't see'd him. He gone."

"He take a white boy with him?" the sheriff says. "A couple of black boys?"

"They was some people visiting, but they gone now. They might done headed back up North."

"With Marvin?" the trooper asks.

"Don't know. Don't think so."

"All right then," the sheriff says.

"Luther ain't talking! Ain't saying shit!" The voice comes exploding out of the window. *"Gon' have to kill this nigger! Haa!"*

"Don't mind him," Mr. Conrad says. "He's just crazy."

The sheriff and Mr. Conrad decide they should try the Loop Road. They pass across the highway, follow the rough blacktop as it curves past shotgun houses and houses built out of cement block. They drive down into Jackson Quarter where small shacks crowd winding dirt roads. Jeremiah doesn't see the car.

Back out on the Loop they pass what Jeremiah knows are soybean fields. He has never worked in a soybean field. People didn't used to plant them, but a family came from way off, bought this piece of land that used to grow cotton, and planted beans. Jeremiah thinks now about how he used to fill his sack out in the cotton field beside his mother and father. That life is so long ago to him at this moment it feels as if it's out of some old book that no one reads from anymore.

They turn left around the Loop, toward Bethel Hill. At the base of the pine-covered slope they approach a trailer in a small clearing. Another dusk-to-dawn lamp shines in the yard. Places lit that never used to be, Jeremiah thinks. He sees the rusted trailer door standing open, and then sees the car, and just as quickly the uneasiness hits him again, that feeling that has slowly taken him over these last years.

"There it be," he says.

The sheriff stops the car suddenly, pulls off the road and into the yard. The trooper and Mr. Conrad follow. Their headlights strike the aluminum and then each driver turns parallel to the trailer. Jeremiah watches as the trooper leaves his car, runs quickly along the edge of the woods, and, pistol drawn, disappears behind the trailer. Jeremiah hasn't even had time to open his door.

The sheriff and Mr. Conrad and his son are already out, too, standing behind their car and truck, pistols out. Jeremiah finally gets out of the car, stands and watches these men as they call out to Marvin. His chest aches and his legs are weak.

A light comes on in the trailer, and Marvin steps up to the door. He holds his hands out in front of himself. His face is caught for a moment in the light from the dusk-to-dawn lamp, and Jeremiah can see absolutely no trace of fear in the narrowed, hard-set features.

"What you want?" he says.

"Who else is in there?" the sheriff says.

"Just Robert Jackson."

"Tell him to come on out."

"He asleep."

"He ain't no more! Now come on out of there. Tell the others, too."

"Ain't no others."

"I said tell them!"

"We's the only ones. What I done? I been here all night."

"Jeremiah says different," Mr. Conrad says.

"Who? Jeremiah? What that old man say?"

"Come down the steps, *now*," the sheriff says.

Marvin walks down as easily as if he is headed out for a night in Demarville. He is followed by a small wiry man who steps much more slowly and carefully. In a moment the trooper walks through the door. "They weren't lying. Nobody else here."

"All right," the sheriff says. "Robert, you just stay back where we can see you."

The sheriff walks up to Marvin now, puts Marvin's arms behind his back, and handcuffs him, then tells him his rights. He walks Marvin to the car and pushes him into the back seat. Marvin's head strikes the car's top.

Jeremiah stands behind the car. The sheriff leaves the door open, walks over and talks with the trooper and Mr. Conrad and his son. They have done all this, Jeremiah thinks. They have taken care of it all. He feels tired again. His arms are weak and his legs are simply numb now. Is this all? he wonders. "Hey old man," Marvin says. "What you tell them? That I robbed you? Well, fuck you!"

He doesn't speak. He feels the fear that comes on him at night. The kind of fear a man might have if he was bound and blindfolded and set out on some unfamiliar ground, alone. A car passes and, for a moment, he thinks about the old road, sees it as it used to be, the old wagon ruts, the dried manure, sees himself walking on it, headed home. He knows it will lead him there. He wants to go home. He turns toward Marvin. His hand grips hard the cool metal deep in the pocket of his overalls. He moves toward the opened door, feels the weight of the metal in his now extended right hand. Above the shouts of the other men, above Marvin's curses, he hears only one voice, Luther's. *"Gon' have to kill this nigger!"*

Kelly Cherry

NOT THE
PHIL DONAHUE SHOW

This is not the Phil Donahue show; this is my life. So why is my daughter, who is 20 years old and, to me, so heartbreakingly beautiful that I think that for the sake of the health of the entire world and probably universe she shouldn't be allowed out of the house without a cardiologist at her side, why is my daughter standing in my doorway telling me she's a lesbian?

She hangs in the doorway, her face rising in the warm air like a bloom in a hothouse. (I have been cooking.) She has chin-length blonde hair, straight as a pin, side-parted. Her skin is bare of makeup. Her blue eyes are like forget-me-nots in an open field. She has a superficial scratch on her cheek, a deep resentment that pulls her head down and away from me.

I'm standing here with a wooden spoon in my hand like a baton and I feel like there is some music that should be playing, some score that, if I only knew it, I ought to be conducting.

If I say it's a phase, that she'll outgrow it, she'll peel herself from the wall like wallpaper and exit, perhaps permanently, before I can even discern the pattern.

If I say honey, that's great, nonchalant and accepting as history, I could be consigning her to a life that I'm not sure she really wants—maybe she's just testing me. Maybe this *is* just a phase.

I can't help it, for just a moment I wish her father were here. I want him to be as shocked and stuck as I am, here in this blue-and-white room with steam rising from the stove, enough garlic in the air to keep a host of vampires at bay. But I remind myself: he would have been glad to be here. I am the one who walked out on him. As Isabel, in her posture, her sullen slouch, her impatient, tomboy gestures, never lets me forget. *Daddy would know how to handle this*, she seems to be saying, defiant as a rebel with a cause. *I dare you to try*.

It is five o'clock. It's already been a long day, which I have spent as I spend most of my days—nursing patients to whom I have let myself get too close. And sometimes I feel a kind of foreclosure stealing into my heart, sometimes I feel like an S & L, sometimes I feel overextended. But I'm always home from my shift at the hospital by four-thirty, while Ian stays late after school to devise lesson plans, tutor the sluggardly, confer with parents.

Now the front door swings open and it's Ian. He's taller than I, who am tall, so tall his knees seem to be on hinges, and he unlatches them and drops into one of the dining-room chairs. I can watch him over the dividing counter that connects the dining room with the kitchen, one of the results of our renovation last summer. Isabel has not moved from her post in the doorway (there's no door) between us.

"Hi, Shel," Ian says to me. "Hi, Belle," he says to my daughter. "Nice to see you."

He wants so much for her to let him enter her life. He has no children of his own—he wants to be, if not a second father, at least a good friend. "Shelley," he says, "What are we drinking tonight?"

"Isabel has an announcement," I say, waving my wooden

wand. I turn around and start stirring, the steam pressing the curl out of my hair like a dry cleaner.

"I'm in love," I hear her say behind my back.

"Hey, that's great," Ian responds and I realize how unfair we have been to him, we have set him up for this.

"With a woman," she says.

Girl, I want to correct her. With a *girl*.

Marlo Thomas would kill me.

"Oh," Ian says. "Well, why isn't she here? When do we get to meet her?"

And I remember: this is why I married him. Because he puts people ahead of his expectations for them, even though his expectations can be annoyingly well defined. Because he doesn't create a crisis where there isn't one.

But this is a crisis. If she were *his* daughter, he'd realize that.

Entirely without meaning to, entirely illogically, I am suddenly angry with Ian for not being the father of my daughter. Why wasn't he around when I was 20—her age, I realize, startled—and looking for something to do with my life, which I had begun to understand stretched before me apparently endlessly like an unknown continent, one I was afraid to explore by myself? Why did I have to wait for most of my life before he showed up?

We are seated at the table from my first marriage, now located under the dining-room window overlooking the leaf-strewn front lawn and Joss Court. It is September in Wisconsin, and the home fires have begun to burn, smoke lifting from the chimneys like an Ascension. The maple and walnut trees are a kaleidoscope of color; the bright orange-red berries of the mountain ash are living ornaments. Soon it will be Halloween, Thanksgiving, Christmas. Across the street, abutting Joss but facing Highland, is my friend Nina's house, in which I lived for a year while making up my mind to divorce

Isabel's father. Directly across from me, behind Nina, lives Sophie, recently widowed. She pushes a hand mower, the last lawncut of the season before raking starts.

"You should go over and offer to rake for her sometime soon," I say to Ian.

"I will," he agrees, drilling a corkscrew into the unopened wine.

Isabel says, "I think she likes doing things for herself."

"I can still offer," Ian says. "She can say no."

During this conversation, a fourth party has been silent; Judy, Isabel's friend. As soon as Ian suggested we meet, Isabel raced out of the house and brought her back for supper.

Judy is not what I expected. For one thing, she's pretty—almost as pretty as my daughter. She has long wavy honey-blonde hair so perfectly cut it falls with mathematical precision, like a sine-curve, around her glowing face. She has this generation's white, even teeth, a kittenish face. It is easy to see why Isabel has fallen in love with her; in fact, I don't see how anyone could *not* fall in love with either of them—so why shouldn't they fall in love with each other?

Thinking these thoughts, I am swept by a sense of déjà-vu. I have lived this scene before—but where? In another life?

Then I figure it out: not lived but read, in all the contemporary novels Nina lends me. Again and again, a mother is visited over the holidays by her college-going son, who arrives with a male lover in tow to explain that he is now out of the closet. Sometimes the father seizes this opportunity to declare that he, too, has all along been a homosexual. I glance at Ian suspiciously. He is in his gracious mode, entertaining the two girls with tales from his life in the Peace Corps, following the fall of Camelot. These stories now have the lustre of legend about them; they are tales from far away and long ago. The girls listen to them, enthralled and cynically condescending at the same time, in both their lovely faces the question, *But how could anyone have ever been so innocent and hopeful?* And I am filled with the furious rush of my love for Ian, my heart pumping, powerful as hydrology, and I want to say to them, *That's the kind of innocence you learn, it takes age and experience to be able to shake off your self-protective defenses and give yourself over to helping someone else.* But I don't say anything, I just look at Ian, reminding myself that later the girls will be gone and we can indulge our heterosexual sexual preferences on the water bed, and he says, "Passez-moi le salt, s'il vous plait."

Ian teaches French at West High.

Two sky-blue tapers burn driplessly next to wildflowers I brought back from the farm a few weeks ago. The wildflowers have dried—it was a delicate transition from life to death, so shaded it would have been impossible to say exactly when death occurred: at what point did these flowers become what they are now?

The candlelight projects a silhouette of the wildflowers onto the wall; it polishes the real gold of Judy's hoop earrings, casts a mantle of light over Isabel's bent head.

I'm not losing a daughter, I tell myself, I'm gaining a daughter.

"They are children," I say to Ian in the kitchen, after they have vanished into the night.

I remember those college nights, full of adventure, philosophy, midnight desperation in the diner over coffee and cigarettes. I had two years of them before I decided to go to nursing school, where nihilism was not part of the curriculum.

I peer out the window as if the children, or my youth, might still be out there, in the dark.

Through the window, which we have opened slightly to cool off, comes an autumnal aroma of fallen apples, bitter herbs. Already, the birds have started south.

"Isabel's almost 21," he says. "You've got to start getting

used to the idea that she's grown up. She has her own life to live."

When he says "life to live," I of course think of one of my patients, only a few years older than Isabel and like her gay, who, however, has but a death to die.

Noting parallels and contrasts to patients' lives in this way is, I discovered a long time ago, an occupational hazard of nursing, and I don't allow myself to be sidetracked. I just say, "That's easy for you to say."

He slams the silverware drawer shut. "No, it isn't, Shelley. As a matter of fact, it's very hard for me to say, because I know you're upset and you're going to take it out on me. It would be much easier for me not to say anything, but someone has to keep you from making a big mistake here."

He's right, but I don't have to be happy about that.

I'm elbow-deep in hot water—literally. I rinse the last dish and he hands me a dishtowel. When we remodeled this kitchen, we made it comfortable for both of us to work in at the same time. We both like to cook. When I think of Ian, I naturally think of spices—"a young stag upon the mountains of spices." Old deer, I have called him, teasing; old dear.

Sometimes he sits at the dining-room table, marking papers, while I make something that can be stored in the freezer for the following day, and as I scoop and measure, doing the Dance of the Cook, I look at him through the rectangular frame created by the counter and cabinets. He is a year younger than I am. His eyes are small, his cheeks ruddy. He would have made a great British colonel, except that he would have liberated all the colonials, at the same time forcing them at gunpoint to call in their pledges to public radio. He is a born and bred Wisconsinite, and I love every contradiction his un-French mind so blithely absorbs. For him, I left a husband who was equally good-hearted but incapable of such contradiction, paradox, surprise.

"Maybe I'm not the one to do that in this case," he continues. "Call Nelson. Maybe *he* can keep you from going off the deep end."

I look at Ian; I pick up the phone; I dial. It rings. "Nel?" I say.

"Shel."

God, we were young. We were young for so long—longer than we should have been. We were still so young even by the time our daughter was born that we thought, amazingly, that the family that rhymed together would stay together.

"I need to talk to you. Can you meet me at Porta Bella?"

"In 20 minutes," he says. "Listen, I know what it's about. Everything's going to be all right."

"She told you first?" I ask. I can't help it, I'm hurt.

Nelson leans back in the booth, and the leather seat creaks. His white hair—it started turning white when he reached forty—looks pink in the red haze of the table lamp, a stubby candle in a netted hurricane shield.

At the bar, male and female lawyers and professors bump against one another, pushing, as if hoping to annoy someone into noticing them. When you are young, you're a sex object because you're *sexy*, but then you reach an age when you have to make someone aware of you as an *object* before it will occur to him or her that you just might possibly be a *sex object*. This is one of the few places near State Street that the students tend to leave to an older crowd.

Nelson's pink beard looks like spun sugar, and for a moment, I remember being a child, wanting to go to the circus and buy cotton candy. My parents said no. It was the polio scare—people thought perhaps children contracted polio from being in crowds. No circus, no swimming lessons, no—

"It's hard on her, our divorce," he says. "I'm happy things have worked out for you with Ian, but you must realize she senses a barrier there now. There's not the same unimpeded access to you that she had."

Unimpeded access. Do I detect smugness in his voice, the way he drapes one arm over the back of the booth like a long, sly, coat-sleeved cat?

"Do you think she's doing this just to get back at me? Will she grow out of it?"

"I think it's the real thing, Shelley," he says. He smiles. "As real as Coke." He means Coca-Cola, I know. We are not the kind of people who would ever mean anything else, I realize, wondering if this is insight, boast, or lament. It could be an elegy. "I think she's in love."

He has brought his arm down, shifted closer to the table. Whatever he wanted to say about my behavior, he feels he has said. Now we can talk about hers. "She's still our little girl," he says.

"She always will be," I agree. "And she's *free to be herself.*" I start to tell him that I'm quoting Marlo Thomas, then don't. The guy has enough to deal with without his ex-wife quoting Marlo Thomas. "It's just that, well, weren't you counting on grandchildren someday?"

"I wouldn't rule out the possibility yet," he says. "A lot of lesbians have children, one way or another. I think she wants to have children someday."

He leans back again, the thick, pink beard like a strawberry milkshake glued to his face. "That wasn't the only thing I was counting on," he says sadly.

We wake to FM. Ian and I lightly touch our mouths together on the corner of Joss and Highland, walking in opposite directions to our respective places of work.

All day at the hospital, I dispense meds, take temps, rig I-V's. I draw blood, turn or ambulate patients, record BP's. It's an unexceptional day—people are dying. September sunlight, that last hurrah of brightness already muted by the foreknowledge of winter, slips across the islanded rooms, making watery squares of shadow on the white sheets of so many,

many single beds, in all of which people are dying. Some will go home first; some will have remissions; some will live long lives; all are dying.

In the hall, I pass Nelson, his white coat flapping behind him like a sail, a tail. If he hurried any more, he would lift off, airborne, a medical kite, a human Medflight. We nod to each other, the way we did before we were married, while we were married.

In the fluorescent glow of the hospital hallways, his beard no longer looks like peppermint. It is as white as surgical gauze.

Gloved and gowned, I duck into Reed's room.

Reed has AIDS. He has been here before, during two other episodes of acute infection. This time he has pneumonia. This time, when he leaves here, he will go to a nursing home to die.

It seems to me that his single bed is like a little boat afloat in the sea of sunlight that fills the room. Reed lies there on his back, with his eyes shut, as if drifting farther and farther from shore.

"Reed," I say to call him back.

He opens his eyes and it takes him a moment to process the fact that I am here, that it is I. I believe the dementia that occurs in 80 percent of AIDS patients has begun to manifest itself, but it's hard to say. I don't know what Reed was like before he became an AIDS patient.

I pull up a chair and sit beside him. The skinnier he gets, the more room his eyes take up in his face. He winks at me, a thin eyelid dropping over a big brown eye that seems, some- how, just a little less sharp than it did the last time he was here.

"Hello, Shelley," he says.

"I thought for a minute you'd forgotten me."

"I still have my *mind*, Shelley," he says, too quick, I think, to assume I mean more than my surface statement. "It's just my body that's going."

I don't contradict him. He knows everything there is to know at this point about his disease. He knows more about it than I do—like many AIDS victims, he has read the research, questioned the doctors, exchanged information. At the limits of knowledge, the issue becomes belief, and I figure he has a right to choose his beliefs. Reed believes he will lick his illness.

I look at the *body that's going:* He has lost more weight since his last hospitalization, despite a rigorous fitness plan. His cheekbones are as pointy as elbows. His brown eyes have lost some of their laughter. When I pick up his hand to hold it, it doesn't squeeze back. There are sores on his arms—the giveaway lesions of Kaposi's Sarcoma. K.S., we say around here. I take his pulse, the wrist between my fingers and thumb not much bigger than a sugar tube.

"Reed," I ask him, "are you sorry you're gay?" I almost say *were.* As in *were gay.* Or *sorry you were gay.*

"Because of this?" He withdraws his hand.

"No. Just—if there were no such thing as AIDS, if nobody ever died from it, would you be glad to be gay?"

"How can I answer that? How can I pretend Eddie never died?"

Eddie was his lover; he died of Aids two years ago, in California. Reed came back home, but his parents, small dairy farmers in northern Wisconsin, have been unable, or perhaps unwilling, to look after him.

He's not having trouble talking; his lungs are much better now, he is off oxygen, and he'll surely leave us in a day or two. I'll never see him again—this former social worker, still in his twenties, now dying more or less alone, whose gentleness is reflected in the sterling silver-framed photo portraits of Eddie and his parents and sister that he brings here with

him each time and props on the night-table, next to the telephone and water tray.

In my imagination, I try to read—Reed!—the dinner scene
from the story of *his* life: His parents are seated at either end
of the old oak table that has been the heart of their family life
for 25 years. Would they place Reed next to his sister, across
from Eddie? Or would they put the two boys together, facing
their only daughter? The former, I think: Eddie is an outsider
in this scene.

I know what they look like, gathered around that table,
because of the portraits. Reed's sister is dark, a little over-
weight; she is the mediator, the one who tries to make all the
emotional transactions among the family members run
smoothly. His mother looks like a blueberry pie—dark and
creamy-skinned, round-faced, plumply bursting out of her
Sears slacks and top. His father is shy, turning away from the
camera, turning away from Eddie not out of any dislike in
particular for him but because he always turns, always has
turned, away from even the merest implicative reference to
sex, and Eddie's presence is an implication. And Eddie—
Eddie is healthy. Eddie is broad-faced and big-shouldered,
Eddie is the one who looks like a farmhand, who looks like he
could do chores all day under a midwestern sun and drink
Stroh's at night, fish for muskie and shingle the roof on Sunday. He does not look like he will be dead anytime soon.

I wonder how the family took it, how explicit Reed was or
how much they guessed or refused to understand. Reed
would have been sensitive about everyone's feelings, wanting
not to hurt either his parents or his lover, wanting his sister
not to be disappointed in her big brother but eager for her to
understand Eddie's importance in his life. I wonder how
Reed felt when, after dinner, they all rose from the table and
said, not impolitely, goodnight, taking him and Eddie up on
their offer to do the dishes, and retired to their rooms—not
condemning him but also, not, not—what did he expect from

them? he asked himself. Had he hoped they would embrace
Eddie as their own, that they would feel, when they looked at
Eddie, the warmth of emotion that sometimes suddenly
welled up in him so intensely he could almost cry, a cup
overflowing? When he turned the dial on the dishwasher, a
red light came on like a point of reference.

While I am musing, Reed is busy fighting off an invisible
force that wants to pull his mouth down, wants to yank tears
out of his eyes. When he wins, his face falls into place again,
at rest, the exhausted victor of yet another round in an intra-
mural boxing match against grief.

"How are Ian," he asks me, "and Isabel?"

We are talking together in low voices, telling each other
about our lives, when Dr. Feltskog stops in with a couple of
residents following in his wake. They are all using universal
precautions. This is a teaching hospital. He introduces them
to Reed, explains Reed's situation, the presenting pneumocys-
tic pneumonia, our methodology for managing the disease.

Dr. Feltskog finishes his spiel, and I am looking at Reed,
trying to measure its impact, when one of the young doctors
steps forward. "Reed," she says—even the youngest doctors
no longer use patients' last names—"how do you feel?"

Reed winks at me again, though so slowly I am not sure the
others in the room recognize it as a wink. They may just think
he is tired, fighting sleep.

"Okay," he says.

The young doctor nods as if she understands exactly what
he is doing: He has said that he feels okay because he doesn't
want to burden them with details about how he really feels. It
doesn't occur to her that maybe he just doesn't want to burden himself with the attention he can tell she is dying to give
him.

"Now, Reed," she says, leaning over him so close it is as if
he has no boundaries at all, leaning into his face, "we know

you have feelings you want to talk about. It's natural. If you like, we can ask a staff psychiatrist to stop in to see you."

There is a silence in which I learn to feel sorry even for her —not just Reed, not just Isabel, not just Ian and my ex, and not just myself but even this jejune, over-helpful (and unconsciously manipulative), too-well-intentioned doctor in pearls and Hush Puppies, the white coat, though she doesn't know it, a symbol of all that she owes to women my age, who made it possible for her to do what she does, have what she has—as I watch Dr. Feltskog register, on his mental ledger sheet, her lack of sensitivity.

To Reed, the suggestion that he see a psychiatrist means he really is losing his mind. It means he will be defeated after all: if his mind is not on his side, how can he combat what is happening to his body? It means he really is going to die before he has had a chance to live.

"I don't want a psychiatrist," he says softly, the tears he had beaten back earlier now overtaking him.

They leap to his eyes, those tears, and others to mine, as he says, with as much exclamatory emphasis as he can command, a look on his face like that of a child who has been unfairly trapped into protesting his innocence even after he knows that everyone knows he is guilty, "Why are you interrogating me about my feelings like this? This is not the Phil Donahue show! This is my life!"

When he says this, I lose track of which one of us is me. It seems to be *me* in that bed, it is *my* body going, *my* mind that's no longer to be trusted. This is the opposite of a near-death out-of-body experience, this experience of being in *someone else's* body near *someone else's* death. Those are my tears on his face, surely; surely, these are his tears on mine.

At first I think he has read my mind. As I begin to regain my ontological footing, I understand that, all over America, people are struggling to prove to themselves that their lives are more than television, that their lives are real, the real thing.

Assembled like this, we have all entered a world outside time, it is as if a collective catastrophe has carried us into a place of silence and immobility, we are a mass accident, a tragedy.

Thus: a moment of stasis, a moment like cardiac arrest, and then we all come to life again, a jumpstart, a fibrillation. And a fluttering, too, a fluttering is going on here: a fluttering of hands, of hearts, of eyelids too nervous to lift themselves all the way up. There is this swift, generalized occupation, and I have a sense as of tents being taken down and away quickly and quietly, a stealth of tents, and yes, now everyone has scattered and I am alone again with Reed. I think of all the things he might have said, the true profanity of his condition, and it seems to me that no words could ever be as shocking as "Phil" and "Donahue" and "Show," words that have brought America into this hospital room, the dream of an essential empowerment so at odds with the insomniac knowledge of our own helplessness, our midnight desperation over coffee and cigarettes.

"Please," I say to Reed, and I am intrigued to note how my voice supplicates, my voice, which is, really, pretty good at both giving and accepting orders and not accustomed to hovering in between like this, "get some rest now, Reed."

He doesn't answer. He turns his face away from me and I wait, but he still doesn't answer or look at me. I am left staring at the back of his head, the bald spot that is the tonsure of early middle age and was once the fontanelle of an infant, and I think—what else could I think—that I don't care what kind of life Isabel leads, so long as she gets to lead one.

I think of my beautiful daughter, her grumpy spirit caged by the circumstances of her own sexuality and her mother's, and of how it will one day—soon, I think—be freed, *free to be itself*, and how, when it is, her sweetly curved profile will disclose the inner strength I know is there, how her blue, blue eyes, deep and true as columbine, will sparkle with the triumph that integrity is.

Not that I wouldn't prefer things to be otherwise; not that I am exactly happy about my daughter's choice. I wouldn't go so far as that—not yet. But what I know, almost annoyed with myself for knowing it because I wish I could surprise myself, but then that is why I married Ian, isn't it, to be surprised, is that I'm going to. I love her too much not to know that the day will come when I will feel however I must feel in order to keep her in my life. This, I realize, was never in doubt, no matter how much I may have been in doubt. The issue always becomes belief.

But back out in the hallway I stop short, confused, almost dizzied, feeling I have lost my place in some book or other. They are paging Nelson—*Dr. Lopate, Dr. Lopate!*— and I remember how I used to call him that our first year together in Detroit. We were the same height, and I'd launch his newly earned title in a low whisper from the rim of his ear, a little raft afloat on the sea of ego. And he loved it, at least for that first year.

I find my way to the locker room and change out of my work shoes into Nikes. Walking home on Highland, I see that we are having what I secretly think of as a Code Blue sky— alarmingly bright, the kind of sky that can galvanize you. A sky like emergency medicine, needing to be attended to on the spot. So when I get home I call Ian at the school. The secretary has to go get him, of course, because he's in his classroom, grading papers. *Nous aimons, vous aimez, ils aiment. Elles aiment.*

"Let's spend the night at the farm," I tell him. "I'll swing by and pick you up."

After supper we go for a walk and wind up down by Beaver Pond. The pond is as round as a smiling cheek, the setting sun a blush on it like rouge, and in the sky a thin crescent moon, the squinty eye of it, the shut eye of it, is already risen, as if it just can't wait, it has things it wants to see, it won't be kept in the dark any longer. Ian and I straddle a log, and we're glad, given the late-day chill, that we are wearing flannel shirts.

Let's face it, things are not exactly quiet out here in the country. Things are going on even out here. We can hear the beavers working away in a scramble against winter. Every so often, there's a crash or a cry, and no way of knowing whether the sound means life or death. There are so many creatures out here, deer and owls and just so many, and the prairie grass, and the abandoned orchard, and wildflowers.

Sometimes I think of the whole world as a kind of hospital, the earth itself as a patient.

There are days, now, when so much seems to be slipping away. Even the things one tends not to think of, like the walnuts. The walnuts are slipping away, going off to be stockpiled by squirrels. The green of summer is slipping away, hiding its light under a bush or a bushel of autumn leaves. There are dreams that slip away in the middle of the night, losing themselves forever in some dark corner of the subconscious. There are stars that are disappearing even as we look at them. There are mothers and fathers and children, all of them slipping away like the fish in the pond, going down deeper for winter. And you reach out to hold on to your child, and she is slipping away, going off into some life that is not your life, and you are afraid to see her go because you know, you know how far it is possible to go, how far it is possible for things to slip away.

"You're thinking," Ian says. "What about?"

But I don't know how to say what I'm thinking, because it seems to me I am thinking of everything there is to think of and of nothing at all, at the same time. "I don't know how to put it into words," I confess. "You have to remember, I had only two years of Liberal Arts."

"I've often wondered," Ian says, "what the Conservative Arts would be. Anything Jesse Helms likes, I guess."

We hear a noise like a senator. "Did you hear that?" I ask. "That must have been a frog."

We listen to two or three frogs bandying croaks back and forth. They're more subdued than they are during the spring, but they still have something to say. "There are throats in those frogs," I say. "Those frogs are talking to one another."

"In French," Ian says. "Frogs always talk in French."

I let out a whoop and get up from the log, but when I do I trip and Ian jumps up to catch me, and he holds me, and my face is buried against his right arm, and my left ear is over his heart, which is making its own happy racket through the walls of his chest, as loud as a neighbor living it up.

Elizabeth Cox

THE THIRD OF JULY

The night kept up one of those almost-silent rains until dawn, and now the mist rose and leaves showed their waxy shine. Nadine combed her hair but decided not to wash it. She pulled on her skirt and the blouse with cornflowers, and put away the pile of sewing she had promised to finish before tomorrow. Nadine was a seamstress. People brought their clothes for her to hem and make alterations.

Today was the third of July. Harold had left early for the field and would work late so he could take off all day on the Fourth. Nadine prepared a lunch for herself and another one for Miss Penny. Two days a week she took lunch to Miss Penny, and she would take it today. The old woman was like a mother to Nadine, ever since the year her own mother died when she was nineteen. The year Bill was born too early. She put chicken salad and sliced tomatoes in a small basket made by Bill when he was six years old. She placed two pears inside and thought of the day he handed it to her.

Nadine Colby had been married for thirty years, but on this morning she wrote a note to Harold after he left. *Dear Harold, I have rented an apartment in Mebane and if you want to see me*

you can call and ask to come by. Things cannot go on as they have.
She signed it, *Love.*

A shaft of sunlight moved into the bedroom as Nadine packed her bags and put them into the car. She had already paid a month's rent for an apartment ten miles away in Mebane. Her sister lived nearby, but Nadine did not like her husband, so the apartment was a perfect alternative.

She left the note in a conspicuous place on the counter. Harold would see it when he came in. She fixed some dinner that could be heated up—a plate of meat loaf, potatoes, and creamed corn. Nadine wondered now if he would still take the whole next day off.

Her reason for leaving was based on one small happening: Harold came in one night, and though she knew who it was when he got out of his truck and started toward the house, Nadine thought he was someone different. His hair stuck up on one side, and he carried his cap, which he usually wore into the house and threw down on the hall table. But on this particular evening she thought he was a stranger, someone coming with bad news—telling her Harold was dead, or hurt. She imagined herself falling into the arms of this stranger and letting him hold her. All of these thoughts came in a few moments while Harold opened the door and said, "Whoa! It's hot!" Then she recognized his voice.

That night Nadine couldn't sleep. She lay next to Harold beneath the sheet and wondered how her life would be without him. If she left, it would have to be quickly and quietly, as though there had been a murder she could do nothing about.

He was foreign to her now, as was Bill. Her son was thirty and had been the reason they got married. Harold and Nadine planned to have four children, though Bill was the only one.

The last time he came home Nadine said, "You don't look a thing like your daddy anymore, you know that?" She picked him up at the airport on Easter weekend. "Not a thing like him. And you used to favor him so strong."

"Lotta changes" was all Bill said.

"No one but me would know you were even kin."

Bill rode next to his mother with his long legs cramped in front of him. He had offered to drive, but Nadine insisted on doing so herself. She wore a navy blue dress with a large white pin at her bosom, bought especially for Bill's visit. She felt pretty as she drove him home.

Bill was a salesman for MetroLife Insurance Company and he had purchased this car for his parents—a Chrysler New Yorker. He had driven it into the driveway one Saturday and said it was theirs. Everyone in town knew Bill was wealthy and that he had bought them the car.

Their son came home on the Fourth. He also made regular visits for Christmas and Easter, but this year he would not come in July. Nadine told him he was getting stingy, though she meant self-centered. She had loved telling people how Bill always spent certain days with them and how she could count on him. But now Bill lived with a woman executive in his insurance company, and they were going off somewhere for the Fourth.

"I don't know what's going to happen if that woman gets pregnant," Nadine told Harold.

"They'll probably get married like we did." Harold didn't think things had changed all that much, but he remembered when Nadine had seemed soft. Her softness had unraveled with the years, and he felt left with just a thin wire of who she was. But he never mentioned it. He loved his wife, even her sharp tongue. And he loved the way she sometimes exploded with laughter at something funny he said.

Yesterday at breakfast, Harold read the paper and Nadine stared at the page that blocked his face. She imagined how he might speak to her, if he knew she was going to leave. *Nadine,* he spoke in her mind, *Don't leave. Please don't.* He would beg. He would kiss her, then kiss her again, hard.

Yesterday when he put down the paper, he asked, "What're we gonna do on the Fourth?"

Nadine didn't know until that moment how much she wanted out. She did not want to spend the Fourth of July with him. She would write the note on the third and let him go. As she thought of it, she felt like the ghost of someone, more than a real person.

"Anything," she said.

Harold kissed her cheek and left for the field.

Nadine washed the breakfast dishes and poured the rest of her coffee into the azalea bushes. She wanted to pick up the dry cleaning in town before going to Miss Penny's house. She placed the note where Harold would be sure to see it.

She had not gone five miles before coming upon an accident. A Ford station wagon had speeded past her only a few minutes before, and Nadine marveled at how this grief might have been her own. When she arrived at the wreck there was still a vibrancy lingering, as after a bell.

The car collided with a truck carrying chickens. It was the kind of crash that occurs in the movies where an audience roars with laughter as some fat farmer gets out stomping the ground and flapping his arms and elbows about—moving as the chickens themselves might move.

She hoped to see that now, even looked for someone to climb out of that screaming chicken truck, but as she drew closer she saw the driver tucked over the wheel. The station wagon's front end looked crumpled and the man driving had been thrown clear. He lay sprawled in the road. Nadine heard him groan for help and felt glad the car had not been her own.

She looked both ways for help, but no one was coming in either direction. She could not hurry toward the accident, her arms and legs felt like rubber bands. The man in the road was barely conscious. She stood over him, then squatted and placed her fingers on the pulse of his neck. She had seen this done on TV.

"My family," the man said. It was a question. He pointed toward the car as though he thought maybe Nadine hadn't noticed it yet. His head lay turned at a peculiar angle.

"Quiet now. You lie quiet." She patted the man's shoulder as if he had a contagious disease, then she moved back. He pointed again to the car. There was no sign of blood and Nadine hoped he was all right. "I'll check them for you," she said. The man seemed grateful to her and closed his eyes.

The man in the truck was still slumped at the wheel. Four crates of chickens had fallen onto the hood. One of the chickens still flapped around, but less now. There were more crates in the ditch where others squawked and fought to get free.

She heard another sound that came from the car. Gurgling. A woman weighing almost three hundred pounds lay across the backseat. She had been sleeping when the accident occurred. Her head was on a pillow and she lay covered with a lightweight blanket, which was soaked with blood. Nadine, who always turned away from such sights on TV or in a movie, opened the door of the car.

The woman was drowning; the gurgling noise came from her own throat, which lay exposed by a low-neck dress, her skin white, supple. Nadine ducked into the backseat to help, and she thought how this woman must be about her own age. The effort for breath came closer now. But the woman's hands jerked as a child's does in deep sleep, and the top of her head was pushed askew, so that it hung precariously like a lady's small hat about to fall off.

Without even thinking, Nadine reached two fingers into the woman's throat and began to dig out debris. She dug again and again as though she were clearing out the hole of a sink.

The woman began to cough and as she did her eyes opened— unseeing.

Nadine could see the place where the forehead split. She reached to put it straight, and the man from the road called out again about his family. Nadine said, "They're fine. You be quiet now." It was the calmest voice she had ever heard. She continued to clean the woman's throat, making her cough a few more times before the breathing came back. "You'll be all right," she told the woman, in case she could hear.

A young boy in the front seat curled slightly forward. About sixteen, Nadine thought. She got out to open the other car door, wiping her hands on her skirt. Some of the chickens wrestled free of their crates and walked around in the road. Another one had flown to a low branch. She glanced to the man at the wheel of the truck. He still hadn't moved. She wished he would.

She searched the highway, but there was no sign of help. As she opened the front car door, she expected to find the boy as she had found the woman, but only a small amount of blood trickled onto his shirt and pants. The dashboard had struck his chest, and he leaned forward onto it like a manne- quin. He wore shorts and his strong legs had planted them- selves to the floor as he braced for the impact. His arms caught the dashboard, but had fallen to his side as the dash- board caught him. The windshield shattered and coated him with a shower of glass that spread fine as Christmas glitter. Nadine wondered if he had ever played football.

When she looked up, she could see Emmett Walker coming across the field. She felt happy to see him though she did not usually wish to see Emmett. In fact, she went out of her way to avoid him. Emmett wore coveralls and his red hair was almost completely gray. His arms and face, though, still ex- posed his freckles from boyhood. Once, for three weeks, Na- dine and Emmett had been sweethearts. Nadine could not imagine that now.

"I heard the crash from the field," he said. "Are they all dead?" He stared at the boy's shimmering back.

"Seems so" was what Nadine said, forgetting about the man in the road. She held her mouth as though it were full of food, then pointed to the woman in the backseat. Emmett peered through the window without commenting.

He turned to the chicken truck. "What about him?"

"I don't know." They walked toward the truck. Nadine wondered if she would be left here all day with Emmett and what she would do. They had seen each other in town, and at gatherings they spoke pleasantly. Now they were suddenly talking in concerned tones and moving together as parents through a room full of sick children.

Emmett pried open the door of the truck. The man's face was hidden by the horn, but his eyes were open and his lips moved in an effort to speak.

"Listen," said Emmett, and he put his head closer to the steering wheel. "He's not moving. Something's wrong with his neck."

They went to each of the bodies, Nadine speaking low, explaining. But as she started to open the door of the car where the woman lay, they heard a siren approaching. Emmett put his hand on Nadine's shoulder and pointed to the ambulance coming over a far hill, arriving more slowly than the siren made it seem.

"I called the hospital," Emmett said.

Nadine went to stand beside the man in the road. He began to scream the name of his wife, *"Mamie, Mamie."*

"Shhh," she told him. The ambulance driver and his attendant secured the stretcher beneath him, then called for Emmett's help. The man asked again about his family, and Nadine said not to worry. "Everything will be taken care of now."

"Somebody's still in the truck," Emmett said and pointed to the tucked figure. "He's not moving." The attendant nodded and motioned toward the car, as if asking a question. Emmett shook his head and the driver reached into the back-seat to check the woman's pulse. He stared boldly at the odd hairline.

"She's still alive," he said to Emmett.

Emmett peered through the window, expecting—he didn't know what—maybe for the woman to sit up, say something.

"Wouldn't be, though." The driver directed his eyes toward Emmett. "Who did this? *You?*" The floor was full of Nadine's work.

Emmett looked at Nadine. She had her back to them as though the whole scene were something she had not yet witnessed.

"Hey, lady. You do this?"

She retreated the way a child does who has been reprimanded, her tongue in her cheek, worried. She nodded and held their admiration, then walked toward them as fragile and blue as smoke.

"Well, you saved her life, lady." He spoke softly and to the side, so that only Nadine could hear him, then he amended his statement. "Might have saved her life."

It took all three of them to lift the woman from the car, then Nadine stood back as they tore the front seat apart, trying to pull the boy from the dashboard. She wished she knew his name and hoped she had saved Mamie's life. They placed the son and his father in the back of the ambulance and Mamie next to them. The man from the chicken truck was strapped near the front. Everyone looked dead.

As the ambulance disappeared, Nadine and Emmett stood beside each other. What followed was a silence as pure as that between lovers. Then Emmett faced Nadine and she turned to Emmett, and they resembled people who see their reflections in a mirror, slouched in a way they never imagined themselves.

Nadine opened her mouth and said, "I hope that woman

lives. You think she will?" She wondered if she should take Emmett's hand or touch him, but didn't.

"Yes." He went to the truck where chickens were scattered in the road. They had stopped their squawking. One was still in the tree. "I'll drive these over to Hardison's Poultry." He pulled the crates together. "What's left of them." He picked up the crates from the road and climbed into the truck. He turned the key several times before hearing it catch. As he drove off, he waved good-bye and Nadine waved back. She walked to the car and checked the salad. It was still cool.

Miss Penny was watching TV when Nadine arrived. She didn't hear the knock on the door, so Nadine walked in and called to her. Miss Penny was folding towels and placing each one beside the chair, fixing them like small bales of hay about to be stored in a barn. She was watching a game show.

When she lifted her head to respond to Nadine's voice, the pupils of her eyes were large and gave an expression of spectral intensity—hollow, not sad. A cataract operation had made them sensitive to light, so the blinds and drapes were pulled. The room, after the full sunlight of the road, seemed to Nadine unusually dark.

"I'll put this in the kitchen." Nadine patted Miss Penny's chair as she walked by. She wanted to scrub her hands and wipe her skirt clean.

"There's a man on here who'll win ten thousand dollars if he can answer this last question," Miss Penny said. Nadine took it as a silencing. The TV blared the question and the announcer declared him winner. Bells rang, people clapped and cried, and Miss Penny told her, "I could've won me ten thousand dollars." She pushed herself from the chair to go to the kitchen.

"Don't know what you'd do with it," said Nadine. She watched the old woman hobble to the kitchen and fall into a chair.

"I'd buy me something."

"Don't know what you need." Nadine spooned salad onto plates and set two places at the table. Her tongue felt dry and she asked Miss Penny if there was some iced tea. Miss Penny pointed to a pitcher. She always made tea and took out the ice trays before Nadine arrived, but today Nadine was two hours late and the ice was mostly water. They put slivers that remained into the tea and sipped it.

"I had the right answer," Miss Penny persisted. She tasted the salad and Nadine gave her a napkin.

"You can't spend the money you have now, let alone ten thousand dollars." They helped themselves to the tomatoes. "What would you spend it on?"

"I'd pay somebody to look after my dogs."

"You don't have any dogs," said Nadine, "and don't need any."

"I would if I had all that money." Miss Penny's words, though simple, were true. "I'd need a lot of things." She thought for a moment, chewing her food with meticulous care. "I'd get some dogs. Not the regular kind, but show dogs. The ones you can train and take to shows."

"You'd like that?" Nadine asked, surprised to find a new interest in a woman she had known as long as she could remember. She thought there were no more surprises left between them.

"Show dogs." Miss Penny's face flushed at the thought of it. "I always have wanted to do something like that."

Nadine wished to say something about the accident, to tell someone what she had done and how she wasn't afraid to see Emmett anymore. "There was a wreck," she began and leaned across the table so Miss Penny could hear. "Over near Hardison's Poultry a truck ran into a station wagon. The whole family got hurt." Miss Penny reached for more slices of tomato. Her face had not yet lost its flush. "It was pretty

bad," Nadine said. "A man and his wife, a boy about sixteen."

"What?"

"Their *son* about *sixteen*." Nadine spoke louder. "He was
killed right off, but the man might live, and the woman." She
stopped leaning and slumped back. "I don't know about the
woman though." Nadine's gaze shifted to something outside
the window.

"*Ten thousand dollars*," Miss Penny said. Her voice empha-
sized each word equally.

From the kitchen window Nadine could see bags of web in
the crab apple trees. "Tomorrow's the Fourth of July," she
told Miss Penny. Neither of them turned away from the window.

Nadine washed the few dishes and put away the bales of
towels into the hall cabinet. She decided not to go to Mebane,
but to go back home. "I'll put these pears in the refrigerator."
She held up the pears. Miss Penny's eyes unclouded and
hardened clear as stones.

On her way home, she picked up the dry cleaning and
stopped at the pet shop to look at dogs not yet full-grown. On
Tuesday she would buy one and take it to Miss Penny. He
would outlive her by six years.

The note to Harold had not been touched but she left it
propped against the sugar jar. The house looked older now.
Each object seemed to have a separate life of its own. When
Nadine saw herself in the mirror over the fireplace, she became aware of the frame around her face.

She called the hospital, but the line was busy. She had already unpacked her bag and put the clothes into drawers
where they had been—her blouses, her good blue dress, two
nightgowns, a sweater, four pairs of shoes. She put her umbrella in the hall closet and went to sit across from the large
picture window.

Twilight made the room silver, drapes shimmering like creek water. The late sun dropped halfway from sight, going down behind the trees like some wild head, and Nadine wondered if everyone wished for life to be different.

When the phone rang, it was Emmett. She heard his voice and her mouth worked itself into a smile. He called to tell her about Mamie and Robert Harkins. "The man will live," he said. "And the woman, she'll live, too." For one moment Nadine could not even straighten her legs. "But that boy, he didn't make it. He was dead when we saw him."

"What about the man in the truck?"

"His back was broke and some ribs. But he's all right, or will be." Emmett coughed as though he didn't have much to say, but wanted to think of something. "The truck driver was Buck Hardison's nephew."

"Why, I think I know him," Nadine said. "I think I met him once when he was a little boy." She wanted the conversation to go on, and she thanked Emmett, so he said she was welcome. "You were fine to help," she told him through the silence in the cord. "I mean, really," and she spoke as if trying to convince him of something important.

"Well," said Emmett.

Nadine watched the sun go all the way down and wondered if Emmett had turned to see out his own window. "It's getting dark," she said.

When they hung up, Nadine sat until she could see nothing but her own reflection in the window, and the reflection of the lamp beside her. Harold would be in soon. She decided to wash her hair. She was bending her head over the sink and rinsing for the second time when she heard him.

"Nadine?"

She wrapped her hair in a towel and went to the kitchen. Harold held the note that Nadine had not thrown out. He held it, but didn't say anything.

"You want something to eat?" she asked him.

Harold said he did.

Nadine did not get the covered plate of meat loaf and creamed corn. Instead, she took out some flounder and began to prepare it for baking with lemon and butter. She cut up new potatoes to go with it and told Harold about the wreck.

She told about the man, the boy, the woman she saved, the truck driver who was Buck Hardison's nephew. She told him she had seen Emmett and how they had worked together. Her telling went from the time she took out the fish, cooked it, and then sat down with Harold to eat.

The note lay on the counter as they talked. Harold had carefully placed it next to the sugar, face down. He listened attentively and ate everything Nadine put before him. When she was through washing the dishes, he walked up behind her to turn her around. He slowly unwrapped the towel from her head. Her hair was damp and frizzy, and he rubbed it dry with his hands.

Terry Bain

GAMES

Sometimes I had to wait for the light to come on in BeaAnne's window, so I'd sit in my car across the street, in front of Pattison's house, and I'd imagine BeaAnne sitting quietly with her parents watching television. BeaAnne would eventually go to her room and turn on the light because she'd rather read. She'd get up and go to her room and turn on the light and lie down on her bed. BeaAnne was a fast reader, and I'd imagine her turning pages, one after the other, quickly passing over the words then pressing them into sentences and expanding them into ideas. I could never force myself to finish a book, so I'd imagine BeaAnne doing it for me, and she would turn the last page, then close the back cover of the book, then put the book away and be satisfied for a while that she had finished it. Then I'd start thinking somebody was going to notice me sitting across the street from BeaAnne's house, right in front of Pattison's house, and sitting there for no apparent reason other than spying on one or the other of them, so I'd start up the car and drive home. I'd turn left at Crystal, then left again at Cherry.

On Thursday nights Pattison's parents went to the Moose

lodge for a prime rib dinner and then sometimes they would go out for drinks afterward. I'd go over to Pattison's then and we'd have the house to ourselves, and maybe his girlfriend, Cheryl Wexler, would come over, or sometimes Pattison would just be talking to her on the phone the whole time. When Pattison was talking to Cheryl Wexler on the phone, I'd try to pass the time by including myself in the conversation.

"Say hey for me," I said.

"Teddy's here," said Pattison into the phone.

Pattison paced back and forth in the kitchen. Pattison picked up a white-handled fork from the kitchen counter and carried it across the room and set it down on the kitchen table. Pattison picked up a crumpled napkin from the kitchen table and carried it across the room and set it down on the kitchen counter. Pattison picked up an empty ketchup bottle from the kitchen counter and carried it across the room and set it down on the kitchen table.

I said, "Is she at BeaAnne's?"

Pattison looked at me without really looking at me, and said, "If she was at BeaAnne's then I'd just walk over there, right?"

Pattison's doorbell rang.

Pattison was trying to get Cheryl Wexler to come on over for a while. It didn't sound like she would do it. Pattison said his parents would be out forever. He said they were out on a binge tonight for sure. It sounded like Cheryl Wexler didn't care.

Pattison's doorbell rang.

I said, "How come she's not there?"

Pattison put his hand over the receiver and said, "Her and BeaAnne had this stupid fight today. You know." Then he took his hand off the receiver and said that Cheryl Wexler should come on over right away and he would give her a treat.

Cheryl Wexler and BeaAnne were always having some

kind of fight. It was probably BeaAnne's fault because Bea-
Anne didn't like to agree with anything Cheryl Wexler had to
say. When Cheryl Wexler and BeaAnne were fighting, I'd
drive past BeaAnne's house at night to see her light on, because I'd know for sure she would be home early, her and
Cheryl Wexler not speaking to each other. So BeaAnne would
be in her room reading a book, and I could imagine her turning the pages, and I'd say "next" to myself after each page
fell to the left and covered the page before it, and I imagined
BeaAnne turning those pages even as I drove away, and I
would say "next" to myself a half dozen times before I got
home.

Pattison's doorbell rang. There was some laughing and
shouting going on outside. I got up and went to the door.
There was nobody at the door. Smashed pumpkin flesh lit-
tered the front step. A candle lay extinguished in the orange
mess of the shattered jack-o'-lantern. I looked across the
street, and I knew BeaAnne's light would be on. If she and
Cheryl Wexler weren't fighting, Cheryl Wexler might be over
at BeaAnne's right then, sitting around in the game room and
listening to music and ignoring the quiet green pool table,
and BeaAnne's bedroom light would be off the whole time
they sat there. And maybe Pattison would go over there after
a while to see Cheryl Wexler, and they would sit on bar stools
in the game room and touch each other and kiss each other,
and maybe I'd be over there too and I'd try to play some pool,
and BeaAnne would try to entertain us for a while, and she'd
give us all 7-Up, and then we'd all leave BeaAnne alone, we'd
go back to Pattison's, and BeaAnne would go into her room
and turn on the light and read a book.

I closed the door and stood there inside Pattison's house for
a while, listening for some more shouting, saying "next" to
myself three times. I could hear Pattison talking to Cheryl
Wexler on the phone, picking up a plastic daffodil from the
kitchen table and carrying it across the room and setting it

down on the kitchen counter, and trying to convince Cheryl Wexler to come on over.

Pattison's doorbell rang.

I went back into the kitchen just as Pattison was hanging up the phone. Pattison picked up a white-handled fork from the kitchen counter and held it in his hand and spun it around between his fingers and stabbed the kitchen counter with it.

Pattison said, "She won't come over."

I said, "Yeah."

Then I sat down at the kitchen table and Pattison leaned against the kitchen counter, tapping the prongs of the fork lightly on the countertop.

Pattison said, "Any parties tonight?"

"No," I said. "Mostly tomorrow."

"What about the river?"

Pattison didn't really want to go to the river. He always complained about the river. So I didn't answer him.

I asked Pattison what Cheryl Wexler and BeaAnne were fighting about this time, and Pattison said it didn't really matter. He said that he didn't know for sure, but he thought BeaAnne was jealous of all the time Cheryl Wexler was spending with Pattison, and that even when BeaAnne was with Cheryl Wexler for a while, Pattison was there too. So any little thing could probably set them off. Who knows what it was this time.

I said, "Why don't you go see her?"

Pattison shrugged and said, "Her folks are fighting about something."

I asked Pattison if Cheryl Wexler was mad at him, and he said probably, and I asked Pattison if BeaAnne was mad at him too, and he said probably, and I asked Pattison if Bea-Anne was mad at me too, and he said, "What the hell have you got to do with this?" He waved the white-handled fork at me, then he tossed it up in the air and caught it on the way back down, and he said, "Listen, you're not hiding anything, so if you want to go over there, I mean, Jesus, she lives right across the street."

Pattison's doorbell rang.

I said it was more difficult than that and he knew it. Then Pattison set the fork down on the kitchen counter, and he picked up the phone and dialed a number. Pattison knew the number because it was where Cheryl Wexler would normally be if her and BeaAnne weren't having a stupid fight. She answered the phone pretty quickly, and a bubble of anxiety came up in my chest, then into my throat, and it tasted like cool steam.

Pattison said into the phone, "Teddy and me were just sitting here bull-shitting, and we started talking about what maybe you were doing." Pattison picked up a white-handled fork from the kitchen counter and carried it across the room and set it down on the kitchen table. "Sure," said Pattison, "If your folks don't mind." Pattison walked slowly across the room and said, "Sure," and hung up the phone. Pattison turned to me and grinned and said, "Let's go."

I said, "Where?"

He said, "Trick or Treating."

So we looked out the front window to see if anyone was coming, then we sneaked out and crossed the street and knocked on the door.

When BeaAnne's mom answered the door, Pattison said, "Just money, please. Paper only."

BeaAnne's mom said, "James! Theodore!" She smiled at us then, and almost gave us a handful of gumballs from a plastic jack-o'-lantern she was holding in her hand, but she stopped and set it down and said, "Bea is in her room." BeaAnne's mom let us in, and I grabbed a handful of gumballs from the plastic jack-o'-lantern and put a few in my mouth and a few in my jeans pocket. The gumballs were sweet and hard as stones, and I sucked on them awhile before I chewed into their soft centers.

BeaAnne's bedroom door was open and she was reading *The Jungle Book.* She closed her book as we came in and tossed it down on the bed as she got up. She walked past us out of her room and down the hall into the game room. We followed her into the game room and she closed the door behind us. BeaAnne went over behind the bar, and I sat on one of the stools in front of the bar. The game room was cold inside and BeaAnne turned the light to about half-on with a dimmer switch behind the bar. BeaAnne asked us if we wanted a 7-Up, and we both said okay. Pattison stood in front of the pool table and pushed the cue ball lengthwise so that it returned off the far bumper, rolling slowly into his waiting hand. The ball seemed to take forever to come back to him.

BeaAnne put the 7-Ups on the bar and I sipped at mine.

BeaAnne said, "So what are you guys doing?"

"Thinking about you," said Pattison.

"Oh?"

"Sure."

Pattison picked up the cue ball and came over to the bar. He sipped his 7-Up and set the cue ball down on the bar with his hand cupped over it. Pattison said, "Teddy here thinks about you all the time."

BeaAnne looked at me and said, "Is that right, Teddy?"

Pattison said, "Let's try the strobe light." The strobe light was mounted near the ceiling in the far corner of the game room and was controlled by an on-off switch next to the dimmer switch. Pattison reached across the bar and dimmed the lights some more, then flipped on the strobe. Pattison grinned and went back to the pool table. He stood in front of the pool table and pushed the cue ball lengthwise so that it returned off the far bumper, rolling slowly into his waiting hand. The ball traveled as if unsure of its existence, disappearing out of Pattison's hand, reappearing slightly away from his hand,

disappearing again, reappearing again, returning off the far
end of the pool table without seeming to have to touch the
bumper, rolling jerkily across the green felt, and leaping from
the table back into Pattison's waiting hand. Pattison brought
the cue ball with him back to the bar.

BeaAnne said, "Is that right, Teddy?"

I had to skip back to pick up the path of BeaAnne's question, the original line having been lost to the strobe and the
returning ball, but finally I was able to blurt out, "Yeah."

"Kiss her," said Pattison, leaning on the bar with his elbow,
chin resting in one hand and the cue ball being cupped over
with the other. And then he looked at me, and then he looked
at BeaAnne, and then he looked at me. He said, "Kiss her,"
again. I stared at Pattison as hard as I could. Pattison said,
"I'll show you." Pattison leaned upward toward BeaAnne,
flashing in and out of the light, and he kissed her on the lips,
and then backed away from her, grinning, and went back to
the pool table and set the cue ball down on the flickering
green felt. Pattison leaned back on the pool table and said,
"You know you want to." He looked at me, he looked at
BeaAnne, he looked at me. I stared through Pattison now.
Pattison said, "I know I did."

Looking at me, Pattison seemed to be pushing me backward. When would he be pushing me from behind? His grin
said, I know you can't do it. You'll never be able to do it.
Outside. Watching the light turn on and off.

I continued to stare through Pattison.

Pattison looked away from me. He looked at the cue ball on
the table. He tapped the cue ball with his finger. He pushed
it. It didn't move very far. Pattison left the room.

Slowly, I turned around and looked at BeaAnne. She kept
going on and off, disappearing and reappearing. My eyes
were adjusting to the nonsense of the strobe, and I could almost see BeaAnne even in the dark, or at least the afterimage
of BeaAnne.

I put both hands on the bar and leaned forward, and Bea-Anne was coming toward me, disappearing and reappearing toward me, and I thought I still had some distance to go when our faces met too hard in the darkness, then softer in the light, and I leaned back and watched her image in and out of the light, on and off with the light, steadily, reassuringly; the light continued to go on and off. And I kissed her twice more, and it was her lips against my lips, and it was her kissing me; I leaned toward her and knew always her position before me; I would not be fooled by her flickering image again.

Or would I.

BeaAnne put her tongue in my mouth and this surprised me at first, but I don't know why I should have been surprised. We kissed like that for a while, across the bar, and then I looked at her face. I turned the strobe off and the steady light on so I could look at her face more clearly, but the world seemed tilted after the strobe, and the skin of her face wouldn't sit still, so I kissed her again. Finally BeaAnne said I should go or her parents would start to think something funny. I said that I might start to think something funny too.

I kissed her one more time.

I said I would see her tomorrow at school, and I closed the game room door as I left.

Pattison had already gone home when I asked BeaAnne's parents where he was, so I took another handful of gumballs from the plastic jack-o'-lantern and said goodbye. I stood just outside BeaAnne's house for a while, wanting to turn around and ring the doorbell again, wanting to go back inside and kiss BeaAnne again. I walked over to BeaAnne's bedroom window and her light was off. I could barely see inside, a wedge of light coming in through her door, *The Jungle Book* laying on her bed. Someone walked past her door, blocking the light for an instant, so I ducked down and crept over to the game room window. BeaAnne was still inside the game room, the strobe back on. She stood next to the pool table. She rolled the cue ball across the table and I watched it disappear into the left corner pocket. BeaAnne turned around and sat on the pool table, then pushed herself farther onto the table and lay down on her back with her legs swinging over the edge. She kicked off her shoes and they flew across the room in a stuttering strobe motion. She turned onto her side and curled up on the hard table.

Her eyes were closed. Her hair was spread out under her head like a thin pillow.

My hands and forehead pressed against the cold glass of the window. I closed my eyes. I would not disturb her.

I walked back across the street.

Pattison was on the phone again, trying to convince Cheryl Wexler to come on over. Pattison picked up an empty ketchup bottle from the kitchen table and carried it across the room and set it down on the kitchen counter. Cheryl Wexler still wouldn't come over and I didn't blame her. I told Pattison I was getting out of there and he waved at me. I turned around and left him behind. I waited inside the front door for a while until Pattison's doorbell rang. I opened the door and three ghosts greeted me: "Trick or Treat!" They were breathing hard and the sheets pulled over their heads were puffing in and out. I reached into my pocket and pulled out the gumballs and put a few in each of the three ghosts' bags. All three said "Thank you" as the gumballs fell in amongst the rest of their treasure. They suddenly ran away from me all at once, as fast as they could. They ran toward the next house they could find, right across the street, with a brightly lit porch, streaking away from me with their white costumes flapping behind them. I wanted them to come back. I wanted to follow them.

Amy Bloom

SEMPER FIDELIS

I shop at night. Thursday nights I wave good-bye to the nurse
and drive off, feigning reluctance. The new mall has three
department stores, a movie theater and hundreds of little
shops and I have been in all but the Compleat Sportsman. It
makes no sense to me but I cannot sit through a movie knowing I'm supposed to be shopping. I eat warm peanut butter
cookies and wander around for almost two hours, browsing
through the very slim jazz sections of the mall record stores,
skimming bestsellers. At nine-thirty, when the mall is closing
and it's just me and the vagrant elderly and the young security guards, I go grocery shopping.

All-night grocery stores seem to be the personal savior and
favorite haunt of dazed young women of all colors, who haul
their crumpled, sleeping babies like extra groceries in the cart;
single middle-aged men and women too healthy and too
lonely to fall asleep at ten o'clock and people like me, who are
scared to go home. It is my belief and sometimes my wish
that my husband will die while I am out on one of my Thursday night sprees.

Max and I have been together for almost ten years, since I

was eighteen and he was fifty. We are no longer a scandal or a tragedy. His wife's friends and the other witnesses have moved away or fallen silent or become friends, the limited choices of a small town. Max and I are close to ordinary, made interesting only by our past and its casualties. Women who would have, may have, spit in my soup at painfully quiet dinner parties ten years ago now bring pureed vegetables for Max and articles on the apricot-pit clinics of Mexico. I have become a wife, soon to be a widow, and I feel more helpless and unknowing after ten years of marriage than I was at eighteen, moving into Max's apartment with two T-shirts, a box of records and no shoes. On our first outing Max introduced me to the chairman of his department and bought me sneakers.

He has not been out of bed for three weeks and he has not spoken since the morning. I always pictured myself as an Audrey Hepburn-type widow, long-necked and pale in a narrow black linen dress. Instead, I am nearly drowning in a river of sugar and covering myself in old sweatpants and Max's flannel shirts. I only dress up on Thursday nights, to go out in a big sweatshirt, as long as a short dress, and black tights, playing up my legs with high-heeled black ankle boots. I have never dressed like this in my life and I am glad to put my sneakers and my jeans back on before I go into the house.

Ray, at the Deli Counter, is the one I've been looking for. He first admired my boots and then my whole outfit and after three Thursdays in a row, I felt obliged to buy another top for him to look at, and he leaned over the counter to tell me how much he liked it and winked as he went back to work. Ray can't be more than twenty-two and I assume he is a recovering addict of some kind, since he is presently the picture of good health and says things like, "Easy does it," and "One day at a time," which are the kinds of things my brother, a not-recovering alcoholic, says whenever he calls to wish me

well or borrow money. I think Ray is a good choice. I think
we would not discuss poetry or symbolism or chemotherapy
or the past and I think I would have a beer and he would not
and I would lay my hand on one thick thigh until I felt the
cloth tighten under my fingers and when we were done I
would climb out of his van, or his room in his mother's house
and thank him from the bottom of my heart and go home to
Max.

I come home to see the nurse leaning over Max, smoothing
his covers as her big, white nylon breasts swing slightly and
shadow his face. He smiles and I see that he is unaware of my
presence and the nurse is not.

"The pearls," she says, continuing their conversation,
"were extremely valuable and irregardless of the will, my
sister and I both think the pearls should have come to us. Our
mother's pearls should have come to us, because they were
already ours."

I cannot even begin to understand what she's talking about
but it feels ominously metaphorical. Maybe the pearls represent Max's health, or his first marriage or our vow to cleave
unto each other; things irretrievably gone and valued more in
their absence than in their presence. I want to shut her up, to
keep her from tormenting us both, but Max smiles again, a
quick softening of his bony, grey face and even I can see that
he is not tormented. I knock against the door frame knowing
that Max as he is now is too innocent and the nurse too self-
absorbed to appreciate the irony of my knocking. I am performing without an audience, which is how it has been for
some time; if you feel sorry for yourself, can it still be a tragedy? Or are you reduced to a rather unattractive second lead,
a foil for the heroes, blind and beautiful, courageously polishing the brass as the icy waters lap at their ankles? It seems to
me—and I would not be sorry to find out—that I have disappeared.

"Sweetheart," he says and the nurse frowns.

"He's been asking for you," she says and I forgive her bitchiness because she seems to care about him, to feel that it matters that he misses me. The other nurses are solicitous of his health, of his illness, but his feelings are nothing more than symptoms to them. For one minute, I love her for loving him; he has made me love people I would dislike if he were going to live.

"Dawn's mother passed away recently, she was telling me." Shaken by love, touched by his effort to keep us together and to keep us his, I smile at Dawn.

"I'm so sorry," I say, trying to be good. "I lost my mother just last year. And I've got a sister, too." That's it. I cannot think of any more astonishing coincidences which will bind us together.

"My sister's my best friend," Dawn says, sitting in the armchair near the bed, as though she'd dropped in on Max for a visit.

"Mine, too." Amazing. My sister, Irene, is my best friend and while my father wept and my mother murmured congratulations from the far side of a scotch-and-soda, my sister took me upstairs, to what had been her room, to discuss my marrying Max.

"You can have anyone, you know. Even after all this. You can transfer to a school in California and no one will ever know. You don't have to marry him."

"I love him, Reen. I want to marry him."

"Okay. Okay, I'll be there. At least he won't leave you for a younger woman. Not without being arrested. Is this justice of the peace or train-and-veil?"

"Justice of the peace. Wednesday."

"All right. How about a suit? Silk suit, roses in your hair? It won't kill you to go to a beauty parlor."

And my sister got my legs waxed, my pores cleaned and my eyebrows shaped in less than forty-eight hours. In the photographs, I look radiant and only a little too young for the

ivory silk suit, which Irene found, unpinned from a manne-
quin, and paid for in less than forty-five minutes. I have ivory
roses in my upswept black hair and Max is laughing at the
camera, held by his oldest friend, who is astonished, amiable
and drunk for the whole afternoon. My sister looks like the
mother of the bride, exhausted, vigilant, more pleased than
not. My own parents weren't there because I didn't invite
them, despite Max's pleas.

Dawn turns to go and I can see that she doesn't love Max;
he is just a better than average case, less trouble than some of
the others. I am free to hate her and I walk her to the door
and open it for her, without speaking, a form of civilized
rudeness I've picked up from my mother.

"Lie down here," Max says, but I cannot lie in that bed.

"I'll lie on the cot." When we left the hospital, a smart,
angry woman in the support group told me to get a cot and
she didn't even pretend to listen when I said that we would
continue to share a bed.

"Undress slowly, sweetheart. I can still look." In the books
I keep hidden, the guides to grief, the how-to books of wid-
owhood and the period that comes before, the authors mention, delicately, that the surviving spouse usually suffers hurt
feelings and frustration due to the dying person's lack of sexual interest. This doesn't seem to be the case with Max.

I throw off my clothes and lie on the cot, like a Girl Scout,
still in my T-shirt, panties and socks. I hear a wet, bubbling
noise, which is how he laughs now.

Max rests one cool, brittle hand on my stomach.

"How was the supermarket?"

"It was okay. I got some groceries."

"And the mall?"

"It was fine. I got some socks."

He strokes my stomach with two dry fingertips and I feel

the flesh at the end of each finger, dragging slightly after the bone. I want to throw up and I want to weep.

"Do you ever meet anybody?"

"Like who?" I ask. Despite everything, I don't think of Max as a jealous man; we have simply misunderstood each other, most of the time. He would remind me, as we drove home from parties, that he had made a point of not admiring the younger women, so people wouldn't think that I was part of his youth fetish, that I was less than unique. He said I owed him the same consideration, and should conceal my impulsive sexuality, lest people think that my marriage to him was just adolescent, hormonally driven mindlessness. We agreed, many times, that he was not jealous, not insecure, not possessive and we must have had that conversation about flirting a hundred times in our ten years together.

Max pokes me lightly. "I don't know, like anybody. Some nice young man?"

"No. No one." I roll over on my side, out of reach of his fingers.

"All right, don't get huffy. Dawn gave me my meds already. Good night, sweetheart."

"Good night." You sadistic old shit.

I lie on the cot, listening to his chalky, irregular breath until he falls asleep and go downstairs to pay bills. His room, our room, fills up at night with a thick wet mist of dark fluids and invisibly leaking sores. This is something else I don't say.

The next Thursday, I smile encouragingly at Ray, who is very busy with the second-shift shopping crowd and I find myself taking a number behind a dark, dark boy, so dark the outline of his whole brown body seems drawn in charcoal. He is all roundness, high, full Island cheeks, round black eyes, rounded arms and shoulders, his pants rounded front and back. My own fullness has begun to shrink and loosen, the muscle sliding down from the bone a little more each year. I want to cut this boy open like a melon and eat him, slice by slice. Cut him and taste him and have him and hurt him. I could tell Max that I understand him better now than I did ten years ago but he would be horrified that I think this mixture of lust and resentment is anything like his love for me. I am only horrified by myself; what I want to do to this boy Max would never do to me.

Ray and I exchange several devoted, affectionate glances; as aspiring lovers we are so tenderly playful and wistful it seems odd that all we really want is to fuck each other senseless and get home before we're caught. My attitude is not good.

I go home to Max and Dawn. She is in my kitchen sipping tea out of my mermaid mug, a gift from Max after a terrible rainy week on Block Island. Her iridescent blue tail is the handle and Dawn's smooth fingers cling to it.

After she leaves, Max questions me again.

"I don't meet anyone, for Christ's sake. Who would I meet? I'm not a girl. I'm twenty-eight and I probably look ninety. Who would I meet?"

"You might meet anyone. Look at me, I'm sixty, I'm a dying man riddled with cancer and I met Dawn."

"Great. I hope you'll be very happy together." I turn out the light so he cannot see me change and I wonder if he gets Dawn to strip for him on Thursdays.

"Really," he says, surrounded by pillows so he can't lie down and be engulfed by his own lungs. "Tell me. Why shouldn't you meet someone?"

I try to see him in the dark as he is, everything that was broad and hard-boned now transparent at the edge, softly dimpled and concave at the center.

"Who would I meet?"

"Some good-looking young man at the mall. Not a salesman, you never like salesmen. They try too hard, don't they?"

"Yes." I want to tell him to rest but I don't think I would be saying it for him.

"Big and dark. Sweet-natured, not terribly bright. Not stupid, of course, but not intellectual. Not an academic. I want to spare you a long, pedantic lecture when you've only got a few hours."

"Good idea. How long do I have?"

"Well, you know your schedule better than I. Two hours at the mall, an hour and a half at the supermarket. We can skip aerobics, I think. I cannot picture you with a man who goes to aerobics class."

He's right. I like them big and burly or lean and lithe but I cannot bear the compulsively athletic, the ones who measure their pulses and their biceps and their cholesterol levels.

"Tell me, sweetheart. Tell me about the man you met in the supermarket."

"Not the mall?"

"Don't play games with me. Tell me what happened."

"He's dark-haired but fair. Black Irish and big. Not tall, but wide. Built like a wall." I realize that I am describing the Max I have seen only in photographs, a big, wild boy with one cocky foot on his Army Jeep; ramming his way through Harvard a few years later, grinning like a pirate as the wind blows both ends of his scarf behind him.

"Go on," Max says, as if I am talking about someone else.

"I do see him at the supermarket. I change my clothes to go there." And I tell Max the truth about my clothes and he says "Ya-hoo" when I came to the black ankle boots. We are having some kind of fun in this terrible room.

"That'll get him. Do you wear a bra?"

"Come on, Max, of course I wear a bra."

"Just slows you down. All right, at least it's one of your pretty ones, I hope, not those Ace bandage things. How about the purple and black one with the little cut-outs?" Max likes silky peek-a-boo lingerie and I buy it but I do not wear sev-

enty-dollar hand-finished bras and garter belts for every day.
Most of the time I wear cheap cotton tubes which he hates.

"I do wear the black and purple one."

"And the panties?"

"No panties."

"Wonderful. The first time I put my hand on your bare ass I
thought I had died and gone to heaven. And then I was afraid
that it wasn't for me, that you just never wore them."

"Max, you asked me not to wear them, remember? I always
wore underpants." I'd had some, more than enough, sex with
boys and by myself when I met Max, but I had never had a
lover. Everything important that I know, about literature,
about people, about my own body, I have learned from this
man and he is leaving me the way we both expected I would
leave him, loving, regretful, irretrievable.

"Tell me about this big guy."

"Big guy" is what I used to call Max who, having been
married to a woman who called him "my dear" and pursued
by highly educated young women who called him Professor
Boyle and thought he was God, found terms like "Big Guy"
and "Butch" to be refreshing endearments.

"He's the night manager." I have given Ray a promotion;
I'm sure in time someone with his good looks and pleasant
manner would be made manager and a sexual encounter
with Ray, the Head Roast-Beef Slicer, seems to demean us all.

"Fine. Where did you do it?"

"Jesus, Max, what is wrong with you?"

"Need you ask? Come on, come on, don't get skittish now.
Where did you do it?" That angry pushing voice used to
scare me to death and I cannot bear that it doesn't scare me
anymore.

"We went to Wadsworth Park." Where Max and I used to
go when I was still living with my parents and he was still
living with his then-wife. Just recently, while sorting out his
pills or shaving his distorted face, I find myself thinking, this

is what a wife is. Now that we cannot see ourselves in the curious excited eyes of other people, the differences which defined us are fading away. We are just a man who is dying and a woman who is not.

"A little buggy?"

"Not too bad." I stall to avoid making a mistake, afraid that I am not telling the right story.

"But you had a blanket and you didn't notice the bugs."

"Max, what do you want from me?"

"I want you to tell me what happened when you got into the woods. You led him to those big rocks, by the stream?"

The woods are thick on both sides of the water, sheltering twin slabs of granite. When we were there Max would press me so far backwards to the ends of my hair trailed in the cold water, collecting small leaves as I lay under him.

"All right. We went to the rocks and we made love. Then I changed my clothes and came home."

"Don't tell me like that," he says and begins to cough, loosely, his whole body bouncing on the plastic mattress. He falls asleep still coughing and I go downstairs and do nothing.

For the rest of the week, he floats in and out of conversations and medicated dreams. On Thursday I put on my shopping costume while Max watches and smiles, alertly. Dawn is reading magazines, waiting for me to leave.

"Tonight?" he asks, barely pushing the words out of his lips.

I don't answer, just tie up my boots and sit down to brush my hair.

"You know who Dawn reminds me of? Not coloring, but the build? Eren Goknar. Remember?"

I remember and I keep brushing my hair.

"I wonder where she is."

"I don't know," I say. "Maybe she went back to Turkey."

"Don't think so. She wrote to me from California, teaching at Berkeley. Marvelous girl," he says, struggling with each consonant. I walk out of the room.

I put up some hot water for me and Dawn and go back to check on Max, afraid that he will die while I'm angry with him.

"Ready?"

"Yeah. I'll be back in a couple of hours."

"I slept with Eren," he says and sighs.

"I know," I say, although I hadn't known until then. And I know that he is pushing me away, furiously, as though I will miss him less because he had sex with Eren Goknar. He can no more lose me than I can lose myself, we are like those housekeys that beep in response to your voice; they practically find you. I kiss the air near Max's face and return to Dawn, who has made tea. We chat for two hours, in between her runs upstairs, and she doesn't ask me why I don't go out. I send her home at eleven.

Max barely opens his eyes when I turn on the night-light to undress. He lifts one hand slightly and I go to him, still in my underwear.

"Off," he whispers. He turns his head and coughs, the harsh, rude sound of a straw in an almost empty glass.

I take everything off and climb into the bed, trying not to press against him, now that even the sheets seem to hurt him.

"Did you?"

I slide closer to him until we are face-to-face and I kiss his dry lips and feel the small bumps and cracks around his mouth.

"Yes, I found him, the one I told you about. The big one. He was getting off work early, just as I got there. I didn't even have to wait."

Max closes his eyes and I put his hand on top of my leg.

"It was so dark we didn't go to the park. We went to a

motel. There was very tacky red wallpaper and the bed was a huge heart with a red velvet bedspread.''

"Route 68," he says.

"That one. Remember that big bed? And the headboard with the little posts, the handholds?"

I move his hand up and down my leg, very gently.

"He undressed me, Max. He knelt down and took off my shoes and then he laid me on the bed and undressed me. He was still in his suit."

"Suit?" Max whispered.

"His work clothes, I mean. Not a suit. He left the light on and he began to kiss me all over but every time I tried to touch him he'd put my hands down. He wouldn't let me touch him until later."

Max moves his head a little to nod and I prop his pillows up.

"He kissed the insides of my thighs and the backs of my legs and then he kissed my back for a very long time and when he turned me over he was undressed. And he pulled me up to him, about two feet in the air and then he threw us both down on the bed and he came inside me and he just kept coming and coming at me until I started to cry and then we got under the covers and we both cried, until we fell asleep."

I lay my wet face next to Max's and listen for his breathing.

"It was the best, Max. Nothing in my life was ever like that. Do you hear me? Nothing in my life was ever like that."

Michael Fox

RISE AND SHINE

At 8:00 AM the view from Steven Paley's rooftop is a hopeful one. That is, it is a view he must rationalize and conquer to retain hope—to inspire a better day. Happily, the view provides him that opportunity. He stands back from the parapet looking south, swinging his arms in an imitation of heartiness and enthusiasm. He is hopeful. He thinks about whistling.

The horizon this morning is a wall of bilious haze. The sun is bleary-eyed and tired; through the haze it squints. Is there anything the least bit valedictory about this day, this particular effort? Steven hopes not. The sun shines feebly—yet enough: the work is done. Between buildings the sun cuts westward into the streets below, casting walls of thin shadow across West End Avenue. And regardless of its strength the sun will rise up through the day steady as a lever; with this Steven reassures himself. Later it will be overhead, another noon. Later the sun's light and shadow will grub in the dirt; the sun will lie down once again, dirty-faced beyond the Hudson. This action is permanent, relentless; Steven knows this, yet as he edges carefully towards the parapet he admits to himself there is cause for concern. It does happen, sometimes, that trajectories lose their arc; mitigating forces interrupt what seem eternal orbits, and bodies stray and fall.

"Down there," Steven thinks, peering over the wall into the street, "Down there in all that pushing you haven't got a chance. There's no moment. Up here the world behaves. I see how it behaves, there are patterns . . . But in the street people are trampled, stampeded, killed, they can't see . . ."

In Steven's opinion, more people should take the time to observe the world from some distant position.

On the roof he is reminded of his childhood, climbing trees. From the uppermost branches the ground beneath the tree looked small and still. People's faces were tiny. People's wide-mouthed, alarmed expressions were the size of acorns. Voices were muted—even his uncle's crazy shrieks—and the broader sound of the wind swaying him in the roost was comfort itself; it was the sound of the wide world brushing against his ears.

Try as he might, Steven can hardly climb high enough. He can't get far enough away from the shoving and falling. Some weeks ago a man threw himself right off the top of the next building—he killed himself. He died in Steven's street. Steven didn't see him fall, thank goodness, but he saw the body. Since then, every morning the view has been here, the perspective has been here, the incident had to be dealt with. The big picture had to be gained, gathered in here: every morning, the rising in the east—that burned-out profligate, the sun—always dubious; and in the west the gulls and planes threading the air, so many regular strands above the river.

This morning it's the usual thing. Along the river's silver length boats run, ripping it open as they go, showing the blue beneath—this river flowing from God knows where past him to the ocean. Relentlessly it flows with swirls of current and the Circle-Line, the oil tankers, the garbage tugs. Probably, this river will never stop. Across the water dim shadows of the buildings fall, and shorten with the sun's sure ascent. For

Steven these recognitions are the conquering, the mastery, the rise of his being over the forces of gravity and chaos.

It is noon when Steven steps down into the tarred stairwell, and he is sanguine about the day. But the birds are the last of the bright outside to catch his eye. Pigeons fly off the clothes-line as the door is closing—and fast, fast they sail beyond the parapet! Above the avenue they lift their wings high, and plummet out of sight.

In the kitchen Alice and Rina are at the counter with a bowl of fruit between them. They are preparing a housewarming gift for the new neighbor down the hall, and quarreling over it; but even so they both hear Steven sneak in the front door, turning the locks softly.

Steven comes in the kitchen and with their backs to him the two women continue to fuss over the bowl, picking up one fruit and replacing it with another, and then undoing that. Rina is stoned again, and Alice is determined to resist her bizarre influence over their presentation to the neighbor. She is meticulously taking out the flower petals Rina's thin fingers have arranged among the fruits.

"What have you been up to?" Alice asks, carefully adjusting her eyeglasses.

"I've been in my room," Steven says cheerfully, "destroying your vacuum cleaner."

Alice is relieved. She sees he won't bring up the suicide again. He'll hide the fact he's been on the roof. It happened *weeks ago,* and Alice, for her part, is tired of the obsession. This is cold of her and she regrets that, but she won't discuss the incident anymore. "Falling bodies" (Steven's words) are not going to rise up for her seriousness anyway. Better to avoid that kind of talk. She prefers it when they lie to each other and have fun.

"You really should *try* the broom and dustpan," Alice says brightly. "You know? It works fine for us, doesn't it Rina?"

"Oh, well, a broom and dustpan . . . Sometimes you want *sound*, like machinery! power!" Rina's eyes spark gleefully. "Did it explode, or what?"

"No, actually I threw it," Steven says. He opens the refrigerator and leans over into the cool white interior, looking for nothing.

Alice says: "You threw it. Out the window I bet. Or did you restrain yourself?"

"Against the floor. It wouldn't eat."

Rina laughs at this. Steven comes out of the refrigerator and watches her replace flower blossoms in the fruit bowl while Alice is not looking. Rina's hands touch the fruit and rise like a heron's feet, stepping carefully among lily pads.

"Well," Alice says with regret, "I guess I'd ask you to come along to this housewarming, but you just might freak out. I guess you have your hands full anyhow. What with repairing our vacuum cleaner and all."

The two women ready themselves and traipse past him, Alice carrying the bowl. She puts her face close to his; "Liar," she says, and kisses him. She hefts the bowl high in front of her and passes on into the living room, very solemn. Rina shuffles in her loose cowboy boots behind Alice and holds a pair of burning incense sticks that she wafts to each side. With appropriate ceremony Steven escorts them to the door and, sweeping it open, ushers them out into the dark hall.

They have been living together, Alice, Rina, and Steven, since they were undergraduates. Steven has since gotten a PhD in clinical psychology—recently he finished his thesis: *Socio-Cultural Pathologies*. Important people are reading his work, and there are publication and job offers, but Steven is putting decisions off. He has stopped answering the phone. The apartment's large, high-ceilinged rooms hold him when Alice goes out to her job, or when, mid-afternoon, Rina wakes and heads out for coffee at La Tacita. From his tall windows, from his perch atop the high stepladder erected in his room, Steven watches Alice and Rina join the throng of pedestrians rushing along West End Avenue.

Alice has the bedroom next to Steven's, towards the back of the apartment. She is a secretary, but Steven is encouraging her to be an actress. Steven is her number one fan. He says she has carriage and bearing, and he will go on to say that Alice is a great beauty and describe in detail her long dark hair and wide-set gray eyes. This might all be in some part true, what Steven says, but this is not how others see Alice. To others, Alice represents an *almost*, a *nearly*, a *potential*. She wears her hair in a very tight, prim little bun, it is never seen long and flowing, and her eyes are obscured behind butterfly-rim eyeglasses that glitter with rhinestones. This is just camouflage, Steven says. Wait until you see her on the stage, he says.

Yes, Alice and Steven are a couple. But Steven, oh Steven— he is a curse to himself. If only he weren't so inconstant, distant, morbid! If only he weren't so . . . repelled—by the world of course, the cosmos!—then he could make her happy. But his world teeters on a precipice, something grim is imminent, and each day he is more peculiar. Of course, Alice gets upset with him. He doesn't blame her or get angry, he only hangs his head when she drops her dignified bearing, shrieks at him and weeps. He is hardly able to react at all when she tells him she won't "live like this," when she demands that he throw her out, *discard her*—when, every so often, with a great show of determination, she packs her bags.

Rina is in a position of being Alice and Steven's child, their misbegotten immaculate. It is usually for Rina that Alice leaves off packing, and stays. The roles are clear: an adolescent daughter with her aging parents. Tender doting, fondness, dependence, and times of sweetness give way to chafing, rebellion, and furious scenes—and reconciliations of the most earnest sort.

. . .

Steven opens his eyes. Daylight has faded, and streetlights have come on, casting a dirty yellow glow onto the ceiling. There is sound out by the elevators, Rina laughing loudly. Then the locks of the front door turn over and the two women come in quietly. They turn on some lights and settle on the couch.

"You've been over there for hours," Steven says. "What were you doing?"

"We had some fruit," Rina says slowly, trying to remember. "The fruit we brought. And we talked . . ."

"Nico *sang* for us," Alice says, gently leading.

"Oh my god, Oh my god," Rina exclaims, and flaps her hands in front of her as though she has just burned them. "He *sang!* Oh, yes, this was so amazing." With a dreamy look in her eye she pulls a rolled joint from her vest and lights it.

"It *was* an amazing voice," Alice murmurs.

Rina passes the joint to Steven. It crackles and smokes as he puffs.

"What sort of thing?"

"Opera—you didn't hear him?"

"Opera?"

"Singing—you didn't hear him singing?"

Steven passes Alice the joint, holding his breath. He plays along.

"Well? I guess I did, but I thought it was a record."

Rina giggles nervously. "Yeah, well, you should have been there," she says, her eyes on Alice. They both begin to laugh. Their laughter sounds like shouts of relief, and Rina's eyes are full of water. Steven laughs then too, with a tight feeling like fear in his chest.

"This was like a voice from fucking heaven," Rina says, and raises her hands to her hair. "We come in, we sit down, we introduce ourselves, right? His name is Nico, he's from Italy. Everything's nice, he's easy, what do we do, what does he do, you know, and he says he's a singer. An opera singer. Really, we say, like—really stupid, you know?—what kind of thing do you sing? He's standing there, getting us drinks or whatever, and suddenly out of his mouth—the man is as big as a house—out comes this great big sound, louder than . . . it seemed louder than anything I've ever heard." Rina laughs. "I mean, there is *nothing* in rock and roll like this." She gets up and stands at the window, looking out. "It was completely beautiful," she says with amazement.

"He sang just for a moment," Alice says. "Just one note, but it made the building shake. I mean it! I thought the windows were going to pop. The sound filled everything up and made it wobble."

Alice and Rina, dewy eyed, are no longer interested in the joint, so Steven sets it on the windowsill, the ash hanging over. He sits down on the couch. Alice gets up. Alice and Rina stand close to each other by the window in tense, stilled postures.

Rina says in a near whisper: "Later he sang again. Like it was coming out of the walls, or the floor, it was just *in the room*—this gorgeous sound. Wasn't it the sexiest thing you've ever heard? Or seen! The way it came out of him!"

Alice's face reddens behind the glittering frames of her glasses. "Oh, well, my lord!" she says, snorting at Rina's suggestion. "What he said to me—as we were leaving? My god, it gives me shivers and I don't know why—it's so ordinary. He said: Alice, I want to eat with you! His laugh afterwards, and his voice: *I want to eat with you!* I nearly died."

Alice and Rina get on a laughing jag. They both laugh until tears come to their eyes. For Steven, something is not funny about this. In the hysteria, the wild eyes, the tears, there is a lot he doesn't understand. He watches them warily, wanting to ask, or say, something arresting, devastating, shocking. He wants to pull them back from this new interest.

Rina catches her breath and holds it, her long fingers covering her mouth. She says solemnly, as though awed by her own conviction: "I'm never doing drugs again, not ever."

Rina lives in the small bedroom up close to the kitchen. There is another bed in the apartment for her, a proper room, but Rina prefers the small room. It is the furthest remove from Steven and Alice's end. This allows her to come and go at all hours, but the more important reason is that the larger rooms frighten her when she is stoned, which she has always been. Rina sings backup for a white funk band. She leads that sort of life, sleeping, when she sleeps at all, from dawn to dusk and living, it appears, on drugs and vitamins. Summers she spends touring with the band. When summer is over she returns paler and more strung out than when she left.

She is a thin wispy girl with sandy eyes and disturbingly pale skin—a thinness and a paleness that are both fragile and elegant, an indifference that appears aristocratic, an expressionlessness that looks knowing. She uses a wide variety of pills daily in a moderate, highly skilled, cheerful manner. Alice and Steven sometimes express their concern and their desire that she get clean, but they are only, when they speak seriously with Rina, performing according to their roles. They like her quite well as she is: fragile, alarming, exotic.

One of the things Rina says—she says it often—is that she has no use for sex. Sex is an addiction, she says. Sex is a "low grade, zip and burn kind of drug," a habit that "most people have no sense about." There are other "indulgences" Rina has little sympathy for—eating and sleeping. Friends of Rina's, male and female, drop in often to spend the day on the couch. They don't exactly sleep, or do much of anything. They are long and thin and quiet people. None of them are, or ever have been, lovers of Rina's.

From Steven's position atop the stepladder in his room, high up near the ceiling, the view encompasses not only the en-

tirety of his large bare room, but the synagogue one street
down, the sidewalks of West End, a glimpse of Broadway
through bare trees along the cross street. From atop the ladder
Steven listens to the sound of the world and shudders. He sits
on high and listens. Whole days pass, a week; the radio reports frightening news—bombings of abortion clinics and a
rash of violent crime against old people.

"The same people are responsible for both," Steven theo-
rizes from the top step. "They've got the credo about invest-
ing in the future. They're pruning deadwood. The body is
saving itself by pruning deadwood, protecting regeneration.
In the social power vacuum people prefer radical solutions."

He sees himself as a limb—tender, exposed, expendable. Or
perhaps calcified, brittle, defoliated. Deadwood.

Into the cross fire of the streets Steven would never go, he
would never come down from his perch if he had a choice.
He leaves the apartment rarely to buy food and pick up a
newspaper, and afterward hurries again to the roof. In the lee
of the parapet sitting on tar paper Steven scans the headlines.
But only the Help Wanted section holds his attention; he
reads the advertised positions and entertains his choices, the
various lives he might live.

"A plumber. A plumber's apprentice. I'll join the union,
make a good wage, work alone. I'll fix pipes. I could do that."

He feels this imagining is a healthy sign, and on other days
he enjoys dreams of being a house painter, a garbage man, a
construction worker. Anything but a psychologist, for which
he has a degree. He dreams of a regular life, a working, physical life, and contentedly settles on his bed for a midday nap.

Alice and Rina he now sees rarely. He seeks them out at
the usual times—breakfast with Alice, coffee with Rina,
late nights with both—but their schedules appear to have
changed. Like well-fed cats in a large house their movements
are mysterious. When he does run into them, he is surprised
to find them so often together—coming home from some-

where, going out, on the run, cheerful, arm in arm and casual. *Ciao*, Alice takes to saying. Steven often hears them laughing out by the elevator, but they are quiet and serious when they enter the apartment. He might find them in the kitchen from time to time, making food together, and the laughter and whispering he can hear from the hall stops as he approaches. They hush up with little smiles on their pusses, and it is clear they are enjoying themselves, some little secret they are harboring. It isn't a dirty secret, the sort hidden to avoid real shame. It is a happy secret, the kind you enjoy keeping from others because you know eventually they will find out.

There is something else: sometimes in their presence Steven is aware they look at him in a sexual way—not with any heat, but with evaluating, probing eyes—as though gauging the ripeness of fruit without touching it. They look at him this way, he feels their eyes on him, and then they turn away, or start talking about some obviously neutral and camouflaging subject. And Steven smiles at them, knowing (but knowing nothing in fact), and they smile back, turn away, very pleased with themselves and almost bursting with their secret. There are times when with a direct question Steven feels he could get it out of them, one of them alone, but he refuses to give them that satisfaction. Instead he grows cold to them, especially Alice, whose behavior is just childish. Her high-flying spirits, her cooling towards him, the way she looks at him as though he were a stranger—all of this, Steven feels, is just a ploy, blackmail. Thus they pass each other in the long halls, each with head high and eyes cool, half-lidded, trying to outdo the other in diffidence and self-possession. But his resentment at their alliance gets the better of Steven, and the women are openly amused at his sullenness.

It goes on for weeks. It goes on so long Steven grows to hate them both for abandoning him, and for teasing him. During this time Alice and Rina change in noticeable, physical ways. Alice loses weight while Rina gains it, and both

come to look healthier and more vibrant than Steven has ever
seen them. Alice wears her hair down, she gets contact lenses
—she allows herself, suddenly, to be beautiful. To Steven it
seems they bloom in front of his eyes, but he knows they do
not; they bloom in secret. Like flowers under their own private sun they mysteriously turn, becoming open-faced and
radiant.

On an afternoon when Alice is out Steven finds Rina in the
kitchen. She is drinking tea brewed in the pot. She invites
Steven to join her.

"Actually I need to ask you a favor," he says casually,
pouring the tea.

"What's that?" Rina is holding her cup up close to her
mouth and peering at him over the rim. Among other things
it is this quiet, watchful attitude of Rina's Steven is unsettled
by—her bubbling, manic eagerness is gone.

Steven explains he wants to rearrange his room. He could
use a hand moving furniture. To himself he notes that the tea
is herbal—chamomile. He senses this must be the true measure of Rina's disappearance—the vanishing of her self—from
black espresso to insipid yellow tea.

"That sounds fun," she says simply. She picks up the tea-
pot and leads the way down the long halls to Steven's room.
He follows behind. He watches the phenomenon of her new
weight, the figure wrestling for space beneath her robe.

"That's got to go, first thing," Rina says, pointing at the
stepladder.

"No," Steven says. "I just wanted to move my bed. I also
need help with the bureau and the desk."

Rina looks at him steadily while sipping her tea. "Let me
help you," she says.

They are finished by evening. Steven's rather spare, practical
room has become a boudoir—a grotto. His desk is gone and

the bureau now fits neatly inside the walk-in closet. But for a single chair, which now adorns the long wall facing the windows, the only other furniture remaining in the room is the bed. Smiling tolerantly, Rina has taken the stepladder away.

The bed is an heirloom, a painted white metal double that Steven's paternal great-aunt and -uncle slept in all their married life. It now appears lonely and somehow lewd, too inviting atop the room's only carpet. Behind the headboard is hung a brilliant red cloth, and the ceiling has been brought low and soft by white sheets hung pillowlike wall to wall.

Rina returns from stowing the ladder and together she and Steven stand by the entrance, looking in at their creation. The total effect, Steven thinks, is summery, light and feminine—and sexy. He says so to Rina.

"Mmmm" she says deliciously. With her hips she makes a rude gesture. "Now all you have to do is get some futons maybe for the corner, some boys and girls to play with on them . . . you'll be rockin'." She tucks a strand of hair behind her ear and, shifting her weight to her other hip, continues to contemplate the room.

"You're into orgies now," Steven says casually. He reaches over his head and smooths a sheet hanging from the ceiling.

"Oh yeah, I'm into everything now," Rina says, and laughs. "Except drugs. No more drugs."

"And you and Alice are having . . . an affair," Steven says. He puts his hands in his pockets as though idly looking for something.

Rina looks at him closely.

"You mean with each other?"

"Yeah," Steven says, avoiding her gaze. He unfolds and examines a scrap of paper from his pocket.

Rina laughs. "Well we're almost, a tiny bit, like, scratching the other one's itch sort of, and I can *see* that, you know? With Alice. I can *imagine* it." She pauses and there is a little smile in her eyes. "But no, we just love the same guy."

Steven pauses for two beats, and says: "Well you sure have a funny way of showing it." His expression is perfectly dead-pan.

Rina looks confused, and then wide-eyed with amazement. She laughs in big gusts of hilarity.

"Oh Steven," she says, "I'm sorry to laugh. But, you know, wow! you really should get out in the world more. You're losing touch. I mean, that's ridiculous. Where have you been, lately?"

Steven only smiles, remembering Rina when she was dizzy and fun.

Steven sweeps the areas of the floor formerly covered by furniture. Dust collects in ash-gray forms that roll like tumbleweed across the room. Steven sweeps them into the pan, deposits them in the trash basket by the window.

It was from this window that Steven watched as, weeks ago, a woman in the building opposite leaned from her window and began to wail. She wailed, and pointed, and there he was—for Steven and the rest of the world to see—a man lying sprawled in the parking lane. The man had fallen silently. No one, or few people, had seen him fall. No sooner had Steven seen the body than someone rushed from the building and covered it with a sheet. Men and women in a quickly forming crowd looked to the roof, squinting angrily, then resumed shaking their heads and staring down at the sheet. A bloom of brilliant red soaked and ran through the cloth.

Some time passed, and then from the long coats a schoolboy stepped forward. A bookbag hung from one shoulder and thin blue hands stuck from his coat sleeves. With eyes fixed on the blood stain, he looked quiet, attentive. He was listening. He picked up the corner of the sheet. Responding to mute command, he held the corner high! The crowd tightened, bowed for a still moment of attention. The boy and the crowd looked until, at once, they were all done looking and turned away. The crowd dispersed and there was a cleared space, a cleanliness in the parking lane around the colorful sheet. Within minutes another group formed.

That was weeks ago. Steven had seen this standing at his window where he is standing now, but the scene is a different one. Now the street is empty but for a young woman sitting on her stoop. Expanses of gray sidewalk and gray facade surround her like an aura. She is dressed in a black shiny skirt so short Steven imagines he sees her underwear, the mannequin-like smoothness of her thighs beneath blue pantyhose. Occasionally she rises wearily and strolls to the curb as a car nears and slows. These are, Steven thinks, signals given and signals received. *Trajectories hitting their targets.* The boy had lifted the sheet obeying a command. Steven now sees an ordering, a cohesion in the street where before there was only chaos and predation.

"In this woman there is a mysterious heart," Steven thinks, vividly imagining her insides. "Her arteries, like mine . . . a bath of red: her lungs billow like sails and I see a boy's face, somehow, squeezing out tears. Why? Each passing face has such blood, such secrets!" He senses, in the clear pictures his mind presents—of blood, of heart, of lungs—the secret of people's relation, the cohesion of their regular motions.

The young woman speaks through a car window; after a moment she opens the door and gets in. A negotiation, an agreement, an exchange! All of it knowledge. The command of finding out, Steven thinks. The dirt and stink of finding out.

The building fills with sound, a vibration rising in melody coming beneath the front door. In the elevator hall the sound rings in Steven's own head as he presses the doorbell of 3C. The singing breaks off, leaving a glancing echo in the place the sound had filled. Nico, his new neighbor, opens and fills the door—large against the light, enormous. He is not tall, but he is as broad as an ox. His face is red and damp like a child's.

"Steven, yes, hello!" Nico says when Steven introduces himself. "Come in. I am glad to see you." His voice is light, mellifluous, with an Italian accent. His face is pleasant. Not handsome, but round and full and moonish—friendly and amusing. He smiles easily, with a lazy interest. His body radiates a damp heat Steven can feel from three feet away. It is this, or it is an actual sound—of liquid rushing, flushing—that reminds Steven, and makes him strangely aware of Nico's blood, flesh, and organs. These are bigger, more red, more alive . . . than what? Steven's innermost impression—that this man is *alive*—has an incoherent urgency and strength that is startling.

There is a smell of fennel, or anise. Nico is chewing something. His teeth, Steven notices, are a dismal shade of gray.

As though it is perfectly clear why Steven is visiting him, Nico proceeds without a word down the hall to a carpeted room. The floor is carpeted, and the walls are carpeted also. In the center of the room there is a small plush couch. It is the only furniture in the room, aside from a music stand.

"I am just practicing . . . a moment more. Please," he says and gestures to the couch. Steven takes a seat, feeling suddenly at ease. He has come to hear him sing. That is why he has come! Other reasons and other questions Steven puts aside. Contentedly he crosses his legs and prepares to listen. At one end of the room sunlight is angling in the bank of windows. It is warm, quiet and pleasant in the large room.

Nico flips the pages on the stand for a moment, and drops his hands.

The sound that rises out of him feels to have come through the floor. It rises as solid as a column through the ceiling, a swelling, soaring note. The vibration gets inside Steven, the sound inflates him. It is only painful—that is how it feels. There is only breathlessness as his diaphragm is pulled with the force of sound up through the ceiling. Steven closes his eyes. The aria rises, and takes off through the floors overhead, through the tarmac roof into the sky over Manhattan, where it dissipates into a whisper and flap of wings, and floats with the wind.

David McLean

MARINE CORPS ISSUE

My father used to keep three wooden locker boxes stacked in the tool shed behind our garage. This was at our house in southern Illinois, where I grew up. The boxes, big heavy chests with an iron handle on each end, were fatigue green, but had splintered in places. Chips of paint and wood had broken off during the miles of travel, and a shiny splayed pine showed underneath. Each box was padlocked with an oily bronze lock, the keys to which my father kept on his key ring, along with his house keys and car keys. I knew that because I saw him open the top box once, when a friend of his came to visit. My father lifted the lid of the top chest, and then a tray within, and pulled out an album or a yearbook of some kind, something to do with the war. The visitor was an old Marine Corps buddy, still active and in uniform. They laughed over photographs and drank whiskey, a whole bottle. I crouched in the hallway around the corner from the kitchen and listened as long as I dared. I don't remember much of the talk, names and places I had never heard of, but I do recall the man's calling my father "gunny," and commenting on his hands. My father had damaged hands. "Look at your hands, gunny—Goddamn it, look at them!" And I think they cried, or maybe it was just drunken giggles. I don't know. That was the only time I ever saw my father drink. That was 1974. I was ten years old.

My original name was Charles Michael, and for the first ten months of my life, my mother tells me, I was called Charlie. I had no father then—that is, he had never seen me. But when he returned from Vietnam the first time, in early 1965, within a week he began the legal proceedings to change my name. Soon after, I was Jonathan Allen; I still am. I learned all this from my mother when I was twenty and needed my birth certificate for a passport application. My father was three months dead then, when my mother explained to me about Charlie, and how I had been renamed for a dead corporal from a small town in Georgia.

I see my father most often in two ways: playing handball or, years later, sitting on the edge of our elevated garden, black ashes from a distant fire falling lightly like snow around him. As I said, my father had damaged hands—a degenerative arthritis, we were told. They were large, leprous hands, thick with scar tissue and slightly curled. He could neither make a fist nor straighten them completely. Normally they hung limp at his sides or were stashed in his pockets. To grip things he had to use a lot of wrist movement, giving him a grotesque bird-on-a-perch appearance. He rarely touched anyone with them, though he did hit me once, a well-deserved blow I know now, and knew even then in the vague way of an innocent.

My older brother, Joe, and I would watch him from the walkway above and behind the handball courts while our mother waited outside. I was six years old, but can still see him clearly, playing alone, as always. He wears olive-green shorts, plain white canvas shoes and long white socks, a gray sweatshirt, the neck ripped loose down the front, and a fatigue-green headband wrapped tightly around his bony forehead. Black thinning hair dipped in gray rises up like tufts of crabgrass around the headband. He wears dirty white leather gloves. He swings at the hard black ball forcefully, as though he held paddles of thick oak. I hear the amplified slap of his hand and then a huge explosion booming through the court as the ball ricochets back. He runs after it, catches up to it, and slaps it again, driving it powerfully into the corner. His tall, thin figure jerks across the court and off the wall, his slaps alternating with the hollow explosions, his shoes squeaking, his controlled breaths bursting out of him as he tries, it seems to me, to break the ball, or maybe rid himself of it forever.

But it always returns, somehow, even dribbling, to the center of the court. Exhausted, he sits against the wall, breathing heavily, his court gone suddenly quiet, though the booming echoes from nearby courts can still be heard. He watches the ball bounce off its final wall and then slowly roll to a stop. I watch it with him, until it again becomes an inert black ball on the wooden floor.

I said that my father had hit me once; it was at our second meeting. The first had been on that six-month home leave when he changed my name. I remember nothing of that, of course. I do remember his second return home, though, when I was five years old. To my new consciousness, Daddy was simply a figure in a photograph, a steely, strong-looking man in dress blues. I remember the disjunction I felt upon seeing him for the first time, how I had trouble believing that this man was the same man as in the photograph. He was thin and gaunt and silent, with deeper eyes and a higher forehead than I had expected to see. He looked at me strangely. He hadn't seen me grow up. I could have been any child, an adopted son, were it not for my resemblance to him.

What I learned shortly after that first real meeting was the necessity of being a noisy child. Noise alerted him to my presence and prevented his being surprised and reacting on instinct. I began to knock on the walls or shuffle my feet or sing to myself as I walked through the house.

I discovered this survival technique one Saturday morning shortly after his return. I had awakened early and had rolled off the lower bunk, my blanket under my arms, a sleepy animal child going to look for his mother. I walked down the hall and into the living room, where my father sat reading. He had not heard me come in. I wanted to play a game. I crept around an end table near his chair, suppressing a giggle, and watched him for a minute. I looked at the back of his head, smelled his sharp aftershave smell, stared freely, for the first time, at his gnarled left hand holding the book in that rolled-wrist way, and then I leaped out from the table and shouted *Boo!*

I saw a white flash—I was airborne, backwards, on my shoulders and over my head. I landed hard on my face and knees, bleeding from the nose and mouth. I looked up and saw him crouched and rigid, eyes on fire, palms flat, fingers as stiff as he could make them.

Then he melted, right there before me, his body slumping down like warm wax, and he began shouting, and crying, "Goddamn it! Goddamn it, Diane! Come and get this God-damned child away from me!" He wouldn't look at me. His hands were in his pockets. He walked out of the house and into the back yard. I didn't see him again until breakfast the following morning. My mother arrived and swooped me into her arms. Only then did I begin to cry.

My mother's life intrigues me. Her strength, well hidden when I was younger, becomes obvious upon reflection. I spend a lot of time reading about the Marine Corps and Vietnam; it is a way of knowing my father. And yet I often find my mother in the books. I cannot read of Khe Sanh or Da Nang without imagining my mother at home with two children under the age of seven and a husband across the world fighting in a war, what I think of as a stupid war at that. She has never spoken about that time, not even about the four continuous years of my father's absence, when, my grandmother told me, she would spend at least two hours every night weeping alone, the children already asleep, and when she could hardly sleep herself. Even after my father's return tension and distance continued for some time. Our family was different from others. I can best describe it as being composed of opposing camps—not camps at war with each other but survival camps: my mother and I in one, my father and Joe in the other. We had no open animosity toward each other, only distance.

My father was in the Marine Corps for seventeen years before beginning his second career in the offices of the Stone City Steel Mill. He was a decorated soldier, a career man forced to retire disabled because of his hands. He had been a drill instructor, a fact that always widens the eyes of those I tell. I can see them reassessing me as soon as I say it—Marine Corps drill instructor—and they look at me in a shifted way that is hard to define. A pity, perhaps, sometimes a fear. I do have a temper comparable to my father's, which usually shows itself in short, explosive bursts of expletives that roll out of my mouth naturally, as if I were a polyglot switching tongues. The violence is verbal only, though I can still see my father, if I make the effort, at my brother's throat. Joe has been caught smoking in the garage a second time. He is fourteen and has been warned. He is pinned to the wall of the garage by my father's crooked paw, his feet dangling, toes groping for solid ground as though he will fall upward and off the earth if he can't find a grip. His eyes are wide and swollen with tears. My father's voice is a slow burn, his nostrils wide. He finishes speaking, drops Joe onto the concrete floor, and strides quickly away.

Despite my father's years of service, our house was devoid of memorabilia. A visitor would have no idea about my father's military career were it not evident in his walk and demeanor. Civilians might miss even these clues. Our house was not a family museum like other houses. We had few family photographs; the decor consisted chiefly of landscape paintings and small ceramic collectibles, dolls and Norman Rockwell scenes and wooden elephants from around the world.

At sixteen I saw the movie *Apocalpyse Now*. I had no interest in Vietnam then; I knew nothing of it. The film left me enthralled and fascinated, even a little horrified in an abstract way. I came home agitated but still had not made any connection. The epiphany came when I walked in the front door. My father was sitting quietly in his recliner, sipping coffee and watching the Cardinals play the Reds on television. My mother sat on the couch crocheting under a lamp, humming a hymn to herself, our Labrador, Casey, resting on the floor at her feet. I stared at them for a long twenty seconds before my father snapped the spell. "Hey, Johnny," he said, "come in here and watch the game. Redbirds are up five to three in the seventh."

"Yeah?" I moved into the room and turned to face the television.

"What'd you go see, hon?" my mother asked.

"What?"

"What movie'd you see?"

I lied. I quickly named some comedy that was showing in the same complex. "It was awful," I added, to cut off the questioning.

I saw the movie again a few days later, and I saw it anew. My father was in there somewhere, dug into a bunker, behind a wall of foliage, there amid the ragged poor and the dripping trees and the sounds of gunfire and explosions. And when I returned home from the movie that night, he was reading a John Le Carre novel, sipping coffee, the silky voice of Jack Buck in the background describing the Cardinals game in Atlanta. The evening was hot and dry. It would be a hard summer of drought in southern Illinois.

The next day I walked to the library and borrowed three books about the Vietnam War. My summer project would be to learn about the war and my father's place there. Under a hot midmorning sun I skimmed the thinnest of the three on the way home, anxious, as though poised to turn the knob of a mysterious door. At home I hid two of the books in my safest place, above the loose tiles of the lowered ceiling in my bedroom, and took the third book and my copy of *The Pickwick Papers* into the back yard.

We had a large yard behind the house, enclosed by a fence of pointed wooden slats five feet high. Against the back fence stood a terraced flower garden, built long before by a previous owner. It ran the length of the fence and was fronted by a red brick wall about two feet high. The three levels were separated by stacked railroad ties. My parents loved the garden and would labor all summer to keep it lush. Even that summer of drought, as the grass was browning under a merciless sun, my parents kept the garden well watered. From April to September we had cut flowers on the dinner table every night.

I kept a private place in the upper left corner of the garden. It was known to everyone; if I was nowhere to be found, my family would always check to see if I was there reading. Before watering, my parents would always shout a warning lest I be rained on. Although known, it was still quiet and just isolated enough. I would lie down on the ground behind a thick wall of day lilies, my back against the fence, and read, or think while staring up at the sky.

That is where I learned about the Vietnam War. I lay on my side and read for at least three hours every day, softly repeating the names of places and operations, marking pages with thin weeds. If called or found, I would rise from the flowers with *The Pickwick Papers* in hand, leaving the history book in a plastic bag among the day lilies, to be collected later. In the evenings, while listening to baseball games, I transferred notes from the weed-marked pages into a notebook that I kept hidden in my sock-and-underwear drawer.

Within two weeks I had finished those first three books. Upon completion of the third I emerged from the day lilies feeling expert. My knowledge of the war—dates, places, names—had zoomed up from zero. I was ready to ask my mother some questions. I approached her one afternoon before my father had returned from work. She was peeling potatoes over the kitchen sink when I padded in nervously. "Mom?"

"Yes, Johnny?"

"Mom, where was Dad stationed in Vietnam?" My throat was dry. I had never before uttered the word to my parents. My mother stopped working and turned to face me, potato peeler held upright in her hand. She looked puzzled.

"I don't remember, Johnny. Lord, that was over ten years ago. I don't remember those funny foreign names. He was stationed in more than one place anyway. Why?"

I felt ashamed, flushed. "Just curious. We learned a little about it at school and I was just curious. That's all."

"I wish I could tell you, but I don't remember. You know me. I have trouble remembering what I did last week." She laughed an unhumorous laugh.

"Should I ask Dad?"

She suddenly looked very tired and thoughtful. "Oh, Johnny, please don't," she whispered. "Don't bring it up with him. It took him so long to forget all of that. Don't ask him to start remembering again." Then she looked directly at me, and I could see that she was pleading with me, and I thought that she was going to cry. But she turned back to the sink and ran her hands and a potato under the tap. She began working again.

"Okay, Momma. I won't. I'm sorry."

"Don't be sorry, honey. You've a right to be curious."

The next day I was with Joe. We were returning from the shopping mall in Fairview Heights, twenty miles away. We were in the old pickup truck he used on construction jobs, trying to cool ourselves with wide-open windows, though even the rushing air was warm and uncomfortable. Joe was eighteen then, and worked nearly every day. I was enjoying the trip all the more because he allowed himself so few days off.

We were speeding down an empty two-lane road through the farmland south of Stone City. It was sickening to see. The corn, usually head-high by the end of June, was barely up to my waist. The ground was cracked and broken in places. Some farmers had recently given up. You could see by the dry brown stalks, standing packed closely together, that they had stopped watering.

"Look at it," Joe said, shaking his head and poking his thumb out the window. He had to shout to be heard over the sound of rushing air. "I've never seen anything like this before. Even Grandma says it's the worst she's seen." I nodded and looked around at the dying fields.

"What'd you buy?" he shouted, pointing at my bag. I pulled out *Great Expectations* and showed it to him. He gave it only half a look and a nod. Then he shouted, "What's the other?" pointing again at the bag. I hesitated, but pulled out *Dispatches*, by Michael Herr. Joe grabbed it and began reading the back cover, completely ignoring the road. We began to drift across the center line into the oncoming lane. I reached over and gave the wheel a slight pull to the right. Joe looked up and grinned. He continued reading, now flicking his eyes up every few seconds.

"Vietnam?" he shouted. "What'd you buy this for?" I shrugged. Joe rolled up his window and motioned for me to do the same. The cab was suddenly very quiet. I looked over and watched a red-winged blackbird light upon a fence post. Joe nearly whispered, "What'd you buy this for?"

"Just curious. I've been reading some history of the war."

"Does Dad know?"

"No."

"Mom?"

"Only a little. Not about my reading." Joe looked down the road. We were already baking in the closed, quiet cabin.

"Just watch out. Keep it to yourself." He threw the book into my lap.

"What do you remember about the war?"

"Hell, not much. I remember Dad coming home, hands all screwed up. Quiet, but I hadn't seen him in so long that I don't remember him being different or anything. Maybe quieter. I don't know. I was only seven. And I remember the POW-MIA sticker. Never understood that until I was in high school. We had a bumper sticker on the old green Impala. Remember?"

"No."

"Well, that's all I remember, really. I never took too much interest. I figured he'd tell us if he wanted to."

"Weren't you ever curious?"

"No, not too much. It seemed all bad and ancient history. Water under the bridge and all that. Jesus, I got to roll this window down!"

I considered asking Joe what he thought about my plan, but didn't. I had decided after talking to my mother that I was going to get into the locker boxes, though I had yet to figure out how. My father was in the garden nearly every day after work, and saw the boxes while getting tools or the hose. Obviously, I needed the keys.

I examined the boxes the next morning. They were stacked in a corner next to a small worktable. Coffee cans full of paintbrushes and nails and loose nuts and bolts stood on top of them. As far as I knew, they hadn't been opened in six years. Spider webs were constructed with a confident permanence between the sides of the boxes and the shed walls. I gave a cursory tug at the three locks, each of which had been scratched with a number.

The locks were the common hardware-store variety that always come with two keys. I began searching for the extras in the drawers in the tool shed. In the days that followed, I rummaged through boxes and cleaned the attic over the garage. I carefully went through my father's dresser, with no luck. I did find one loose key at the bottom of a toolbox, and raced out to the shed to try it, but it wouldn't even slide into the core of the locks. I would have to take the risky route for the operation. The useless old key would help.

I spent three scorching days in the garden reading *Dispatches* and an oral history of the war while I looked for the courage necessary to put the plan into effect. The plan was simple, but I wasn't certain it was safe. I would switch the old key I'd found for one from the key ring, rummage a box and switch the key for a second the following day, and then switch the one after that, for a three-day operation.

The next morning I rose as early as my father, much to his and my mother's surprise. My mother was in the kitchen scrambling eggs, and my father was in the shower, as I'd hoped. I slipped into their bedroom and with nervous, fumbling fingers forced the key numbered one off the key ring, replacing it with my found key. The key ring was tight, and I slipped in my haste, gouging my index finger in doing so. I left the bedroom with my slightly bleeding finger in my mouth, jamming it into my pocket as I passed my mother in the kitchen.

Later, quietly, with an archaeologist's caution, I removed the coffee cans from the top box and set them on the worktable. I then slipped in the key and flicked open the lock. Despite the heat, I felt a shiver through my back and shoulders, my body reminding me that I was crossing some line of knowledge, transgressing some boundary of my father's. My hands shook and I held my breath as I lifted the lid.

The first thing I saw was a yellowed newspaper clipping: the death of James Dean, carefully cut to keep the date intact. I read the whole article with interest. I knew nothing of his death. Then I saw my mother's high school diploma, class of 1955. Stacks of old photographs. Family snapshots, black-and-white with wavy white borders. I found my old report cards from early grade school and all of my brother's report cards up to the sixth grade. I found a baked-clay saucer with a tiny handprint pressed into it, and "Johnny 1968" scratched on the back. It was all interesting, but not my reason for the risk, so I lifted out the tray full of family memorabilia and set it to one side.

Underneath I found uniforms. Dress blues neatly pressed and folded. A shoeshine kit. A drill instructor's Smokey the Bear hat. Little plastic bags full of Marine Corps emblem pins like the one on the hat. A tan uniform. And the yearbook my father had pulled out six years before for his visitor. It was a thin platoon book dated 1964, San Diego. I flipped slowly through the black-and-white photos, looking for pictures of my father. The photos were mostly head shots of similar-looking boys in dress blues and white hats. I found action shots of boot training, of the mess hall, of track-and-field competitions. I saw my father here and there, leading a parade, demonstrating a hand-to-hand hold. He was still youthful and very muscular, stern-looking but not weary. The picture of him in his dress blues was the same I'd learned to call Daddy before I'd met him. His hands looked normal in the photographs, the vulnerability gone, his arms strong and well shaped, like solid tree limbs. Upon looking through again, I noticed small notations next to a few of the photos: "KIA," followed by a date. I was looking at dead men. I didn't know it then, but I would go back years later and find a picture of my namesake, Jonathan Allen Whitney, of Hinesville, Georgia, in that book.

But that was all, and it amounted to little. I replaced the tray and closed the lid, reconstructing the tool shed as well as I could.

That night at dinner I waited for the explosion, the accusation, my father holding up the key ring, his tight voice burning through me. I saw it all, but it never came. Later, in my room, I sorted through what I'd seen and made notes in my journal. I hadn't learned much, except that my mother loved James Dean and was a curator of her young sons' lives. As for my father, I'd found little new except the images of a younger, stronger man.

I opened the second box with less trepidation, half expecting to see my mother's junior-prom dress folded neatly inside, a dry corsage still pinned to the front. Instead, I found the memorabilia that probably should have been hanging on the walls inside the house. In the top tray were three wooden plaques commemorating different things my father had done, all before the war. They were homely little plaques given to him by platoons or friends. His dog tags lay wrapped in a green handkerchief underneath the plaques, "Joseph D Bowen" pressed into the thin aluminum. The tags read "Methodist," which surprised me, since he never went to church and mentioned God only as a prefix to "damn it." I found a pile of old letters written by my mother which had been mailed to an address in San Francisco. I couldn't bring myself to read them. I did, however, find three letters dated shortly after my birthday, and opened them. One contained the expected photograph, the usual hideous newborn, with the words "Hi, Daddy! Love, Charlie" written on the back. There was another photo, of my mother with Joe and me. Joe was two, and I was just weeks old. The picture was taken at my grandmother's house and dated June 30, 1964.

Beneath the tray I found more uniforms. Khakis this time, combat-style fatigues with "Bowen" stenciled onto them. There was also a pair of worn black boots, a canteen, two thick belts, and a cigar box full of uniform ribbons and their matching medals. Vietnam service, the crossed rifles for marksmanship, and others. There was an unexpected find: a Purple Heart. He'd been wounded. I wondered where. His hands, perhaps, or the fairly large scar on his left thigh—a childhood farming accident, he'd told us. I was staring at the medal, trying to open my imagination, when I heard the back door of the house swing out and bang against the siding. I threw the medal back into the box, and the box into the locker, and hurriedly shoved everything else inside. I pushed on the lock as the footsteps left the patio, and heaved the first box back on top. I was arranging the coffee cans when Joe walked in. "Hey, what are you doing?" he said. I was sweating, but felt a twitching relief that it was only Joe.

"Looking for a nut. I need one for my bicycle." I dumped one can over and began sifting through the dirty nuts and bolts. Joe walked around me, glanced down at the wall, and began sifting through the pile with me. "I need one for the seat," I told him. He quickly handed me a nut. "That'll do it," he said, and then added, "Hear what happened?"

"What?"

"Some old farmer set his fields on fire this morning. Acres and acres are burning like hell."

"Where?"

"Just east of town, off one-eleven. You can see smoke from the front yard. I thought we could drive out and see it."

"Why'd he do it?"

"I don't know. Just mad, probably. Wasn't doing him any good, dying there in front of him."

It wasn't much to see, really. The flames weren't huge, just crawling slowly across the field of dry stalks, crackling softly. Large glowing leaves swirled into the sky and became flocks of black birds in erratic flight. A few other people had pulled over to watch from the highway before a patrolman came slowly by and moved them along. Joe asked him if the fire department would put it out, and he said no, that it was no real danger, though the farmer would be fined or something. He said it would burn itself out in a day or so. We saw a man near the farmhouse, about a hundred yards from the road. He was old, wearing a red baseball cap, sitting on a tractor watching the wall of black smoke rise from the field. "Probably him," Joe said.

That night my father came home with two tickets to a Cardinals game against the Mets. "Box seats," he said, dropping them onto the table. He was as excited as we ever saw him, shining eyes and a slight smile, nothing showy or too expressive. "Let's go, Johnny."

From the car I watched the thin sheet of black smoke rising harmlessly like a veil on the horizon, not the ominous black plume that comes from a single house burning. I told my father about Joe and me driving out to see the fire and about the old man on the tractor. My father just shook his head. We were driving by his office at the steel mill, a different kind of fire and smoke shooting from the stacks. "Poor old man" was all he said.

I kept looking at the keys hanging from the steering column, expecting a wave of recognition to light up his face any second. I couldn't imagine how he would react, though I considered anger to be the best guess. What I was doing was wrong; I knew that and felt bad about it, especially since he was in such a good mood. His face was relaxed and peaceful, and he was smiling. He'd fought in a war; he'd been wounded in some unknown place; his hands gripped the steering wheel like arthritic talons; his friends had been killed and his sons had grown without him. I imagined him weathering bitter nights; he was driving us to a baseball game, sliding easily through traffic. I kept glancing at his profile, the thinning hair touched with gray, the deep circles under his eyes, the rounded nose—my nose. We were crossing the Mississippi River on the Poplar Street Bridge. The Arch was a bright filament in the afternoon sun. The river was remarkably low, looking as though you could simply wade across the once unswimmable, strong-currented distance. I considered telling my father everything right then. I was consumed by guilt, tapping my fingers on my leg. "What happened to your finger?" he asked.

"Nothing. Caught it on a nail in the tool shed. I was looking for a key to my old bike lock." I'd had that excuse saved for two days. I couldn't look at him. I watched people in the streets. He began talking baseball. It had always been the bridge between us. There had always been the gap and one bridge, a love of the game.

The game that night was exciting, a pitchers' duel with outstanding defensive plays. We had never sat together in box seats before, and we marveled at seeing everything so close up, how quickly the game really moves. We talked baseball all night. I kept score; I marked every pitch on the card, like a memory. The game went into extra innings. I didn't want it to end. I knew even then that this was the first time I had ever felt really close to my father. We shared a soul that night, and then, in the bottom of the twelfth, the game ended suddenly with one swing by Ted Simmons, a crack, and a long home run disappearing over the left-field wall. We drove home happy, though quiet from fatigue.

Strangely, he passed our exit and continued around town to the east. "You missed our exit," I said.

"I didn't miss it" was all he said. He was pensive. I was puzzled, but only for a few minutes. We turned onto Route 111 and headed south on the dark highway. Suddenly the

land to our left was a glowing pile of embers. We could see
little smoke, but the field was alive with orange fires, flickering and rising like fireflies. My father clicked on his hazard
lights and pulled onto the shoulder. He stepped out of the car
and walked across the still road, with me trailing behind. The
unseen smoke was too thick. I coughed and my eyes burned.
"I just wanted to see it," he said quietly, and we stood in
silence watching for ten minutes before driving home.

I didn't notice the ashes falling until after I'd changed the
second key for the third. I was walking back through the
kitchen when I saw, out of the corner of my eye, a leaf fall
against the window screen, break into pieces, and then disappear. I looked up and out the window. The wind had shifted
in the night, and the ashes from the cornfield were swirling
above like elm leaves in autumn, some falling gently to earth
like a light November flurry, except that the flakes were
black. In the back yard I held out my hand to catch one, and it
disintegrated in my grasp. The temperature was already over
ninety degrees. It was a wonderful and hellish sight. Ashes
blew across the patio and collected in the corner against the
house.

After my father left for work, I went into the garden to
read. Ashes drifted down, breaking between the pages of my
book and landing in the day lilies and roses along the fence. I
felt strangely uninterested in the third box. The previous
night had left me content with my knowledge of my father's
past. A new understanding had come to our relationship. I
felt guilty opening the third box, as though I were breaking
some new agreement between us.

The top tray contained nothing of interest. I found shoe
polish, dried and cracked, two more plaques, socks, two dun-
garee hats. I sifted through these things mechanically and
quickly, wanting to be done with it all. The compartment
beneath was only half full. A musty smell rose out of the box.

It came from the clothing—an old khaki uniform tattered and worn, filthy but neatly folded—that lay on top of the items inside. Also within sight was an old pair of combat boots, unpolished and ragged. They, too, smelled musty. I lifted out the uniform and found a small box made of dried palm fronds. It was poorly woven around narrow sticks with an ill-fitting lid on top. Inside it were yellow newspaper clippings folded up into squares, and a small paper ring box. I unfolded one of the clippings carefully, so as not to tear its tightly creased edges. The headline read "LOCAL PRISONER OF WAR TO COME HOME," and was accompanied by that same photograph of my father in his dress blues. The clipping was dated July 13, 1969. I read the article slowly, trying not to miss any details. It explained that my father had been a prisoner for just over three years, that he was to be released July 30, and that he would be returning to the base in San Diego within days. He was being held in a prison camp in the North, just above the DMZ, and had been captured while on patrol near Khe Sanh in 1966. It gave details about the family in Stone City.

I set the clipping aside and quickly unfolded the others. They all told the same story. One was from the Stone City paper, dated the day of his release. I read them all twice, almost uncomprehendingly, before carefully folding them and returning them to the homemade box. I was a little afraid to go further, but I picked up the small paperboard box, felt it rattle, and opened it. Inside were teeth, all molars, yellowed and with black spots in places. I picked one up. On closer inspection the black blemishes became legible: painted on the side of the molar in tiny letters was "N.V. 3.3.66." I picked up a second. It read "N.V. 5.12.66." All six of them had dates, three from March third, one each from three other days. I was breathing through my nose in a deep, mechanical way, sweating heavily in the hot late morning. I put the teeth back in the box and set the box aside. I was shaking and didn't want to continue. There was more to see, a few letters, some folders, a small book.

The book was a paperback, a Marine Corps field manual bound with a manila cover. It was titled *Escape and Torture*. I began flicking through the pages. There were some small, meaningless diagrams, a dull text about techniques for escaping from some generalized prison camp. Then there was a section on Vietnamese torture techniques. I began reading the clinical, distant descriptions of various forms of torture. Naked men in small, cold concrete cells, sleep deprivation, swelling legs, tied hands, beatings. A few pages into the text the notations began. They were written in black ink, always the single word "this" in the margin next to an underlined passage. The first, as I recall, described something with the feet. Then beating on the legs, "this." Then the hands. "This" was bamboo splinters under the nails. "This" was a beating of the knuckles. "This" was being strung up by the wrists. I felt my stomach go hollow and my comprehension numb as I stared at that awkward, childlike scrawl in the margin of each page.

I didn't hear my father walk into the tool shed. He appeared suddenly, as though he'd sprung from the ground. I felt a presence and turned to see him standing there in the doorway of the shed, holding his key ring in his right hand and my useless bronze key in his left. I have never seen such confusion on a man's face. He was startlingly angry, I could see, his body stiff, his nostrils flared, his breathing heavy, his jaw muscles rolling beneath his skin. But his eyes were weary, even desperate. We stared at each other while he decided what to do. I didn't move. I said nothing, only watched him. His eyes welled, and bright molten tears ran down his cheeks. Then he dropped the single key and walked away.

I rose and walked out of the dark shed into the hot sun and falling ashes. He was sitting on the edge of the garden with his head down and his eyes closed as if in prayer, his hands lying loose and unattached in his lap. He then moved them to his sides and began clawing at the dry dirt in the garden until he had dug two holes and half buried each hand under the loose dirt. He sat as still as a memorial statue, and I realized that I didn't belong there. I left him with his head down and eyes closed, and walked into the house. I see him there every day.

In the four years that he lived beyond that moment he told me a little about the war. It was a topic I could never raise. On occasion, if we were alone, he would begin talking about some aspect of the war or of his service. These were heavily guarded moments, slow monologues as he groped for the correct words to tell me. It is another way I remember him, speaking the things that he knew he wasn't capable of saying. This is how I love him the most, this great man. Semper Fi.

Elizabeth Graver

THE BOY WHO FELL FORTY FEET

The girl he loved was shy and quick and the smallest in the class, and usually she said nothing, but one day she opened her mouth and roared, and when the teacher—it was French class—asked her what she was doing, she said, in French, I am a lion, and he wanted to smell her breath and put his hand against the rumblings in her throat.

The boy he loved was in the class above and came from a faraway Arab country and was called Rachid. When the others wore navy blue, Rachid wore red, and when the others cut their hair short, he let his curl well below his ears, and when the rest of the boys joined in a huddle before soccer games, wrapped their arms around each other's shoulders and cried out, the Arab boy stood by himself and closed his eyes, and with him they always won.

The boy didn't know how anyone could move that fast, Rachid a churning tangle on the field. He didn't know how anyone could hug that close to the ball or arc it so smoothly toward the net. In the end it didn't matter, because a dark, thick happiness almost choked him at the moment time ran out and he knew that nothing could change the score, and he breathed the clinging, sour smell of grass and mud and leapt with the other boys. Then, in the locker room comparing bruises, they sang together, school songs or something vaguely bawdy, or the National Anthem tinged with sarcasm. Only a few things equaled this for the boy: having his feet measured for new shoes, bending a piece of orange peel until a fine spray shot up, falling asleep in the car—when they had a car—and the smell of gasoline. There were so many things to think about, so many different ways, he thought, to get it off his mind. That was what his aunt said to his mother: "Go to a movie, get a haircut, anything to get it off your mind." And the boy pictured his mother's mind like a breakfast tray, bent in the middle from overuse.

At home, alone in his room, he would start at the top of his head and run his hands down over his face, over his narrow chest, down to his knees and feet, and then sometimes he would lie on the floor and try to force his legs back behind his neck like the Pretzel Man. He had plenty of time for this lately and was sure that eventually he would succeed.

His mother had a job to bring home money, but also, she said, because going to work as a secretary forced her to think a little about things like lipstick, stockings and cutting her hair. She had a microwave, so fast and simple, and bitter pine oil for baths so hot they burned—the only remedy for muscle ache and city grime. Often at night they would get ready for bed at the same time, and then the boy's mother would settle down in her room to watch an old romance or western on TV. Later the boy would wake to voices and wonder who could possibly be talking in their house.

At school, the teachers saw him as nicer and more inclined to help than he really was, and often they asked him to open the windows, shut the blinds or erase the blackboard, which he did with a tight, obliging smile on his face, and with his mind on the lion girl or Arab boy or other things. Every once in a while, knowing his situation, his teachers tried to talk to him outside of class, but his eyes would wander to the door or window, and he would answer, "I'm fine, she's fine, he's fine, we're fine," as if conjugating a verb. His mother left him notes: "Hi. Back at nine. Do your homework and there is a nature special on TV at eight if you want." Or: "Please do *not* answer the phone because it could be the insurance people." She brought him pens from work now and then, and when she got home from the hospital she came in to say goodnight and express her thanks that he was such a grown-up kid and bearing up so well under the pressure, because any added trouble and she would crack, she said, although he could not imagine it.

When she brought him with her, which was not often, he bought candy in the gift shop and scuffed his shoes across the glossy floors. One day a nurse gave him a rubber surgeon's glove which he blew up like a cow's udder, and a woman in a wheelchair waved him down in the hall and asked for the story of Bessie the Cow. The boy said he didn't know it; he grew diffident and shy, yet stood there frozen with the inflated glove. What he wanted very badly was the facts—was it her legs or an invisible something else? The woman smiled, and her head didn't wobble. She asked his name, and her words didn't blur together at each end. He wanted to yank the afghan from her lap and peer below, but there was his mother apologizing to the woman, chiding her son for not reading his comic book on the bench. That was why kids could only come visit now and then, she said. The staff was afraid they would catch things or make noise.

Sometimes the boy wrapped himself around his pillow at night, and other times he played word games and chanted to himself: "My old man is kicking the bucket, my papa is passing away, my dad will soon be dead." I am the only one in my school like that, he thought, although he couldn't be sure, and often he imagined that he lived alone, for it was almost true, and that he had always lived alone. One day they read

about the Mayan Indians who were waiting for the end of the
world, and he realized that his life had grown calm and
stretched like the insides of a balloon, and that since he had
turned eight two years ago and his body had begun to wake
him up at night, and his father's body had begun to nibble on
itself from the inside out—since then, he had been quietly
waiting for everything to end and begin.

Coming out of school, he spied on them: the girl, who set
off alone, wearing a plaid raincoat even on the sunniest of
days; Rachid, who leaned against the brick wall waiting for
his brothers and sisters, and broke into that language when
they appeared, noisy as a clattering subway car, and left without looking back. His house, thought the boy, was probably
so full of people you couldn't help bumping into them everywhere you went, and probably all the children slept in one
wide bed. The lion girl had an older brother at the high
school—she had said it once in class—and if she ate too much
sugar, something happened to her blood so that she grew
pale and brought her hands to her face, her face to her knees.
He knew everything she wore, the colors of her notebooks,
and her locker number: S417. He had nearly mastered the art
of looking at her sideways or through lowered lashes, but
when she caught him, he wished he had never begun, and a
taste like the tip of his pencil filled his mouth.

His father said the drugs they gave him made him feel all
soft and changed the way his skin felt, so that he wondered if
he were growing fuzz like a peach. Once he had been the
manager of a large sporting goods store, and often now when
he couldn't sleep, he told his son, he counted inventory in his
head. The boy pictured the rows of football jerseys and tennis
rackets, the hockey pads to protect the athletes from each
other, the smooth white chapsticks to protect them from the
sun and wind.

"See how he's glad to see you," his mother said when her
husband closed his eyes. "He's having a real good day."

"I have to go to the bathroom," whispered the boy.

"Just tell him goodbye."

"I have to go," he said, and his mother took him out.

Most afternoons, he went home to read her daily note and make sure nothing had changed, then put on the dirty yellow baseball cap they wouldn't let him wear in school, hunched up his shoulders, and went to roam or prowl. It was his mother who called it roaming, "senseless roaming," but the boy preferred the word prowl, which was what animals did, because it made him think of secrecy and grace, and some kind of final catch. He knew his neighborhood at least as well as the postman, and probably, he thought, as well as the bums, and maybe as well as the stray dogs, who could see around corners before they got there.

One afternoon in May while his mother was at work, the boy perched on a mailbox like a gargoyle, examining the bottom of his sneaker. He was wearing it out in a funny way, he saw, so that the sole on the inside of the foot was thinner than the rest.

Do something, he said to himself, so he jumped down from the mailbox, walked into an alley and kicked a trash can, then bashed at it again until the front of his foot tingled, and he had made a small dent.

Something else, he told himself. Walk down by the river, where there are rats.

So he walked past the Chinese Grocer with its squares of tofu plunged like soap in a tub outside, past the curb where he had seen a man vomit into his hands, past the basketball court where his father had once played with him in the hot sun, and the boy had not known whether to be happy and pleased with the new orange ball, the afternoon devoted to sports, or embarrassed at the slight paunch his father had (and then lost), and the way he yelled too loudly and told the boys on the other court that their ball could use some air.

Someday, thought the boy now, shoving his hands into his

pockets, there will be no more court, and no more basketball, and every one of those boys will be gone, and he tried to strip the city to what had once been there, which must have been air, and a skinny dog or two, and dirt.

When he saw a penny on a manhole cover, he picked it up, and when he passed a woman making snowcones, he stopped to watch, and when he saw scaffolding and men in hard hats and flannel shirts, he snuck around back where they were no longer working and began to climb. On the first level, he found an empty paper bag left from someone's lunch, and on the second level he found a pile of screws and pocketed a few. Climbing reminded him of his body, of pulling himself up by his arms, and he wrapped his hands around the sun-warmed metal pipes and felt his jeans stretching with his legs. He passed the windows like a shadow and assessed the height as he reached the fifth level, then the sixth level, then the top. At the top, he lay down on the rough wooden boards and looked down through the cracks. Below, he could picture them standing in a circle—his mother, his father, the Arab boy, the lion girl. His father was draped between his mother and Rachid; the girl was off by herself a little—four faces tipped toward him like different-sized planets, only narrowed by the crack. They were there to look up at him, after him. They were there to marvel at the distance. The boy looked down again and saw a taxi and a moving van, a man with a shopping cart, one kid shoving another up against a wall. He put his head down on the board to smell the girl and smelled instead the pitchy scent of wood. He pressed down on the platform and felt his heart crowd against the sharpness of his ribs.

At the end of the alley was the river, and next to the river was the building site where he often looked for rats, and at the edge of the site, stretching its neck over a makeshift sidewalk and a pit, was a yellow crane. A woman was walking that day along the sidewalk. It had never happened before and would probably never happen again, but as the crane leaned forward to hoist its load of metal rods, it lost its balance and tumbled forward like a 35-ton bird. For a moment, movement: the pavement cracking, weight shifting as the crane's base pushed the plywood barrier halfway down the pit's slanted side. A crumbling of earth. Then a creaking sound, a settling in, and the tipped base came to rest precariously against the displaced plywood barrier and lodged, overgrown and awkward, across the fallen woman's lap.

From the scaffolding, the boy saw the glint of yellow and heard the scraping noise, and then he heard sirens and began to scramble down. By the time he had run the length of the alley to the site, the woman had opened her eyes to a crushing weight on her legs, pushing the sense out of her, knocking her silly, so much pain she felt she had been lifted to another world.

"There's a lady down there," said a teenager to the boy, and they stood with the others at the edge of the roped-off area. Some people bit their nails and others prayed, for they had already brought in a priest.

Maybe, thought the boy, they needed someone small and careful to bring her things, because the police and medics had succeeded in communicating with the woman, and she had tugged twice on the rope they had lowered to say, "No, I can't move my legs," and once to say, "Yes, I'm all right," and once more to say, "Yes, a priest."

"They know she's alive but they don't know how to move the crane," said the teenager to the boy, and they peered at the machine tipped against the side of the pit at a crazy angle, as if waiting to slide further down the hole. "Move it wrong and she's a goner, huh?"

The boy nodded and ducked off, tunneling his way through the crowd to the edge of the roped-off area, stretching his neck to see.

I'm small, he thought. I could fit down there no problem

and help her out, but as he peered over the edge of the pit, a policeman pushed him back as if he were a pesky dog and told him to get on home.

The boy stood like a statue, as if he hadn't heard, and the policeman waved a hand before his face. "Yoohoo kid, I'm talking to you! No kids on the premises. Scram, or I'll have to bring you in to the station."

So the boy left the lady and the crane and went back to the scaffolding, but they were working where he'd been. He went down another alley, closer to home, and kicked at an empty metal garbage can lying on its side until it rolled. Then he leapt on top of it, lost his balance, fell, and got up to leap again, balancing and falling his way down the alley like a half-broken machine until his jeans and shirt were streaked with grease and dirt, and bruises painted his cheeks and arms. When he got to the end of the alley, he turned the other way and started back. This time he whispered "All right! All right!" and pressed his fingers to his palms, knowing he'd caught the rhythm of the thing.

It was a question of moving your feet at the same speed as the can, or no, moving them a tiny bit more slowly, because the feet pushed the can forward and made it go. It was a question of leaning back just enough to avoid going over the front edge, but not so much that you got left behind. Timing and balance, he thought, balance and timing, and he remembered the athletes who came to his father's store, the careful way they talked about their sports. He found he could go ten, twelve, twenty feet at a time, arms flailing like a madman's, teeth clenched. He was the only one in the alley, and he could hear nothing but the hollow sound of the can, the pounding of his feet, the ragged intake of his own breath. He could feel nothing but his own body, until the pressure of a hand wrenched him from the moving garbage can, landing him hard on his left ankle so that he fell forward to his knees.

"You always screw around with other people's property?" said a voice as the boy stumbled up, and the hand came down on his shoulder to shake him hard. The boy winced at the pain in his ankle and shut his eyes the way he used to when his mother yelled at him. He heard: "Where you from? You think this city is a goddamn playground? You've got nothing better to do with your time?"

Then the voice stopped talking, and the boy opened his eyes to find it belonged to a bulky man in a red t-shirt, with a small ratty girl at his side.

"You got nothing to say for yourself?" said the man.

"My father died," said the boy, and the words hovered in the alley like suspended bells, so clear he knew they must be true.

"Aw shit," said the man, reaching out to touch the girl's head. "Today?" he asked, and the boy nodded and watched his sneakers, which were coated with a fine layer of dirt.

"Aw shit," said the man. "You better get on home. You got a mother at home?"

The boy opened his mouth to say no, to tell the man he lived alone, that he had always lived alone, but instead he found himself nodding, and the man said, "Okay, good," and rubbed the girl's neck. "You better get on home," he repeated, so the boy said "yeah" and turned to go.

On the way back, he mumbled it: "My father died, my father died," and nobody noticed because it was the city. Limping from his twisted ankle, exaggerating how much it hurt, he tried to picture his father with a pain like this, with a worse pain—so hot it lit you like coals until you turned white, then gray, then disappeared. Once, the boy had not known about hospital smells, or how beds went up and down like dentists' chairs, or the way people could eat through rubber tubes. He had not known the elastic possibility of change, and then one day he had come home to find the world on a whole new axis, everything slightly tilted, like a bike on crooked training wheels.

My father, he thought, was a goddamn honest man. His mother had said it on the phone to her sister: "How could I not tell him what the doctor said? You got to talk straight to him. He's such a goddamn honest man." His father was tall, a jokester, with hair in his nostrils and on his back and a way of tossing his head like a horse. That's all I know, thought the boy—all I remember, because the rest came from after. He sat down on a stoop a block from his house and lowered his head to his knees.

You dummy, he said to himself. You dumbhead—get up, and he tried to think of something he might like to do, but he was so tired, as if someone had drained away his blood. He tried to think of things he liked, but his mind went blank, so he thought of things he disliked and remembered the time his father had smacked him on the side of the head because he had stuck a pen into the pilot light of the stove. It had not been a gentle slap, meant to teach. It had wrenched the boy's neck and left a red mark on his face, and later he had snuck out and poked tiny holes with the pen in the seat of his father's car.

"Shit, shit, shit," whispered the boy into his hands, because he missed his father so much he couldn't move.

When he got home, his mother was not there, and he pulled down his shade, crept into bed and held himself. Later she came to the door, peered into his room and said, "Asleep already? It's only nine," and he turned to display his cuts and bruises in a swatch of light. His mother wore an orange sweater and lavender skirt—she wore only the brightest colors—and her shoulders drooped. When she looked at him she sighed and said, "Oh no, not a fight," and turned on the light by his bed.

"Was it a fight?" she said, unbuttoning his pajama top to see where he was hurt, and he shook his head dumbly, and then, for the first time in front of his mother in at least a year, he began to cry.

"It was. Those bastard kids," she said, lowering herself to perch on the edge of his bed. "Those little bastard city kids. We have to get you into a different school." She put out her hand to pat the blanket covering him, and breathed in, as if gathering herself. "Tell me about it," she said.

So he told her how he had been down by the river, and there was this big crane—you know, over where they're building that apartment building—and he had been walking along looking for rats, and suddenly the earth had fallen out from under him.

"No!" said his mother. "I heard about that! They were talking about that at the hospital, all the nurses."

"Yeah, well I fell twenty, maybe thirty or forty feet," he told her, and she moved closer to him and took his hand.

"It's crazy. Thank God you weren't badly hurt. They should have taken you to the hospital."

"I know," said the boy, wiping his face on the cuff of his pajama top. "Except nobody saw me, and there was this lady buried by the crane. They had this ladder over on the other side, and I just sort of climbed out alone."

"Really?" said his mother. "Really, did you do that? All alone?"

"Yes," he said, and he knew she didn't believe a word of it.

She was holding his hand, and he was leaning toward her, and then she was saying something, but he couldn't make out the words.

"What?" he said, but she shook her head.

"He liked your drawing, I think," said his mother, and for a minute he couldn't remember which drawing, but then he knew it was the one in India Ink, the face of someone he had invented, a girl.

"Come here," said his mother, and for the first time in a long time she held him as if he were a young child, and he breathed the warm air against her chest until she pulled away, too soon, and said she was tired and would get ready for bed.

"It'll be okay," she said as she turned to go, and he blocked his ears with his fingers and burrowed down under the quilt, but he could sense his mother hovering in the room, so after a minute he surfaced and lowered his hands.

"I'm sorry," she said from the doorway, half in, half out. "I'm so sorry about all of this," and her voice sagged, then rose again. "Rest is important, isn't it? Sleep well, pumpkin, all right?"

What she didn't know was that he couldn't fall asleep, not for the first hour after she left, not for the second hour, not for what seemed like the entire night. He drummed his fingers against the wall to the beat of songs. He took his flashlight from the milk crate by his bed and inspected the corners of the room. He got up to run his fingers over the books and cars on his shelf, then climbed back in with the flashlight and a mystery, but the print was small and strained his eyes. I should count, he told himself, so he turned off the light and thought of thirty pairs of skis, eighty baseball bats, but the numbers stretched before him to infinity and made him more awake. His leg ached from where he had fallen, and he pressed on the tender spot until his hand grew stiff.

My mother is sleeping, he thought, and he knew just how she looked, flat on her stomach in her blue flannel nightgown under the plaid comforter, her head buried under her arms. Next to her bed, he knew, was the lamp shaped like a soldier holding a torch, and under the bed were her pink quilted slippers and some wadded kleenex and some dust and maybe a gum wrapper, and on her night table were her gold rings and the clock they had gotten free from the bank, the alarm set to six-fifteen. And my mother is breathing, he thought, first shallow breaths and then deeper breaths, and her mouth is slack and her fingers are limp, and my mother is sleeping.

My father, he thought—but they had put his father in a plain old hospital room, nothing special about it, and the boy didn't know how to go on.

Susan Starr Richards

THE HANGING IN THE FOALING BARN

Here it was three-thirty in the morning. Between foaling mares and nursing sick foals, Luther hadn't slept more than three hours straight in the last two weeks. Tonight, at last, everything looked quiet, and he had gotten to bed with the prospect of being able to stay there all night for a change.

And then the night man called up to tell Luther he was going to hang himself in the foaling barn.

Luther sat there a minute, thinking something serious was happening—a mare was ready to go, a foal had a fever. "Tell you what, Maurice," he said at last. "If you want to die so damn much, why don't you just go in Brownie's stall and stand behind her and touch her once on the butt? You'd get your picture took in a hurry."

"Why Luther—" intoned Maurice's vague, startled voice— "She might just hurt me."

Luther smiled sweetly at the telephone. "That's true. You probably wouldn't stand anywhere near the right spot, and she'd probably just kick you someplace internal, and you'd crawl out into the hallway and lay there all night turning blue, and I'd have to fight all the mares past you in the morning before I could even turn out."

Luther took a big breath. He thought about it. "All right," he said. "All right. Only for God's sake don't hang yourself in front of the foaling stall. Wiggy's been snorting and staring in there every evening, still looking for that dead meadowlark the cat left in the corner last week. She won't go in, and then she keeps looking in all the corners and snorting that way. And in the morning she runs over top of you trying to get out. She'll never relax enough to have that foal. And if she does, she'll probably think it's a dead meadowlark, she's so dumb.

"Not as dumb as you are, though, Maurice. You got to call up and want to kill yourself here in the middle of May. Couldn't you wait till June, at least, when foaling season's over?"

He slammed the phone down. Then sighed.

When Luther had first known him, Maurice was leading apprentice at River Downs. He'd ridden a lot of winners for Luther over two summers there. Back in those days he had yellow hair like bright wheat straw, and those tall slender girls that always love jockeys leaning all over him. A strut to go with it, and a flat back in the saddle. And a way of waiting on a horse most bug boys had no knowledge of, sitting still till it told him to move, and then only moving to disappear into it as it ran, till it was all one beast, man and horse, running together at the wire. Luther had believed Maurice had a chance to make it at the real races.

But even then he was drinking, and then the weight got to him. He was an exercise rider for a while, and then a groom, and then Luther lost track of him entirely. When at last he showed up working at a gas station in town, still talking horses all the time, Luther had given him the night job for old time's sake. He still drank, of course, but then most night men did. He didn't smoke, at least, so he wasn't likely to burn the barn down. And he claimed to have nightmares so bad that he never would sleep at night. It might even been true—in eleven years of foaling, he'd never missed a mare.

The only trouble was, toward the end of every foaling season, Maurice started considering suicide. Of course, that just made him normal. Everybody started thinking about killing themselves, or someone else, this time of the year. But Maurice would get into ways and means. One night he tried to drown himself by driving into the farm pond, but since it was only four feet deep, he'd only managed to drown his Chevrolet truck. Luther bought him an old car to replace it, and then the next spring he tried to ram the car into the big oak by the driveway. His aim wasn't too good, so he made several passes at it, and by the time he gave up, he'd taken out about a quarter of a mile of fairly new plank fencing and let the barren mares loose all over the farm.

But he'd never tried to kill himself in the foaling barn. Luther found himself not just irritated but indignant at this. The foaling barn was where the heavy-in-foal mares came swinging in every day with their huge bellies swaying rhythmically, and the new foals staggered up on their feet for the first time and tried to kick somebody right away. Everything there wanted to live so much, was so full of life. That was why you always felt so bad when sometimes they didn't make it. To try to kill yourself in the foaling barn, Luther believed, was sacrilegious.

Of course, he never thought for a minute that Maurice had any real intention of doing it. "But he's fool enough that he might just accidentally get it done," he said to himself.

He sighed again. His clothes were right there by the telephone, ready, waiting for some mare to call him up and say she was foaling, waiting for life to call him up, instead of some dummy saying he wanted to kill himself. "Hang on, Maurice," he said. Then laughed out loud, once.

. . .

A branch came out and slapped at Luther's arm as he jerked the truck around the corner by the woods. Luther slapped back at it. The yearling colts came swirling up, blazing white-and-green-eyed in the headlights, racing the truck down the fence at a dead run, sliding on their butts like baseball players to stop in a scramble half an inch short of ramming through the gate for the second time this week. "That's right," he said. "You all keep trying to kill yourselves, too."

The lights were on in the barn hallway, a big floating square of light with the dark trees outside touching the roof. Grids of shadows in the squared-off reaches above. The mares looked up, big-eyed, interested, some of them speaking to him, ever-hopeful of extra grain rations. The tackroom was empty. He called. No answer. But he heard a little shifting noise up in the loft, like something afraid to move and afraid to sit still. Maurice was up there, all right. He was sitting in the hay bales. Luther could just make out the top of his hair, which didn't look like wheat straw any more—more like old grass hay, by now.

Luther went in the foaling stall to check on Wiggy. "She do any more digging?" he called up to Maurice.

Maurice didn't answer for awhile. "Been real quiet," he said at last. "Don't worry," he added, in his sing-song, mournful voice. "You ain't going to need me tonight."

"What about that new baby? You see him pee yet?"

"I done wrote you a note about that."

There it was, on the clipboard by the door, written in Maurice's own edifying style: "The colts kidney acted."

"Be with you in a minute, Maurice," Luther said. "My kidney's about to act." He went into Twinkle's stall to pee. There she was, talking to her little sick baby, so happy to see it on its feet again and nursing on its own. Not a bit happier than he was, though, after getting the foal up every two hours for the last two days.

Luther calmed down some as he stood there, listening to

the foal slurp its milk. All around him were the mares, munching slow and peaceful in their stalls, and some lying down and talking in their sleep to their new foals that hadn't been born yet, the way they do toward the end, having baby dreams. And here it all was in the middle of green fields stretching out in the dark, and the fireflies outside going on-off, on-off, and the air smelling like a grape popsicle the way it always did down by the woods this time of year.

And there was Maurice hiding up in the loft, wanting to kill himself. Talk about racehorses being crazy. At least if a horse killed itself, it was because it was trying to do something else, playing or fighting or just running.

Luther started climbing up the ladder, cursing silently as he maneuvered himself up over the top. He did not like heights—not even the twelve-foot height of the loft.

A rag-tag rope made of a bunch of shanks tied together looped up to the central two-by-eight above the hallway. At the other end of it was Maurice, huddled up on a hay bale like some stray cat waiting to be kicked, holding a makeshift noose in his hands. "Look at you," Luther said. "Forty-one years old. Still healthy, in spite of all the alcohol you've put in your system. Sitting up here on a hay bale wanting to hang yourself with a lead shank. Couldn't you just kindly wait awhile? We ain't always going to be alive, you know."

Maurice said in a pitiful voice, "I waited long enough. I'm just doing what I should've done a long time ago."

"That's the truth," Luther said. "At least you sure should've done it before three-thirty in the morning. How come you didn't want to hang yourself just after supper? I had about twenty minutes then. I could've worked you in."

Maurice was silent. The mares chewed, stopped, thought about it, chewed again. A foal whinnied in its sleep, jumped to its feet, its mama spoke to it softly. Maurice glanced out into the middle of the space above the hallway, as if he saw something there.

Luther didn't like that look. It reminded him a little of Crazy Harry, a horse that saw things—spooks—and no matter how many times you told him, "There ain't nothing there," he wouldn't believe you. He was always so sure there was something just up ahead of him that was going to jump on him that he would almost get you to believing it. Harry would freeze, and snort, and arch his neck, and bug his eyes, and start looking both ways to decide which way to bolt, till you'd find yourself saying, "What the hell is it? Where is it? What's it going to do?" You just couldn't pay attention to Harry at all, or he'd convince you the world really looked like he thought it did. What you had to do, Luther reminded himself, was to give him something else to think about.

"Suppose you get it done," he said, nodding at the rope, settling himself on the bale opposite Maurice. "Then what? How do you know you won't come right back again? How would you like that?"

Maurice stared at him kind of cock-eyed, the way he did. "Come back as a ghost, you mean? Ghosts can't feel nothing."

"But you'd remember feeling things. How it feels to be hanging in the middle of the barn, for example, with your head ripped loose from your body." Maurice hunched up a little bit more on his bale. Luther sank back on his. It was beginning to feel soft already.

He tried to calculate what he could do that would get him back home and to sleep quickest. He could hit Maurice on the head and tie him up with the shanks and leave him here until morning. Or he could leave him alone and let him jump. But that rope probably wouldn't hold, and he'd wind up just breaking his leg, and then Luther would have to do something with him in the morning. And anyway, Luther was against things breaking their legs in his barn. Even humans. Even Maurice.

"If only they hadn't taken me off of He's No Angel," Maurice said.

"Hell. They took you off that horse twenty years ago. And they didn't even take you off. You only rode him the once, remember? When that other boy had days?"

Maurice nodded dreamily. "He win by twenty. I never asked him for a thing. If I'd just stayed with him, I'd be riding in New York today."

Luther shut his eyes, feeling sleep right there behind his eyelids, dark and soft. "Yeah, and if things were different, I'd be breeder of the year. But I ain't planning to hang myself about it. What you need to do is to cool out a little. Life ain't all that serious to be worth killing yourself about."

Maurice was silent again for awhile. Then, "You remember that time I win on Circus Cat?" he said.

Luther grinned, reluctantly. This was one Maurice could always get him in on. Circus Cat was one of Luther's all-time favorite horses—not the best he'd ever bred, but probably the bravest—a tiny little filly who ran against the older horses at marathon distances on the local tracks, sometimes fifty lengths out of it in the backstretch, always hopelessly beaten going into the turn, and more often than not on top at the wire. In the race Maurice was talking about, even the winner's circle photographer had been faked out—she was still second when he took the picture of them all running at the end. Luther himself had turned away, saying, "Not this time," sure she was second, till he heard the shout as they put her number up.

"You remember what that guy said about her afterward?"

They recited it together, as wondering and staccato as the trainer of the second horse had said it after the race, shaking his head in disbelief. "That-sucker-came-from-freaking-Tennessee!"

"She did, too," Maurice said. "I can still feel it."

Luther could still see it, himself—the filly still trailing the

field clearly when she came out of the final turn, then bur-
rowing into the pack until she was almost invisible, just
an impression of speed, a bay shadow, slipping sketchily
through all those great, big, solid horses that seemed twice
her size, to emerge third as the two leaders ran for the win.
Then disappearing again between those two, then suddenly
there, diving like a demon for the wire. "She was a wonderful
little filly," he said softly. "You suited her down to the
ground, too, Maurice. I have to say that."

Maurice nodded. His eyes had dropped to the rope again.
"She was the last winner I was ever on. You put me on. When
nobody else would. You was always good to me, Luther. And
I let you down. I let everybody down. But I'm going to make
it all up to you now. You ain't never going to have to worry
with me no more."

Luther leaned back against the bales, nodding. "Whatever
you think, Maurice. I wouldn't want to tell a man his business. But all I want is to get back in the bed." He closed his
eyes once, nodded, opened them again. He wasn't sure how
long it had been. But Maurice had stood up, and he had the
noose around his neck. He turned away vaguely toward the
edge of the loft, holding his arms out from his sides, as if he
might explode. The rope lifted up a little around his neck; he
tugged at it daintily with one finger. But he didn't move.
"Standing tied," Luther said to himself.

Maurice straightened his shoulders. "I'm going now," he
said in a loud voice. "I want to go. It's now or never." Then
he stood there, as if he were waiting for something to happen.

"Looks like never to me," Luther said.

Maurice glanced over at Luther. "Life don't make no
sense," he said, in a cracked, inspired voice. Like he'd finally
figured it out. "At least, my life don't. You think your life
makes sense, Luther?"

Luther thought. "Not this part of it. Here I am sitting in a barn loft at four in the morning discussing life with a party who's ready to kill himself. What do you care?"

"That's right," Maurice said. He took a deep breath. He wiggled the rope around his neck, once, like straightening a necktie. Then he started walking toward the edge of the loft. He was taking baby steps, but he was heading that way.

Luther growled. He got up and took two big steps and caught up with him. "Give me that," he said, reaching out to snag the noose. Maurice walked faster. "No. Stop, I tell you."

He grabbed Maurice, turned him around. Maurice backed up. The rope pulled tight. Luther grabbed the rope. Maurice grabbed Luther. A slow waltz, Luther stepping forward, Maurice backward.

"Stop, now, what are you pulling on me for?" Luther said.

"I ain't pulling. You're pushing. I want to do it. Just let me go on and jump."

"You ain't jumping. You're hanging on to me. Give me this rope, I tell you."

They swung toward the edge of the loft together, their shadows huge, flapping against the light.

"Take that thing off your neck, now." Luther was breaking a sweat. "Here. Don't crowd me, you crazy booger. I ain't going to jump with you. This ain't no lover's leap." He was on the edge with his back to it, the space opening dizzily in the back of his head. They teetered forward together, and for a moment he was sure they were going over flat-out, heading for a great big double belly-whopper on the floor of the barn. Then they teetered back again.

Luther lunged forward, swung Maurice around with one big jerk of his arms. His heart was pounding wildly.

Now Maurice stood with his back to the opening. He still had a stranglehold on Luther. His eyes, close up, were blood-red, filling Luther's vision, like the eyes of a horse that had been in the stall too long and was fighting you to get out, banging on the walls, climbing all over you. Luther wrestled himself loose and stepped back.

But then it was as if all that red had gotten in his own eyes. He saw Maurice crouched before him, looking strange, black lines running all over his face like it was a cup about to crack. Talking in a funny, screechy voice, saying "Don't, Luther," or "No, Luther," or "Whoa, Luther" over and over again. Behind him was the great complex orderly opening above the hallway. Luther could feel the push coming all the way from his heels, could see Maurice rocketing off into the clean space behind him.

But then there was a big blow in Luther's middle, like he'd been kicked. And he was sitting on the floor, alone in the loft. And the rope was holding. It was swinging back and forth like a pendulum, while Luther watched it in disbelief, certain that Maurice had to be the weight at the other end of it, since nothing else could be, but trying hard to think of some other explanation.

The rope started swinging and started jiggling, twitching, like someone was fishing with it. There was an unfamiliar noise, coming with the twitches, grunts of effort it sounded like. The rope's motions got tighter and tighter, the grunts got louder and louder. His breath knocked out, sucking for air himself, Luther listened respectfully. Was it that much work —hanging?

Then the whole barn seemed to shift, get up and crawl a little under him. Maurice's hay-colored hair, sticking straight up, was reappearing over the strawy edge of the loft.

Now, when he had discussed the possibility of Maurice coming back from the dead with him a few minutes before, it had never occurred to Luther that he might really do it. The rope was still taut. It still held his weight, clearly, it still twitched and wiggled. But Maurice's hair was not down there at the end of it where it should have been. It was, somehow, bobbing or floating or flying back up toward the loft again, back toward Luther.

And there was Maurice's whole head, staring at Luther over the edge. It opened its mouth several times to speak, but there was just a gurgle. At last it said, in a surprised, interested voice, "This mare's foaling." There was a little whistling sound, and the head disappeared again.

Luther sat there staring. Maurice had just come back from the dead to tell him his mare was foaling. Then he said, "What?" He jumped up and ran over to the edge. There was Maurice, all of him, head and arms and legs, wrapped around the rope, grinning up at Luther, looking livelier than Luther had seen him in years. "Hell, Maurice," Luther said. "You're going to have to do better than this. You ain't anywhere near dead." He grabbed hold of the rope and hauled Maurice in hand-over-hand, like a big fish, and they both scrambled back down the ladder.

And there was Wiggy, the silver birth-sack already sticking out of her like a great big light bulb. A front foot already visible in it. Luther walked in and looked at it. "Big foot," he said, looking at Maurice. "Real big foot."

And she was a little mare. They pulled, she pushed. She got up and she lay down. The head was hard. "Pull, Maurice," Luther said. "He just winked at me." The chest was harder. "Come on, baby," Luther said to Wiggy. "You're getting it." The hips were impossible, it seemed. "We've got to rock him," Luther said. They grabbed the forelegs of the foal and swung them in half-circles. "Like twisting the cork out of a bottle," Luther said, grinning at Maurice. "You ought to be good at this." The foal thrashed, throwing them around. "Hold on, boy," Maurice said. "You're about there." At last the mare gave a huge groan, and the whole thing came squirting out with a big rush.

Then there was all the navel-painting and cleaning up and rubbing on the colt and talking to him and getting him up to nurse, which took forever because he was so big. At last they sat at the end of the stall full of clean new straw, one in each corner, while Wiggy took her ease at the other end, with her new colt beside her. Not yet gray or bay or brown, his soft, mysterious, undersea color, indefinable, silky, shining from within, his beautiful neck arched as he rested, nose on the ground. He had a great big white star, just like his mama did.

Luther had seen that star in a lot of winner's circle pictures. Wiggy had been a good racemare, but she hadn't become the broodmare he had meant for her to be. She'd had some nice horses for him, though—the best he'd bred, in fact. And he still believed in her, unlike some of the mares he'd kept. And last year, because she'd foaled so late, he'd gotten her to a better horse than he'd ever dreamed of being able to breed to. It was more money than he'd wanted to spend. "But you've got to keep gambling," he said to himself, "to keep your mind limber."

Still, Luther had always been amazed by how much class his horses lost just in the process of growing up. When they were born they were all Derby or Oaks winners. As weanlings, they won major stakes. When they were yearlings, it was just minor stakes. And when they went off to the races, he just hoped for a good solid $7,500 claimer.

But that's the way it is with all of us, I guess, he thought. Look at Maurice—riding high at seventeen, then retiring early, as they say in the *Form*. Wanting to hang himself at forty-one. And here he himself was. He'd made a little splash early on, raised some nice horses, sold some high-priced yearlings. But the champions he'd known he was raising when he was young had somehow become just horses. He was still just a small breeder. He still mucked his own stalls and rubbed his own yearlings. And he still had his hand on every one of his horses, every day, and he knew by now that was what he did it for.

But he looked now at the foal in the straw before him, his

quick breathing and perfect little head and the complex of bones that would round out into sweet, smooth horseflesh and carry him to his fate. And he saw that white star getting larger and larger, coming down the lane at him like the engine light on a fast freight train, while the others in the field rattled along, behind forever.

"He could be any kind," Maurice said, startling him, reading his thoughts. And then doing it again, speaking softly, kindly, almost laughing, "You was trying to kill me. Wasn't you?"

Luther grinned at Maurice. "For a minute there I thought I might have to," he said. "You can kill yourself all you want," he added, "but you ain't doing it in my foaling barn." He knew all that didn't make any sense. But Maurice nodded, as if he understood it perfectly. Luther rubbed his sore middle. "What did you hit me with, anyway?"

Maurice grinned back at him. "My head. I rammed you so hard I went over backwards."

"That figures," Luther said, nodding. "I thought you was a goner. But you grabbed onto the rope, didn't you, when you went off? And then you climbed right back up it, like a bobcat on a leash." He shook his head. "I should've tied your hands back behind you, you know. Like they do in the cowboy movies. Do a job, do it right."

"Don't worry about it," Maurice said, quietly, drowsily, watching the foal. "It don't matter."

Luther groaned and pulled himself upright, ready at last to go home to bed. But he stood there a minute, listening to the meadowlarks outside singing their high, sweet songs, the sound reaching out to the edge of hearing and beyond, till it seemed to him, as he listened, that the whole world was just one great, big, green meadow starred with dandelions and full of racehorses, their long silhouettes sliding along fluid and silent, their reverent, long necks bowed to the earth. He glanced over at Maurice, wondering if he could understand that, too.

But Maurice was asleep, his face looking softer and younger in the coming light, delivered from his nightmares into morning dreams, as they had both been delivered back into their innocence by the neat, smooth, strapping, velvet fellow they had just helped into the world. His mama was up now and eating around him in a circle, her nose turned always to him as if she were tethered. Around them, in the foaling barn, all the other mares were standing quiet in their stalls, looking out the windows at the rising sun.

Janice Eidus

PANDORA'S BOX

Pandora was a phone sex worker. She worked in an office in a dingy building in SoHo. About six other women worked the shift with her, from eight at night until three in the morning. "I give phone," was the way that some of the other women described what they did. Pandora preferred saying, "I'm a worker in the phone sex industry."

Pandora was not a prostitute. She resented the term "phone whore." Her clients didn't know her real name. They couldn't touch her, see her, give her diseases, make her pregnant. She sold words and images and voices, not her body. Never her body.

Unlike some of the other women with whom she worked, Pandora lived quietly; she didn't drink or take drugs. She didn't trust herself to. She feared that if she allowed herself even one glass of wine, one pill, it would all be over for her. She would be opening a box that wasn't meant to be opened.

Pandora's job didn't pay much. She lived in a dark studio apartment on the first floor of a building on Eighth Avenue, in Times Square, next door to a strip show joint. The neighborhood was rampant with muggers and crack dealers, but Pandora couldn't afford to move. She kept her hair short, and wore loose-fitting jeans and T-shirts, so as not to call attention to herself. And it wasn't as though rich women on Sutton Place never got raped or murdered. Where you lived didn't matter, not really. The world was a dangerous place.

Many of Pandora's clients wanted her to be a dominatrix. As a dominatrix, she used the name Queen Bee. Her slaves liked her to order them to get down on their knees so she could whip them until they bled. They liked for her to humiliate them in various ways—to call them filthy names and pretend she was smearing excrement on them, for instance, and then not allow them to clean themselves up. The slavemen also liked to be ordered to wear diapers. They liked her to shove high-heeled shoes down their throats.

Other of her clients asked Pandora to be a little girl, a little girl who deserved a spanking for being so naughty. She spoke to those clients in a lisping, breathy, sing-song voice. Poutingly she would say, "Oh, Daddy, I've been such a bad, bad little girl!" Those clients knew her by the name of Angela, a name she chose because it sounded angelic and innocent, and because innocence was precisely what those clients wished to abuse.

Sometimes, she was asked to have sex with a dog—usually a mean-looking German shepherd—or a horse. Frequently, she was raped. She was asked to throw grapefruit at men and to lick the juice off their bodies. She was bound and gagged and tied up with nylon stockings. She was suspended from the ceiling on meat hooks.

She never actually did any of these things. Never. She, herself, was inviolate. Untouchable. Always in control. It was just fantasy, just impersonal dialogue transmitted over phone wires between strangers. The name of the company she worked for was Phantasy Phone-Phun. Pandora never felt sexy, or sensual, over the phone. She believed that what she did was a kind of social work—helping frustrated and lonely men to obtain a small bit of pleasure in their lives. She was also contributing to society, helping to prevent these men from acting out their very dangerous fantasies, from really going out on the street and raping or murdering women. She was offering these men an outlet. She understood their loneliness, their fantasies. In her heart, she knew these men, had always known them.

A lot of the other women at Phantasy Phone-Phun wanted to be glamorous movie stars. Like Pandora, they had fled to New York from small towns and unhappy homes. Most, like Pandora, had never finished high school. But unlike Pandora, the ones who wanted to be movie stars perceived what they did at Phantasy Phone-Phun as theater, as a rehearsal for bigger and better roles to come. Pandora felt sorry for those women because they were deluding themselves. A few of them made porn films, and were hoping to be discovered that way. A few stripped in the strip joint next door to her building in Times Square.

Pandora, Pandora, come here, Pandora!" her father, the judge, the powerful judge, in the sleepy upstate New York college town, used to call out to her when she was a little girl. She had no choice but to go to him. He would lock the door. "My little girl," he would say, "my little Pandora and her little box." When Pandora got into the big, creaky bed with him, everything turned abruptly to a dream. It had to be a dream, because her real daddy, the man who bought her sweet candies and salty, crunchy pretzel sticks, the man who loved her more than anyone else in the whole world, the man who was respected by all the people in their town—that man

would never do anything mean to her. Real daddies didn't
hurt their daughters; real daddies protected their daughters.
So, she wasn't there, not really, when this dream thing happened with this man who was not her daddy—this man who
had stepped right out of her dark nightmares, out of her most
frightening and horrid fantasies. Afterward she didn't remember what had happened. She didn't even remember having dreamed him.

When Pandora was a little girl, she resented her name. She'd
read the tale of Pandora in a book of mythology for children.
She hadn't liked the girl Pandora in the myth, even if she was
beautiful and even if her name meant "the gift of all." It
seemed to her that the other Pandora was a very, very bad
and guilty little girl for doing such a thing, for having so little
self-control, for opening the lid of that box and unleashing
sorrow and evil and plagues upon the world, despite having
been warned never, never to open the box. That other Pandora had too many desires, too much passion, for a nice little
girl. And Pandora didn't like the ending of the myth, either,
when the other Pandora finds Hope at the bottom of the box,
in the guise of a butterfly. The other Pandora must have been
a ninny to believe in Hope. Pandora, herself, already knew
better than to believe in anything.

One afternoon, her heart racing, she found the courage to tell
her father how much she hated her name. In a soft voice, she
asked him, please, to change her name to something very
simple, like Margaret or Mary. Her father was sitting in the
deep brown leather armchair in his wood-paneled den. He
poured himself a drink. When she was finished explaining
her reasons for hating her name, he spoke very slowly. He
said that she should remember that she wasn't the real Pandora from the myth. Nobody blamed her for evil; and at the
same time, nobody was forcing her to feel hopeful if she

didn't feel that way. Myths aren't real, he said, myths explain the unexplainable, offer rationales for the irrational. He described myths from other cultures: the myth of Gilgamesh from ancient Sumeria; the myth of the Native American trickster. Many people, he told her, believe that the Bible is one big myth. Besides, he said, the world was filled with self-involved, narcissistic people who cared only about themselves, and nobody else really gave a damn whether Pandora was named Pandora or Athena or Aphrodite. He waved his drink and spilled some on his lap, and said he was tired of explaining all this to her. "You're just paranoid, Pandora," he said finally, "and paranoia is the ultimate narcissism."

Paranoia was a major subject in their household, which consisted of Pandora, her two older brothers, and her father. This was because her mother had been diagnosed as a paranoid schizophrenic and was in the hospital. Or, as Pandora liked to say—*in hospital*—the way she'd heard it said by British characters on TV.

Pandora had few memories of her mother, who had died *in hospital*. These were the memories she did have: herself, as a very little girl in a pink flared dress, watching from her seat on the curb where her mother has deposited her, while her mother stands in the street directing traffic in her ripped ankle-length housedress, until the police come and take her away, and her mother claws and spits at them, as Pandora begins to cry.

Another memory: her mother walking naked in their garden, with a checkered bandana tied rakishly around her neck, dancing and twirling her arms, shouting, "I am a butterfly!" over and over again, scaring Pandora, who is watching from a window, wondering why her mother is stealing the butterfly image from her myth, wondering if her own sad mother is trying to communicate something to the world about Hope.

And another: her mother not getting out of bed for months and months, so that Pandora has to get ready all by herself for school, has to remember to put her clothes out the night before, has to learn how to iron and wash clothes, how to cook meals for her father and brothers, how to give her father massages just the way he likes them late at night after he's worked all day at the courthouse where he's a very important man, and it's crucial that Pandora learn to relax him just the way he likes, although she hates to do it, hates the way her father's flesh feels beneath her small hands.

When Pandora was in seventh grade, her father wouldn't allow her to go to boy-girl parties even though the parents of all the other girls let their daughters go, as long as the parties were supervised. Her father said that Pandora was not as responsible as the other girls, and that she would get in trouble at an earlier age than the rest of them because she was so vulnerable and silly, because her head was too easily turned by flattery.

On a Saturday afternoon, when she was in ninth grade, she put on a pink, gauzy, short dress, which she'd bought at the mall with her allowance money the week before. The dress was so beautiful, she felt like a princess in it. As she stood staring at herself in the mirror, her father walked into her bedroom. He yelled at her and told her to change her clothes, told her that she looked like a tramp. She protested, "Daddy, all the girls wear short dresses now! Barbara wears them, and Linda and Suzie and everyone . . ." He said, "Barbara and Linda and Suzie and the other girls don't have bodies like yours!" His voice was cold. "No," she said, defying him at last, hating him with all her heart, her voice throbbing, her jaw clenched. He ripped the dress right off her, shredding its delicate fabric. She began to cry, standing there in her white cotton panties. He turned away from her and left the room, throwing the ripped dress at her feet.

Pandora's middle brother killed himself when he was sixteen. Pandora was thirteen. She was the one who found him. She opened the front door and found him in the living room, on the sofa. The gun was in his mouth. He had made a mess. Pandora vomited, and then cleaned up after herself before calling her father at the courthouse. Nobody knew how her middle brother had gotten hold of her father's gun. Pandora's father held her and comforted her all night long. He told her it wasn't her fault. A suicide note was found the next morning on her brother's bureau. The suicide note was incoherent and ranting, declaring that Satan was living in their midst, right in their house, and that Pandora should run for her life, should flee the devil. Her father, who hadn't wept when he saw her brother, wept when he read the note. Later, he threw the note into the fireplace and burned it right in front of Pandora.

When Pandora was a senior in high school, she had a crush on a boy she sometimes saw. Although his father was a banker, he affected a street boy's stance and attitude. When the boy asked her out, Pandora defied her father, who forbid her to date. She agreed to meet the boy at Suzie's house, so her father wouldn't know. She had sex with him the very first time they went out. But she felt nothing, nothing at all during the act, although she yearned to feel something—arousal, contentment, fear, anything at all—but she was numb. In that boy's arms, she had gone somewhere else. Being with him had become a dream. Yet in the midst of that dream she knew exactly what to do to the boy to give him pleasure, although she wasn't sure how she had come to have this knowledge. The boy told his friends about her the very next day. She had sex with the rest of them, one after another, for a period of three weeks, sometimes with two a night, until one of the boys' mothers found out and called Pandora's father and told him.

When Pandora's father got home that night, he made her pull down both her pants and her panties, even though she was much too old to have to do that in front of him, and he beat her with a strap. She held in her screams. She didn't want him to see how much he could still hurt her, although a part of her wished she could scream so loud that the whole world would know what he was doing.

The very next day, after her father had left for the courthouse, she packed a large bag and took a train to New York. She bought a newspaper in the train station, and by that evening, had found herself the apartment in Times Square and the job at Phantasy Phone-Phun. She was eighteen years old, and she felt very adult; she didn't write or call her father. She did call the boy, the one she'd had a crush on, but he didn't want to talk to her.

Pandora had a very high I.Q. She had been told this by her seventh-grade English teacher, who'd heard it from her guidance counselor. The day she learned this, she raced home, proud and eager to tell her father the good news. Her father said, "Don't think you're special just because some old battle-ax of a teacher thinks you are." Pandora learned the next day from her oldest brother that her mother, too, had been extremely smart and had been at the top of her college graduating class, had even written poetry that had been published in magazines—before she'd been diagnosed as crazy.

Pandora began to fear that, like her mother, her high I.Q. would drive her to madness. Already, Pandora secretly suspected that she was crazy, different, not like other people, not really like Barbara and Linda and Suzie, even though they were her very, very best friends. Pandora promised herself that she would never again let anyone know how smart she was, that she would never read or write poetry, or do anything to call attention to her mind, so that her father would never be able to put her *in hospital*, the way he had her mother.

In high school, Pandora had been sent to the school psychologist by the principal because her low grades didn't match her high I.Q. The school psychologist wore thick glasses, a beard, and a nubby wool sweater with a reindeer design. "Close your eyes," he said, "and imagine that a boy is touching you, fondling you." Pandora, sitting across the room in a leather chair, wearing a plaid jumper, crossed her ankles and did as she was told. "What do you feel?" he asked her. "Nothing," she answered, truthfully. He told her to keep her eyes closed. She heard him rising from his chair, which creaked. He touched her breast through her jumper. "What do you feel now?" he asked. "Nothing," she whispered. He put his hand beneath her skirt, inside her white cotton panties. "And now?" he asked. Although Pandora continued to sit very still and to do as he told her, she didn't answer, because she was no longer really there, no longer in the room with him.

Pandora called her father the day of her nineteenth birthday. She'd been living in New York and working at Phantasy Phone-Phun for a full year. She expected him to yell and scream. Instead, he began to cry, saying he'd missed her and how sorry he was that he'd taken the strap to her that time, and how he wanted her to forgive him, he needed her to forgive him, he'd lost control because he'd been so worried about her, what he had done may have been misguided but it was for her own good, and he hadn't deserved to be abandoned by her. He knew she was still a good girl despite what she had done. He'd hired a private detective, but nothing had turned up. He'd feared she was dead. He had nightmares. He couldn't sleep. He was sick with worry.

She agreed, finally, to meet him for lunch. He took the long train ride down to Manhattan. They met at a restaurant she knew, west of Times Square on Tenth Avenue. She wore the only dress she still owned from when she'd lived at home and had been a high school student—it was rayon, with a polka-dot design, and she felt like an imposter in it. Her father walked into the restaurant, fifteen minutes late, because his cab driver had deliberately taken a long way around. He looked much older and frailer than when she'd last seen him. He wore bifocals and his nose ran. It broke her heart to see him that way. But she resisted the urge to hold him and comfort him and say she was coming back home, which was what he wanted. When he asked her how she supported herself, she said she was a secretary. He offered her money. She refused. She stood and said she had to go. But after that she agreed to have lunch with him every few months.

Her father brought her oldest brother and his wife along to one of their lunches. They met at a French restaurant on the East Side that her brother's wife had seen advertised in a magazine. Pandora felt out of place in such an elegant restaurant. Her brother was now a lawyer in their hometown, living only five minutes from their father. He drank three martinis during lunch, and hardly spoke. Whenever their father said anything, her brother looked away and shut his eyes tight. When Pandora excused herself to go to the Ladies Room, her brother's wife followed her. In front of the brilliantly-lit mirror over the sink, as Pandora washed her hands with the restaurant's lavender-scented soap, her brother's wife said angrily, "Your brother is a drunk and a basket case, and I don't know how much more I can take!"

Soon after that lunch, her father died. Her brother called Pandora to tell her. Their father had left most of his money to various charities. Pandora and her brother each received a very small amount. Pandora didn't care. She didn't want his money.

Her brother made all the funeral arrangements. Pandora took the train upstate. Her brother's wife met her at the station, but she and Pandora said nothing to each other during the drive to the funeral parlour. Pandora remained dry-eyed during the entire service. Before she left, she hugged her brother, who was also dry-eyed, and whose breath reeked of alcohol.

A few weeks after the funeral, Pandora remembered for the very first time what used to happen after her father would call to her, "Pandora, Pandora . . ." She remembered what took place behind those closed doors, in his bedroom, on his bed, beneath his covers, on top of his sheets, in the bathroom, in his car, everywhere. For the first time, she remembered the nightmare of her childhood, the horror that lay at the very core of her being, the horror that had always defined her, that had marked and branded her, although she'd never known it. She screamed. She howled like a beast, wrapping herself in a blanket. She held a razor to her wrists, to her throat. She thought about putting her head in the oven, about running into the streets and jumping off a subway platform. Instead, she lay rigidly on the cold floor of her apartment, willing the memories out of her head, willing them far, far away, willing herself to feel nothing.

About a month later, while she was riding the subway downtown to work, the memories returned. She had convinced herself that she could will them away forever, but now, as she clung to the overhead strap in the crowded, hot subway car, as her body swayed with the subway's movements, she saw that the memories were far more powerful than she, and that they would continue to surface and haunt her whenever they chose—only they didn't feel exactly like memories now, not so distanced, they felt more like visions, hallucinatory visions, like the flashbacks she'd heard that soldiers had after a war. The subway kept lurching, and the flashbacks kept coming, clearer and clearer: "Pandora, Pandora," her father would call. She saw her middle brother touching her while her father stood above them, ordering her brother to touch her harder, harder, and deeper, deeper. When the subway reached her stop, she ran out of the car, onto the platform, and upstairs to the street. She walked the streets of SoHo for an hour until she felt calm enough to step into the offices of Phantasy Phone-Phun, not caring that she'd be docked an hour from her paycheck.

Her first call that night came from one of her regular clients. He wanted Queen Bee to call him filthy names and to tell him over and over how worthless he was. When she was finished with him, another regular client called for Angela. He wanted Angela to wear a frilly, transparent little slip and no panties, and he wanted to tie her by her wrists to a closet door. A third client, a new one, wanted her to listen as he called her a bitch and a whore and a slut.

After work that night, Pandora invited one of the other women, Nilda, out for coffee. She didn't feel ready to go home; she dreaded getting back on the subway. She and Nilda decided to walk uptown to a coffee shop in the West Village. Nilda, who was just five feet tall, always wore very high heels and walked slowly.

While they waited for a light to change on Sixth Avenue, Nilda said, "Pandora is such a different name. Is it real?" Pandora had long ago stopped thinking much about her name one way or another. She figured that Nilda, who'd grown up in a poor village in Puerto Rico, had probably never heard of the myth. Pandora shrugged. "It's real enough," she said, and the light changed.

Because it was three a.m., the coffee shop was filled with hookers, pimps, transvestites, and a few other haunted-looking women who reminded Pandora of herself. Nilda ordered scrambled eggs. Pandora sipped a cup of black coffee. Nilda was sleepy, slightly rambling. She had two kids, and had kicked a major drug habit a few years before. She lived with an aunt in East Harlem who thought she was a private nurse working a late-night shift. Pandora only half-listened to Nilda's complaints about how little they were paid at Phantasy Phone-Phun, and how expensive children's clothes were. The flashbacks were threatening to start up again, and Pandora was trying to will them away; at the same time, she longed to confide in Nilda about her father and what he had done to her. But what if Nilda didn't believe that such things could happen, or what if she blamed Pandora? Even though Pandora liked Nilda, she didn't trust her—she didn't really trust a soul in the world—and besides, it wouldn't change a thing either way, whether she told Nilda or not.

Pandora paid the check for both of them. "Catch you tomorrow, Pandora," Nilda said, as they parted outside the restaurant. Pandora almost called her back to tell her, but didn't. Instead, she stepped out into the street and hailed a taxi, dreading too much getting back on the subway while the flashbacks were threatening once again to overtake her.

The phone rang a month later, waking Pandora out of a half-sleep. It was her oldest brother's wife, calling to say that Pandora's brother was dead. "How?" Pandora asked. His wife spoke coldly: "He threw himself off a bridge." Pandora pictured her brother sinking beneath deep black water, helplessly gasping for air.

The flashbacks came again, stronger than ever, as soon as she'd hung up the phone. This time she saw her oldest brother looking sleepy, with his hair all mussed, standing in his pajamas at the foot of their father's bed, watching as her father did something to her that looked like tickling, but wasn't. She heard her father telling her brother to join them in the bed. She wished then, more than anything else in the world, that her oldest brother were still alive. She wanted to tell him that she, too, had remembered, and that she didn't blame him for what their father had forced him to do when he'd been far too young to understand, or to resist.

Pandora took a lover. She had never had one before, hadn't craved sex or intimacy since the day she had run away from home. But now, after her oldest brother's death, sleep came less and less easily to her, and she found herself wanting to be held. Her lover's name was Charlie, and he lived in a studio apartment on the top floor of her building. He was her age, and handsome, with dark hair, and a cleft chin. Although he acted in porno movies, he had no illusions of becoming a famous movie star.

One summer night, in Charlie's apartment, after Pandora had cooked dinner for him, and after Charlie had had a few beers, they made love, which had become their usual pattern. As always, Pandora felt neither desire nor arousal during the act, because she saw her father's face, and felt her father's hands upon her skin, even though she knew that it was Charlie lying on top of her, Charlie entering her so forcefully she feared she would split apart and die. She knew, too, how to pretend desire, and she didn't think Charlie suspected.

Afterward, she lay quietly in Charlie's arms. His bed was too narrow for the both of them. It was hot, and the windows were wide open. Pandora's skin was sticky and wet. A radio outside was blasting rap music. But despite everything—her lack of desire during sex, the narrow bed, the heat, and the pounding music—Pandora felt closer to Charlie at that moment than she had ever felt to anyone. He had been her steady, nightly lover for three months; she, who deserved nothing, had been given a gift.

The music outside stopped, and as she lay very still in his arms, almost before she knew she was doing it, she was telling Charlie the truth about her childhood, about her family. At first she spoke hesitantly, but soon her voice grew more forceful. She told him about the suicide of her two brothers, and about how her middle brother had looked when she found him. She told him about the coldness in her oldest brother's wife's voice when she had called with the news of his death.

Pandora also told Charlie about her mother, the naked, dancing butterfly-lady who had died *in hospital*, and whom Pandora could not forgive. "I believe," she said to Charlie, speaking aloud what she always had been afraid to articulate, even to herself, "that my mother *chose* to go crazy rather than to admit what was happening, rather than to try to rescue her own children." Charlie lay his head upon Pandora's shoulder, and her eyes filled with tears, so that finally she was able to tell him everything, all the terrible things that her father used to do to her after he'd called her into his room. "He was a monster. A *monster*," she repeated. It felt good to say the word aloud to someone else, to shame her father and to lay blame on him, at last.

Pandora described to Charlie the way she felt when the flashbacks came, the way she couldn't breathe and felt as though she would never be able to breathe again. For a long moment, Charlie didn't say anything. Then he said he believed her completely. She was so grateful she lifted up his hand and kissed his fingers one by one—the sort of impassioned, romantic gesture she'd seen actresses make in movies but which she had never before been inspired to make—and she allowed her lips to caress each of his fingers slowly and lovingly.

Pandora wanted to make love again, thinking that perhaps this time she would experience real desire, but Charlie sat up and began complaining about his poorly-maintained apartment and the rough Times Square neighborhood. He told Pandora that he was thinking of moving to L.A., where it was so much warmer and prettier, and where he could live in a house right on the beach.

After Charlie fell asleep that night, the flashbacks came. Pandora bit into her wrist to stifle her sobs, and lay rigidly so as not to disturb and wake him on the narrow bed.

Soon after, Charlie moved to L.A., and Pandora saw no point in taking another lover. She preferred her solitude once again, preferred to be alone with her feelings of self-loathing and shame and rage when the flashbacks came.

During the next few months, Pandora noticed that Nilda was losing a lot of weight. Nilda had also developed a raspy, hoarse cough that wouldn't go away. The doctors finally told Nilda what Pandora had suspected: Nilda had AIDS. Her condition deteriorated rapidly, and very soon she was too weak to come to work.

A timid girl from Korea who wanted to be a fashion designer took Nilda's place at Phantasy Phone-Phun. Pandora missed Nilda. One afternoon, Pandora rode the subway uptown to visit Nilda in the hospital. There were no other visitors. Nilda lay, tiny, shrunken, hairless, covered with sores, almost unrecognizable.

Nilda tried to lift her head to greet Pandora, but couldn't. Pandora reached for Nilda's hand and held it gently, fearing that even normal pressure would break those fragile bones. "I'm so sleepy," Nilda said. Her voice was soft, and Pandora had to lean way down in order to hear her. "Pandora . . . your name is so different . . . ," Nilda whispered, and then drifted off to sleep.

Pandora continued to sit at Nilda's bedside, continued to hold her wraithlike hand in her own, watching as Nilda slept a troubled sleep. Pandora longed to lie down beside Nilda, longed to share in her pain and her dying. And she saw for the very first time the terrible irony—and the terrible truth—

of the myth after which she had been named. She saw that her myth, like all myths, had no real ending, that it was destined to be repeated and repeated, in different guises, forever and ever. She saw that there were girls like herself, and boys like her brothers, all over the world, girls and boys who were destined to remember, and then not to remember, destined to open boxes, and then to close them tight, destined to reach out as far as they could to grasp onto Hope, only to see Hope fly away just beyond their reach, forever and ever.

Judith Ortiz Cofer

NADA

Almost as soon as Doña Ernestina got the telegram about her son having been killed in Vietnam, she started giving her possessions away. At first we didn't realize what she was doing. By the time we did, it was too late.

The Army people had comforted Doña Ernestina with the news that her son's "remains" would have to be "collected and shipped" back to New Jersey at some later date, since other "personnel" had also been lost on the same day. In other words, she would have to wait until Tony's body could be processed.

Processed. Doña Ernestina spoke that word like a curse when she told us. We were all down in *El Basement*—that's what we called the cellar of our apartment building: no windows for light, boilers making such a racket that you could scream bloody murder and almost no one would hear you. Some of us had started meeting here on Saturday mornings— as much to talk as to wash our clothes—and over the years it became a sort of women's club, where we could catch up on a week's worth of gossip. That Saturday, however, I had dreaded going down the cement steps. All of us had just heard the news about Tony the night before.

I should have known the minute I saw her, holding court in her widow's costume, that something had cracked inside Doña Ernestina. She was in full *luto*—black from head to toe, including a mantilla. In contrast, Lydia and Isabelita were both in rollers and bathrobes: our customary uniform for these Saturday-morning gatherings—maybe our way of saying "No Men Allowed." As I approached them, Lydia stared at me with a scared-rabbit look in her eyes.

Doña Ernestina simply waited for me to join the other two leaning against the machines before she continued explaining what had happened when the news of Tony had arrived at her door the day before. She spoke calmly, a haughty expression on her face, looking like an offended duchess in her beautiful black dress. She was pale, pale, but she had a wild look in her eyes. The officer had told her that—when the time came—they would bury Tony with "full military honors"; for now they were sending her the medal and a flag. But she had said, "No, gracias," to the funeral, and she sent the flag and medals back marked *Ya no vive aquí:* Does not live here anymore. "Tell the Mr. President of the United States what I say: *No, gracias.*"

Then she waited for our response.

Lydia shook her head, indicating that she was speechless. And Elenita looked pointedly at me, forcing me to be the one to speak the words of sympathy for all of us, to reassure Doña Ernestina that she had done exactly what any of us would have done in her place: Yes, we would have all said *No, gracias* to any president who had actually tried to pay for a son's life with a few trinkets and a folded flag.

Doña Ernestina nodded gravely. Then she picked up the stack of neatly folded men's shirts from the sofa (a discard we had salvaged from the sidewalk) and walked regally out of El Basement.

Lydia, who had gone to high school with Tony, burst into tears as soon as Doña Ernestina was out of sight. Elenita and I sat her down between us on the sofa and held her until she had let most of it out. Lydia is still young—a woman not yet visited too often by *la muerte*. Her husband of six months had just gotten his draft notice, and they have been trying for a baby—trying very hard. The walls of El Building are thin enough so that it has become a secret joke (kept only from Lydia and Roberto) that he is far more likely to escape the draft due to acute exhaustion than by becoming a father.

"Doesn't Doña Ernestina feel *anything?*" Lydia asked in between sobs. "Did you see her, dressed up like an actress in a play—and not one tear for her son?"

"We all have different ways of grieving," I said, though I couldn't help thinking that there *was* a strangeness to Doña Ernestina, and that Lydia was right when she said that the woman seemed to be acting out a part. "I think we should wait and see what she is going to do."

"Maybe," said Elenita. "Did you get a visit from *El Padre* yesterday?"

We nodded, not surprised to learn that all of us had gotten personal calls from Padre Alvaro, our painfully shy priest, after Doña Ernestina had frightened him away. Apparently El Padre had come to her apartment immediately after hearing about Tony, expecting to comfort the woman as he had when Don Antonio died suddenly a year ago. Her grief then had been understandable in its immensity, for she had been burying not only her husband but also the dream shared by many of the barrio women her age—that of returning with her man to the Island after retirement, of buying a *casita* in the old pueblo, and of being buried on native ground alongside *la familia*. People *my* age—those of us born or raised here—have had our mothers drill this fantasy into our brains all of our lives. So when Don Antonio dropped his head on the dominoes table, scattering the ivory pieces of the best game of the year, and when he was laid out in his best black suit at Ramirez' Funeral Home, all of us knew how to talk to the grieving widow.

That was the last time we saw both her men. Tony was there—home on a two-day pass from basic training—and he cried like a little boy over his father's handsome face, calling him *Papi, Papi.* Doña Ernestina had had a full mother's duty then, taking care of the hysterical boy. It was a normal chain of grief, the strongest taking care of the weakest. We buried Don Antonio at Garden State Memorial Park, where there are probably more Puerto Ricans than on the Island. Padre Alvaro said his sermon in a soft, trembling voice that was barely audible over the cries of the boy being supported on one side by his mother, impressive in her quiet strength and dignity, and on the other by Cheo, owner of the *bodega* where Don Antonio had played dominoes with other barrio men of his age for over twenty years.

Just about everyone from El Building had attended that funeral, and it had been done right. Doña Ernestina had sent her son off to fight for America and then had started collecting her widow's pension. Some of us asked Doña Iris (who knew how to read cards) about Doña Ernestina's future, and Doña Iris had said: "A long journey within a year"—which fit with what we had thought would happen next: Doña Ernestina would move back to the Island and wait with her relatives for Tony to come home from the war. Some older women actually went home when they started collecting social security or pensions, but that was rare. Usually, it seemed to me, somebody had to die before the island dream would come true for women like Doña Ernestina. As for my friends and me, we talked about "vacations" in the Caribbean. But we knew that if life was hard for us in this barrio, it would be worse in a pueblo where no one knew us (and had maybe only heard of our parents before they came to *los estados unidos de América*, where most of us had been brought as children).

When Padre Alvaro had knocked softly on my door, I yanked it open, thinking it was that ex-husband of mine asking for a second chance again. (That's just the way Miguel knocks when he's sorry for leaving me—about once a week—when he wants a loan.) So I was wearing my Go-to-Hell face when I threw open the door, and the poor priest nearly jumped out of his skin. I saw him take a couple of deep breaths before he asked me in his slow way—he tries to hide his stutter by dragging out his words—if I knew whether or not Doña Ernestina was ill. After I said, "No, not that I know," Padre Alvaro just stood there looking pitiful until I asked him if he cared to come in. I had been sleeping on the sofa and watching TV all afternoon, and I really didn't want him to see the mess, but I had nothing to fear. The poor man actually took one step back at my invitation. No, he was in a hurry, he had a few other parishioners to visit, etc. These were difficult times, he said, so-so-so many young people lost to drugs or dying in the wa-wa-war. I asked him if *he* thought Doña Ernestina was sick, but he just shook his head. The man looked like an orphan at my door with those sad, brown eyes. He was actually appealing in a homely way: that long nose nearly touched the tip of his chin when he smiled, and his big crooked teeth broke my heart.

"She does not want to speak to me," Padre Alvaro said as he caressed a large silver crucifix that hung on a thick chain around his neck. He seemed to be dragged down by its weight, stoop-shouldered and skinny as he was.

I felt a strong impulse to feed him some of my chicken soup, still warm on the stove from my supper. Contrary to what Lydia says about me behind my back, I like living by myself. And I could not have been happier to have that mama's boy Miguel back where he belonged—with his mother who thought that he was still her baby. But this scraggly thing at my door needed home cooking and maybe even something more than a hot meal to bring a little spark into his life. (I mentally asked God to forgive me for having thoughts like these about one of his priests. *Ay bendito,* but they too are made of flesh and blood.)

"Maybe she just needs a little more time, Padre," I said in as comforting a voice as I could manage. Unlike the other women in El Building, I am not convinced that priests are truly necessary—or even much help—in times of crisis.

"*Sí, hija,* perhaps you're right," he muttered sadly—calling me "daughter" even though I'm pretty sure I'm five or six years older. (Padre Alvaro seems so "untouched" that it's hard to tell *his* age. I mean, when you live, it shows. He looks hungry for love, starving himself by choice.) I promised him that I would look in on Doña Ernestina. Without another word, he made the sign of the cross in the air between us and turned away. As I heard his slow steps descending the creaky stairs, I asked myself: What do priests dream about?

When El Padre's name came up again during that Saturday meeting in El Basement, I asked my friends what *they* thought a priest dreamed about. It was a fertile subject, so much so that we spend the rest of our laundry time coming up with scenarios. Before the last dryer stopped we all agreed that we could not receive communion the next day at Mass unless we went to confession that afternoon and told another priest, not Alvaro, about our "unclean thoughts."

As for Doña Ernestina's situation, we agreed that we should be there for her if she called, but the decent thing to do, we decided, was give her a little more time alone. Lydia kept repeating, in that childish way of hers, that "something is wrong with the woman," but she didn't volunteer to go see what it was that was making Doña Ernestina act so strangely. Instead she complained that she and Roberto had heard pots and pans banging and things being moved around for hours in 4-D last night—they had hardly been able to sleep. Isabelita winked at me behind Lydia's back. Lydia and Roberto still had not caught on: if they could hear what was going on in

4-D, the rest of us could also get an earful of what went on in 4-A. They were just kids who thought they had invented sex. I tell you, a *telenovela* could be made from the stories in El Building.

On Sunday Doña Ernestina was not at the Spanish mass, and I avoided Padre Alvaro so he would not ask me about her. But I was worried. Doña Ernestina was a church *cucaracha*—a devout Catholic who, like many of us, did not always do what the priests and the pope ordered, but who knew where God lived. Only a serious illness or tragedy could keep her from attending mass, so afterward I went straight to her apartment and knocked on her door. There was no answer, although I heard scraping and dragging noises, like furniture being moved around. At least she was on her feet and active. Maybe housework was what she needed to snap out of her shock. I decided to try again the next day.

As I went by Lydia's apartment, the young woman opened her door—I knew she had been watching me through the peephole—to tell me about more noises from across the hall during the night. Lydia was in her baby-doll pajamas. Although she stuck only her nose out, I could see Roberto in his jockey underwear, doing something in the kitchen. I couldn't help thinking about Miguel and me when we had first gotten together. We were an explosive combination. After a night of passionate lovemaking, I would walk around thinking: Do not light cigarettes around me. No open flames. Highly combustible materials being transported. But when his mamá showed up at our door, the man of fire turned into a heap of ashes at her feet.

"Let's wait and see what happens," I told Lydia again.

We did not have to wait for long. On Monday Doña Ernestina called to invite us to a wake for Tony, a *velorio*, in her apartment. The word spread fast. Everyone wanted to do something for her. Cheo donated fresh chickens and island produce of all kinds. Several of us got together and made *arroz con pollo*, plus flan for dessert. And Doña Iris made two dozen *pasteles* and wrapped the meat pies in banana leaves that she had been saving in her freezer for her famous Christmas parties. We women carried in our steaming plates, while the men brought in their bottles of Palo Viejo rum for themselves and candy-sweet Manischewitz wine for us. We came ready to spend the night saying our rosaries and praying for Tony's soul.

Doña Ernestina met us at the door and led us into her living room, where the lights were off. A photograph of Tony and one of her deceased husband Don Antonio were sitting on top of a table, surrounded by at least a dozen candles. It was a spooky sight that caused several of the older women to cross themselves. Doña Ernestina had arranged folding chairs in front of this table and told us to sit down. She did not ask us to take our food and drinks to the kitchen. She just looked at each of us individually, as if she were taking attendance in a class, and then said: "I have asked you here to say good-bye to my husband Antonio and my son Tony. You have been my friends and neighbors for twenty years, but they were my life. Now that they are gone, I have *nada*. *Nada*. *Nada*."

I tell you, that word is like a drain that sucks everything down. Hearing her say *nada* over and over made me feel as if I were being yanked into a dark pit. I could feel the others getting nervous too, but here was a woman deep into her pain: we had to give her a little space. She looked around the room, then walked out without saying another word.

As we sat there in silence, stealing looks at each other, we began to hear the sounds of things being moved around in other rooms. One of the older women took charge then, and soon the drinks were poured, the food served—all this while the strange sounds kept coming from different rooms in the apartment. Nobody said much, except once when we heard something like a dish fall and break. Doña Iris pointed her

index finger at her ear and made a couple of circles—and out
of nervousness, I guess, some of us giggled like schoolchil-
dren.

It was a long while before Doña Ernestina came back out to
us. By then we were gathering our dishes and purses, having
come to the conclusion that it was time to leave. Holding two
huge Sears shopping bags, one in each hand, Doña Ernestina
took her place at the front door as if she were a society host-
ess in a receiving line. Some of us women hung back to see
what was going on. But Tito, the building's super, had had
enough and tried to get past her. She took his hand, putting
in it a small ceramic poodle with a gold chain around its neck.
Tito gave the poodle a funny look, glanced at Doña Ernestina
as though he were scared, and hurried away with the dog in
his hand.

We were let out of her place one by one, but not until she
had forced one of her possessions on each of us. She grabbed
without looking from her bags. Out came her prized *minia-
turas,* knickknacks that take a woman a lifetime to collect. Out
came ceramic and porcelain items of all kinds, including
vases and ashtrays. Out came kitchen utensils, dishes, forks,
knives, spoons. Out came old calendars and every small item
that she had touched or been touched by in the last twenty
years. Out came a bronzed baby shoe—and I got that.

As we left the apartment, Doña Iris said "Psst" to some of
us, so we followed her down the hallway. "Doña Ernestina's
faculties are temporarily out of order," she said very seriously. "It is due to the shock of her son's death."

We all said *"Sí"* and nodded our heads.

"But what can we do?" Lydia said, her voice cracking a
little. "What should I do with this?" She was holding one of
Tony's baseball trophies in her hand: 1968 Most Valuable
Player, for the Pocos Locos, our barrio's team.

Doña Iris said, "Let us keep her things safe for her until she
recovers her senses. And let her mourn in peace. These things

take time. If she needs us, she will call us." Doña Iris shrugged her shoulders, "*Así es la vida, hijas:* that's the way life is."

As I passed Tito on the stairs, he shook his head while looking up at Doña Ernestina's door: "I say she needs a shrink. I think somebody should call the social worker." He did not look at me when he mumbled these things. By "somebody" he meant one of us women. He didn't want trouble in his building, and he expected one of us to get rid of the problems. I just ignored him.

In my bed I prayed to the Holy Mother that she would find peace for Doña Ernestina's troubled spirit, but things got worse. All that week Lydia saw strange things happening through the peephole on her door. Every time people came to Doña Ernestina's apartment—to deliver flowers, or telegrams from the Island, or anything—the woman would force something on them. She pleaded with them to take this or that; if they hesitated, she commanded them with those tragic eyes to accept a token of her life.

And they did, walking out of our apartment building carrying cushions, lamps, doilies, clothing, shoes, umbrellas, wastebaskets, schoolbooks, and notebooks: things of value and things of no worth at all to anyone but to the person who had owned them. Eventually winos and street people got the news of the great giveaway in 4-D, and soon there was a line down the stairs and out the door. Nobody went home empty-handed; it was like a soup kitchen. Lydia was afraid to step out of her place because of all the dangerous-looking characters hanging out on that floor. And the smell! Entering our building was like coming into a cheap bar and public urinal combined.

Isabelita, living alone with her two little children and fearing for their safety, was the one who finally called a meeting of the residents. Only the women attended, since the men were truly afraid of Doña Ernestina. It isn't unusual for men to be frightened when they see a woman go crazy. If they are not the cause of her madness, then they act as if they don't understand it, and usually leave us alone to deal with our "woman's problems." This is just as well.

Maybe I *am* just bitter because of Miguel—I know what is said behind my back. But this is a fact: When a woman is in trouble, a man calls in her mamá, her sisters, or her friends, and then he makes himself scarce until it's all over. This happens again and again. At how many bedsides of women have I sat? How many times have I made the doctor's appointment, taken care of the children, and fed the husbands of my friends in the barrio? It is not that the men can't do these things; it's just that they know how much women help each other. Maybe the men even suspect that we know one another better than they know their own wives. As I said, it is just as well that they stay out of our way when there is trouble. It makes things simpler for us.

At the meeting, Isabelita said right away that we should go up to 4-D and try to reason with *la pobre* Doña Ernestina. Maybe we could get her to give us a relative's address in Puerto Rico—the woman obviously needed to be taken care of. What she was doing was putting us all in a very difficult situation. There were no dissenters this time. We voted to go as a group to talk to Doña Ernestina the next morning.

But that night we were all awakened by crashing noises down on the street. In the light of the full moon, I could see that the air was raining household goods: kitchen chairs, stools, a small TV, a nightstand, pieces of a bed frame. Everything was splintering as it landed on the pavement. People were running for cover and yelling up at our building. The problem, I knew instantly, was in Apartment 4-D.

Putting on my bathrobe and slippers, I stepped out into the hallway. Lydia and Roberto were rushing down the stairs, but on the flight above my landing I caught up with Doña Iris and Isabelita, heading toward 4-D. Out of breath, we stood in the fourth-floor hallway, listening to police sirens approaching our building in front. We could hear the slamming of car doors and yelling—in both Spanish and English. Then we tried the door to 4-D. It was unlocked.

We came into a room virtually empty. Even the pictures had been taken down from the walls; all that was left were the nail holes and the lighter places on the paint where the framed photographs had been for years. We took a few seconds to spot Doña Ernestina: she was curled up in the farthest corner of the living room, naked.

"Como salió a éste mundo," said Doña Iris, crossing herself.

Just as she had come into the world. Wearing nothing. Nothing around her except a clean, empty room. Nada. She had left nothing behind—except the bottles of pills, the ones the doctors give to ease the pain, to numb you, to make you feel nothing when someone dies.

The bottles were empty too, and the policemen took them. But we didn't let them take Doña Ernestina until we each had brought up some of our own best clothes and dressed her like the decent woman that she was. *La decencia.* Nothing can ever change that—not even *la muerte.* This is the way life is. *Así es la vida.*

Mary Tannen

ELAINE'S HOUSE

Janet, an editor of children's books, and Alice, who paints wooden jewelry for a living, are sitting on the terrace of Elaine's Nassau house, which Janet has rented for the long Easter weekend, Thursday through Sunday. Alice is disoriented. She always is the first day in a new place; it doesn't matter that the flight was short and there was only an hour's time difference to adjust to; it's the light and heat, the colors—so many shades of blue in the sea and sky after months of New York gray. She thinks she hears Janet asking her to name the Seven Deadly Sins, decides she must have imagined it, and drifts back into heat-induced reveries.

"Seven letters," Janet says. She's sitting with her chair tipped back, her ankles crossed on the wall that surrounds the terrace, and—Alice notes with relief—working the crossword puzzle, not launching them into a discussion of metaphysics.

"Adultery?"

"Too long. Anyway, you're thinking of the Ten Commandments," Janet says. She rubs suntan lotion on her midriff. Since they arrived, she has gotten Elaine's car jump-started, found the supermarket, bought groceries, unpacked and gone for a half-hour swim (she timed it). Alice, who stayed behind because she was expecting a call, rummaged in her duffle bag until her bikini came to light. She has yet to go swimming.

"Sloth—but it's not long enough," Janet says. She runs her fingers through her hair, which is short, pepper-and-salt, and stands up energetically on her head. Alice's hair is wavy, reddish gold, shoulder-length, but most of the time she keeps it pulled back with a rubber band, where it doesn't get in the way when she paints.

"I think Pride is one," Alice says. She is watching a boy— eighteen, maybe twenty—trying to windsurf. Elaine's house is on a cove and the wind is tricky close to shore.

"Pride wouldn't be a sin. It's a good thing. Anyway it's the same length as Sloth."

"A Catholic might know," Alice says. The boy has no sense of where the wind is. He's fighting it instead of letting it bring the sail up for him. "Is Elaine Catholic?"

"Episcopalian, but sometimes she talks about converting."

It's the incense that attracts her, Alice thinks, that and wearing black lace veils, confessing to priests in little booths. When Elaine's husband, Mo, dies, she will turn to religion, after having had a few beautiful young lovers. Aging coquettes always turn to religion. Alice leans her head back to expose her neck to the sun. "Lust!" she says.

"Lust is good. Sloth, Lust. Maybe Pride *is* one. Envy! Sloth Lust Pride and Envy," Janet says.

"That poor boy has no idea of how to work a sail. He's only exhausting himself," Alice says.

"Why don't you wade out and show him how? Maybe he'll let you use his board."

"I don't want to emasculate him."

"Do you really know how to use one?"

"Sure. It isn't hard if you understand wind. Maybe we could rent them at the hotel. I could teach you."

"That would be fun," Janet says, being a good sport, a game girl. It actually looks frustrating; the pain of learning probably doesn't equal the joy of doing. She'll be happy to use the long weekend just to catch up on her work, do some swimming and jogging, but she doesn't want the vacation to be boring for Alice, who consented to come along at the last minute when Jake, Janet's son, suddenly went off skiing with his father for spring break. Janet didn't mind—for years she's been trying to get her ex-husband to take more interest in their son—but it left Janet with the prospect of spending the weekend alone in Nassau, when she'd only planned the vacation in the first place because of Jake. Maybe Alice won't need entertaining. She brought a bag of wooden bracelets to paint. She has orders to fill.

"You haven't taken out your paints yet," Janet says.

"I decided to get seriously into Sloth for the first day."

"And what else?"

"What do you mean?"

"Why are you watching the windsurfer? Is it Envy for the surfboard or Lust after his body?"

"Envy. I can't lust after anyone who doesn't do as well as I can. That's why I couldn't marry Mo, for instance."

"Because he can't windsurf?" Janet asks.

"Probably never tried."

"He *is* fifty-four years old," Janet says. She wonders if Alice remembers that Janet dated Mo, briefly. In fact, Elaine and Mo met at Janet's Christmas party the year before last. Afterward, Elaine was sweet on the phone, wanting assurance from Janet that she hadn't *stolen* Mo from her, and Janet absolved her, saying it had been more of a friendship really, that she was delighted Elaine and Mo were so mutually smitten, a rare occurrence in this day and age, etc.

"I bet they don't even go swimming. I can't picture them climbing the wall," Alice says.

The house is part of a complex of attached houses and condominiums. In order to get to the beach, you would have to walk all around the row of houses or scale the terrace wall,

which isn't an athletic feat, but Janet agrees with Alice that
she can't see Elaine and Mo doing it.

"Why do you think Elaine decided to go all white and pastels? If you had a house down here wouldn't you want hot
pink, turquoise, bright yellow? The light is so strong that pale
colors bleach down to nothing," Alice says. It is Friday morning. In shorts, sitting with her legs apart on Elaine's sofa,
Alice looks enormous, as if she grew in the night. The bracelets she is painting in brilliant colors are spread out across
Elaine's glass-top coffee table. Janet admits the room is very
white: white drapes on either side of the sliding glass doors
(which Elaine calls French doors), white sofa and armchairs;
on the dining table is a white linen cloth, hand-painted with
dashes of blue. Under the coffee table is a dhurrie rug in
muted shades of lavender, pink, mint green.

"But Elaine is pale. She decorated to compliment her coloring. She told me she wears mostly white when she's down
here," Janet says.

"I feel like I'm sitting inside an eggshell. The only practical
thing is the carpet."

The dark green carpet came with the house. Elaine hates it
but she hasn't gotten around to changing it. "Why don't you
go out to the terrace to paint?" Janet asks. She's secretly fearing for Elaine's dhurrie.

Mo bought the house for Elaine last fall. "I need it," Elaine
told Janet over lunch in New York. "I need something of my
own, to connect me to the earth." With her whispery little girl
voice, Elaine did seem a wraith to be pitied with no place to
call her own. She and Mo live in a duplex in Manhattan and
spend weekends at their farm in Connecticut but these are
places Mo shared with ex-wives and therefore are not truly
Elaine's. Only later, back in her office, did Janet remember
that she herself rents and doesn't own the place she lives in

(fourth-floor walk-up; Jake has the bedroom) and that shelter, not real estate, is one of the basic necessities of life.

"I'll help you move your paints," Janet offers.

Alice and Janet are reclining on lawn chairs they found on the beach near the house, admiring the evening sky and drinking straight rum on the rocks. Alice has a red nose and shoulders. Janet, who used sun-block and cover-ups, has turned an even brown. The day was hot and still and for some reason the whole complex ran out of water in the afternoon. The toilet flushed with a dry asthmatic hiss. Showers were out of the question; the women rinsed under a trickle of cold water from the outdoor shower by the condominiums.

"Avarice," Alice says.

Janet is puzzled, then she laughs. "Oh, we're back to the Seven Deadlies. Sloth Pride Lust Envy Avarice. Sounds right. What made you think of Avarice?"

"Elaine. She gets Mo to buy her this house and then she asks you, her friend and under-paid editor, to give her money for staying in it, when Mo provides her with everything she wants."

"That was the deal with Mo, I think. She has to take care of the expenses on the house so she rents it to her friends."

"To teach her responsibility." Alice has taken the lime out of her drink and is sucking on it, pursing her lips in a disagreeable way like an old maid. Alice has never married. The men she gets involved with are always too young or unstable or they live in foreign countries. A few weeks ago, Alice was very enthusiastic about someone she'd met—Peter—but she hasn't mentioned him lately and Janet wouldn't ask. She wonders if Peter is the friend who was supposed to call but hasn't.

"How old are you, Alice? Thirty-five?"

"Thirty-seven . . . Why are you looking at me like that?"

Janet laughs and spills a drop of rum on her blouse. "That's the trouble with women living together. We're too attuned to each other's signals. Jake would never notice."

"Well?"

"What?"

"Why were you looking at me, what were you thinking?"

"I was wondering if you were committing the sin of Envy."

"Elaine, you mean? Envious of Elaine?"

"Mmmmm."

"Why should I be?"

"She's an artist, same age as you—"

"I wouldn't call her an artist. She's an illustrator. You don't call that art, do you, those pie-faced children and bunnies she turns out?"

"O.K., not an artist. She's someone with an art background who leads a very easy, pleasant life. And you—work. You work twelve hours a day, even on vacation."

"I wouldn't trade a day out of my life for hers. Be married to Mo?"

"He adores her."

"Never." Alice gets up to check on dinner, chicken curry cooked with some interesting root vegetables, and leaves Janet to watch a planet glowing on the horizon—Venus, it must be—and the colors changing to deep indigo, black and silver.

Alice puts a glass into her hand, filled again with rum and ice and a fresh slice of lime.

"Oh Alice, should I be doing this?"

"It's your vacation, isn't it?" Alice stretches out on her chair with a second glass of rum. "All you have to do afterward is get your body back over the wall and eat dinner. Besides, you might need it. I burned the curry."

"Oh, that's what I smelled. I thought it was the tropical air—"

"No, it's burned curry. I rescued it, though, most of it."

·   ·   ·

In the morning Janet sees that the blouse she brought for going out at night has curry stains on it. The second rum was a mistake. It spoiled the mood of the evening. Alice went all sad and confessional. It seems Peter told her he was married and Alice took him to bed anyway, the night before she left. She gave him the number here and told him to call but he hasn't. Janet couldn't think of anything to say that wouldn't sound judgmental. Downstairs a metamorphosis has taken place in Elaine's living room. Sand is moving in on the green carpet. The dhurrie rug is curling and waving like a restless sea. Lamp shades are askew. All over the glass table are Alice's bright works, like toys, or seashells washed up by the tide. A gravy boat stands abandoned on the dining table. They ate inside last night because of the little mosquitos that came out. Janet lifts the gravy boat and catches her breath as if she's seen a hideous truth revealed: there's a yellow stain on the hand-painted cloth. She balls it up and sticks it into a cupboard. Dishes, greasy and yellow, are piled in the sink along with the burned curry pan, which she scrubs until the enamel comes off. She throws the pan in the garbage and leaves to go jogging.

Opening the door on her return, she hears the sound of falling water. She thinks that somehow it is raining on the other side of the house until she realizes that the water is inside, not out, coming from the ceiling. It looks weirdly natural, with the wall of sliding glass doors beyond, an extension of the outdoors. And yet it's horrible, such quantities of water coming from the ceiling, splashing off the dining table, soaking into the carpet. Upstairs, the toilet, bone-dry yesterday, is a steady fountain. Wads of toilet paper float on top as water flows out all around. There's a puddle on the kitchen floor. Water is seeping in from everywhere through secret channels, a localized disaster come to destroy Elaine's house.

Janet rushes outside, not really expecting to find anyone this early on a Saturday, but there is a maintenance man in a neat brown uniform who receives her news with a calm smile. He tells her they are expecting a lot of trouble today because there was no water yesterday. It's a mistake to flush the toilet when there is no water in it. The pipes clog. He will repair the pipes, but it would only be right if she paid him something because, after all, it is her fault that they are blocked.

Of course she'll pay. She'll be glad to. She gives him twenty dollars. He tells her that the water will soon stop coming through the roof. Roof? She doesn't understand. Oh, the ceiling. Maybe he doesn't have a word for ceiling. Most Bahamians live under roofs, not ceilings. Ceilings are a mainland concept, as are upstairs bathrooms.

Janet pounds the floor with towels, but no matter how hard she sponges, water still comes up between her toes when she walks across the carpet. She would have thought the noise would wake Alice, but she sleeps on, oblivious. Didn't she mention she'd started her period? She wouldn't have flushed her tampons, would she?

It's the ringing of the phone that wakes Alice. She flies downstairs, her mind still half-asleep, her heart racing, only to hear Elaine on the other end. As Elaine talks, Alice reads the signs in the sodden squish of the carpet, the wet brown stain in the ceiling, the towels drying on the terrace wall, and in the cadence of Janet's arms rising and dipping in the water a hundred feet from shore.

"Elaine called. She wanted to know what the hell was going on and I told her to get down here quick, that you were destroying her house." Alice enjoys her own joke hugely. Janet looks around for a dry towel but there aren't any. She stretches out on the wall to bake herself dry. "Actually, she did call," Alice says.

"I knew she would. I felt it when I was swimming. She has sixth sense. What did you say?"

"Nothing. I told her everything was fine."

"Thank God I wasn't here. You know me. I would have been compelled to tell her everything," Janet says.

Alice is calmly painting bracelets with pyramids and spheres, arcs, ladders, intersecting lines, creating patterns with another part of her mind, not the part she uses to speak with Janet. "Elaine gave me a list of things she wants us to do."

"Oh?"

Alice produces a piece of paper from the pocket of her shorts. "I like her style: rent your place to friends and then ask them to do favors for you."

"What's this?" At the bottom of the list are written: "Pride Lust Avarice Covetousness Envy Sloth Gluttony."

"Elaine knew them."

Janet, shivering in the breeze (the sun's gone behind a cloud), ponders the words. "These are mainly sins of wanting, wanting too much or what belongs to someone else."

"Medieval inventions to keep the peasant in his place," Alice says.

"But they're still sins today, aren't they? Sloth? Lust?"

Alice says they're more like positive attributes, that people go to sex therapists to work on Lust; they practice relaxation technique to learn Sloth. Janet is watching a lizard on a piece of driftwood. He does rapid little pushups, moving his head up and down. It must have something to do with perception: he gets the whole scene going up and down and then he can pick out an insect because it isn't moving with the background. "I can't believe there isn't some reward for virtue, some punishment for sin," she says.

"If you believe in heaven and hell, or that you'll come back as a cockroach in the next life—"

"No no, not that. But I do think there is a price to pay, there has to be, in this life."

"Who's keeping track? Who's got the scorecard of sins? Who's meting out punishments? God?"

Another lizard has come out and is also doing little push-ups. With both of them facing each other nodding their heads up and down, it looks as if they're sending signals or performing a ceremony. Janet argues that the idea of sin wasn't merely an invention by priests to keep the flock in line, it also had to do with how a person felt, within himself, and in that sense, the idea of sin is still valid today. "When one of the Seven Deadly Sins takes over, you get out of balance. Your emotions run haywire. When you're in balance you feel good. It's a state of grace."

"It's guilt that makes you suffer, not sin," Alice says. "The Seven Deadly Sins look like basic biological drives to me. The only sin is in repressing them. That's what leads to cancer and hypocrisy." Alice flicks her brush over the bracelet she is painting. It leaves a trail of red across a sphere, making it look like a bleeding planet. But Alice always insists there are no messages in her art. The shapes are only shapes, not symbols.

Janet spends the rest of the day accomplishing Elaine's list of errands. She also takes the towels and the tablecloth to the laundry (where they can't guarantee that the curry stain will come out) and buys a pan to replace the one that burned. Alice paints and goes for a swim in the late afternoon. When she comes in, she sees that the dhurrie has been hidden away somewhere. Janet is looking at the brown blot on the ceiling. "Do you think it's gotten smaller since this morning?" she asks.

Alice hadn't really noticed how big it was before. "Oh definitely," she says. She throws her used towel on the back of an armchair and Janet snatches it up.

"I think you need to get out," Alice says.

The restaurant, one Elaine recommended, is the kind of place where the people all know each other. They're packed in three deep around the bar, shouting over the juke box and the roar of the blender which is constantly whipping up pink and yellow drinks. Everyone is dressed differently—swimsuits and sweatshirts, tennis whites, evening clothes—but they have one thing in common: they all dressed for something else and have dropped in before or after. Only Janet and Alice, outfitted specifically to come here, seem out of place.

Alice and Janet look terrific. Alice used the blow-dryer and her hair is fluffed out and curly. She's wearing lipstick and makeup, a big white shirt belted over tight jeans, sky blue cowboy boots. Janet didn't have anything but her curry-spotted outfit to wear so Alice persuaded her to borrow something of Elaine's, who had plenty of things hanging in the closet, and Janet and Elaine are exactly the same size. Alice picked out a long white skirt for Janet to wear with a matching top that's ingeniously cut so it looks like a jacket with a little buttoned vest beneath. It shows just an inch of midriff. "I can't wear this; I'm a mother." Janet laughed in front of Elaine's full-length mirror. "You're about the only one who can," Alice said. "Look at you. There's not an inch of fat around your middle. You should show off more. Show off your tan." Janet didn't have any shoes to wear with the dress so why not borrow Elaine's red high-heel mules, the kind of shoes that encourage you to shorten your stride and sway in the hips a little, the way Elaine does?

The red mules are not a good choice if you are standing at a bar waiting endlessly for a table. Janet thinks back on her jeans and sweatshirt, her sneakers, things she was going to wear before Alice persuaded her to disguise herself as Elaine. For whom did she think she was dressing? These people who all know each other? That man with the interesting face and prematurely gray hair who looked them over when they came in, then turned back to the bar?

Suddenly the place clears out and everyone goes off to whatever they had planned. Alice and Janet are given a table.

They begin discussing marriage, Elaine's and Mo's. Alice wants to know if Janet thinks Elaine loves Mo.

"It was a marriage of convenience, I suppose, but it seems to be working all right. He has a rough-hewn charm."

"He looks like a toad next to her. Whenever she sees a good-looking man her own age she's got to realize she's made a mistake." Alice is eating ribs. Janet ordered conch stewed with tomatoes and onions. "Does he love her?" Alice asks.

"He's proud of her. He likes to show her off. And she enjoys that." Janet imagines them coming in the door, Mo holding it open for Elaine, she stepping in with her chin held just a little higher than is natural, flicking her blond hair back from her shoulder.

"What do they do when they get home?" Alice asks.

"What do you mean?"

"When the show's over, what then?"

"We don't know. No one knows."

"I bet they sleep in separate rooms."

"Maybe they make love all night and she comes five times, each one better than the last," Janet says. She stops herself from adding that, after all, Mo is a practiced lover. Janet knows this because she and Mo did have a night together— just one—before that Christmas party. Janet was so quick to absolve Elaine, and so averse to playing the part of the woman wronged, that she had almost forgotten that night. She's certain Mo has.

"I don't think Elaine likes sex all that much. She's too fastidious," Alice says.

"She might have another side."

"Maybe they're into bondage. Maybe he ties her up."

"You're determined to find the dark side, aren't you?"

"She has to suffer, goddamnit! It's not fair. You can't marry an ugly old man for his money and live happily ever after," Alice says.

"She has to pay!" Janet says.

"Damn right!"

People are looking at them. Janet wonders if they've been screaming "Mo" and "Elaine." Someone here might know them, might even recognize Elaine's clothes and shoes, but they would look different on Elaine, more dashing, sexier, more expensive. Some of the conch in tomato sauce slips off her fork and rolls down the front of Elaine's dress.

The spots do not come out under cold water. In fact, as Janet stands in the ladies room with the front of Elaine's skirt in the sink, it seems that they are spreading. In fairy tales, that's how you tell a troll: you give her a stain to wash out and the more she rubs, the worse it gets. The figure in the mirror could be a troll, with wild smudged eyes. It's the makeup, the eyeliner Alice lent her, insisted she use. And Alice talked her into wearing these clothes. Alice is so careless that it almost looks intentional, fed by hidden springs of envy for what Elaine has. Janet will have to be more vigilant, prevent Alice from doing any more damage.

Alice has ordered two cappucinos; they turn out to be coffee laced with rum and topped with whipped cream from the can. Janet drinks hers anyway because it's hot and the wet skirt, the bare midriff, are giving her a chill.

The gray-haired man is still at the bar when Janet teeters past in the ruined skirt. If she can make it in these shoes through the parking lot, which isn't a lot really but a hard-packed dirt clearing with trees standing among the cars, she'll be able to drive home safely, she tells Alice, who hasn't expressed concern.

Someone has painted the trunks of the trees white so they will show up even in the dark. Later, Janet is convinced she saw the trunk clearly through the rear window as she backed the car into it. That's how it always seems in hindsight, Alice tells her, driving home because Janet has become catatonic, staring straight ahead at the curves in the road. "The crease

on the fender hardly shows. Elaine won't even notice it,"
Alice says.

That night Janet dreams that Elaine's house has crumbled and
washed out to sea, leaving a gap in the row of townhouses.
Inside the broken shell tropical plants are growing, birds with
brilliant plumage fly in and out and cat-size lizards signal to
each other. It's disturbing yet beautiful at the same time, like
water cascading from a ceiling.

Dennis Trudell

GOOK

When I was young our suburb had a prep school that later closed and sold its forty acres for a county park. Among its wooden buildings were two gyms—and friends and I would sneak into the older, "girls'" gym to play basketball on winter Sundays. We knew the Asian janitor who lived on the grounds might kick us out, but we'd unlatch a locker-room window after jimmying open a door, so that was no problem. We'd climb back inside once his slight form trudged out of sight. Often we continued the same half-court game he interrupted.

The school had seen better days: paint flecking on clapboards, locker room moist and smelly, showerhead dripping. . . . Yet my friends and I were too cushioned by economics to imagine how little the janitor was paid, probably little more than apartment and meals. To think why he seldom bothered rechecking the gym, despite his threats ("No come back! Much wrong I tell you other time. Go before call police —no come back long time ever!"). We sort of *liked* his appearing; the games we returned for were sweeter once he'd reminded us they were illegal.

Maybe he was, too, and that's why we sensed he wouldn't

call police. I don't know what country he was from—only that, in that winter of 1965–66, it was most likely not Vietnam.

It wasn't much of a gym: just six feet between baselines and wall, wooden backboards, one rim an inch too high . . . but on those Sundays we considered it ours. In love with basketball and ourselves, we felt an unused gym on a winter day was a crime against nature—ours anyway. What happened was part due to our adolescent belief that a moral issue was involved. One Sunday the janitor *did* return, found the unlatched window before again confronting us:

"No play here! I lock window, you no come back! Police for sure if return you. This time go *for always!"*

What happened was also due to our wish to find two or more wrongs *can* make a right. We were romantics in ways suburban teens a decade later could no longer be. We didn't need drugs: we felt the world and future grinned at us.

Me, Len Grunwald and Cy Rabb versus Rob Beauchamps, Fred Chunka, and Mel Duncan that mid-afternoon. Parklawn School gym; sleet beating on it and Rob's car nearby—and melting from the cap of this small man beside the court. Grun held the ball. He was maybe our best player, though Fred Chunka was the deadliest shot our school had produced, held the varsity single-game record. Grun frowned at the man, and the rest of us frowned.

If we left now, there'd be no more basketball that day. Our sweat in the cold car would feel like it did after bouts of just necking on dates. Something moved among us, defter than any pass. Then Grun dribbled to a corner. No other of us moved except Fred Chunka—a step late to stop Grun's sudden drive for a lay-up. *"The leader does it again! Catches Chunka dreaming of Sandy Krebs' boobs,"* called Cy Rabb, who came mostly to amuse us and himself by announcing our play. His pudgy form, with discernible "boobs" of its own, shuffled around ineffectively. I think he spoke from habit just rather than to defy the janitor. I think none of us, including Grun, knew what our terms for leaving were before Grun spoke again:

"That's 12-10. Game of 15. We'll finish it first, okay?"

The man didn't understand, or didn't realize the words were for him. None of us looked his way as Fred passed to Rob, took a return pass, sank a long one-hander. "Chunka hits another! He cans it, pots it; he flushes it down!" Cy announced.

For it *was* a decision now. We moved the ball quickly—Grun to me to Cy, who skittered it back to me. I was aware of the janitor's stare as I shot, and it banged off the rim. "Ryder *misses!* Crops fail in Iowa, floods cover the Sahara!" Cy said.

Fred Chunka rebounded, looked to pass. But I had Rob covered, and Mel Duncan was now facing the janitor. The man stomped one of his boots.

"Go *now*, you law-breaking! Why you not leave fast fast? *No play this building!*"

The rest of us stopped. Then Mel noticed drips under the man.

"Floor's getting kinda wet," he said, pointing. He wasn't mocking; Mel was the largest and gentlest of us. He'd quit football that fall after an opponent he blocked was carried off.

"YOU LEAVE!" shouted the janitor. The vinyl cap moved down over his eyebrows as he stomped again. I think if he hadn't touched Mel, we would have just shrugged and left. Surely if U.S. troops weren't in Southeast Asia, Grun wouldn't have said what he did moments later.

Mel still pointed at the floor. The man took a step and pushed his hand aside.

"Jeez . . ." Mel said.

This moved a quiver up the man's body, ending with a throb of his head. Which bent, aiming the cap's top at Mel. Then lurched into his stomach, driving Mel's breath out. He fell down, gasping.

"Holy balls," said Rob Beauchamps.

The janitor spoke in another language. Grun stood closest to him. He was an honor student, read newspapers. "Watch yourself," he said, then said: "Gook!"

We never knew if the man understood that. He'd maybe heard it from Parklawn kids since March, when U.S. Marines had landed at Danang. Anyhow, he took off the cap and flailed it at Grun. He missed, but drops flew on Grun's face.

"God *damn!*" said Grun. Beside him Mel got up, and the man's gaze darted between the six-footers. Then he kicked out; his boot got Mel in the crotch, doubling him over.

At that moment the man's face looked more puzzled than angry. Then Mel's groan jerked him into motion. He turned and ran from the gym.

"Hey, *fucker!*" called Fred Chunka. We heard the boots run past the front door toward the locker room. Mel was red-faced, murmured that he was okay.

"Gooks . . . they call them gooks over in Vietnam," Grun told us. He spoke softly, as if half-apologizing for the word. Fred's jaw was thrust like during arguments in our games. He never argued back, just shot whenever he got the ball. And seldom missed.

"What you think?" Rob asked. "We go scare the shit out of that gork?"

"Gook," Grun repeated.

"What do you say, Mel?" said Rob. His father had left home that year, was living with another woman. Recently at school a teacher most of us feared grabbed Rob's arm for making noise. Rob jerked it away so hard the man slammed a wall. He just stared when Rob hissed to never touch him again.

"You don't kick a guy's nuts," Grun said.

"It's a technical against the East team," announced Cy. "But, fans, that team has left the court."

"Let's scare *his* nuts," said Fred—and we moved into the

hallway. The sound of sleet outside seemed to push us faster to the locker room. We couldn't find the janitor there.

He hadn't gone out a window; all of them were latched. He wasn't in the john or shower room. We saw only dank towels and gym clothes by the lockers. Rob knotted a towel as Fred called that the gym office at the far end was locked, empty.

We stood inhaling the scent of mildew, damp plaster, rusted lockers.

"Folks, the Far East team has vanished!" Cy said. His announcer voice was high-pitched; it could be fun to hear or could rasp the nerves.

"Where the hell'd he *go?*" said Rob, snapping the floor with his towel.

"Look, this is dumb," Mel said from the doorway, having trailed us from the gym. "The poor jerk was just trying to do his job. Besides, you know I got steel balls."

"If he got outside, he could be phoning the cops," Rob said.

I haven't mentioned myself speaking since the janitor reappeared. I was the shortest of us, the only one not on the varsity team; Cy was the manager. I was grateful being included in the Sunday games. "Bet he's more scared of cops than he is of us," I said now. "And we could say the gym door was ajar —we thought it was open house or something. Asshole comes and yells stuff we can't understand. Next he's kicking Mel."

"You do not," Grun told us, "kick someone's testicles. Not in this country."

"Let's just leave now," said Mel.

"Sure he isn't hiding in that office?" Rob asked. Fred shrugged, so we went and looked through the office door's glass. No one was under the desk, nor between it and the wire-mesh panel to the gym for handling equipment. We returned to the lockers, might have given up and left if Rob hadn't noticed a locker open.

"Hey, that was shut before! They all were. He was in there!"

We gazed at it. Rob reached into the locker, held up a pair of panties.

He snapped them. "Probably not his . . . but he should get twenty flicks for being so sneaky."

Rob smiled, but I didn't. The man had been hiding ten feet from where I'd devised our possible lie.

"Come here, guys!" we heard Fred call from the shower room. We found him by a manhole-like cover in the drying area. It was cast iron, with a ring for lifting, and of course it was rusted.

"I heard something. He's *down* there," Fred told us.

Rob bent to the cover and listened. He nodded. The leaky showerhead dripped, echoed. I felt something danker than the air near my flesh. This was *weird*. Either the man was panicked out of his mind, or he was making fools of us. I thought how quiet he'd been in that locker. How *fast* he'd gotten from there under the iron cover.

Now Rob lifted it, revealing a shaft with some rungs leading to pure darkness. For the first time, I wondered why the man hadn't run outside after kicking Mel.

"Can't see shit," Rob said. "We know you're down there, guy!"

Nothing answered; we heard no movement.

"Must lead to a crawlspace or whatever," said Grun.

Rob looked angrier than before. *"Come on out, jerk-off! You're just making it worse for yourself."*

"Bet he's halfway to Hell by now," Fred said, voice strained. Mine would have quavered just then, and even Grun looked dubious. Maybe nobody had to get hurt that day if one of us had said then: "Hold on. This is getting too strange—and I need it to stop."

Instead, Rob said, "Anyone want to climb in? Or should we close this and wait awhile?"

No one volunteered. The blackness under the third, vague rung looked almost solid.

"What's the shit *doing* there?" Fred said. "Wetting his pants? Trying to enter a sewage pipe and climb out a toilet?"

"*Here, gooker, gooker, gooker*—" Rob called. He was my best friend, though all five were friends I enjoyed more than ones I have now. I mean, I loved them.

"Should we check if there's another way out of there?" I asked.

"You guys, this is *dumb*," Mel insisted. "Let's just go."

"How about I shut and guard this while you guys check?" said Rob. "We don't find one, it means he's trapped. We could pitch a wastebasket in there. Turn him into one huge gook-bump and call it a day."

Grun nodded. "Right. By the time he gets the nerve to come up, his supper'll be cold. Fish-heads or whatever. His old lady'll be pissed off and wailing."

So we'd mouthed some venom to counter our anxiety—and everyone but Rob and Mel left the shower room. Now it was reassuring to hear Cy's announcing, as if nothing unusual were happening: "With a new strategy, the West team's back in action. Their eyes have a confident glow. Which reminds me to say this game is brought to you by Colgate Palmolive. . . ."

I left it behind to check the gym with Grun, while Fred and Cy searched around the locker room. The two of us were in the hall when we saw the gym lights go out.

Grun swung around. I saw the uncertain look on his face again as he shoved me back toward the others.

"Hold it, fellas!" he said in the locker room. "Lights just went out in the gym! He's either there now or else—"

"Maybe yanked some wires down below. I'm gonna yank *his*," said Fred.

"Electric wires don't run underground," Grun replied. He

liked knowing things we didn't. "Downtown in cities they do, but not in a place like this."

"So he used the gym switchbox," I said. "The gym must be where that crawlspace leads."

"Let's go find out," said Fred. *"Hey, gook, you farting around in there?"*

"Hold a sec," Grun said; I heard in it that he needed to take charge. I believe now that uncertainty was literally painful for him. He would captain the varsity next year, later be president of a fraternity. "It's possible that the crawlspace leads *outside,* and he's pulled or cut wires there. What we do is split up—not stay bunched while he plays his little games."

"Look, all he wants is us to get out of his gym," said Mel. "Wouldn't any of us do the same?"

"What, crawl around like some rat?" Rob said.

"We split up," Grun said more firmly, nodded at me. "Ryder here and Fred check the gym. Rob and I'll go outside, look around the building. Cy, you guard the iron cover."

Mel began to argue, then just shook his head. No one else objected, so the rest of us moved. Fred followed me into the hall. I didn't want to enter the dark gym, but made myself picture the janitor—whose head only came to about my chin. Fred and I moved into the large room.

Our eyes adjusted, and the place looked empty. Near the doorway were our jackets and Rob's basketball. We could see only the dim gray of protective mat down by the switchbox. We moved slowly toward it. I was feeling angry at the man for the fear I'd carried from the lockers. At the switchbox I hesitated, in case he'd done something to shock anyone touching it. Then I made myself move one of the switches. As the light came on, there was a step behind us; an Asian syllable climbed my spine.

It filled my brain so I couldn't see clearly as I spun toward the figure emerged from behind the mat. Fred made a sound like a child as he turned.

It wasn't until the man had run from us, again left the gym, that I had an image of him with a hand swinging something. Wasn't until running after him that I realized he'd snapped his *belt* at us. Its buckle had hit my leg, and stung—stung hard!

"Get the shit! Coming your way, Cy!" Fred shouted in the hall as we saw the main door hadn't opened. We came to Mel in the locker-room doorway, blocking it.

"He get you, Fred?" I asked. "Bastard caught me good. Get out of the way, Mel—he's trapped in there now." I touched my jeans, expecting blood.

There was none, but he'd torn the denim. Mel stayed where he was. Beyond him I saw Cy come from the showers.

"Damnit, outta the way!" Fred told Mel. But Mel pushed him gently backward and shook his head.

"Guys, could we just *think* a sec?" he said.

Grun and Rob came in from the sleet. Grun's voice was loud, smug: "He *was* out there, studs. We found a hole with torn screen in the foundation. But there's no wires. . . . He must've snuck back inside to the switchbox. Any sign of him there?"

"Fuck took off his belt, hit me with it," I said. "Then ran back to the lockers. Meanwhile, Mel's flipped or something."

Mel still blocked the doorway. He spread his arms, as if appealing to a jury. I thought again how *fast* the janitor had moved—to get through the crawlspace, tear the screen, return to the gym while we stood by the manhole.

"What's the deal here?" Mel asked. "We really gonna *hurt* this guy? Gonna stand over him kicking and pounding? Snap him bloody with that towel, Rob?"

"Let's just find him. You're in the way!" Rob said, and touched Mel's chest. He was the second shortest of us, and either he or Mel was the strongest. He was expected to break the school 100-yard-dash record that spring.

Mel looked surprised. He stayed in the doorway, arms still

spread. Rob shoved him, and Mel pushed back. Rob swore and charged, arms pumping. The two jittered back and forth in the doorway as we yelled at them. Then they lurched inside, holding one another. Suddenly Mel's greater weight swung Rob into Cy—who was thrown against a wall.

Rob backed away from Mel with fists raised. "Fuckface bastard!" he said.

"Hey, man. Easy, easy—"

"Gook-loving *fairy!*"

Grun stepped to keep them apart. Seeing that, Fred Chunka did too, and then I did. Grun turned toward poor Cy—who was down on one knee. Cy's soft body shook; he tried to catch his breath.

"If he gets away because of your shit . . ." Rob told Mel, but he didn't try to get past the three of us.

Mel's shirt was torn, but he looked mostly sad gazing from Rob to Grun to Cy. Neither he nor Rob was hurt, though both were flushed, breathing loud. All our breaths were audible in those moments our six faces were close together.

Someone had to speak next, and of course it was Grun: "No sweat, Rob. Mr. Suey won't get away . . . and we won't beat him bloody, Mel."

"Suey?" I said.

"Right. First name's Chop."

The rest of us had to smile then, and Cy had to try for something funnier: "West team just ran a tricky pattern, fans—" He paused, still gasping. "But decided to save it for football. Your announcer calls time-out to pry lungs from kidneys."

"So where *is he?* In a locker again?" Rob said. His hands were no longer balled in fists. Mel was touching his ribs, wincing. Grun led four of us past the lockers while Mel stayed there.

We found a window open—the same one we'd climbed in

before. We stared out at the weather, and no one spoke. Then a row of connected lockers tipped over on us.

"YOU LEAVE NOW!" was shrieked as they crashed; I glimpsed the man atop the next aisle's lockers—having pushed the others with a boot.

Fred's elbow hit my face, and I was knocked across a bench with his weight on me and lockers on him. My back sirened pain from the bench-edge; I tasted blood from biting a lip. I felt Cy jam against me, also caught between the lockers and bench. Grun was beside him on knees, back supporting a locker at the end. Fred was swearing. Rob swore at him and the rest of us to get the lockers back upright.

The janitor's shriek seemed to ricochet off walls like a handball.

After getting the lockers off us, we found no one was really hurt. Cy was worst off, a wide scrape down one arm. It turned from pink to red as we stood touching ourselves for cuts, ripped clothes. The janitor, of course, had vanished again.

"Did he run out the door past you, Mel?" Grun asked.

"Nobody went by me."

"That shifty yellow *fuck*," said Fred Chunka. His long face glared; there was a rip in his sweatpants. His gaze looked suddenly older.

"He set us up," I said. "Opened that window, crouched on lockers till we were bunched. Then pushed them on us."

"Damnit, he's *creaming* us. Don't do any funny announc-ing," Grun said. He looked as if Cy had pushed the lockers. Cy shrugged; his eyes were moist.

"You okay? That arm looks mean," said Mel.

Cy averted his eyes. He picked up a towel, pressed it to his arm.

"Where'd he go, if not out to the hall?" Rob asked. None of us thought Mel would lie about that—Mel never lied. Rob looked strange. I expected rage from him, but he appeared muted. He stared up where the man had been with something like respect.

Not Fred, though; he knotted a towel. "That gook made us bleed. So now he's gotta pay some blood."

"Please, you guys," begged Mel. "Let's knock it off. I just hate . . ."

"The gook's smart," Grun said. "Fast and smart—doesn't go by any rules. Got me *mad*."

"Hate this violence. . . ." Mel's lips trembled, and he turned away.

"Suey needs to learn a lesson," continued Grun. "I'll see if he went back to his crawlspace. Fred, you and Cy check the office again. Rob, you and Ryder try the gym."

"I don't know," Rob said. "Maybe Mel's right. Maybe we ought to just—"

"You don't swing belts or push lockers on people," Grun declared. His mother had gone to Smith and his father a two-year college. Grun's father got excited when the varsity did poorly, would murmur to his wife; we'd see her tap the coach and repeat the words in her cool, patrician voice. The coach would nod.

Fred took his towel toward the office. Cy Rabb looked frozen in place with his bleeding arm. I followed Rob into the hall.

We were almost to the gym when Cy shoved over another row of lockers. The crash rushed Rob and I back to the doorway. We saw Cy lift a bench to his chest, then above him; I hadn't thought he was that strong. He threw the bench at a wall, where it gouged plaster. The others had run back, too, and tears on Cy's face embarrassed us.

"Not there," Grun said at the shower entrance. "Didn't climb back in his gookhole."

What's happening to us?, I wanted to yell. I didn't; I was afraid to have others look at me like we looked at Cy.

I heard him throw another bench as Rob and I returned to the gym. We found it empty. Its lights were still on. We shrugged at each other and at Mel, who'd followed us. All three of us were about ready to give up; I know my stomach felt like rusted lockers. We might have gathered jackets and tried to convince the rest to leave if Rob hadn't noticed his basketball missing.

He told us that, and Mel and I gazed with him at empty corners of the gym. I had a sense that all of us, six teenagers and the janitor, were trapped in the building. That each time he outwitted us, turned out lights or pushed lockers or whatever, we had to stay longer—get someone else hurt and sobbing. . . .

"Where's my damn ball?" Rob said, and I shrugged. There was nothing to do but return to the locker room and tell the others.

When Cy heard it, panting at where the second thrown bench had a crack, I saw he was *glad* Rob's ball was gone. As if that justified his tantrum. I hated him just then; Cy looked as weak and phoney as I felt.

Then his announcing started again as we stood there: "This is a first, hoop-fans. Far East team stole the game ball. Have they eaten it? Have they ball-napped it back to Asia?"

Cy later became a talk-show host: a minor celebrity by the end of the Vietnam War. People called in and he made fun of them, whatever their views. He ridiculed both hawks and doves; and if someone called him a cynic, Cy accepted that. "Asked where I *really* stand, folks. I don't, I sit. This is sitting cynic Cy Rabb, saying come on, kiddos. Phone in, spit-brains. Make jerks of yourselves. . . ."

The locker room was a mess. The two rows of overturned lockers and thrown benches filled much of the space. We moved past them to the office again.

"Okay, this is still locked," Grun said. "So if he's not in there, where *is he?*"

"Hold it. Look!" said Fred, pointing inside.

Our stares passed the desk and equipment boxes to the wire-mesh panel leading to the gym. We saw it was unlatched. It had been opened and shut again, but not all the way.

"Fucker unlocked this door and climbed out through there," Fred said.

"Right, locked it again—got to the gym and took the ball," said Grun.

I recall waiting for Cy to make a broadcast-quip. I eyed Fred's knotted towel, hoped it would smack Cy's face if he did. But Cy said nothing, and Fred placed the towel on the door's glass. His other hand rapped it firmly—and the second rap broke the glass. Meanwhile, Rob hurried past lockers to return to the gym. I saw Mel flinch as Fred rapped again and glass fell into the office.

"Jesus, guys, more damage. We got to stop . . ."

Fred ignored him, reached in to open the door. Then he and Grun moved inside. Grun went to the panel while Fred stopped at the desk and lifted its telephone. He jerked it hard, ripping the cord from the wall.

"*Hey, fellas—check this one out,*" Rob called from the gym.

Grun and Fred blocked the panel, so I hurried out around through the hall to the gym. I felt nauseous—wanted to be alone if I threw up. But I heard Cy and Mel behind me. Then I was again under the gym lights, and the nausea seemed rising to my brain. I felt I'd projected a fantasy-image as I joined Rob at midcourt.

His basketball was there; placed beside it was a shard of glass.

The janitor's magic: he's the fucking Devil, I almost shouted, thinking it was a fragment Fred had just rapped to the office floor.

Then I saw this glass was thicker. Mel touched me, nodded where Rob was gazing at a wall. It held a fire-alarm box, with a shard of glass missing. We looked at Rob's ball—at the pointed end of glass facing it.

Grun and Fred ran into the gym, and we all stood by the ball and glass. "Okay, what's it *mean?*" Rob said.

"This some Asia gook symbol?" Fred asked Grun.

They spoke softly, yet the words seemed to bounce louder off the walls. We didn't doubt the ball had been set just there, on the midcourt line. I looked around again: still no shape hunched in a corner, no boots visible under mats at either end. Grun appeared dazed, like he'd received a D on a test.

Yet I felt something like hope replacing my nausea. This time the janitor must have left the building. Put the ball and shard there and *gone.* My hope widened; it would mean the contest was over. Somehow it might mean we'd *won.* . . .

Grun's voice dimmed it: "Look, the sharp end points at the ball. It means, 'I could've slashed your stupid toy if I wanted.' "

"Right on," Fred said. "Goddamn warning. Fucking *threat!*"

"And then he went where?" Cy asked. He was afraid; Cy's gaze jerked around, above us, and said he didn't want to bleed elsewhere on his body.

He's still here in the gym, I suddenly knew. And then I knew where. While Cy tried for his broadcast tone and failed, so that his quip hung like a fart: "Fans, can the East team be *inside* the ball?"

I knew where the janitor was, where he had to be—because he wouldn't leave the building with us still there. In 1966 I didn't know *why* he wouldn't: am not certain I do now. But he wouldn't leave, had placed ball and glass as one more plea for us to.

I faced the mat he'd hidden behind before snapping me with his belt. Then turned to the end where we had played— faced that backboard and beams from the wall holding it in place. I was thinking: *You could just say nothing.* . . .

Then Grun said, "Tell you, I'm shit out of ideas."

"Up behind the backboard—at that end," I told them, pointing at wall-hooks for a volleyball net you could use to climb atop the protective mat. From there you could climb onto a beam.

I had been cut from the varsity, but wanted Grun and the rest to know I was smart. Otherwise the day might have ended with no more harm than Cy's scraped arm plus the locker-room damage. Instead, we all went to look behind the blackboard; and that's where he was.

Squatting on one of the beams from the wall. The janitor's face gazing down was smaller than his boot-soles over the beam's edge. It looked calmer than I'd seen it before.

"Okay, better come on down now," Grun said. He spoke with more authority than since dividing us up when the lights went out.

"Got a choice, gooker," called Fred. "Climb down—or we *knock* you down with the ball."

But he wasn't the one with Rob's ball. Mel had picked it up, and now he said, "We're not touching him."

And I don't know where that would've led because Mel didn't want to hurt *anyone*. But he may not have been able to keep Fred and Grun, and maybe Rob—and maybe me—from shoving the man around any other way.

Then Rob Beauchamps went to the wall, gripped the higher net-hook. He pulled himself up so his sneaker rested on the lower one. Rob, the most eager and restless of us: whom I remember as a boy running with hair flying, lips parted in a grin as air moved against them. Saying nothing, he put a knee on top of the mat and grabbed the man's beam. He pulled himself onto it.

He didn't seem angry; Rob's anger seemed drained away after the fight with Mel. He might even have helped protect the man once they were down. I think he climbed there more to know he could *do* it than anything else.

But one of his knees, maybe damp from the locker-room floor, slid off the beam. He swung abruptly under it, holding the beam with one hand. Then kept swinging as his grip wouldn't hold . . . so that he made a half-turn on the way down.

He hit facing the floor; and what hit first, with a *crack* that brought my nausea spewing out instants later, was his right knee. Shattering bone there forever.

That sound turned the air crimson for me: wild crimson. When I looked up from my vomit, from Rob's writhing, and saw through that color—it was the janitor's eyes I saw. They were full of pain, as if he too felt a knee break. He jumped down from the beam and landed softly, just a rubber squish two yards from Rob.

He was bending to help Rob when Fred Chunka slugged him in the face.

Hit him with a fist and all his might, the fist of his shooting hand. The sound wasn't loud; nothing could seem loud after that crack. But some teeth were knocked out . . . and I've wondered often if the jaw wasn't broken. I've wondered if surgery weren't need to restore the face's bone structure, and who would pay for that.

I don't know. I was one of the three, with Fred and Cy, who ran from the gym to bang on doors of nearby houses. We tried several before someone was home who agreed to call an ambulance. The paramedics would have come ten minutes sooner if we'd phoned from the gym office. But no one ever said that would've made a difference to Rob's knee. When we three returned to wait for the siren, the man was gone, and I never saw him again.

There were two teeth and part of a third, and drips of his blood, on the floor. We cleaned that up along with my vomit. Then Fred and I got the lockers upright before the ambulance came. The paramedics didn't ask why we were in the place— nor did anyone from Parklawn School ever learn who'd damaged the wall and bench. As I said, the school closed a few years later; its buildings were torn down, and the grounds became a park. My parents wrote me about it. I was in college then, with a student deferment from the draft. So were Grun and Fred and Cy.

Fred wore a sling briefly, but his hand was sprained, not broken, from slugging the man; it soon healed and he went on to more scoring records. Rob had two or three operations on his knee and still walks with a limp. Our parents never doubted our story that he'd climbed onto the beam as a dare. We never went back to that gym. Cy Rabb grew from pudgy to fat and became a radio personality. Mel Duncan went to a two-year college but dropped out and was drafted. He went to Vietnam, where they made him kill some young men.

Helen Fremont

WHERE SHE WAS

Jana and I were in the bathtub on a drizzly afternoon, miles from anywhere. She was turning the hot water on and off again with her foot. I leaned against her, comparing legs. It made me think I was seven again, at the Albany Art Museum, copping a feel of those rich velvet cordons when none of the guards were looking. Her legs wove around mine and just kept on going. You could string them along an art exhibit for half a city block. Her left foot hung over the edge of the high-lipped bathtub—one of those tubs that's perched on four porcelain paws, like it's fixing to walk away.

No, my mother doesn't know. She thinks Jana and I are friends. I love that word: friends.

We were up to no good, lolling around on that rain-soaked winter afternoon in Dix Notch, Virginia. Two streets, a flashing yellow light at the center, and a white Victorian mansion to one side, on a hill. Downstairs, three cats did a slow slalom between the legs of chairs. The innkeeper was snoring in his bed, a book of crosswords open, upside down on his chest.

Actually it really doesn't much matter where the innkeeper was: he could have been in the kitchen, cooking a slow-burn veggie dinner on that gas stove the size of a twin-engine plane. Or leaning over the sink, cutting cucumbers in the salad. Plink, plink, plink. Green wax skins sliding off the peeler like snakes. You'll just have to take my word for it, and hope for the best.

So we were back in the tub, fumbling with paper-thin bars of Ivory on a steel dish, the water plunging from silver faucets. The tub was deep and old, a creamy yellowed porcelain. Cracks in its Victorian skin. I sank my breasts and shoulders underwater, and the soap slipped between my legs. I felt for it, and it squirted through my fingers.

The water rose, and a green cloth fanned out just below the surface. I could go on and on. You're more interested in Elmer, in dinner, in his reasons for leaving New England twenty-two years ago, quitting his job as a math professor, and coming here, buying this old wreck of a Victorian, and coaxing it back into an inn. But I don't know that story. If you want to know all that, you can stop in and read the brochure.

But listen.

We'd been for a walk in the woods that day. Pouring rain. Wet leaves, puddles of water in every leaf. The Great Wetness. The air was thick with big juicy drops of rain, translucent apples of water. It curled my hair and slicked it to my scalp. Jana's hair is thick and black. It turned blacker.

The trail was covered with leaves, covered with water. It climbed high above the town in a lazy switchback. The ground shimmered. The air felt like cotton, and our breath hung in our faces, there was no room for it to go anywhere. Jana was talking. I walked ahead, and the words drifted up to me over my left shoulder. She was telling me how she felt.

"I don't know," she said. "I can't say right now." Jana was like that. Water was starting to seep into my boots. For all their triple-stitched leather and heavy steel shanks, they were helpless against this much rain. The water crept in softly, without a sound, grabbing at the instep, and then gradually spreading out, filling my feet. My boots had nothing to say for themselves. We walked on in silence.

We reached an outcrop of rock overlooking the town. A frothy strip of silver roiled below in the heart of the valley: the Three Dames River. There was a story behind that, but I didn't know it yet. The world was a wall of grays. It made me want to hold Jana, so I leaned against her and stretched my arms around her knapsack, my face plunged into the slick, wet sheet of her parka. We stood there, on the crumbly white rock, with the whole suffocating mist swallowing us up in its mouth.

"What would you do with a million dollars?" she said.

Jana could never stick to the point. The point was Us, or at least that's what I was trying to get a reading on today. "I'd invest it wisely," I mumbled into her jacket.

"No, really, I mean it. A million dollars. Would you quit your job?"

I shrugged. "Maybe." I worked Social Services at the jail, shared a government-issue metal desk with three other social workers, and inhaled other people's Marlboros. "I'd miss it," I said. "I'd miss the people."

Everyone I knew was at the jail, including Jana. She did part-time work for Corrections, and had a private practice on the side. About a year ago she did a tooth extraction on one of my guys, and I was never the same after it. Those long thin fingers, the bright lights, her shiny silver instruments. "I might do Social Services some more," I said. "I don't know."

We walked on. "What about you?" I asked.

She giggled. Obviously she had given it a lot of thought. "The truth?" she asked.

I nodded, irritated for some reason. I could never get a straight answer out of Jana. Two years we'd been together, two years of late nights and long talks, and I still didn't know where she stood. She seemed to be thinking it over now.

"I don't know," she said finally.

.   .   .

Elmer had rung the gong for breakfast at 6:15 that morning. It was a twelfth-century Tibetan gong the size of a satellite dish. It was greenish, thick, and dull; it sounded like the bombing of several small villages. Elmer had bought it on a trek to the Dhali Harahm, and had let UPS figure out how to get it back to Dix Notch, Virginia. It had taken eight months.

Elmer Doyle was a vegetarian. So was the Dhali Harahm, as a matter of fact. Jana, on the other hand, was a renowned eater of stews, steaks, and hamburger. She could eat half a fried chicken in one sitting without even stopping for breath. Quick and quiet, no crumbs on the counter. Her jaw worked like a piston till her plate was clean. Consequently she was in danger of losing weight this weekend.

We reached a level grassy knoll, a sort of détente between up and down. The path snaked through a thin stand of trees, their trunks clammy and dark, their heads tossed in a fuzz of rain. A small dip, and then a trail junction. We turned left, on a blue-blazed trail that plunged back into the valley. We followed the stream, through tall green streaks of grass.

It grew steep and muddy. The stream flew over its banks, and flooded our trail. Soon it was no longer a stream but a river, a forest of rushing water. Our path went under and came up for air on the other side. We tried to follow it, crisscrossing the stream again and again. We'd walked through that river and back across it so many times, I didn't know which side I was on anymore. The water was ice and it filled my boots, my feet swimming in suitcases of leather, but I kept walking anyway. Pretty soon my feet didn't matter, and they kept quiet. After a while it didn't even feel like I was touching ground much anymore, and it was just my arms swinging, and my breath flowing in and out. It made me feel lighter, and I probably would have floated away, except I had a backpack on, which reminded me what I was there for. I kept hiking.

Breakfast that morning had been biscuits with soybean sausages that I won't go into right now. We'd gone back to the room before our hike and flopped onto the bed—I felt we deserved that much. Jana had thrown back her head and laughed, because it was the only thing to do just then. Her hair was a jungle: black, thick, tangly, daring. But oh, her teeth. Ears of baby corn. I ran my tongue over them, she hated that. "If you're going to kiss me, kiss me," she said, "don't lick my teeth." She had teeth that had never grown up. They were small, meek, obedient; all lined up like that with no place to go.

"They need attention," I said.

She pushed me aside lightly and started up from the bed.

"Don't," I said, trying to wrestle her back down. "I'll behave, I promise."

But she twisted free and marched to the little porcelain sink in the corner of the room, a cereal-sized bowl of white enamel. Snapping open the toothpaste tube, she fed a fat line of blue paste onto her toothbrush with one hand. Classy. Left hand on hip, head thrown back, chin thrust forward, she brushed her teeth with defiance: a dental flamenco dancer. Then she leaned over the sink, flipped on the water, and rinsed her mouth.

I stepped behind her, standing tiptoe, and rested my chin on her shoulder. We looked at each other in the mirror. I leaned closer, touched my lips to her neck. She looked pensive, almost sad. "I love you," I whispered. She turned away, dried her hands on the towel, and packed her knapsack for the hike.

The trail leveled out towards the bottom, and Jana and I found an old log to sit on. My legs ached, a rich warm brooding in the muscles. I rubbed them so they wouldn't stiffen up. Jana was fiddling with the map, following our trail with her finger. The stream we'd crossed was a thin blue wire, falling through V-shaped rows of brown topographic lines like strings of spaghetti. Our path was dotted in black.

"Water?" I said, offering her my bottle.

She shook her head. "We're almost there," she said, looking up from the map to the trail ahead. A blue blaze stood out on a wet black tree trunk.

It was quiet: soft sounds of water seeping through layers of leaves, soaking into the earth. A mist hung from the trees. Somewhere, far away, the hushed grumble of a motor. Jana's eyes closed. I could see her breath puffing from her lips, rising over the curve of her nose, her eyelids, beads of water on her lashes. I couldn't tell what she was thinking.

The inn was creaky, unpretentious as an old man in overalls, wrinkled with age. Our room glowed with gray light from full-length windows. Braided rugs wove colors of the woods: muted mahoganies, wine, wheat. It was a fat old house leaning back on its haunches. It didn't try too hard. When you walked through the hall, the floorboards gave slightly—just slightly—enough to feel like the floor of the forest. The wallpaper was faded, a dull oxblood. Although not shabby or neglected. Relaxed.

The fireplace in the living room sputtered and coughed, or crackled sharply if the wind blew overhead. It smelled of almonds. We sank into the olive sofa, studied the cindery front page of the *Dixville Gazette*, and let our eyes close gradually under the weight of all that wood and rain. Elmer shuffled in, a scratchy plaid shirt bulky over his white stretched T-shirt. I glimpsed him from a quarter-inch crack in my eyelid. He stared at the fire, took in the seating, and sighed. He sounded like Jana's father with that sigh: a little sad, some tired, and solitary as an egg.

"Want a seat?" I offered, lifting my head slightly and nodding to the space next to me. I was overcome by a terrific lethargy, as if my body were silently weaving itself into the couch as I spoke.

He pointed his finger and raised his hand slowly, until his outstretched arm was at the level of my eyes; then he moved it back and forth between me and Jana, as if warding us off.

Jana threw me a glance, which I caught and tossed back. We played pitch and catch with it for a little while. Finally he spoke.

"Go for a walk?" he said, withdrawing his hand and rocking back on his heels.

"Yeah." I nodded.

"Wet," he said.

We both nodded.

The fire took over then, and dropped a log off the stand. It rolled.

"See that?" he said. "That's good wood. Strong. It jumps." He was perfectly serious.

"Wood that jumps is rare," he continued. "In these parts, you got to take your house apart to find wood like that."

I wasn't sure what he was trying to say, but I believed him.

"You don't believe me?" he asked.

"Oh no," I said, "I believe it."

He seemed somewhat mollified. "They bring round the tractors down there, to the other side of the river." He scratched the side of his face, a sound like day-old bread being ground into crumbs. "Then they start hauling out logs right out from the houses, just like that." He demonstrated hauling a log out of a house, using his hands. One hand was the tractor; the other hand was the house. He tugged on the pinky of his right hand till it looked like it would snap off. "When the tension reaches a critical point . . ." He yanked on the pinky, and I heard a loud pop. "Like that," he said. "You get that."

I felt pressure on my toe. Jana's foot was pushed against mine. I glanced down at it, then up at her. A smile—very faint —snuck across her face.

"Uh-huh," I said. "I see." Jana's smile became sweeter.

Elmer scratched his chin again. "Well," he said.

He turned and shuffled out of the room, touching the lampshade lightly with the tips of his fingers, as he might touch the brim of a hat, if he'd been wearing one. "O.K.," he said, and wandered out to the kitchen again.

Jana's eyes were on me, but for some reason I couldn't look at her. "Hey," she said, "what's the matter?"

I shrugged. Nothing was wrong, and everything was wrong. Jana leaned towards me, but she seemed, somehow, very far away. I could never really figure out where Jana was: whether she was with me, or only a little with me, or only sometimes with me.

She held up her right pinky and pulled on it with her other hand, as Elmer had done. "Pop," she said softly.

What did we do, Jana and I, left on the couch with the innkeeper gone? We necked. It wasn't a wise thing to do, maybe, but we couldn't help it. It just seemed right. We found ourselves doing things like that more and more those days, and it was a welcome change. It's a lot of tension to withstand, always doing unlikely things, going against the grain, finding yourself in unexpected places doing difficult things that no one can fathom. This, on the other hand, was easy. We necked.

But what it was, the moment I wanted to tell you about, happened earlier, in the bathtub. It was the way she covered my face with the washcloth, and brought it slowly down over my eyes, like falling off a cliff, slow motion. Through the terry cloth, I could feel her fingers, thin and delicate. There was a gentleness to her touch, and a deliberation. She kept repeating that motion over and over again—like a curtain coming down over my face again and again, till the play was over, and never over, till it didn't seem to matter whether we were at the beginning, or middle, or end—till all that mattered was the love in that gesture, the certainty of night falling, and the promise in her hands of another day coming.

Elizabeth Oness

THE ORACLE

I'd been home, out of college, only a few hours; I hadn't even unpacked the car, when my mother told me that she had met someone. He's a dentist, she said, and he's been saved.

"Saved from what?" I opened the refrigerator to survey its contents. Whenever I came home from school, the abundance of her refrigerator amazed me. At school, the staples in our refrigerator were ketchup, mustard, and beer.

"Saved?" I prompted her.

"Philip, don't be smart," she said.

"No, really, what brand of Christian is he?"

"Oh, I know it doesn't matter to you. But he told me about it on our first date, how everything's changed for him, how he gets along with his ex-wife now, and how he really feels like he's helping people, much more than fixing their teeth." She smiled a little as she repeated his happiness.

I had noticed a difference in her at graduation, but I thought it was relief that I'd made it through college un-scathed. She seemed more relaxed, less precise. She no longer moved things and straightened them when she talked, a habit she picked up, or maybe I only noticed it, the year my father died. After the first months of mourning I waited for her to break out of herself, to become less restrained, but she continued in much the same way. She was a pretty woman with a small, square jaw, and long brown hair just starting to turn gray. Every year she asked if she should cut it, and every year I said no.

"Mom, I think you're in love," I said.

"Oh, I'm not," she smiled as she denied it, then set the plate she was holding back in the dishwasher.

"You don't even know if you're loading or unloading." I took the clean plate from the rack. "So he's divorced. Does he have kids?"

"He has a fourteen-year-old daughter who's just started to live with him again," she said. "And he's having a cookout tomorrow. He asked if you'd come, he wants to meet you."

Whenever she was flustered, my mother inspected some insignificant object as if its stillness would steady her. She examined the calendar on the kitchen wall as if it were new. I walked over and hugged her; she felt smaller, her rib cage like a brittle basket. I squeezed her lightly and released her. She looked up at me, reassured, and smiled.

The following night, on the way to his house, I tried to get her to describe Hal. She blushed and said I would meet him myself. It was strange to see my mother fidgety over a man. As far as I knew, in the years since my father's death, she had never even been out on a date. Of course her friends encouraged her to get out more, meet someone else, but she always refused. This devotion to the memory of my father was antiquated, probably even wrong, but my mother had a quiet stubbornness at times. She would summon a formality that kept people from pressing her further. We drove through a wooded development, winding down smoothly paved roads with those peculiarly feminine suburban names: Natalie Court, Caroline Lane. We finally stopped in front of a large, modern house. Wind chimes hung from a Japanese maple in the yard. A slender window divided the house; starting by the front door, it rose up to the second story. Hal opened the door before my mother had a chance to knock.

"Hello, Deirdre." He kissed her on the cheek and turned to me.

"Philip, it's a pleasure. I've heard a lot about you." He shook my hand firmly. It was a humid day, but Hal seemed freshly scrubbed, as if he'd just stepped out of the shower. His light crewcut was edged with gray; his blue eyes were pale-lashed, rimless. A large gap separated his two front teeth. No wonder he was a dentist.

We walked through the house, which shone with polished wood floors and sleek, modern furniture, and into the kitchen, where the back wall, almost entirely glass, looked onto a lush backyard. Hal guided my mother through the doors, placing his palm against the small of her back. His fingers were short and thick. Peasant hands, my father would have called them. He started to lead us down to a small group of people standing around the grill when a young woman, dressed entirely in black, walked over.

"Philip, this is my daughter Megan," Hal said.

It didn't seem possible she was only fourteen. I was careful with my eyes; I tried to stare only at her face.

She smiled briefly and brushed her hair from her cheek. A clutter of black plastic bracelets and silver chains slid down her arm.

"Philip just graduated from University of Virginia," Hal told her.

"How impressive." She wrinkled her nose at me.

Hal looked uncomfortable.

"Deirdre, you look nice." Megan kissed the air near my mother's cheek. Her lips puckered, then relaxed into their fullness. It wasn't your usual fourteen-year-old gesture. I later came to associate those airy kisses with girls I'd known in college—when I ran into them after many years. Women I'd never touched would greet me with that pressure on the arm, a softness aimed at my ear.

"Would anyone like a drink?" Megan asked.

"I'd love a beer," I said.

Megan went into the house and my mother and Hal joined the group at the grill. I lingered awkwardly, waiting for Megan. She returned with two tall-neck beers and nodded at our parents.

"Well, what do you think?" she asked.

"About what?"

"About them." She gazed at me, unblinking. She had light gray eyes, darker near the pupils. She seemed to be deciding if I was playing dumb. "They really like each other," she said. "My father keeps hinting they might get married."

"I just got back yesterday." I wanted to defend my ignorance. "I'm trying to take it all in." Then cautiously I said, "My mother says your dad's been saved."

She snorted and looked across the lawn at Hal, who was talking to his friends, one arm gesturing, the other around my mother's shoulders. Megan took a long drink of beer. I wondered if he let her drink or if she was just showing off.

"Yeah, he's been saved all right," she said.

"What about you, have you been saved?"

"Hell, no," Megan laughed.

"What do you believe in?"

"Oh, I don't know." She twisted up her mouth, chewing on the inside of her cheek. Her hesitation made her seem closer to her age.

"What do *you* believe in?" she asked.

"Elliott's," I said.

"What?"

"Elliott's Apple Juice. It has little quotations written on the inside of the caps."

She shook her head.

"I meditate for an hour every morning before I choose my

first bottle." I leaned closer, lowered my voice. "I believe in the cosmic synchronicity of my choosing a particular quotation. I live every day by the wisdom inside a bottle cap— unless I drink two bottles, then I have to change my whole philosophy in the middle of the day."

She laughed, then looked at me sideways to make sure I was kidding.

"It's as good a thing to believe in as any, I suppose." She looked out over the yard. She was one of those girls who tried to look bad, but couldn't really pull it off. Her hair was cut in bangs and fell just below her ears, a stylish cap of dark hair that showed off her long neck. She affected the attitude of a streetwise flapper, but her face gave her away. Her cheeks were slightly round, childlike; she had a sprinkling of freckles. Megan. It was hard to be tough with a name like that. Her black T-shirt, cut wide and ragged around the neck and cropped along the bottom, ended a few inches below her breasts and stayed out there, not tucked into anything. I wanted to slide my hand up underneath it.

"I have to make a phone call." She turned abruptly and walked toward the house.

My mother introduced me to the other guests. We listened to a tall woman with waving arms tell an elaborate story that turned out to be a movie plot. A man in camouflage pants talked to Hal about target practice and a new rifle he'd bought. I ate as food was handed to me. I was aware of the dark smell of charcoal, Megan's bare shoulders, scents of dark and light circulating through the blue evening. Hal worked his way around to my mother and me.

"So you had a chance to talk to Meg?" he asked.

"Yes," I said. "She seems quite grown up."

Hal looked at me hard, trying to decide what I meant.

"I hear you did well at school, magna cum laude. Maybe you can encourage Megan. She's bright, but she doesn't apply herself."

I nodded and tried to look understanding. He was reminding me of her youth. I was afraid whatever I said would
be wrong.

Later, as my mother prepared to leave, I watched Hal draw
her over to him, circling his arm around her waist, so that
both of them could wish his friends good-bye.

"Did you have a good time?" Megan's question startled
me.

"Not exactly my type of party," I said.

"What is your type of party?" Her voice was low, flirta-
tious.

"I don't know." I stumbled, afraid her father would hear
her tone if not her words.

"Well, I'm sure we'll be seeing each other again." She
looked at me, wide-eyed, from under her bangs.

Washington, D.C., was a tropical city in the summer. The sky
could threaten rain all day, and after it finally poured, the air
was still thick and hot. I spent that summer working on my
resume, studying the classifieds, and meeting with alumni
who worked for companies I might be interested in. I felt like
I was moving into a borderless cloud. I drank apple juice,
hoping for clues to my future. In my cap one day:

> There is only one success—to be able to spend your life
> in your own way.
>
> (Christopher Morley)

I had no idea what my own way was. I went out at night
with friends who were in the same postgraduation haze. I
read *The Washington Post* completely, every morning, as if one
day I would find in its pages the exact thing I was meant to
do. I thought about Megan almost constantly. I tried not to. I
thought about her when I woke early in the summer heat,
filled with the shadows of my dreams. I thought about her at

night, too: her mouth, the way she put a bottle to her lips. I tried to imagine living in the same house with her. I imagined her getting out of the shower, walking past my room in a towel, wet.

My mother occasionally asked about girls I'd gone out with at college, but her questions were random; she might have been asking about a professor, or a difficult course I'd taken. I assumed she didn't want to know anything too specific, my answers might embarrass her, so she ironed my shirts and asked about my interviews, which weren't real interviews at all, but a series of talks with men who had established specific places for themselves in the world. I looked forward to weekends, when I wouldn't have to answer her questions; but when I woke up alone, sunlight filling my room, the house silent below me, it seemed that Hal had everything in that glassed-in house several miles away: he and my mother eating brunch in the kitchen, Megan upstairs sleeping late. I imagined her face, flushed with sleep and creased a little from the pillow, her smooth hair awry. I wanted her before she put on her grown-up edginess; I imagined her arms around my neck, how she would curl her long legs around mine. I tried to picture exactly what she looked like under those flimsy clothes, and I lay in bed for what seemed like hours, wondering whether she was a virgin or not. I fantasized until I exhausted myself. Then I slept, and when I woke, I tried to think of how I would distract myself for the rest of the day.

One Saturday morning my mother called from Hal's and asked me to dinner. I'd just gotten up and I stood in the kitchen, listening to her on the phone while I waited for the coffee to finish dripping. It was strange to be invited to another man's house by my mother. Driving over that night, I thought about Hal; my opinion of him shifted slightly each time we met. That night he seemed confident, self-sufficient, but there was an odd difference between him and my mother, as if they were the right and left shoes of a slightly mismatched pair. Hal insisted on cooking and serving, as if his kitchen wasn't my mother's territory yet. He moved around the table serving us, and I watched his reflection in the large window. He was substantial, squarely built—each of his polo shirts was the exact same tightness across his chest—but he seemed like a pasty shadow superimposed over my memory of my father, a dark, transparent man of air.

Megan hurried into the kitchen and grabbed an apple off the counter. She wore a short black skirt, high-topped sneakers, and a long T-shirt. She moved as if she hadn't grown into her body yet.

"What's the hurry?" Hal asked.

"I told you, I'm going to the movies with Jill."

Hal stopped for a moment, holding a dripping spoon above a pan.

"I asked you last week. It's *Gone With the Wind*." Megan's tone was highly reasonable, as if she were talking to a child. "We went through the whole thing about how it's a long movie, remember?"

Hal smiled, but his tolerance seemed strained.

"What about dinner?"

"Mmm, lasagna. Save some for me. Don't let Philip eat it all." She grinned at me and hurried out the door.

At home that night, I sat in front of the television, flipped through all the channels twice, and turned it off. I tried to remind myself what I'd learned about women in the past few years. I found that the girls who dressed most wildly, who seemed so sure of their looks, often wanted talk more than sex. Of course you could never be sure, but it was the straight ones, those preppy girls in button-down shirts who seemed a little awkward, shy even—those were the ones who had their diaphragm in their purse.

·   ·   ·

"So has Hal decided what he thinks of me?"

My mother and I were sitting in the kitchen. I'd made dinner, spaghetti with clam sauce, because she seemed tired and I'd had another long week that added up to nothing. My mother managed a print shop in Bethesda. They did stationery, fliers, advertisements; it was not a bad job, but it was hectic at times. The owner kept saying he was going to retire and leave my mother in charge.

I bought a bottle of wine for dinner, although my mother didn't usually drink. I poured a glass for each of us, and when she gestured for me to stop at a small amount, I kept pouring. I missed this hour at school, sitting on the porch with a few beers, grumbling about professors, telling stories or lies, and watching the sun go down over the Blue Ridge Mountains.

"I need a new dress for church on Sunday," she said.

"You're going to church?"

"I've been going for a few weeks." She twirled her spaghetti on a spoon and took a large bite.

"What's it like?"

"It's fine."

"It's church, of course it's fine. What's it *like?*"

"Well, it's a regular service, but everyone seems very sincere. It's a little embarrassing. When they pray they sort of raise their hands in the air." She showed me, raising one arm, then the other almost shyly, her open palms in a gesture of supplication. "Sometimes," my mother started to giggle, "they only raise one hand, like asking to be called on in class."

"Does Hal do that?"

"No," she said, relieved. "But it's strange. Sometimes I wonder if there's something wrong with me. I don't feel anything."

She smiled a little, lightened by her admission, and tapped

her glass for more wine. She had made two completely un-characteristic gestures, the raising of her palms, tapping her glass for wine. The unnatural movements made her seem younger, confiding.

"The thing is," she hesitated, "it's important to Hal, he wishes I were more interested. I don't mind going, but . . ." her voice trailed off.

"But what?"

"I guess if I were more involved, he would be more sure of me, somehow. Of course he's never said it like that, but . . ."

I looked out the window. The sky was pale behind the trees.

"If he really loved you, he'd want you either way," I said.

"I suppose." She sighed and picked up her plate.

The next morning my mother announced that she and Megan were going shopping.

"You and Megan?"

"Hal said he'd buy her some clothes if she'd get something that wasn't black."

When Hal's car pulled in the driveway, I picked up the newspaper as if I hadn't been waiting. My mother answered the door, and I heard her and Hal making plans for later on. Megan's shoes clicked across the kitchen floor. I listened to her opening up the cabinets and getting something to drink. When my mother went to get her purse, Megan came in and sat down on the sofa next to me.

"So you and my mother are going on shopping?" I put the paper down.

"My father set it up, he wants us to be friends." She said it evenly, as a statement of fact. When she looked around the room, I thought how small our house seemed. She leaned back and stretched, looking up at the ceiling. I wanted to run my finger along the tendon at the back of her knee.

"But I do like your mother, she's a good person, innocent in a way."

"Innocent?"

"She always believes the best about people."

It surprised me, her seeing this. It was true. My mother always had a theory to account for someone's bad behavior. Serial killers, rapists, thieves, she believed that given enough time, a person's goodness would ultimately rise to the surface. I'd never known whether to call it optimism or foolishness.

When they left, the house seemed drained. I picked up a novel and put it down. The oak wall clock ticked louder, almost faster, as if it might rattle the china in the cabinet below.

My mother returned with a whole outfit—a skirt and blouse made of pale brown cloth with brightly colored threads running through it. A loose-fitting vest went over the top.

"They're wonderful for you." Megan grinned and held them up against my mother.

"Do you think your father will like them?" My mother touched the cloth with her forefinger.

"He'll like anything you wear." Megan's voice was encouraging. She took a soft purple belt from the bag and playfully dropped it over my mother's head.

"What about you?" I asked.

"He said he'd pay for whatever I wanted as long as it wasn't black and it didn't show my navel." She pulled out a pale green shirt made out of silky cotton. "It's kapok, it's made out of milkweed—the way it hangs is terrific." She stared at me, daring me to imagine her in it, then held it up, turning it around. "Backless. It looks great on."

Then, finished with me, she hugged my mother and thanked her for being so sweet, for taking her shopping.

.   .   .

A few days later my mother asked me to have dinner with her and Hal. She asked in a careful way that hinted it was important.

"Is Megan coming, too?"

"I don't think so," she said.

"She likes you." I remembered Megan hugging my mother.

"The divorce was hard on her. Hal's had a little trouble with her, but they seem to be working it out. It was a big step for her to move in with him."

"What kind of trouble?" I asked.

"Oh, that's not for me to say."

"Mom, if you're going to start, I wish you'd finish."

"I only said it's been a bit difficult."

My mother could be annoyingly proper. She didn't gossip. What had Megan done? Drugs? Possibly. Gotten pregnant? Too young. Well, not technically. I went round and round in my head. Imagining the possibilities made me jealous.

When Hal came to pick us up for dinner, Megan wasn't with him. He opened the car door for my mother, touching her arm as she got in. I slid into the back seat, watched the fast-food restaurants and chains of stores as Hal maneuvered down Rockville Pike, neatly cutting through traffic, a few aggravated horns honking behind him. When we climbed out of the car, heat rose up off the pavement, matching the heat in my head. Inside the restaurant, nets and fake sea memorabilia were strung along the walls. The smell of fish and melted butter made me hungry. Hal asked about the job hunt. I recited my growing list of dead ends.

"Well, it's hard to know what you want to do. I didn't decide to be a dentist right out of college."

"What did you do when you graduated?" I asked.

"I went to California, surfed for awhile, then I went to Alaska. I had this romantic notion about working there, but the emptiness drove me crazy, so I came back and joined the service. I knew they'd pay me to train me."

"Why did you choose being a dentist?" I asked.

"I was good with my hands. I could talk to people, and I figured if you have to work, you might as well make money."

I liked his honesty if not his reasoning. Over the meal we talked about work and school. He mentioned shooting, and I asked a few questions about skeet shooting. It seemed that I'd been having the same conversation for weeks. Finally, Hal took a drink of water and aligned his silverware next to his plate.

"I just want you to know that I love your mother very much. She's a rare woman. I also want to tell you that I've come to God in the past few years. He's the center of my life. I know that each person comes to Him in their own way, and I don't ever want you to feel that I'm pushing you when I express my feelings about the Lord."

I couldn't look at my mother. His honesty was painful. I felt myself blush.

"Well, I appreciate you talking to me," I said.

"I also want you to know that you're always welcome at the house. Don't worry if it takes you a while to find the job you want. I know you're a real self-starter. Be picky about that first job." He took my mother's hand and squeezed it.

"Thank you."

I reached for my wine glass. It was empty and I lifted it up, feeling that Hal's words called for some comment, but I had nothing to say. I felt the silence as my arm came down. There was only a single glass of wine left and I didn't want to pour it for myself. Hal did it for me.

"And Megan looks up to you. Don't worry if she acts smart. She has a little growing up to do."

"She's a lovely girl," I said, feeling myself redden.

The waitress returned with coffee, and our conversation floated back to the surface.

．　．　．

I woke the next morning knowing that Megan was out of the question. I had to stop thinking about her. Finding a job so I could afford my own apartment was the only way out. At eleven o'clock I had an appointment at World Bank with the father of an old roommate. Getting ready to leave, I looked myself over in the mirror and felt better. I would get a job and get my own place. I bought an apple juice when I got off the Metro, and my bottle cap confirmed me:

For he who has no concentration, there is no tranquility.

(Bhagavad Gita)

I was shown into an office that looked like a private library. The walls were filled with bookcases, oil paintings, and photos of Paul's father shaking hands with important people. A set of golf clubs rested in the corner. Paul's father gestured toward a leather armchair. A secretary appeared in the doorway to ask if I wanted coffee. When she shut the door behind her, the hum of air-conditioning sealed us in. After looking at my resume and asking a few questions, he let me know that my background was mediocre, that studying French meant practically nothing. I should have studied Spanish, German, Japanese, or Russian—those were the important languages. I listened to his polite advice and excused myself as quickly as I could.

Down on the sidewalk, I watched the people hurrying by and I wondered how it was that they all had something specific to do. A bicycle messenger wove down the sidewalk and through the standing traffic; pedestrians flattened themselves against solid objects and glared in his wake. I took off my tie. I was wet through to the back of my suit. At the entrance to the Metro, a man with no legs was propped up on a cardboard square. He held out a paper cup, and I glared at him and stepped onto the moving staircase.

When I walked in the front door, the house seemed small. I

looked at the photographs of me growing up, my mother and father; they seemed at once familiar and generic. The house was still. I went to take a shower, to wash the morning off, and when I got out, the phone was ringing.

"Hi, Philip. Is your mom there?" It was Megan.

"She's at work. Do you want me to give her a message?" I didn't want to let her off the phone yet.

"No." She was quiet for a moment, then her voice picked up. "Well, I guess you had the God talk last night."

"Well, there wasn't a whole lot of discussion."

Megan giggled, "Look, do you feel like going into the city, just walking around or something? I want to get out of the house."

"Sure." I said it before thinking.

"Great. Come by in about half an hour, OK?"

I tucked the towel around my waist and went to get dressed.

"So what did he say last night?"

We were driving toward D.C. without a specific destination. I was aware of being in the same small space with her. She leaned against the car door, her knees tipped toward me.

"Come on, what did he say?" she asked again.

"He said that he loved my mother a lot, and he talked about how important church was, all that." I was too embarrassed to repeat the words he'd used.

"That's all?" she asked.

Megan directed me as we got closer to the city: turn here, go left up there. It was funny the way she ordered me around. We parked in Adams Morgan, an old Hispanic neighborhood now gentrified with restaurants, record shops, and bars.

"I'm starved," Megan said. "I know a Mexican place that's cheap, and they make terrific margaritas."

She led me down the shopping street into a seedy part of town. A runny-eyed woman shared a stoop and a bottle with two men. On the corner, a check-cashing store was crowded. The restaurant was empty except for a Mexican family in the corner. The dim quiet was soothing; we were hidden from the daily world. Megan explained how she'd found the restaurant, but I didn't always pay attention to her words. I watched her mouth, her long fingers, ten perfect crimson dots at the tips. The icy lime and salt blended in my mouth, became warm in my stomach. Megan ate slowly, fishing around in the salsa for bits of tomato.

"I can't wait to go to college," she said. "No one around to watch what you do."

"Is it better living with your father?"

"Dad's weird, Mom's weird, it's kind of a trade-off." She stirred her drink, wiping salt down into the slush.

"How did your dad die?" she asked.

The question surprised me.

"He had cancer. One of the kinds you're supposed to survive."

"How old were you?"

"Thirteen."

"It's a rough age to have that happen," she said.

I laughed out loud. Her expression shifted from concern to anger.

"What?" she demanded.

"Rough age, as if you're the voice of experience."

"You don't have to be any special age to know things." She stared at me and sat back in her chair. Then she looked off at the mural on the wall. The slight roundness under her chin trembled.

"I'm sorry."

She crossed her arms and looked away. "Never mind," she said. "Maybe we should go."

"I really am sorry."

"Then pay." She leaned over the table and pushed the check toward me.

We left and walked into the late afternoon sun. I wanted to touch her, to cup my hand around the nape of her neck. We strolled down the shopping street, and, as we paused to look at some of the more bizarre store windows, I felt her anger ease.

On Columbia Road we turned west and sat down near a playground at the top of the hill.

"Do you think being saved has really changed him?" I felt philosophical; drinking sometimes made me think about God.

We looked out over the playground. The sky was pink and orange behind the apartment buildings that bordered the park. Two chubby little boys started to fight over a plastic tractor.

"He's changed all right, but he had to. He got caught. And he's sorry." Her voice was bitter.

"He got caught?"

She paused, weighing something.

"He needs to make something out of everything. He couldn't have all the ruckus and just go on his merry way. He had to do something positive." She sneered when she said *positive*.

"Positive?"

"Yeah." She kicked her foot against the wall. "Jerk. Once I got a really good report card—all A's except one B. My dad has always been real big on grades, and I was so excited that I went over to his office right after school, which is something I never did. The waiting room was empty, so I went back to where the offices were, and no one was there. I started to feel scared, everything was so quiet. His office door was closed, but I heard sounds of moving behind it, so I walked up to the door to knock on it, and then I heard a woman's voice, little sounds, then not-so-little sounds. They got faster and louder, and I just stood there, listening. Finally they stopped and I heard my father's voice and a woman giggle and I just turned around and left."

"How old were you?"

"Eleven, twelve, I guess."

"You didn't tell anyone?"

"No, my mother found out some other way."

My stomach felt as if I'd hit a sudden bump in the road. I thought about my mother, wondered if he would do that to her.

"So when all this got found out, that's when he got saved?"

Megan nodded.

She put her arm around my waist. Then she leaned against me and I slid my hand down her arm, smoothed her hair.

"I'm sorry," I said.

"You had nothing to do with it." She sounded mad, as if she were going to cry.

"I just mean I'm sorry it happened."

"Well, things happen all the time. I still think my father's a jerk. And I hate all this Christian shit. I know the reason for it."

"But you said you think he's really changed."

"I think he has. That's why I'm mad, too, because he feels all better now, and I still feel like a kid standing outside his door with my stupid report card, listening to him fuck his hygienist."

Our arms were still around each other and I was suddenly aware of my limbs, as if I were singing in public and I had to decide what to do with myself. I held her lightly, unsure of what to say. Two teenage girls with bright shopping bags walked by, and I imagined Megan at twelve—standing outside a door, her face pale and freckled under the fluorescent lights, listening to her father and his nurse. I rubbed her arm, but she ignored me and stared out over the playground. I bent to kiss her shoulder, and she turned and studied me, then she slid her arms up around my neck and kissed me, a little shyly at first, then not shyly at all. We stayed like that for a long time, talking and kissing until dark.

When I walked in the door, my mother was watching TV with the lights out. Usually she read, curled up in a chair with her feet underneath her. The blue light deepened the lines in her face. A burst of canned laughter spilled out of the television. She asked how my interview went, and at first I couldn't remember what she was talking about. Then I remembered that morning and started to explain why it was lousy. Even in the dark I saw she wasn't listening, so when I said I met a friend for dinner, the lie came easily.

"Are you OK?" I asked.

"I suppose." Her voice was low.

"Did you and Hal have a fight?"

"I wouldn't call it a fight," she said. "I don't feel like talking about it now."

She forced a smile. I wanted to help her, but I was too full of Megan. When I kissed my mother's hair and said good night, she didn't move.

"Do you want me to turn off the TV?" I offered.

"No," she said.

I touched her arm and left her in front of the television.

I stretched out on my bed and thought about Megan, the way she tasted, the small sounds she made. I wondered what Hal had told my mother. I would have to say something to her, and I dreaded it.

The next day I was afraid that Megan would retreat into her prickly self, but when I called her, she suggested that we meet. Before we could arrange it, Hal must have walked into the room, because her voice changed and she hung up.

The whole week was a series of interrupted phone calls and aborted plans. I couldn't pick her up because Hal's office was adjacent to his house and my car would be recognized. There

were no buses in her neighborhood. I started to hate the sub-
urbs.

I told myself that I'd talk to my mother after I saw Megan
again. I put it off because I couldn't think of a way to say
what I knew. Finally, one Thursday night, my mother came
home early from dinner with Hal. She sat down in the kitchen
and pulled off her shoes.

"Mom, did Hal tell you about his marriage, his divorce,
and all that?" I tried to sound casual.

"Yes, he did." She was sorting through the mail, placing it
in small piles on the table. The definiteness of her answer
surprised me.

"What did he say?"

"That's between us, don't you think?"

I stood by the bulletin board, poking a large plastic tack in
and out, making a circle of tiny, dark holes.

"Well, you've seemed kind of upset. I thought it might be
something to do with that."

She looked up at me surprised.

"His first marriage has nothing to do with it. He's a much
different person now, anyway."

Her words started me, *much different now.*

"Is there anything I can do?" I didn't know what else to
say.

"No, Philip," she smiled, weary. "It's really between us."

I stuck the tack into the wood molding and decided to go
for a drive.

The following night Megan called after I'd come home from
having dinner with some friends. She sounded as if she'd
been crying.

"What happened?"

"My friend Barry was in a car accident."

"Is he alive?"

"He's in a coma."

"Do you want me to come over?"

"Yes."

"Where's your dad?" I asked.

"Out with your mother."

On the way to her house, it occurred to me that Barry might be an old boyfriend. I switched off the radio and rolled down my window. The night air was cool as I drove past the dense woods. Her front door was unlocked, and I let myself in. Megan was on the phone with another friend of Barry.

When she got off the phone, she seemed calm, as if she had settled some question. Without saying a word she went to the refrigerator and poured two large glasses of wine. She wore the backless shirt she'd bought with my mother; the fabric fell in a deep loop that showed the curve of her waist, the indentation of her backbone, all the way down to the small of her back. She padded down the hall and I followed her long legs, shadowed in the dark. We lay down on her bed and I let her talk about what happened until she started to cry again. My heart was beating quickly, out of rhythm with her sorrow. I slid my hand up under her shirt and touched her very slowly and softly. She moved against me when I put my mouth to her breasts. I was afraid to ask my question, so I touched her and waited. When she unbuttoned my shirt, reached for my pants, I knew it would be all right, and the rest of our clothes came off quickly, awkwardly.

I looked down at her face, the slope of her shoulders, her flattened breasts pale in the half-dark. Her mouth was open but she made no sound. She moved with me, but her motions seemed more a mirror of mine than her own. I slid my arms up under her knees. Her body was pliant, but she was somewhere far away, somewhere only in herself. I waited as long as I could before letting go.

Afterward, dozing, everything inside me settled into place. Then I heard voices in the living room, my mother and Hal. I started awake, sweating. I strained to hear what they were saying. What if they found me here? Then I remembered my car in the driveway. They already knew. My stomach felt like it was being squeezed by a cold hand. I heard Hal's voice, loud and angry in the living room, and I looked at the clock by Megan's bed—one-thirty-five. Megan lifted her head from the pillow and heard them. She cursed under her breath.

We lay still for a moment, then she threw back the covers and got out of bed.

"What are you—"

She took the chair from her desk and placed it under the doorknob.

"I don't want him bursting in here," she said.

The air ticked behind my thoughts. I thought of Hal talking about target practice; I wondered if he had a gun.

"He is going to kill me," I said.

"No, he's not. Besides, it's nothing he hasn't done himself."

I couldn't see her eyes in the dark, but her voice was bitter and calm.

We lay still. Hal was shouting in the living room, and then my mother's voice was raised back, something I hadn't heard in years. The front door slammed. I wondered if she'd take the car. Blood pounded in my ears. If she took the car and left me here, Hal would kill me. I was sure of it. I felt for my jeans on the floor and rattled my pockets. I had the keys.

Then my mother's voice again:

"Take me home."

"Drive your son's car home."

Her voice lowered. She must have told him there were no keys in it, reasoning with him.

Finally, they left. We lay still, listening, making sure they were gone. The house creaked. Outside, the trill of crickets and peepers shifted into high gear.

"What will he do to you?" I asked.

"He'll be furious, but he won't *do* anything." Her voice was quiet and defiant. "I'll just tell him I haven't been saved yet."

"You're not afraid of being left alone?"

"No, but you should go."

I tried to dress quickly in the dark, but my fingers felt stiff and uncoordinated.

Megan didn't dress. She got up with me and took the chair from underneath the doorknob. We stood by the door, and I slid my hands down her back, wanting to feel what I had an hour ago, but I was too nervous and shaky to feel her smoothness under my hands.

"I'll call you later in the morning."

"OK, you better go," she said.

I hurried out to the car, keys in hand. It stalled once and my heart started to pound again, but it caught the second time and I pulled out of the driveway.

When I got home, my mother was waiting. She stood by the kitchen table; the part in her hair was crooked, her eyes were bright.

"You had to do it, didn't you?" she shouted.

"Mom, I wasn't trying to—"

"It really was the last straw, do you know that? The last straw, to come back to Hal's house and realize that you two are in bed together."

My mother focused on me as if I looked different than I had that morning.

"She's just trying to get at Hal. She doesn't care about you. I hope you know that. She's a confused young woman. She'd sleep with almost anyone if she thought it would hurt him."

My mother's mouth was dark, rectangular, as her shouted words floated out. I leaned against the doorjamb and looked past her; I couldn't see outside through the kitchen light's reflection. I remembered Megan's calm defiance, her efficiency as she set that chair under the doorknob, as if it were something she had practiced. I felt the connection of everything I wanted to believe was separate—Hal gently guiding my mother through a door, Megan moving underneath me in the dark. My mother stopped to catch her breath, and her features settled back into what I knew.

Katherine L. Hester

LABOR

MONROE'S HANDS:

Monroe's hands are hard and calloused. The jagged crescent of scar gouged in the fleshy part between his thumb and forefinger. Where a chisel slipped, maybe. It was a while ago. His right index finger stubby and lopped off. Some industrial accident, he says. A faint hairline of grease under every fingernail. He keeps a can of Go-Jo in the bathroom by the sink, plunges his hands in it when he gets home from work. Twists them under the running faucet but they don't come clean, completely, ever.

"My hands," he says, surveying them bitterly. Dried blood across his knuckles, always, where he drags them across something. Insulation, wood, roofing, concrete. "My mother always said I had *artistic* hands." He splays them on his thighs. "Shows how much *she* knew." Jane takes Monroe's hand between hers.

"Artistic hands," she repeats. Trying to make him think of something else. She presses her breast, her body, her heart, into his hands. A roadmap of every job he's held, the lifeline of his labor.

MONROE'S EYES:

Monroe has faint creases in the corners of his eyes. It's what she notices the first night they're together, when he stops at the corner of a building and bends his head to the flicker of a lighter, cupped in his hands. Like a young Paul Newman, maybe. Vision's shot, he mutters, later, squinting drunkenly at the restaurant menu. Too much sun and wind and work. At night he dreams he's running wire; his hands stir the bedsheets blindly. He twitches like a dog in its sleep. "I don't dream," he says flatly, positively, when she inquires. "Those aren't dreams. They're cramps, that's all."

When Monroe gets home from work he turns his television on, in an apartment complex full of doors, huddling towards each other, with blaring television sets behind them. A good location, out near the industrial parks. A free VCR when you move in. It's moving *up*, that's what it is, and the asphalt lot in front is full of dirty pick-up trucks and company vans which must be washed every weekend or the risk is run of employee demerits. The laundry room is always full, full of bachelors who could be Monroe's brothers: hair receding slightly, the muscles in their stomachs almost washboard smooth, their biceps hard, but getting softer. Labor is a young profession.

Monroe's neighbor's sister, she drives over to the apartment complex to do his laundry. *What'll happen when he's not so quick, when his back goes bad?* she asks Jane, folding clothes in the laundry room beside her. The brother that she worries over builds the highways, their foundations firmly rooted in the broken bodies of crane operators, welders, builders. Her brother's eyes dream blankly at the alkaline dirt scraped clean, the dust, the wide, white sky. The jack-hammer keeps

him awake, the thought of four o'clock's six-pack of beer
keeps him going. Monroe's neighbor's sister believes in drug
testing, George Bush. Her mother had religion. Her brother
will be dragged down soon enough, she wants to save him
the plunging, snapping, faulty wire, the clutching fingers of
the coworker who's falling, screaming.

Duane, on the other side, he does his own laundry, bewil-
dered. The brown uniform shirts tumble, boneless, in the
dryer. You can never get them clean, completely. He's outside
the door, fumbling for a cigarette. "I need me a good
woman," he informs everyone who struggles in the door under the weight of their dirty laundry. "A good one, one
who'll wash my clothes." He used to have a girlfriend but he
doesn't any more. Monroe saw him through that, the week
Duane moved in, without any furniture, Monroe handing
him the cans of Miller out of his refrigerator. The ashtray in
the living room filled with half-smoked butts. Monroe went
down to Dan's, for a bottle of cheap bourbon. Duane picked
up the telephone. Called the house where he used to live and
hung up when his girlfriend answered. He circled the living
room edgily, turned the bottle of bourbon up until it pointed
at the asbestosed ceiling. Next door, in his apartment, the
smuggled-in rat-terrier bitch yelped and moaned, scraped at
the door until her toenails bled. The lights were off but the
television set was on. From the screen, Tom Cruise surveyed
the wreckage of the living room; the radio turned up too
loud, the trash can in the kitchen overflowing, beer cans and
McDonald's wrappers, all of it leached out under the television's heated gaze. Duane wandered to Monroe's window
and stared down at the parking lot. Maybe she would change
her mind. He took another swig of bourbon. She'd thrown his
work clothes out into the yard, the television set, the box of
tools, the half-grown dog. He used to have a girlfriend, he
said wildly, and just what did he have *now*? She'd said she'd
have the dog put down, if he didn't find a place to keep her.

He looked out at the parking lot. A girl locked the door of a red pick-up and walked across the asphalt. "Hey, honey," he yelled loudly. She turned her face toward the window and held up her hand. She pointed to the ring on her finger. Duane shrugged and leaned further out the window. "Why don't you just come on up *here?*" he instructed. "All I want's a little of your time."

Behind every door a television set is blaring. Monroe says it's education. He watches CNN, public TV. He watches "Cops," "America's Most Wanted." Leans forward intently when the policemen shove the lawbreaker face first into the mud, the booted foot square on the writhing back. "That's it," he says triumphantly, *"that's how it's done."* If Jane isn't in the apartment when he gets home, he checks the closets carefully, to make sure she hasn't been hung up, like clothes someone has worn out, a bad man, a man like one on "America's Most Wanted," one that would break into the apartment and chase her past the breakfast nook with a long knife in his hands. It happens. He's seen it on TV.

MONROE'S LEGS:

"My old man," Monroe says. "My old man, all the hair worn off his legs. I'll quit my job before I let that happen."

All those years of wearing polyester pants. Monroe's old man, run out of Baton Rouge and into Houston when he got the goods on the wrong rural policeman. Everyone knows about Louisiana.

"You're *investigating* the wrong place, boy," the three cops who stopped him on the swampy, dark shoulder of the highway told him, with Monroe watching, hunched over on the passenger seat, trying to hide his eyes from the cops' flashlight, his awkward, fourteen-year-old's knees hitting the dashboard.

"Boy," Monroe says. "Like he wasn't *nothing."* The largest cop flung his father's private investigator's license out into the sucking bayou. There was more to it than that, but that was all Monroe saw, that night. It was enough for him. His old man slid, then on, going out to the store for butter and coming back seven hours later.

Monroe's mother never asked. They lost the house, the brand-new Ford. His father swore that he was on some kind of *list,* by God. Bottles of bourbon hidden in the carport and the trunk of the car, in the wheel wells, his father's voice; raving, trailing off, under the yellow lightbulb on the screened front porch, as constant as the crickets from the stand of pines down by the rotting dock behind the house. Monroe's mother twisted her hands, bit her lips until they bled. Monroe hunched his shoulders, his arms and legs too big, hands dangling at his sides. Went down to the dock with his bamboo pole and flung the carp onto the warped boards just to watch them flop. Bringing his foot down on their dull, fishy bodies. Their cold eyes watching his booted foot descend. Not even any eyelids. He wanted them to blink.

Monroe's old man: now he's old, really *old,* and the master of the scheme, the scam. He sniffs them out like dogs onto meat. Monroe's mother takes each new one to heart like religious salvation. For a while it's water purifiers he sells door to door. Free enterprise, he calls it. When a 'client' says he can't afford one, Monroe's father puts his shoulder to the door and patiently explains it. If you sell four you can have your own, well, not for free, but at half the regular price. It's a *steal,* Monroe's old man insists, but it's just a steal for him: he gets the percentage, each time he hooks some sucker in, convinces him to sell them.

"A pyramid, then," Monroe points out, in Houston for

Christmas day. It's ninety-two degrees outside his parents' apartment complex. His father is brandishing a check to prove the value of it.

"A pyramid's fine if you're the point man," he says heartily.

And then it's the Mr. Auto-Fix-It franchise and his father's up in Dallas at a seminar, learning how to charge his customers for parts they didn't need, how to cut the largest corner and come out with a profit. Then Amway. Monroe's mother puts dollar bills in chain letters and watches for the mail. His old man has lost three houses now; "*lost* them," Monroe says, "like they were his car keys!" When they own a split-level, Monroe's mother can convince herself they're still okay. Two cars totalled, forced around the trunks of trees. One repossessed.

MONROE'S BACK:

There's a picture of Monroe, one Jane found in a box shoved under the bed, and he can't be more than twelve. His father must be riding high: there's a boat propped up, slant-wise, next to the garage. The person holding the camera must have been standing at the farthest edge of the back yard. Monroe's father sits at a metal patio table. Monroe's mother is caught beside him, in the act of pouring something from the top part of a blender into the glass he holds up to her. Her hand is on his shoulder and her face is solicitous, wiped smooth. Her high-heeled sandals sink into the grass. Her hair is swept back from her forehead in a stiff blonde dome. There are rings, gaudy, costume, on each finger of her hand. The look she gives the camera, unsteady in her high-heels, is resigned. As if she knows the rings, the boat, the brand-new Osterizer blender are all about to disappear.

Monroe is in the farthest left-hand corner of the picture. He's sitting on the ground, his knees drawn up to his chest. His back is to the patio table and his shoulders are slumped forward. He is looking at something beyond the scalloped edge of the photograph, not because it's particularly interesting, but just because it's there.

MONROE'S BODY:

Welts all over his body from sweating outside in the heat. His legs shiny where the hair's worn off. His back is going bad. He worries about hernias and lay-offs. In the morning, he drinks burned coffee in the warehouse and eyes the chart taped to the door, the chart designed by upper management to record the rise of the most productive worker, the employee who will be recognized as "Top Gun" for the month and rewarded with a ten-dollar bonus in his paycheck. Monroe hasn't been Top Gun for months. One month he called in sick, another, someone called the number painted on the back panel of his van. TELL US HOW WE DRIVE. They told his boss instead. " 'Tell us how we drive'," Monroe says. "I know how I drive. Like anybody would who has to drive this fucking interstate all day long across this fucking town." At least he hasn't gotten a speeding ticket. Then it's drug tests, reprimands. Each employee of the Company has been issued a slick, official pamphlet reiterating the problem of illegal influences. *"Watch the employee who wears sunglasses, who has called in sick, who curses over extra hours, who uses slang, whose productivity is down. . . ."* But Monroe knows it could be worse: he could be filling out forms, standing bleary-eyed in lines that snake around the Employment Commission parking lot at seven-thirty every morning. Could stand exchanging cigarettes and small-talk with the rest of them, holding their styrofoam coffee cups with broad, beat-up hands, shuffling forward and then stopping, patient, in a line that stretches, stops, bunched up until ten, maybe eleven every morning. There's always that. *Displaced workers*. Like the hand of God has scooped them up, shaken them in a meaty fist, and tossed them out, to bounce like dice along the dirty pavement. Staring snake-eyes in the unemployment line. Bones. Shook out and scattered, waiting for the wind to pick them up and blow them someplace better. There's always that. There's a bad disc in his back from lifting, stooping, carrying. The backs of his hands bloody inside the work gloves that he wears. *Laid Off*. It could be worse. Monroe stands in the shower after work, leaving a ring of gray grit around the drain. When the water runs down his face it tastes like salt, like sweat, like metal, like blood.

MONROE'S VOICE:

No matter what, Monroe sings in the shower. His voice, it swoops and stalls like the highway across the border, past the dirty customs station, down into Mexico.

"The Baja? Ruins of Spanish forts up in the mountains? Concrete huts with bananaleaf roofs down in the jungle on the Yucatan side? Tangerines you pick right off the trees?" He's seen it in the *National Geographic*. His eyes gleam, bloodshot, weary. His vision's shot, he says. Jane just can't see exactly what it is he pictures.

"We could do it. Really. Just disappear down in there and never come back. No one would ever fuck with us, no one would even know just *where* it was we'd gone. I heard it only takes three hundred bucks to live a year. . . ." He lifts his beer can to his lips. Catches Jane's stare. "Down there I wouldn't need to drink, honey."

"In Mexico," he continues, "they give you a metal driver's license. So that if your car goes over the edge of some road, bursts into flames, they'll be able to identify you." He lights a cigarette. "Your *remains*," he says with satisfaction.

JANE'S HEART:

Jane met Monroe at a party. "What do you do?" she said politely, slightly bored. "I'm a *laborer*," he said wryly, crushing his beer can with his hands.

"Well, *everybody's* a laborer," she said brightly. She didn't know a thing.

"But I can sing like anything," he told her quickly. Picturing himself on the cover of *Rolling Stone?* Inside the house, somebody put on Patsy Cline. He danced her in a circle in the bare dirt, putting his feet down carefully, as if he was balancing them along the steep ridgepole of some half-constructed house, as if they were on a broad, iron, rusty beam and that was all there was between him and the ground. He laid his hands against her back and they were big and certain, warm. She felt the callouses through her shirt.

"I have a bike," he said shyly. He made it like a question. "If you'd like to take a ride?"

No matter what, Monroe sings in the shower when he gets home from work. Towels himself off and scrubs fiercely at his greasy hands. Jane's in the bedroom. Her bags are packed. For leaving him, for Mexico? She doesn't really know. There's the hiss of the pop-top of a beer can in the kitchen, and Monroe holds it tightly, in his hands.

Thomas E. Kennedy

LANDING ZONE X-RAY

I picture the FBI that year on 83rd Street in Jackson Heights across from St. Joan of Arc's Church where years before I'd gone to dances, the spring I was fifteen, doing the lindy in a powder-blue suit with a plump, sweet-mouthed girl named Luanne.

But now it's another time; I am not a boy but a young man, a senior in college with the Army behind me and political ideas that may have consequences. I picture two men in suits climbing out of an unmarked car, chunking the doors shut, entering the wide, dim lobby of my apartment house. I picture them crossing to the elevator; one gets in, the other ducks out back to cover the fire escape. I see him stand there against the wall, chewing gum with his lips closed, dawn light shadowing the acne scars in the pit of his cheek. I see the other man's thick finger stab the elevator button for five, hear the moment's silence before the machinery hums into movement and the car lifts up the shaft past floor after floor of sleeping families, the Cohens, Mendozas, Taylors, Rakovecs, O'Connors, Giannasios.

And I see those families in bed behind locked doors in their three and four room apartments, some with little kids asleep in cribs, some old, retired, some alone, divorced, never married. I can hear the newspapers thump on their door mats as a sleepy kid jogs from floor to floor, delivering the *News*. I see the FBI man in the dim light of the ascending elevator car.

I see him, but I cannot see what he is thinking. His face is impassive, his mind, his heart closed to my reach. He is, say, forty-five years old (my age now), has a family I can barely glimpse, a smudged vision in a dream: a woman in a bathrobe, a house somewhere, a suburb, kids, two boys. Does he cheat on her? Is he a bully, a tyrant at home? Did she give him a plate of eggs this morning before he left to do this? Does he think patriotic thoughts about what he is about to do? Is he reluctant, grim? Did he himself fight in WWII or Korea and feel cheated by our type? Is it a meanly agreeable task, cornering the enemy in their sleep?

I see his face only fleetingly through the round window of the elevator door as the car lifts past, up toward where I see myself now, asleep in Apt. 5D on a box-spring mattress beneath the high ceiling, within the shadowy walls, pale bars of light falling through the slats of the venetian blinds across my sheet-draped body.

I open my eyes. Danny is no longer snoring on the sofa. He stands on bare feet on the dusty wood floor, buttoning his plaid shirt. I sit up on my elbows. He says, "Something wrong," cocks an ear, eye whites luminous in the shadowy light. A clock ticks on the window ledge: 5:00 a.m. The elevator grinds and echoes in the shaft. I watch Danny's sockless feet find tennis sneakers. Then he is through the kitchen door, mounting the window ledge, out onto the fire escape, looking down through the bars. "Damn!" he sobs.

I hear the elevator stop on my floor, hear the tiny creak of its door opening, hear a finger stab at my dead doorbell, then a fist slamming the door itself as Danny climbs up instead of down, and I see the fire escape trembling under his weight and the weight of someone coming up from beneath, hollering.

Sometimes on a winter afternoon I sit at my desk here by the window, miles, years away, and look out at the water and the sky, gray as lead and just as still, and everything seems to make sense. The sky seems to take me to it, take my heart, and my stomach moves like when you look off a high building, and you know in your body suddenly how small and fragile and frightened you really are.

All I want to do then is pack it in for the day, go down to the kitchen and have a cup of coffee with Stephanie or yell out to the kids, "Hey! Jack? Kathy? Emergency up here! Come on up and give the old man a hug!" And rejoice in the fact they will come running, they will still do that for me.

We get to thinking things are stationary sometimes, but of course they're not. Everything is changing constantly, from minute to minute. A week, a month is nothing. A year goes like a dream. I waited so long in my life before having kids and now, in five years already both of them will be teenagers, off on their own most the time, that great sense of closeness we've developed will turn to secrecy, aversion, impatience. They will begin to take their own positions on things, will take chances, risk themselves on actions whose meanings will later seem to change, open to question. This is what parents know.

It was the same for us with our own folks. It's all in the natural order of things. They'll be off learning for themselves, beyond my control, uninterested in my advice; and I'll sit up here at my desk, stare out at the sea and pray they come to no serious harm, knowing there is a real risk they will, and I'll have to face it on my own, whatever it is I see there that gives me this scary feeling of merging with forever. Stephanie and I will have to learn to live together with quiet again, see if we can face it together.

"It's incredible how short a life really is," she said to me the other day, dazed by the sudden realization that it had been twenty-five years since her little brother was shot to death in the war. She said it in a way that went straight to my heart, made me feel the way I do when I sit here and look at the sea in the dead of winter.

When I was a kid, ten or fifteen, my father used to say, "That was, oh, twenty, twenty-five years ago," and I used to think how strange to be so old you can remember history.

Now I think of Danny that morning they got him and *that* was twenty-three years ago. I never saw him again. We exchanged a few letters, then I lost contact with him. I saw his mother once or twice on the street in Jackson Heights before I moved away. She was about fifty I suppose, a tall, slim woman with short red hair and Danny's big broad nose. I don't think I ever saw her smile. She was divorced, and very strict with Danny, whose father lived in Florida. She stared at me on the street, watched me with her pale eyes. She despised what Danny had done, called him a coward and a traitor, praised his older brother in the Navy, told Danny he was just like his no-good run-off father. And she never forgave me for hiding him, would not speak to me, only stared, with those hard, pale eyes. That was so many years ago. She might well be dead now.

Danny got a dishonorable discharge and four years at Leavenworth, came out to do some small-time dealing, worked as a mule, lived in communes in California, disappeared in Mexico during the seventies. That was his story, history. I knew him since high school, a nice enough fellow to start with, a year younger than me, a tall big-nosed guy who seemed always uncertain of things, but good humored. He was always nodding to some private music, rhythm and blues, or plucking an invisible electric bass and miming notes with his lips, singing blues lyrics, "You know I feel so bad/ Like a ballgame on a rainy day . . ."

In 1968, after he finished advanced infantry training at Fort Dix, he drew orders for Vietnam. He was given a week's leave first, and he ran for it. He lived where he could for a couple of years, spent the last six months at my place until they came and took him away.

I learned later that it was his girlfriend turned him in, Kathy Giovanni, a small, slight, green-eyed girl with overlapping front teeth she used to hide with her tongue when she smiled. Why she did that to him I cannot imagine. She was always quiet with him. For a few years there, the two of them were always together. I don't ever remember hearing them speak, just standing together, or walking with their arms around each other, Danny very tall beside her, going off by themselves, walking to Mass together on Sunday mornings, speaking quietly, intently.

Then he ran from his orders, and she turned him in. I try to picture her getting out the phone book, turning pages to *F, Federal, Federal Bureau of Investigation,* dialing, saying, "I want to report a military deserter." I picture her lips, overlapping teeth near the mouthpiece of the phone, and I try to look into her mind, her heart, but cannot understand why she would do that to him. Was she bitter that his becoming an outlaw also meant leaving her? Did she hope he would only serve a few months in jail and then come back to her? Did she have her own political convictions, that a boy should be willing to give his life for his country even in a war like Vietnam?

The one FBI man already had Danny in handcuffs up on the roof when I opened the door to see a broad-faced man in a suit flash a wallet with a piece of metal in it, say something, shove me into the room before him, looking around at the blankets on my sofa, my bed, the banged up furniture.

Then Danny was being stuffed back through the kitchen

window from the fire escape, and the other Fed with the acne scars was there. Danny looked young and slight next to him in the kitchen, his pale hair and light skin, his features clear, still young, untouched. He was twenty-two years old. Legal age. Expected to fight for his country. Old enough to vote. But he looked like a boy there, standing beside that man.

"He don't know anything about it," Danny said to the cop, jerking his head at me. That was when I noticed his hands were cuffed behind his back and there was blood between his teeth and his mouth was swollen.

"Did I ask you something?" the broad-faced cop asked quietly, staring into Danny's face. Then his hand shot out, and he smacked him. Danny's head jerked to the side, and he looked at me, smirked. I was too scared to pull faces. I just stood there in my pajamas, shivering while the cop poked through my things.

I had a poster on the wall that was a close-up photograph of a derelict staggering down a city street over the caption *We have all come from lovers*. The cop ran his hand in behind the poster, tearing one corner of it, feeling the wall. Then he looked at the picture, smirked. "Beautiful," he said. "Just beautiful." He opened my bureau drawers, jerked them all the way out so the contents spilled on the floor as he checked beneath them. He opened the freezer section of my refrigerator and ran the ice cube trays under the hot water tap, watching them carefully as the frost melted from them. He went into the bathroom and lifted the porcelain lid off the toilet tank and peered in.

"Better watch out," Danny said. "Could be some dangerous crap in there." I shook my head to silence him.

Then the cop came back inside and looked at Danny. "You *stupid* jerk," he said. "You're screwed. And for *what?*" He jabbed the tip of his finger against my chest and asked my name. I told him, Paul Casey, and he asked my draft status, what kind of discharge I had, where I'd served.

"Fort Ben Harrison," I said. "Honorable discharge."

He snorted. "Chairborn cowboy. Private pencil." The other cop put his face close to mine, so I could smell the coffee and cigarettes on his breath, and he said, "I want you to wait right here, Casey, 'cause I'm coming back for you with a warrant. Now don't you touch a thing here, I got it all memorized, and you touch a thing, I got you for tampering with evidence in addition to being an accomplice to a felony. You got that, Casey?"

They led Danny out, reading him his rights, and that was the last I ever saw of him, with his shirt hanging out and blood between his teeth, tennis sneakers with no socks, and his wrists cuffed at the small of his back.

As soon as they were gone, I flushed the two joints I had in my cigarette pack down the toilet. I watched my fingers tremble as I broke and emptied them into the water. Then I scrubbed the bowl with Ajax and sat down on my sofa and waited.

Five blocks away, my mother and father were just getting up out of bed in their shingle-and-stucco house on Hampton Street. My father, a squat, bull-faced man, would be standing at the bathroom sink shaving, while my mother put on coffee down in the kitchen. They never spoke about the war. If I brought it up they would only stare, or change the subject, look away. The only thing they ever said was, "Thank God you got out before it started for real." My mother said that. My father said nothing. He had never been a soldier himself, too young for the first war, too old for the next two. He was a kind, quiet man, who would never allow anyone to use the word *nigger* in his presence without calling them on it. For many years, I did the same.

They used to call me *Paul X* in the neighborhood, many of my old friends who inherited their parents' racism. I argued with them. If they said, "Nigger," I corrected them, "Negro." Then it became a joke, so that if I said, "Negro," *they* corrected *me*, ''Nigger,'' and I had to give it up then because they turned it into a joke.

But for a while there, a short while in the Sixties, it seemed as though many of them changed. In the end, none of them wanted to go to Vietnam, and those who did go came back opposed to it. Their general view of things seemed to soften. Racism went out of style. Everyone was suddenly more open to one another, or so it seemed, for a time.

I didn't know anyone who *wanted* to go. I knew one guy who said he was gay to get out of going and was haunted by that for the rest of his life, others who got doctors to testify to false disabilities, chronic skin diseases, back disorders. I knew two guys who moved to Canada before they were called, and several who were called and went against their will, a few of whom came back in body bags or missing a leg or an arm or limping, or broken in other ways. One guy named Brian Macauley came back and never left his house, sat in the front window staring out at the street, and you could see tears spilling out of his eyes, although his face was perfectly still. My wife's brother got killed there, five years before they came and took Danny.

Danny is the only guy I knew who deserted. Aside from marching a couple of times, and signing petitions, things like that, sheltering Danny was the only active thing I ever did against the war. Nothing to speak of, really.

It is hard to fathom the mistakes a nation can make, mistakes that mean the death of thousands of men and women, blown-up, burned, maimed, shot. I sit in my living room or at the window of my study looking out over the sea, warm, comfortable, and try to imagine Danny, try to understand his life, or the life of my wife's brother, Jimmy, who got called in when he was nineteen and got shot in the stomach and the leg and the face. I see a rifle bullet enter his face alongside the nose, tear through his brain, open the back of his head, others burning into his stomach, shattering his thigh bone. I see

Jimmy, with whom I used to play basketball in the P.S. 89 school yard, set shots, twenty-one, a black-haired kid with a quick grin who was called and went and got killed so fast no one even knew there was a war on yet. They didn't even have the notification teams organized yet. Stephanie's parents got a telegram delivered by a cab driver. I sit safe and warm in my home now a quarter of a century later, and I still see Jimmy's grin, see him duck and feint and jump, drop the ball into the hoop. And I see him fall, know pain, horror, at nineteen, beyond anything I have ever known or am likely to experience in my life, hopefully beyond anything my own children will ever know.

I can't really picture it. I can *see* him hit, bleed, fall. I can force my mind to create an image of his face shattering around a rifle bullet, but I cannot really experience it in my imagination, no more than I can experience Danny's fate at Leavenworth. Was he raped, broken, *protected, educated?* His letters revealed nothing of what his real life there was like, and I didn't ask. When he got out, he headed straight for San Francisco, the Haight-Ashbury, then full of criminals, as was the East Village in New York, and for that matter the whole so-called Peace and Love Movement.

Danny wrote a few more letters about *muling,* about trips into Mexico, about a score so good he bought a new Ford Fairlane, about a commune where he stayed out in the desert, in the mountains. And then there were no more letters and the ones I sent to his last address were returned *unknown.* That was a good fifteen or eighteen years ago. I no longer know where his mother lives, or his older brother, and I have moved so many times that if Danny tried to get in touch with me it is unlikely he would succeed. Most likely he is dead. Or in prison in Mexico.

I sat for nearly three hours waiting for the FBI men to return to my apartment after they took Danny away. Finally I realized they were not coming back for me, that I was free, off the hook. Well, it actually took some time before I really felt free of them. In some respects I continued to wait, felt them watching me. Every tear at the corner of a piece of mail, every click on the telephone made me think of them, but they never came back, never made themselves known in any way. Maybe my name still sits in some file somewhere and would ring a bell if I ever applied for a security clearance, but at least I was never interrogated, never had to spend even a day in jail. My life was allowed to go on without any disruption. I did not have to enter a penitentiary, see the hard faces there, waiting for me, did not have to die.

I had gone into the Army after six months of college, volunteered for the draft to get it out of the way, and was discharged in 1964, the year the Gulf of Tonkin Resolution was adopted and President Johnson started getting serious about Vietnam. So I was spared that. My first six months in college I was an ROTC student—that's how abruptly my life changed in the Sixties—so if I had gone on to finish according to plan, I would have been graduated as a second lieutenant in 1967, would no doubt have gone right to combat in the Nam. I would have been forced to make a choice that might have drastically changed my whole life one way or the other, death or prison or exile. But I was spared that.

How arbitrary it all seems. Danny's life, mine. A president makes a bad choice, thousands of people die violent deaths. My life has been more or less normal. I married, have a house, children, a job. I live a quiet life. I wear my political convictions, such as they are, quietly. I am old enough now to glimpse that place up ahead where my days will end, a natural death probably, although who knows? Perhaps I will be killed by someone shaped into a murderer by poverty, misery, the chance turning of events. Or perhaps not. Perhaps I will die as quietly as fall becomes winter, a withering, fading.

Sometimes darkness, gloom, is a comfort. One chill dark day, early winter, you look at the frozen earth, and you know that some winter will be your last one, you will miss the next beat in the rhythm, we all will, and that is actually a comfort sometimes, in the way it is a comfort on a chill dark day to see a light in the window of a strange house, a yellow lampshade on a table behind gauze curtains. Mysteries.

Like the mystery of Danny's life. I try to picture what it was like for Danny in jail. He didn't say much about it in his letters, not about the actual conditions, but it must have been a cruel experience. I ask myself why Danny did what he did, why I hid him. What was really in my heart, in Danny's? Why was he ruined by the war? Because he was altruistic? Naive? Did he simply decide he could not kill, could not bear to risk his own life for an historical mistake, and lost it anyway? Did he just use poor judgment? Try to save his skin in a foolhardy way? Or was he just unlucky? A historical casualty? We didn't really discuss it. We didn't talk much about the war. We watched it on TV most nights, of course, shook our heads, groaned, but we were not political, didn't discuss the whole situation. Danny just deserted and, when the time came, I let him stay with me.

What about the generals, the politicians, the people who marched, the people who stayed home, the people who supported the war, and the ones who were just indifferent to it all? I know what my father believed. He said it once finally to me, reluctantly. "We *need* an army, son. People can't just go and run off." I smirked.

"But do we *need* this war?"

I saw Danny's girlfriend, the one who turned him in, once more, many years later. It took me several moments to recognize her. She had gained a lot of weight, but slowly her face appeared from amidst the heavy jowls and sagging wattles. I could see her face, the crooked tooth, the pale green eyes. She was wearing a gray cloth coat, standing outside the projects in Jamaica, near where I teach, and she was shouting after a child of ten or so. I stared at her, recognized her finally, and she looked back at me, but her face showed nothing. It was an empty face, or seemed so, one without emotion, neither joy nor sorrow, but who can judge from a moment's glance?

Now, so many years later, I try to recall Danny's face. I can remember he joked a lot, that he loved rhythm and blues music, used to play an imaginary bass guitar and mime the notes with his mouth. I can remember him with his girlfriend, the two of them with their arms around one another off by themselves, talking quietly. But in truth that is all I can remember. I can hardly remember him at all, cannot call his face to mind in more than the vaguest details, cannot close my eyes and see it there. It is almost as though I never knew him, as though none of it ever happened, although of course it did.

He did run from the army, I did hide him, I did see two federal policemen lead him out of my apartment in hand-cuffs, shirt out, blood between his teeth, his young innocent mouth swollen.

Twenty-two years later, on an airplane flying to a conference in the Midwest, the stewardess offers me a magazine, and I select *U.S. News & World Report,* in which I read a story about the 25th anniversary of a battle at Landing Zone X-Ray, judged to be the first real battle of Vietnam, on November 14, 1965. The story recounts in detail the five-day encounter, which took the lives of 234 Americans and 2,000 Vietnamese. The article narrates the battle, discusses tactics and strategy, the use of helicopters, tells about many of the individual soldiers who fought, plots their movements on a map through each day of the encounter, describes their wounds, an eyewitness-account of a lieutenant bleeding from the neck, another whose brains literally spill into his helmet, corpsmen squeezing bloodbags into the veins of men bleeding to death.

I know about this battle; it is here that Stephanie's little brother was killed. The article does not mention his name.

The story ends with a piece about a meeting between the two generals who ran the battle, the American Lt. General "Hal" Moore, the Vietnamese General, Vo Nguyen Giap. General Moore is now 65 years old, General Giap is 80, an aged smiling man. They meet and converse for ninety minutes under the observation of a reporter who had been present covering Landing Zone X-Ray 25 years before. When the time comes for the two old generals to part, General Moore, a big red-headed man with an underslung jaw, takes off his wristwatch and presents it to Giap—*A small gift from one old soldier to another.*

Giap cups the watch in both hands. Then he embraces his former enemy. The article leaves the two old generals in one another's arms.

I stuff the magazine into the seat pouch in front of me, glance out the window at the landscape below which looks like quadrants of sheet metal rivetted together. It occurs to me that, with a quiet impartiality, I am observing the history of my own years.

I feel no rancor. I have read the article with interest, with a certain enthusiasm even, curious to know the details of the men who fought that battle, to know what became of the survivors. I am sad for the dead, shaken by LBJ's mistake, America's mistake, baffled by revisionism that would have us no longer feel shame about it all, baffled by my own quiet acceptance of it all. I feel no anger. Not toward Johnson or Nixon or the generals or those two FBI men who took Danny away, or the political mistakes that murdered my wife's brother.

This is my story, the story of my time. This is what was going on when I was young. I think of Danny, probably dead now, and maybe his last hours were terrible, his last years, or maybe he is still alive, huddled against an adobe wall in Mexico, broken, rotting in his own dirt, ill, soon dead. We all will be one day, and at the hour of our death, we will look back over our time and regret its passing and puzzle over it, and all of our friends and all of our enemies will be the people we shared our time with. All the dead men and all the women will turn their hollow gazes toward us then, and I do not think we will wish that we had done more or less or something else.

I think death, finally, will become the passage we choose. Resistance will dissolve, and the mystery of all the people we ever touched or who touched us will fold into our hearts at that final moment, like the embrace of an enemy, very old now and smiling.

BIOGRAPHIES
and Some Comments by the Authors

Terry Bain: "I served for one year as managing editor of *Willow Springs* magazine. I earned an M.F.A. at Eastern Washington University, and since then I've been working as a technical and advertising copy writer. My fiction has appeared in *The Gettysburg Review* and *The Quarterly*.

"About four years ago I wrote a poem, or tried to write a poem, called 'On Kosmos Lane.' As with most poems, I was simply never happy with the process, nor the product. A few Augusts ago, I visited Kosmos Lane again, the place where the poem supposedly occurred, and I jotted down the names of the streets, and turned the corners a few times in my car. Then, while house-sitting for one of my writing teachers, feeding rabbits and cats, lounging in the swimming pool, and reading all I could from her bookshelves, guilt began to pile up because I wasn't writing much. Ideas were rolling around in my head about the nature of myth and repetition and rhythm, and I knew I should vent them on paper. I needed a springboard for a story, and I stumbled across my notes: 'Left on Kosmos, Left on Crystal, Left on Cherry.' I decided to salvage the poem, which I thought might work better as a story anyway. Luckily, I didn't have the poem at hand, so my only reference materials were from memory and my notes on Kosmos, Crystal, and Cherry. I sat down at my teacher's desk and, after rifling through all her drawers for the proper pen, I wrote the first draft of 'Games,' as well as sketches for several other stories based on the main character, Teddy. This collection of stories, which my friends call 'The Teddy Stories,' is slowly becoming a book, which I have entitled *Calling Them Rain and Calling Them River*. 'Games' is only my second published story, and is the first published from this collection."

Alison Baker was born in Pennsylvania, grew up in Indiana, has lived in Chicago, Maine, and Utah, and now lives with her husband in the Rogue Valley of southern Oregon. Her story collection, *How I Came West, and Why I Stayed*, was published in 1993 by Chronicle Books.

"A friend of mine once mentioned in passing that one of his colleagues had changed sex. He said it was a little unsettling, and then we went on to discuss other things. But the idea lingered somewhere in the bowels of my mind, and one day when I sat down at my desk a man popped his head through a door in my brain and said 'I'm changing sex.' Another man, sitting at a desk not unlike my own, said, 'For the better, I hope'; and so Byron Glass and his friend Zach/Zoe sprang into action. They carried on from there, and I scrambled along behind them, typing as fast as I could, trying to record their conversations and experiences accurately.

"One of the pleasures of writing fiction is that you can lie or you can tell as much truth as you want to, and no one can be quite sure which you are doing when. So I do both, usually at the same time. It is a comforting way of revising both my own past and the apparent present, as well as foretelling the unlikeliest of much-to-be-desired futures."

Marlin Barton: "I grew up in the Black Belt of Alabama and graduated from the University of Alabama. I received an M.F.A. from the writing program at Wichita State University, and I now teach at Clemson University. My stories have appeared in *The Southern Review, Shenandoah,* and the *South Carolina Review.*

"Before I began writing 'Jeremiah's Road,' I thought that it was going to be a short simple story that probably wouldn't take long to write. I couldn't have been more wrong. As I wrote, Jeremiah became more and more complex, and his story grew in ways that I hadn't anticipated but was glad to discover. This is the only story I've ever written in the present tense, but it seemed right somehow."

Amy Bloom is the author of *Come to Me* (HarperCollins, 1993), a collection of short stories. Her fiction has appeared in *Story, Antaeus, Mirabella, The New Yorker,* and other magazines.

" 'Semper Fidelis' is another slightly twisted tribute to love. I wrote about the things that scare me (lingering illnesses), the things that charm me (the way women care for each other through beauty trivia), and the things I believe (fidelity is not about where you put your body)."

Kelly Cherry is the author of ten books, including *God's Loud Hand* (poems), *The Exiled Heart* (an autobiographical narrative), and *My Life and Dr. Joyce Brothers* (a novel in stories).

"The first line of this story, and hence the story, came to me while I was walking my dog. I had published a sequence of stories about a woman living in the Midwest, and now I realized that I wanted to follow her life a while longer and also that I wanted to know more about her neighbors, among whom were Shelley and Ian Wallace.

"My dog and I were home in twenty minutes, but it took me six years to complete the story. I'm a slow writer. I like to work on a draft of something, set it aside to turn to a draft of something else, and then set that aside to turn to a draft of something *else.* I need all those drafts before I can see all the dimensions and aspects, in each case, of the thing I'm doing. The payoff, as a friend pointed out, is that while one thing will be far from finished, another will be nearly done. 'It's like keeping your money in C.D.s that come due at different times,' he said. And I guess it is rather like that."

Judith Ortiz Cofer: "I was born in Hormigueros, Puerto Rico, and spent part of my childhood on the island with my mother and brother while my father was on sea duty with the U.S. Navy. The rest of the time we lived in Paterson, New Jersey. Some years it was six months in each place, so I can honestly say that I lived a bilingual, bicultural life. 'Nada' and the other Paterson/Island stories are part of my new collection of prose and poetry, *The Latin Deli*.

" 'Nada,' like many of my poems, essays, and stories, arose out of a meditation on a Spanish word or phrase. The power of my native language is concentrated not just in the word spoken, but also on the intonation, the nonverbal signals that pass between people. This is true for most cultures, I know, but as I have of necessity distanced myself from my sources of Spanish, I have begun to focus on the triggering effect that a word has on my imagination, bringing back not just memories, but also emotional associations that motivate me to pursue the word to its real meaning in the culture. This is often the beginning of the creative process for me.

"*Nada* means 'nothing.' There was a triggering incident to my interest in the word: I had heard a woman friend say that when she lost her mate, she felt like giving everything away and almost did. And this is a woman who collects for pleasure: antiques, knickknacks, books; her house is a museum to her eclectic interests and joy of life. Yet it was all meaningless in the face of her loss. I wanted to explore the depths of a woman's anguish when she was left with nada. I also wanted to give voice to the strong women of the barrio—the ones who understood the word's power to destroy a life, who supported each other in *la lucha* of their daily lives, and who defended one another's right to die with dignity. I hope my work is a tribute to the women of my childhood, who taught me by their example that self-respect is the key to a woman's, and an artist's, survival."

Elizabeth Cox: "I grew up in Chattanooga, Tennessee, on the campus of Baylor School where my father was headmaster. From the window of my bedroom I could see the Tennessee River and Williams Island in a valley of mountains. I have never gotten over the vision of the mountains and river I saw each morning. I often write of that place, but my story, 'The Third of July,' has a more rural setting. I based the story on an accident seen during a Fourth of July weekend in the 1960s.

"I like to dramatize the needs of women whose lives are not exciting or flamboyant, but who prove to be necessary to the people around them. These women are often defined, or even criticized, as complacent. I see Nadine as a solid though restless soul. I see her as unselfishly loving."

Stuart Dybek grew up in Chicago, and currently teaches writing at Western Michigan University. He is the author of two books of stories and a collection of poems.

" 'We Didn't' began as a poem that I tinkered unsuccessfully with through several drafts until finally, in a hotel room in Anchorage on a borrowed typewriter, it evolved into a story. That same process—a poem becoming a story—has occurred in my work often enough so that it shouldn't still surprise me, but it does. What was unique for me in this particular instance was that, rather than an image or an incident from my own memory or imagination, what initially generated 'We Didn't' was a poem that I'd read titled 'We Did It.' It's a poem by Yehuda Amichai, an Israeli poet, whose work I've long admired for its wise, humanistic vision and comic vitality. In his poem, he—or in any case his translator—takes 'doing it,' a phrase that has always struck me as one of the more tacky, inarticulate variations of the many, mostly inadequate terms to describe making love (a pretty misleading term in itself) and playfully elevates it. I had the notion of engaging his poem in a sort of dialogue, of playing an American-Judeo-Christian 'Thou Shalt Not' off his psalmlike 'Thou Shalt.' It seemed like an entertaining idea for a poem, but as I worked on developing it, characters began to emerge from anecdotes and I surrendered to them. Once the characters began running things, I realized that what interested me most about the idea was how often we allow our experiences to be defined by what they supposedly should be, so that sometimes such experiences—intense and haunting as they are—can finally only be expressed in the negative: what they are not."

Janice Eidus: "I grew up in the Bronx, New York—and have lived all over since then—and now live in midtown Manhattan with my husband and cat. My new novel is *Urban Bliss* (Fromm, April 1994). My first novel, *Faithful Rebecca*, was published in 1987, and my short story collection, *Vito Loves Geraldine*, appeared in 1990.

"This story, 'Pandora's Box'—which I wrote while I was in residence for a month at the artists colony Ragdale—will appear in a forthcoming collection of stories. It was a painful story for me to write, and being away from my home and my 'real life' helped me enormously to focus on it, to enter Pandora's world, which I very much needed to do. And I was passionate about wanting to write this story about a woman so abused, so mistreated throughout her life, that the very fact that she discovers ways to survive—and to survive still with a generosity of spirit toward others, in fact—takes on almost mythic proportions. For me, although Pandora is a victim, she is also a female hero."

Michael Fox grew up in New York and Vermont. He is living in Ann Arbor, Michigan, working toward an M.F.A. degree from the University of Michigan. "Rise and Shine" is his first published short story.

" 'Rise and Shine' arose out of a dream I no longer remember (fiction has superseded it) and a nauseated mood inspired by living badly in New York City. The first draft had to do with bugs and spilled soup and a vacuum cleaner, configured as illustration of a cosmic order inverted . . . something like that. Nothing but the mood of the first version remains in what is (re)published here."

Helen Fremont was raised in Upstate New York and lives in Boston, where she writes fiction as an antidote to her job as a public defender. A graduate of the Warren Wilson M.F.A. Program for Writers, she has worked as a Peace Corps Volunteer in Southern Africa, a prosecutor of corrupt lawyers in Massachusetts, and a hut caretaker for the Appalachian Mountain Club. Her fiction has appeared in *The Harvard Review*, *Phoebe*, and *Ploughshares*.

" 'Where She Was' was born in a bathtub and went through several revisions during a rainy year in Boston. The characters and sections tumbled together somewhat haphazardly, and to this day I have no idea who Elmer is, or what he is doing there. Less mysterious is the rain, which appears with uncanny predictability the moment I set Vibram sole to mountain trail. But essentially, I think, I was interested in exploring the hope born of a lifelong commitment to uncertainty that is at the heart of the story."

John Rolfe Gardiner, a fiction contributor to numerous magazines, is the author of the novels *Great Dream from Heaven*, *Unknown Soldiers*, and *In the Heart of the Whole World*, and the story collections *Going on Like This* and *The Incubator Ballroom*. He lives in Loudoun County, Virginia, with his wife Joan and daughter Nicola.

"Composition of 'The Voyage Out' began with the recollected anecdote of a small boy asking his mother to explain the Trinity. My family kept two English schoolboys during W.W. II—brothers who had lost their headmaster to a German bomb. Each fall we packed them off to a Canadian boarding school according to their parents' instruction. As a child, I doubt I ever considered the details of their ocean journey to America. I would have been preoccupied with the real wail of the air raid siren on top of our suburban Virginia home, and the blackout drills my father could command with a lever on the siren's control box. The story must have had a long incubation, but how it developed into the present tale of a boy's tragicomic displacement and maturation I couldn't hope to explain without concocting a list of half-truths and conceits. With this invitation to analysis it's probably more forthcoming to say that if I sat long enough at the typewriter I could hope to be visited by a few happy accidents."

Elizabeth Graver's short story collection, *Have You Seen Me?* was awarded the 1991 Drue Heinz Prize and published by the University of Pittsburgh Press, and in paperback by Ecco Press. Her short stories have appeared in *Best American Short Stories, 1991, Antaeus, The Southern Review, Story, Southwest Review*, and elsewhere. She currently lives in Somerville, Massachusetts and teaches English and creative writing at Boston College.

"A few years before I wrote 'The Boy Who Fell Forty Feet,' I taught English to French junior high school students in a suburb of Paris. On my first day of teaching, I walked into the classroom to find a tiny, long-haired girl roaring like a lion in the back row. Years later, she reappeared in my mind and became the first line of this story, which unwound from there in a rather mysterious way. Though the crane scene is based partially on an event I read about in the newspaper, I see this largely as a story about what might either be called imagination or lies. The boy invents stories as a way both to get through to his mother and comprehend the loss of his father. And yet it is not until the end of the story, when the boy realizes he cannot imagine his way into his father's situation in the hospital, that he truly comes up against the unthinkable nature of the loss."

Katherine L. Hester, a native of Texas, grew up in Athens, Georgia, and now lives in Austin, Texas, where she received her master's degree in English from the University of Texas at Austin in 1993. She currently holds a James A. Michener postgraduate fellowship in writing awarded by the Texas Center for Writers. Her fiction has appeared in the *Indiana Review* and is forthcoming in the *Cimarron Review*. She is currently at work on a novel.

" 'Labor,' my first published short story, was one of those stories that sometimes comes to writers almost like a 'gift.' Stories like that don't come to me very often, and when they do, I can't help but feel both happy and grateful. I wrote the first paragraph of the story while sitting in my car in traffic snarled by road work, one typically sweltering Austin day. Once I got home and typed that first paragraph out, the rest of the story came quickly, and almost seemed to write itself."

Thomas E. Kennedy grew up in Elmhurst, New York, and has lived many places since, currently in Copenhagen, Denmark, where he serves inter alia as European Editor of *Cimarron Review*. He started trying to write when he was seventeen and published his first story when he was thirty-eight in 1982. In the following ten years he has published five books, including the novel *Crossing Borders* (Watermark, 1990) and about sixty-five stories. His "Years in Kaldar" (from *The Literary Review*) won the Charles Angoff Award in 1988, and "Murphy's Angel" (from *New Delta Review*) won a Pushcart Prize in 1990. He has just completed his second novel, *The Book of Angels*.

" 'Landing Zone X-Ray' contains a few scraps of personal

biography—the apartment at the beginning is a real place where I once did shelter a deserter, but he was nothing like the character in the story. While I did have a powder-blue suit and dance the lindy at St. Joan's, my wife does not have a brother who died in Vietnam. However, I lost a number of friends due to the war, killed in action or damaged in other ways, and there is a friend who disappeared many years ago whose fate I never learned. But the story as such and all the characters are invented, including the narrator and his family. The impulse to write it started with the ending. When I learned about the meeting between the two opposing generals in 1990, that they had survived to embrace and pay respect to one another, I was reminded painfully of all those whose lives were damaged during those years. I was angry at the generals, embracing like players after an exciting game, the dead forgotten like so many plastic pieces. My initial anger at them, however, was resolved in writing the piece as I came to recognize that we are all more or less powerless in the face of history, that history only appears in retrospect, and though we live our youth with fervor—as, I suppose, we should—in the end, looking back, we seem to have been mere spectators of that which will have become the history of our own time, that sometimes a holocaust rages around us and passes, leaving us by dumb luck still standing, unscathed other than by the pain of what we have witnessed. With my story, I hoped to put that pain to rest for myself—not to forget, but to find a deeper peace."

David McLean was born and grew up in Granite City, Illinois. He graduated from Bradley University in Peoria, Illinois, in 1987. He has lived and worked in London, Boston, and Slovakia and currently lives in Brookline, Massachusetts. "Marine Corps Issue" was his first published short story.

"I remember reading *Escape and Torture* as a teenager. My father was a career Marine and our house always contained a lot of Marine Corps memorabilia. Years later it occurred to me that it was a strange book for a fifteen year old to have on his shelf, there with Sherlock Holmes and *The Baseball Encyclopedia*. My father's career had always impressed me, but I had never put two and two together: the young recruits we had watched him march across the parade grounds in San Diego between 1969 and 1972 were going off to war, a place my father had already been. The gap between what I grew up witnessing and how removed I actually was from this part of my father's life sparked the story. I went back to *Escape and Torture* and wondered what it could reveal if found hidden in a locked box.

The first half of the story took numerous drafts as I groped for a voice. The second half seemed to know exactly where to go. I had been starting and quitting stories for a few years before I finally finished one—this one—and mailed it to *The Atlantic Monthly*."

Lorrie Moore is the author of two collections of stories, *Self-Help* and *Like Life*, and of the novel *Anagrams*. Her second novel, *Who Will Run the Frog Hospital?*, will be published in September 1994. She has also edited *I Know Some Things*, an anthology of short stories about childhood, and is currently a professor of English at the University of Wisconsin in Madison.

"These kinds of opportunities for comment always stump me. But I love to read other people's responses—so noble, cooperative, anxious, bestruggled! So maybe it would be mean of me not to offer *something*.

" 'Terrific Mother' is about an improvised convalescence and its incongruous setting. Its inspiration comes from a number of different sources—like furniture bought and arranged eclectically so as not to refer to any particular store. My hope was that the story's disparate parts would come together with enough friendliness to make something sturdy and at least temporarily real.

"I'm very honored to have it included in this book."

Susan Starr Richards: "I was born and raised in Florida but have spent my last thirty years in Kentucky. I've never figured out whether I'm a fiction writer who happens to raise racehorses or a horse breeder who happens to write fiction. I've spent a lot of long nights alone in the barn waiting for my mares to foal. On quiet nights it's a good job for a writer. I started 'The Hanging in the Foaling Barn' several years ago; it began as a serious and rather grim tale about a contest of wills that turns into an actual attempt at murder. I wasn't happy writing it; it seemed inhuman, somehow. So I put it away. When the *Thoroughbred Times* announced its first fiction prize, I got the story out and looked at it again. I recast it as a comic story, and had a very good time writing it that way.

"My husband and I live and raise horses on six hundred acres of rough, half-wooded, Outer Bluegrass land. I'm putting together a collection of stories. I'm now in the last stages (I hope and pray) of a novel called *In the Chapel of Carnal Love*, based on the Arthurian legends. I've managed to get a horse farm and a horse race into it."

Mary Tannen is the author of three novels—*Second Sight, After Roy,* and *Easy Keeper*—as well as three children's books. Her work has appeared in *The New Yorker, Mirabella,* and *Allure*.

" 'Elaine's House' is very loosely based on a vacation we spent in the borrowed beach house of a friend. Things started going wrong with the house and naturally I felt terrible and responsible, although I really couldn't have predicted that the toilet would overflow. By the end of our stay the house didn't look too bad but I was a wreck. The family, having put up with my over-the-top attack-dog behavior in defense of the house, said that at least I should be able to get a story out of it.''

Dennis Trudell: "High school friends and I used to sneak into a prep school gym to play basketball. But this was in the 1950s—not the '60s, as in my story 'Gook.' And though we were sometimes kicked out by an Asian janitor, we never entered a vicious skirmish with him—and we grew away from our Buffalo, New York, suburb unscarred by a winter afternoon's violence.

"I moved us ahead ten years to see if that would help me imagine what it was like being drawn into battle over a place we didn't belong—as U.S. teenagers were in Vietnam. And to be outsmarted there, outmaneuvered, *outpassioned*, though our eighteen-year-olds were passionate. I had no trouble envisioning my friends' and my own qualities—'Grun's' confidence, 'Cy Rabb's' wit, 'Rich Beauchamps's' spontaneity, my own appeasement—becoming exaggerated and ugly, dangerous to strangers and ourselves, in a society gone to war. War makes humans crazy. Basketball is a sane passion—and so my friends and I were lucky. At least one of us later did go to Vietnam, and at least one marched against the war. But we never heard the ugly word that titles my story until we had left our boyhood courts.''

Elizabeth Oness has previously published a story in *The Hudson Review* and a chapbook of poems, *In the Blue Before Night* (Heatherstone Press, 1991). She was selected as the poet for "Options," sponsored by the Washington Project for the Arts, and she spent six years working at the Taoist Health Institute in Washington, D.C., before moving to Columbia, Missouri, with her husband, the poet Chad Oness.

" 'The Oracle' began with Philip's voice and a question: what happens when a parent remarries and a child finds himself attracted to the child of the new spouse? The more I thought about it, the more it seemed that this was probably not an unusual situation. As I was writing, I realized that each person in this quartet of characters was grappling with a central lesson of adulthood—that sexual desire is complicated, and the one who is desired represents much more than the satisfaction of longing or lust. I imagined that Philip's predicament would have its own momentum, but mostly I wanted to write a story that would be realistic, not sensational. I also tried to convey that miasmic confusion that sometimes comes with graduating from college, being reasonably intelligent, and having no idea what you want to do with your life."

MAGAZINES CONSULTED

Agni, Boston University, Creative Writing Program, 236 Bay State Road, Boston, Mass. 02215

American Short Fiction, Parlin 108, Department of English, University of Texas, Austin, Tex. 78712-1164

American Way, P.O. Box 6199640, DFW Airport, Irving, Tex. 75261-9640

Another Chicago Magazine, Left Field Press, 3709 N. Kenmore, Chicago, Ill. 60613

Antaeus, 100 West Broad Street, Hopewell, N.J. 08525

Antietam Review, 7 West Franklin Street, Hagerstown, Md. 21740

The Antioch Review, P.O. Box 148, Yellow Springs, Oh. 45387

The Apalachee Quarterly, P.O. Box 20106, Tallahassee, Fla. 32316

Arizona Quarterly, University of Arizona, Tucson, Ariz. 85721

Ascent, P.O. Box 967, Urbana, Ill. 61801

Asimov's Science Fiction Magazine, Davis Publications, 380 Lexington Avenue, New York, N.Y. 10017

The Atlantic Monthly, 745 Boylston Street, Boston, Mass. 02116

Boulevard, P.O. Box 30386, Philadelphia, Pa. 19103

California Quarterly, 100 Sproul Hall, University of California, Davis, Calif. 95616

Canadian Fiction Magazine, P.O. Box 1061, Kingston, Ontario, Canada K71 4Y5

The Chariton Review, The Division of Language and Literature, Northeast Missouri State University, Kirksville, Mo. 63501

The Chattahoochee Review, DeKalb Community College, North Campus, 2101 Womack Road, Dunwoody, Ga. 30338-4497

Chelsea, P.O. Box 5880, Grand Central Station, New York, N.Y. 10163

Chicago Review, 5801 S. Kenwood, Chicago, Ill. 60637

Chicago Tribune, Nelson Algren Award, 435 North Michigan Avenue, Chicago, Ill. 60611-4041

Christopher Street, 28 West 25th Street, New York, N.Y. 10010

Cimarron Review, 205 Morill Hall, Oklahoma State University, Stillwater, Okla. 74078-0135

Clockwatch Review, Department of English, Illinois Westleyan University, Bloomington, Ill. 61702

Colorado Review, 360 Eddy Building, Colorado State University, Fort Collins, Colo. 80523

Columbia, 404 Dodge Hall, Columbia University, New York, N.Y. 10027

Commentary, 165 East 56th Street, New York, N.Y. 10022

Confrontation, Department of English, C.W. Post College of Long Island University, Brookville, N.Y. 11548

Cosmopolitan, 224 West 57th Street, New York, N.Y. 10019

The Cream City Review, University of Wisconsin-Milwaukee, P.O. Box 413, Milwaukee, Wis. 53201

Crescent Review, 1445 Old Town Road, Winston-Salem, N.C. 27106-3143

Crosscurrents, 2200 Glastonbury Rd., Westlake Village, Calif. 91361

Denver Quarterly, Department of English, University of Denver, Denver, Colo. 80210

Downstate Story, 1825 Maple Ride, Peoria, Ill. 61614

Epoch, 251 Goldwin Smith Hall, Cornell University, Ithaca, N.Y. 14853-3201

Esquire, 1790 Broadway, New York, N.Y. 10019

Fiction, Department of English, The City College of New York, N.Y. 10031

Fiction International, Department of English, St. Lawrence University, Canton, N.Y. 13617

The Fiddlehead, UNB, P.O. Box 4400, Fredericton, New Brunswick, Canada, E3B 5A3

The Florida Review, Department of English, University of Central Florida, Orlando, Fla. 32816

Four Quarters, La Salle College, Philadelphia, Pa. 19141

Free Press, P.O. Box 581, Brooklyn, N.Y. 10463

Frisko, Suite 414, The Flood Building, 870 Market Street, San Francisco, Calif. 94102

Gentleman's Quarterly, 350 Madison Avenue, New York, N.Y. 10017

The Georgia Review, University of Georgia, Athens, Ga. 30602

The Gettysburg Review, Gettysburg College, Gettysburg, Pa. 17325-1491

Glamour, 350 Madison Avenue, New York, N.Y. 10017

Glimmer Train, 812 SW Washington Street, Suite 1205, Portland, Oreg. 97205-3216

Grain, Box 1154, Regina, Saskatchewan, Canada S4P 3B4

Grand Street, 131 Varick Street, #906, New York, N.Y. 10013

The Greensboro Review, Department of English, University of North Carolina, Greensboro, N.C. 27412

Harper's Magazine, 666 Broadway, New York, N.Y. 10012

Hawaii Review, Department of English, University of Hawaii, 1733 Donaghho Road, Honolulu, Ha. 96822

High Plains Literary Review, 180 Adams Street, Suite 250, Denver, Colo. 80206

The Hudson Review, 684 Park Avenue, New York, N.Y. 10021

Indiana Review, 316 N. Jordan, Bloomington, Ind. 47405

Iowa Review, 308 EPB, University of Iowa, Iowa City, Ia. 52242

Kalliope, a Journal of Women's Art, Florida Community College at Jacksonville, 3939 Roosevelt Boulevard, Jacksonville, Fla. 32205-8989

Kansas Quarterly, Department of English, Denison Hall, Kansas State University, Manhattan, Kan. 66506-0703

The Kenyon Review, Kenyon College, Gambier, Oh. 43022

Ladies' Home Journal, 100 Park Avenue, New York, N.Y. 10017

The Literary Review, Fairleigh Dickinson University, 285 Madison Ave., Madison, N.J. 07940

Manoa, English Department, University of Hawaii, Honolulu, Ha. 96822

The Massachusetts Review, Memorial Hall, University of Massachusetts, Amherst, Mass. 01002

Matrix, c.p. 100 Ste-Anne-de-Bellevue, Quebec, Canada H9X 3L4

McCall's, 110 Fifth Avenue, New York, N.Y. 10011

Michigan Quarterly Review, 3032 Rackham Building, University of Michigan, Ann Arbor, Mich. 48109

Mid-American Review, 106 Hanna Hall, Bowling Green State University, Bowling Green, Oh. 43403

Midstream, 110 East 59th Street, 4th Floor, New York, N.Y. 10022

The Missouri Review, 1507 Hillcrest Hall, University of Missouri, Columbia, Mo. 65211

Mother Jones, 1663 Mission Street, San Francisco, Calif. 94103

Nebraska Review, Writer's Workshop, ASH 210, University of Nebraska at Omaha, Omaha, Neb. 68182-0324

New Directions, 80 Eighth Avenue, New York, N.Y. 10011

New England Review, Middlebury College, Middlebury, Vt. 05753

New Letters, University of Missouri-Kansas City, 5100 Rockhill Road, Kansas City, Mo. 64110

New Mexico Humanities Review, The Editors, Box A, New Mexico Tech., Socorro, N.M. 57801

The New Renaissance, 9 Heath Road, Arlington, Mass. 02174

The New Yorker, 20 West 43rd Street, New York, N.Y. 10036

The North American Review, University of Northern Iowa, 1227 West 27th Street, Cedar Falls, Ia. 50614

North Atlantic Review, 15 Arbutus Lane, Stony Brook, N.Y. 11790-1408

North Dakota Quarterly, University of North Dakota, Grand Forks, N.D. 58202-7209

Northern Lights, P.O. Box 8084, Missoula, Mont. 59807-8084

The Ohio Review, Ellis Hall, Ohio University, Athens, Oh. 45701-2979

OMNI, 1965 Broadway, New York, N.Y. 10012

The Ontario Review, 9 Honey Brook Drive, Princeton, N.J. 08540

Other Voices, The University of Illinois at Chicago, Department of English (M/C 162), 601 South Morgan Street, Chicago, Ill. 60680-7120

The Paris Review, Box S, 541 East 72nd Street, New York, N.Y. 10021

The Partisan Review, 236 Bay State Road, Boston, Mass. 02215

Playboy, 680 North Lake Shore Drive, Chicago, Ill. 60611

Ploughshares, Emerson College, 100 Beacon Street, Boston, Mass. 02116

Prairie Schooner, Andrews Hall, University of Nebraska, Lincoln, Neb. 68588

Puerto del Sol, College of Arts & Sciences, Box 3E, New Mexico State University, Las Cruces, N.M. 88003

The Quarterly, 201 East 50th Street, New York, N.Y. 10022

RaJah, 411 Mason Hall, University of Michigan, Ann Arbor, Mich. 48109

Raritan, 31 Mine Street, New Brunswick, N.J. 08903

Redbook, 224 West 57th Street, New York, N.Y. 10019

Sailing, 125 E. Main Street, P.O. Box 248, Port Washington, Wis. 53074

Salamagundi, Skidmore College, Saratoga Springs, N.Y. 12866

Sandhills/St. Andrews Review, Sandhills Community College, 2200 Airport Road, Pinehurst, N.C. 28374

The San Francisco Bay Guardian, Fiction Contests, 2700 19th Street, San Francisco, Calif. 94110-2189

Santa Monica Review, Center for the Humanities at Santa Monica College, 1900 Pico Boulevard, Santa Monica, Calif. 90405

Sequoia, Storke Student Publications Building, Stanford, Calif. 94305

Seventeen, 850 Third Avenue, New York, N.Y. 10022

The Sewanee Review, University of the South, Sewanee, Tenn. 37375

Shenandoah, Box 722, Lexington, Va. 24405

Short Fiction by Women, Box 1276, Stuyvesant Station, New York, N.Y. 10009

Snake Nation Review, 110 #2 West Force Street, Valdosta, Ga. 31601

Soma, 285 Ninth Street, San Francisco, Calif. 94103

Sonora Review, Department of English, University of Arizona, Tucson, Ariz. 85721

South Carolina Review, Department of English, Clemson University, Clemson, S.C. 29634-1503

South Dakota Review, Box 111, University Exchange, Vermillion, S.D. 57069

Southern Humanities Review, 9088 Haley Center, Auburn University, Auburn, Ala. 36849

The Southern Review, Drawer D, University Station, Baton Rouge, La. 70803

Southwest Review, Southern Methodist University, Dallas, Tex. 75275

Stanford Humanities Review, Stanford Humanities Center, Stanford University, Stanford, Calif. 94305

Stories, Box Number 1467, East Arlington, Mass. 02174-0022

Story, 1507 Dana Avenue, Cincinnati, Oh. 45207

Story Quarterly, P.O. Box 1416, Northbrook, Ill. 60065

The Sun, 107 North Robertson Street, Chapel Hill, N.C. 27516

Tampa Review, Box 135F, University of Tampa, Tampa, Fla. 33606

Thoroughbred Times, P.O. Box 8237, Lexington, Ky. 40533

The Threepenny Review, P.O. Box 9131, Berkeley, Calif. 94709

Tikkun, Institute of Labor and Mental Health, 5100 Leona Street, Oakland, Calif. 94619

TriQuarterly 2020 Ridge Avenue, Evanston, Ill. 60208

The Village Voice Literary Supplement, 36 Cooper Square, New York, N.Y. 10003

The Virginia Quarterly Review, University of Virginia, 1 West Range, Charlottesville, Va. 22903

Vogue, 350 Madison Avenue, New York, N.Y. 10017

Washington Review, Box 50132, Washington, D.C. 20091

Webster Review, Webster University, 470 E. Lockwood, Webster Groves, Mo. 63119

West Coast Review, Simon Fraser University, Burnaby, British Columbia, Canada V5A 1S6

Western Humanities Review, University of Utah, Salt Lake City, Ut. 84112

Whetstone, P.O. Box 1266, Barrington, Ill. 60011

Wind, RFD Route 1, Box 809K, Pikeville, Ky. 41501

Witness, Oakland Community College, Oakland Ridge Campus, 27055 Orchard Lake Rd., Farmington Hills, Mich. 48334

Yale Review, P.O. Box 1902A, Yale Station, New Haven, Ct. 06520

Yankee, Main Street, Dublin, N.H. 03444

Zyzzyva, 41 Sutter Street, Suite 1400, San Francisco, Calif. 94104